SHADOWED DOUBT

BAY TOWN BOOK THREE

KATHLEEN J. ROBISON

ISBN: 978-1-951839-94-9

Celebrate Lit Publishing

304 S. Jones Blvd #754

Las Vegas, NV, 89107

http://www.celebratelitpublishing.com/

"Fear not, for I am with you, be not dismayed, for I am your God; I will strengthen you, I will help you, I will uphold you with my victorious right hand." Isaiah 41:10 (RSV)

CHAPTER 1

Lacey let the screen door slam behind her. Standing on the front porch, she gazed across the gulf. Calm waters, clear skies. A perfect day for a wedding. She glanced back at the house.

"Don't be too long," Melanie, Lacey's mom, called from inside.

Don't be too long? She'd never heard that before. Not when it came to going for a run and not from her mom, the runner in the family. But Lacey finally experienced the value of pounding the pavement, especially along the gulf coast. Good for the body and soul.

Sticking in her earbuds, Lacey tightened her ponytail and skipped down the porch steps. She jogged the walkway from their chic, little cottage home. Their home. Just the two of them. A pang hit her heart. Grandpa and Grandma. Lacey blew out a breath, wishing they were still here. Although, it had always been just her and mom in Bay Town. But today, their life would change forever.

Lacey eyed the mailbox perched at the side of their property. Spring wildflowers, irises and hollyhocks bloomed from the earthy bed below, like good news beckoning her. She could sure use some. Walking over, she reached out her hand to the mailbox's metal flap opening and pulled back. *Not now.*

Instead she crossed the street, breathing in the gulf air. Releasing a whoosh from her lungs, she stepped up her pace. The waters danced, and the clouds seemed to sweep in rhythm while seagulls overhead screeched to accompany the heartache pounding in her chest. She ran harder, passing the familiar private piers. She recalled how much her mother loved running the coasts. First in California and now here. And how many of those years had she begged Lacey to run with her? When they'd moved to Bay Town Lacey finally took up jogging. Therapy after the horrific trials she'd lived through in her short, young life.

Lacey ran past the sprawling lawns of the restored, old homes that the last big hurricane hadn't completely destroyed. An old familiar fishing boat chugged up the inlet. The lines and gaffing swayed in the light breeze and made Lacey smile. She took out her earbuds and strained her ears, trying to catch his voice above the loud clanking noises of the rust-stained vessel.

"Hey, Lacey. Today's the day, huh?" The pilot of the vessel yelled, removing his navy beanie and waving it high in the air.

"Yup." Lacey looked at her watch. "Five o'clock tonight. You going to be there?"

"Sure thing." He waved. "The good Lord's blessing this day, that's for sure."

Lacey gave a thumbs up. She slowed a little, recalling her quiet time devotions. The Bible promised hope and a future, yet something like a kinked spring twisted inside. God had always been there. No matter what. But how many more "whats" could she endure? Lacey ran harder. Her chest burned, and her pulse pounded in her temples.

Reaching the turnaround point, she slowed and walked up to Bubba's Catch Shack. The round plastic canister dripped with condensation from the ice water it contained. Filling a paper cone cup, she lifted it to her lips and swallowed, but the cool liquid did little to loosen the knot in her throat.

"Hey, Lacey." Bubba raised a hand. His long red beard waved with the blowing breeze. "Can I get ya' something?"

"Thanks, Bubba. It's a little early for breakfast."

"You sure got a big day ahead of ya'."

"I do." Crumpling the cup, she tossed it into the dented metal can. "See you tonight."

"I wouldn't miss it for the world."

The world. Lacey's eyes welled. *Whose world?* "Great. See you tonight. Bye, Bubba." Her voice cracked, and so did her heart.

"Hey, Lacey?" Bubba called after her.

She turned.

"Any word from that fancy sewing college?"

"Design school." Lacey shrugged. "Not yet."

"It's all in God's hands, eh?"

The sweet aroma coming from Bubba's grill smelled so good. She wished she could stuff her stomach full of the cinnamon French toast he cooked. Deflecting the subject, she asked, "Did you ever apply for culinary school?"

His belly laugh filled the air, and Bubba's stomach jiggled. "Yeah, right. My old lady's not gonna have none of that. We're both working two jobs as it is. She'd kill me if I took up school."

"There's always online. Distance learning."

"For cooking?" Bubba's heavy red brows knit together.

"Well, it's a start. Maybe you could begin with the food health safety classes."

"Did you do that online for your dress stuff?"

"Yes, some of it, through the community college. But I went on campus for the clothing construction."

Bubba nodded. "I'll think about it. Thanks for the idea, Lacey."

Waving back, she turned and skipped a step continuing

her run. The home stretch stared back at her, and she stopped. She blinked repeatedly, and tears threatened. Lacey leaned on the short concrete sea wall. The water lapped below, lulling her to remember God's promises. She knew she could trust Him, but doubts swam in her head. After rejections from design schools in Los Angeles, New York, and San Francisco, only one remained—the smaller school near her Aunt Charlene in Washington D.C. Still hope. Dare she dream? The clouds parted and a ray of sunshine shone down.

"Yes! I will dream," Lacey yelled. Swinging away from the wall, she pushed to the center of the boardwalk.

"Whoa!" A man's voice startled her.

He gripped her shoulders from behind, shoving her aside. As he did, she bounced off the railing and tumbled to the ground, but she didn't hit as hard as the body lying next to her. He moaned, rolled over, and hopped up faster than she could gain her footing.

"Are you crazy?" he asked.

She pushed back loose strands, scowling at the figure standing in front of her. She couldn't see the face because of all the hair falling over it.

"Me? You ran into me." Lacey rubbed her hip.

"Yeah, because you didn't give a warning before you jumped out on the sidewalk." He offered a hand.

"Boardwalk," Lacey said, scrunching her nose. He resembled a cute, wet labradoodle. Wild, thick hair stuck to his neck, and the soaked tank shirt clung to his drenched body. His extended arm and muscled biceps held the invitation to help. She took it, and he yanked her up.

"Who were you talking to?" he asked.

"What?"

"Before you sidelined me, you yelled, *Yes I will.*"

Lacey bent to brush the dirt off her calf and noticed his bleeding knees.

"Nobody. I wasn't talking to anybody." She winced and

pointed. "You know Bubba's got a first-aid kit back there. Can I help you clean up?"

He bent over touching his knees. "Oh, man." Straightening, he placed his hands on slim hips. "Who's Bubba?" His wide eyes scrunched, but the mellow brown pools glistened. He swiped a hand over his hair, so plastered with sweat that it stayed slicked back. A second later, waves sprung loose. "Never mind. I'll wash it off somewhere." He looked around.

"You're not from around here, are you?"

A corner of his mouth threatened a sneer, but he grinned instead. "No, ma'am." He cleared his throat. "Just here on business."

"Business?" Lacey tipped her head. "How old are you?"

He threw his head back and laughed. Swiping a hand over his face, he shook it in a downward motion, and droplets dotted the sidewalk. His smile remained, and Lacey's heart warmed. She hadn't felt this good all morning.

"Now, if I was a girl, you couldn't ask that."

"Oh, please. I'm nineteen, almost twenty, and I don't think you're much older than me."

He pointed a finger at her. "Got you beat. I'm twenty-two."

"Like I said, not by much. What kind of business?"

He cleared his throat and kicked the ground. Before he could answer, Lacey's cell, strapped to her arm, buzzed.

"You better get that," he said rather quickly.

She checked the screen. "Oh shoot. I have to run." She winced, glancing again at the red trickling down his shin. "I'm so sorry. Please, go see Bubba. You don't want that to get infected."

He started walking backward. "I don't know. That's a greasy spoon." He threw out his arms. "But nice running into you. What's your name?"

"Lacey." Her name rushed out so fast that she surprised herself.

"Okay, Lacey." He tipped a hand to his brow. "Remember. Yes, you will."

"Huh?" Lacey scrunched her face.

He pointed at her. "You said it. Yes, I will." He turned and jogged toward Bubba's.

Fingering the cross hanging around her neck, she nodded. "Yes, I will." Lacey watched him run and giggled. *I will dream, and I will hope.* Orange rays peeked through a break in the clouds, and the load Lacey carried seemed a little lighter.

Reaching home, Lacey walked into the house. She slid her hand across the floral chintz sofa and glanced around the cottage's chic living room. Plants, candles, fresh flowers. All her mother's perfect decorative touches.

"Lacey? I thought something had happened to you. Are you all right?" Her mother walked from the hallway, meeting Lacey in the living room. "I can't believe you ran without me."

"Mom, I've been doing that for a year now."

Kissing her mother's cheek, Lacey stroked it. "You can't keep up with me anymore."

"Anymore? I've been running all my life, sweetheart." Melanie's eyes watered a little.

Running. *Had they run here from California?* No. God had moved them here. Although they needed to leave the heartache of devastating loss back there, unfortunately it seemed to follow them.

Lacey pulled her mom into a tight hug. "No more, Mom. We're not running from anything. God's got our backs."

"He always has, hasn't he?" Melanie kissed Lacey's head. "Ewww. Go wash that hair."

Teasing, Lacey nuzzled her mother's neck with her sweaty head. Their hair tangled together, and as Lacey pulled away, she stared at her mother's long chestnut waves. The same color as hers, but Lacey had her father's thick, coarse curls. She yanked her tresses apart from her mom's.

"Ouch," Melanie said, untangling Lacey's hair from her necklace.

Lacey started the tickle fest, and Melanie tried to run away. "Lacey, no. Stop."

But they poked and prodded one another, and Lacey tried to catch a breath while giggling. They'd always been so close. Her mother was only nineteen when Lacey was born, and it had been the two of them all their lives. They played much like girlfriends, but Lacey couldn't help but feel all that would end today. She lessened her grip, and her mother escaped. Lacey didn't chase but watched her run back down the hallway. Melanie stopped.

"Lacey? I'm sorry I didn't run with you this morning."

"I'm a big girl. I can run by myself." Loving sarcasm laced her words.

"I know, but it's just that it's our last run. Oh, I didn't mean the last."

"Shhh," Lacey said.

Melanie narrowed her eyes, but Lacey laughed. Her mother hated to be shushed, especially by her daughter.

"Hey, today's a fresh start for both of us." Lacey joined her mom. "Come on. Let's go pray for your wedding."

A sob escaped, and Melanie shook her head. "Who's the mother now?"

The girls slipped into Melanie's room, but the monochromatic soothing color scheme didn't work its magic, and Lacey's heart weighed heavy. She bit her lip, turning her face away from her mother. Even the lemongrass scent of the burning candle on the nightstand did nothing to soothe her heavy heart.

Mother and daughter sat on the edge of the bed in a sweet embrace that Lacey never wanted to end. Tonight, her mom would be in Pastor Desmond's arms. The embrace broke, and Lacey recoiled at the thought.

"Ewww," Lacey moaned.

Melanie dropped her arms, staring at her daughter. "Ewww, what?"

"Nothing. A weird thought. That's all." She took her mom's hand. "I want to pray for you, Mom. You and Pastor Desmond." She swallowed hard, but it didn't stop the first drop. "I'm so happy for you. I've wanted you and Pastor together since the first day I met him. You deserve this." Lacey swiped at her cheek and prayed. She thanked God for her mom and Desmond and for their community in Bay Town. She especially prayed for joy for everyone, including herself.

Her mother choked back little sobs. "This isn't the end for us, Lacey. It's a new beginning for you too." Melanie gripped her daughter's hands.

Light from the window swept across the room, and Lacey turned. The sun burst through, and she randomly thought of the gulf, and the young man with the unruly hair, much like her father's. Before she let her heart go to the sad memory of his death, a sigh escaped.

"I could use a fresh start." She jumped up. "Did you check the mail?"

"No, I totally forgot," Melanie said.

"Slacking there, huh?" Lacey pinched her mom's arm. "I meant to check this morning. I'll go."

Melanie followed Lacey to the front door. "Lacey, it's going to be okay. I'm praying you get accepted, but whatever God has planned, it's all good."

"But you don't want me to move to Washington D.C. I know. Don't worry, Mom, if I move in with Aunt Charlene, I'll be fine. She's an activist, right, a fighter? She won't let the evil, big city eat me up."

"I know. But I still like the idea of you living here with some girlfriends. Is Allie still thinking about moving? I know she needs to finish the semester first. Never mind, Desmond is moving in here until we have your life figured out."

"I thought you said God has my life figured out," Lacey said. "Besides, Allie is still thinking about it, and you'll be away for a two-week honeymoon before you need to start worrying." She tried to smile.

All these changes. If only one would be favorable in her direction. Something hitched inside her, and Lacey wanted to surrender it all to God. That moment of decision, when she knew she'd feel peace once she did, but something held her back.

"Yes. About that two weeks." Melanie paused. "I told Desmond I thought a two-week honeymoon is a little long. A week is long enough."

"Mom, no. You need this. He needs it." Lacey reached for the door.

Melanie laughed. "I don't need it. I'm not doing anything. The wedding planner I hired is going to put me out of business. She's that good."

"No one's as good as you, Mom. I'm glad you turned it over. This is your day." Lacey pushed open the front door.

"Lacey?" Melanie frowned. "What happened to your leg?" She pointed.

A raspberry patch swelled on her knee, but it didn't even hurt, and she grinned at the memory of the young man down at the harbor. "I fell."

"Fell? Well, let's get that cleaned up. It could get infected. You know the boardwalk isn't that clean. What with all the fish guts, and bait and hooks. Oh my. You didn't get a hook in there, did you?"

"Mom, stop. I'm fine. You need to stop worrying about me. Start worrying about Desmond." Not waiting for an answer, Lacey ran out the front door.

"I love you, Lacey," Melanie called after her.

Her mom's voice did the soothing thing, and Lacey slowed

down as she approached the mailbox. She lifted her hand and rested it atop. It stayed there for a long time. Closing her eyes, she sent up last-minute prayers. Praying that a letter would be in there—one expressing congratulations.

"Good morning, Lacey," a voice called from across the street.

Lacey turned. The sun warmed her face, and the voice heated her heart.

"Hey, there." Lacey waved. It was him. Hair flopping, face grinning as he jogged, bandaged knees and all. He even seemed to limp a little, but he didn't stop.

What's your name? She wanted to ask, but he seemed in a hurry. She opened her mouth to speak as he faded away. Making a mental note of the time, she promised herself to jog tomorrow morning at the same time.

Shoot. Tomorrow's Sunday. The doubting shadow loomed again. *Here on business.* That's what he'd said, which meant she'd never see him again. Maybe she could jog before church tomorrow, on the chance he would too. *Ridiculous.* Why should she care? Lacey stared after him and returned to the mailbox.

Pulling out a pile of mail, Lacey frowned. Junk. Junk. Junk, but then her eyes widened. Stuffing all but one piece back into the box, she ripped open a white envelope and skimmed the letter. Short but not sweet. Lacey crumpled it and threw it to the ground—the last rejection from design school. She slammed the mailbox with an open palm.

Her eyes burned, but tears didn't come. The letter darkened as moisture seeped from the morning dew. She lifted her foot, pressing it into the grass, and twisting until the paper almost ripped...like her heart.

CHAPTER 2

Tapping an unlit cigarette against the gold case, he fixed his eyes on the cross atop the classic white steeple. The setting sun dipped over the roof, and the steeple bell rang. Crowds of happy people he assumed were wedding guests flooded out. Stroking back his groomed hair, he turned and stepped off the lawn, retreating to his car.

Lacey ushered all the guests to line up along the walkway leading from the veranda. The guests formed two rows, raising their clasped hands high, creating a tunnel. Whistles and screams resounded as her mom and Pastor Desmond emerged from the sanctuary. Lacey stepped aside and gazed at her mother, and her heart swelled.

The champagne-colored dress sparkled, and with every move her mother made, it swirled with precision, just as Lacey designed it to. An original. Her original. Although she would have loved to have constructed it herself, Lacey marveled at a local dressmaker's handiwork. Victoria owned a high-end boutique in town and had amazing tailoring skills.

Melanie stepped forward, and the floor-length tulip hem swished around her feet. The sound of crystals lining the bottom half of the dress sang a soft tune of joy, and her mother looked like a starlet from a black and white movie. The shimmering satin gown fit Lacey's mother like a glove, and Lacey giggled thinking about how she and her mother adored the old forties classics and fashions. Although her mother wasn't keen on wearing a gown for the wedding and it took much pleading, she finally gave in to please Lacey. Her mother and the dress' dazzling effect exceeded Lacey's expectations.

Desmond swiped a loose tendril from Melanie's cheek and stared. Lacey watched and hoped that one day some godly young man would love her the way he loved her mother. He leaned in and kissed Melanie, and the crowd cheered.

The wedding consultant stood next to Lacey. "I've done my share of weddings, and I don't think I've ever seen any couple more in love."

Lacey's eyes watered, and she pointed upward.

"But we better get this show on the road. Would you like to take the lead? We need to get the reception started," said the consultant.

"Sure." Lacey nodded, then tapped her mother. "Okay, enough of that for now. Are you ready, Mr. and Mrs. Brooks? It's time for the gauntlet." Lacey pointed to the tunnel.

Desmond raised Melanie's hand, and as they gazed into one another's eyes, their chests rose with simultaneous deep breaths. Melanie picked up the hem of her dress and turned toward Lacey. Their eyes connected, and Melanie mouthed, "I love you."

A tear fell, and Lacey nodded. "I love you too, Mom." She blew a kiss.

As Melanie and Desmond started down the steps, rice flew through the air, bubbles floated around them, and squeals of delight deafened the moment.

"It's about time, dude." Bert, the chief of police, managed to slap a hand on Desmond's back.

Sally Trotman and Bethie Cook, the two senior women in the church, held one another shedding happy tears.

The youth group cheered the loudest and pelted the couple with more than a few sprinkles of rice. The wedding consultant frowned at Lacey.

"I don't remember ordering rice packets. That's a bit eco-unfriendly."

Lacey scrunched her nose. "Eco-unfriendly? Is that a word?" She twisted a tulle packet of rice behind her back. "Oh well, it's good for the birds, right?"

"Birdseed would have been a better choice."

"Oops. Guess I watch too many old movies." Lacey hunched and followed the crowd, now heading for the reception.

Standing in the doorway of the Community Hall, Lacey stepped back and gasped. Garden lights crisscrossed the room —white magnolia centerpieces graced each table. The floral masterpieces surpassed any she'd ever seen, compliments from Max who owned the Pink Rosette on Main Street. Crystal glasses shimmered off the flames of flickering candles scattered about.

They had many potlucks here, but the transformation surprised Lacey. She'd half expected to break down in tears at the thought of celebrating her mother's wedding in this room. She had received the news of her father's death here a few years before.

Lacey's father and mother had divorced before Lacey was born so she didn't know him well, but days before his unexpected death, he'd expressed the desire to be a father and husband again. A last voice mail to her mom said it all. But this wasn't the same room. Thoughts of that awful night floated away, and tonight held magic. Looking around, Lacey felt God's presence.

She watched as her mom and Desmond sat up front at one of the round tables. She knew she had a place next to them, as did Aunt Charlene, Melanie's sister. Her mother insisted on not having a head table. Melanie felt a little foolish having a full-blown wedding and reception, but Lacey wanted it for her. Her mother had never had a wedding. At nineteen years old, Melanie had a quick Las Vegas ceremony, and the marriage ended a few months later. *Nineteen.* Lacey's age now.

"Hey, Lace, get over here." Aunt Charlene waved. "It's time for the toast. Then we can eat."

Lacey waved back and started across the dance floor. Forgetting to pick up the hem of her chiffon dress, her high heel caught, and her body fell. Propelling forward in perpetual motion, she couldn't stop herself, until strong arms enveloped her preventing the disaster. Her eyes caught her rescuer. Him again. The runner. The one with the bloody knees. His face lowered to just inches above hers, and his eyes sparkled. He grinned and his biceps relaxed in her grip, but her stomach fluttered.

"Do you have a hit out on me or something?" he said.

He continued holding her in his arms, and the embrace felt enchanted. The moment surreal. Suddenly the crowd cheered. Glasses tinkled and Lacey glanced around. Everyone tapped their champagne flutes with silver spoons and pointed to her mother and Desmond.

Lacey pulled away and straightened. "What are you talking about? And what are you doing here?"

"You're welcome." He tipped a hand to his head.

Lacey watched as he walked away. Her brows knit together, and she felt her insides do the same.

"Lacey?"

She turned. Her mother stood next to her.

"Aren't you supposed to be kissing or something? Didn't you hear the glasses tinkling?" Lacy gazed after her rescuer.

"I saw you stumble. Are you okay?"

Lacey nodded but glanced down. Her silver heel punched

a hole through the hem of her dress. "Oh, man." Holding on to her mother, she bent and wiggled her dress free.

Melanie held her daughter, but asked, "Do you know that man?"

Lacey cleared her throat. "He's not a guest?"

"I assume he's a server with the catering company."

"So he's not a guest?" Lacey asked again.

"Did you even see him? He wore all black like the rest of the servers," Melanie said.

"Oh. So, he is here on business," Lacey whispered.

"What?"

"Never mind. I better do that toast before Aunt Charlene has a heart attack." She waved at her aunt and Desmond as both mother and daughter headed to their table.

Before Aunt Charlene could quip anything, Lacey raised a flute filled with sparkling cider.

"To my mom and Pastor. I mean, Desmond." And Dad, she thought, as her eyes watered. She took a deep breath and exhaled. "There couldn't be a better match. Mom, what can I say? You're perfect. You've always pointed me to Jesus. And Pastor Desmond, I know that's your job, but you're the real deal, and so is your faith." She paused and looked around. "We all have benefited from your example, your counsel, and most of all your love." Lacey choked as she gripped the mic.

Melanie joined Lacey and Desmond followed, enveloping the girls in a group hug. The solidifying embrace representing their new family. Sniffling and clapping broke the momentary silence, and the resounding applause accompanied by whistles lightened the moment.

"I love you, Mom," Lacey whispered, as she clutched her mom's neck. Leaning into Desmond, she nodded. "And you too, Pastor."

Lacey faced the guests, raising her glass. "Let the games begin," she yelled.

Blank faces stared back. She looked around at the puzzled

crowd. The runner caught eyes with her from across the room, laughed, and gave her a thumbs-up.

"Uh, the party. Let the party begin," she called.

After the toast, the DJ played mellow tunes as the waiters began serving. Pastor Desmond walked up to the microphone.

"Hey, I'd like to ask God's blessing on the food before we eat."

"Make it a fast one, Pastor. We's all hungry," Big Joe said.

"He will. He's got a new wife to get back too. Besides, it ain't you praying, or we'd be here all day." Chief Bert laughed, and Big Joe's loud guffaws matched. But when Bert's wife Lina elbowed him, he cleared his throat. "Okay, Pastor, take it away."

"Please join me and bow your heads. Lord, your goodness abounds, and I thank you for my beautiful wife, for Lacey, and all of Bay Town. We ask your blessing on this food and upon all our lives. Let us bring you glory in everything we do." He paused. "In the blessings and the trials, we trust you. In Jesus's precious name, and all God's people said…."

"Amen!" roared through the crowd, almost breaking the sound barrier.

Dancing, eating, and mingling, the magical night continued, but Lacey noticed a worrisome brow gracing her mother's beautiful face after the cake cutting.

"Mom? What's up?"

Melanie huffed. "I hate to leave you tonight, Lacey."

"Shhh."

"Lacey…"

"I mean, stop. Don't worry about me. Are you serious? Besides, Tina's next door."

"Actually, I asked Tina to spend the night with you."

"Mommm." Lacey moaned.

Ever since the attack in their carport a few years back Lacey's mom refused to let her be alone, and most of the time she didn't mind. This wasn't one of those times. "Stop. I'm a big girl, and if I get scared, I'll call Tina. Besides, isn't Aunt Charlene staying too?"

"No, I told you, Desmond is moving in until you get some roommates."

"We'll talk about this later. You have a honeymoon to get to." Lacey leaned over her mom. "Right, Pastor? A two-week honeymoon."

"You're not getting me in the middle of this. However, I do have a preference," he said.

"See, Mom, it's done. Enjoy your road trip. I hear New England is beautiful in the spring."

"That's the fall, and we're not going there. Change of plans," Melanie said.

"Your mom misses the ocean, so we're going to Ocean Beach in Alabama, instead," Desmond said.

"It's only two hours away," Melanie added.

"Great. Then no reason to cut your honeymoon short. If I need you, I'll call." Lacey stood. "It's settled. Get dressed, mom. I'll see you in two weeks." She winked at Desmond.

"Thanks," he mouthed.

They exited in a whirlwind complete with more tears and shouts of congratulations. As Lacey ushered the guests out, the catering company cleaned up, and the wedding coordinator finalized everything with Lacey.

"We're almost finished here, Miss Thompson. I can lock up if you'd like to leave."

"Thank you so much. You did such an amazing job here."

Walking through the kitchen, Lacey thanked the crew and her eyes roamed. The mysterious jogger, the server, had made himself scarce all evening. But Lacey had been so busy she barely had time to think about him. Not that she'd know what to say or do if she did meet him. She slipped out the back door with a yard of blush chiffon hanging over one arm and high heels dangling from her fingers.

Breathing in the cool night air, Lacey thought she saw a

flicker of light coming from the street, but it disappeared. She gazed upwards at the shining stars, and her eyes pooled. "Thank you, Jesus."

"Hallelujah." A voice shouted in the darkness.

Lacey jumped and spun around. The runner, the server, whoever, leaned against the building.

"Oh my gosh. You scared me half to death. What are you doing out here?"

"I could ask you the same." He brushed back the brown waves falling across his forehead. Curls flicked out along his collar.

"Aren't you supposed to be in there cleaning?"

"I'm off the clock. My job is done."

"Oh, the business you were in town for?" Lacey mocked.

"Don't laugh. Someday, I'll own that catering company."

"It's the catering spin-off from a hotel in New Orleans, isn't it?"

"Right. So I'll own the hotel, or at least manage it. Someday."

"Wow. Big dreams."

"It can happen. So, what are your plans? Throwing a rager with Mom gone?"

Lacey scrunched her face. "Rager?"

He chuckled. "You don't know what a rager is?"

She stared back at him. She didn't have a clue.

"Oh, you're one of *those* girls," he said. "A rager is a wild party."

Lacey whacked him with her shoes. "I am not one of those...whatever those girls are."

He laughed and rubbed his arm where the heels hit. Then he looked at her. Really looked at her. She glanced down. Heat rose within her, despite the cool night air. "I better go."

"Yup. Me too." He pushed off the wall and walked into the dark.

Lacey's throat felt thick, and the thought that she might

never see him again caused her heart to flutter. She twirled her shoes.

"Hey, do you need a ride home?" The voice in the darkness again.

Before caution could work common sense, she blurted. "Yeah, sure." And too eagerly she asked, "So, what's your name? I mean, who are you?"

His laugh bellowed, and he emerged once more into the light. "Wade Gardner at your service." He swept out his arm and bowed deep.

"Gardner? I know a Gardner. Do you know—"

"Lacey?" A shrill voice cooed from inside before the door swung open. "Oh, there you are, sweetie. Rudy and I are headed home. Your mother said you're coming with us, and I'm spending the night. We'll pull an all-nighter. You, me, and your Aunt Charlene."

Their next-door neighbor and Melanie's best friend, Tina, smiled. A gorgeous woman. Her dark smooth skin glistened, and her full taupe lips were perfectly shaped. Lacey loved her hair. Black and golden ombre ringlets bounced all around her face.

Wade laughed. "Looks like Mom's got it all planned out."

Lacey glared at Wade, then turned to Tina. "Yeah, sure. I'll be there in a minute. Meet you at the car."

"Okay. Don't be too long. Rudy's a party pooper, and he's all tuckered out." Tina peered into the dark. "Who is that?"

Stepping forward, Wade reached out a hand. "Wade Gardner, ma'am."

"Nice to meet you, Wade." Tina shook his hand. "Charmed, I'm sure." She giggled. "Are you from around here?"

"No, ma'am."

"He's with the catering service," Lacey said.

Tina winked at Lacey and whispered, "He's cute. But you're coming home with me. Don't be long."

The door shut, and Lacey exhaled.

"Like I said, one of those girls." Wade chuckled. "Hey, I'm staying in town tonight, but how about we meet for coffee tomorrow morning?"

Lacey froze. *Was he asking her out?* She swung her arms, the shoes hitting her thighs. "I'm one of *those* girls that go to church in the morning." Instantly, she thought of going to the late service so she could say yes.

"Fine, how about after?"

A light flickered in the darkness again, and Lacey peered past Wade. It came from the street, and she'd ignored it when she saw it earlier, but this time she thought she saw someone on the sidewalk.

"Is that a friend of yours?"

Wade turned. "Who?"

The stranger and the flickering light disappeared. Without moonlight and the streetlights spaced so far apart, Lacey thought maybe her tired eyes were playing tricks.

"Never mind."

Wade stepped forward, and his gaze searched her face, and the twinkle in his eyes seemed to express a funny joy. Lacey's body tingled. He reached out a hand, and she hesitated before taking it. He shook but didn't let go.

"Hi, Lacey. I'm Wade, and I work part-time for this catering crew. I live in New Orleans, but I'm staying with my great-grandfather tonight in Bay Town."

Lacey's brows furrowed. "Wait a minute. Did you say your last name is Gardner? Any relation to Reginald Gardner?"

"Do you know him?"

"Sure. Doesn't everyone?"

"He's my great-grandfather, and he owns the catering company." Wade kicked at the ground. "So, coffee?"

"I don't know. I'm not sure."

"Look, I'm not stalking you. It's just like we keep running into each other. So why not?"

Lacey's pulse increased, and she feared he'd feel it in her palm, which was starting to sweat. She pulled her hand back. "Why not what?"

He laughed again. "Why not have coffee?"

Nodding her head caused the few pins holding up her messy bun to fall out, and her thick hair fell around her shoulders.

Wade's eyes widened, and his mouth gaped. Silence. Too much silence. No one had ever stared at her like that, and she squirmed. She ran a hand through her hair, trying to finger comb the tousled tresses.

"Wow. The backlight makes you look like an angel." He grinned. "Maybe you are." He chuckled. "Listen, meet me for coffee, and I'll tell you anything about me you want to know."

Lacey pulled her bottom lip through her teeth and sighed. "Okay. Meet me at the Mockingbird Café at 8:30." She reached for the door, her heart pounding. *I'll hit the late service.*

"Okay, then." Wade tipped his hand to his head.

Lacey ran through the kitchen and the community hall. She stopped to thank the wedding coordinator and picked up her maid-of-honor bouquet. Holding the flowers to her face, she breathed the sweet gardenia scent, and it added to the elation rising. She gazed over the room, and she couldn't help but smile. Sauntering to the exit, Lacey relished the cool tile flooring that tingled her bare feet as she floated to the door. The wedding had been magical for her mom, and maybe her too.

"Lacey, let's go, sweetie," Tina called from the parking lot. When she reached Tina's car, she jumped in and slid down the back window. As the car pulled out onto the street, she heard muffled voices coming from the sidewalk.

CHAPTER 3

"What are you doing here?" Wade said.

"Aren't you happy to see me?" A gravelly voice spoke, and a laugh followed.

Wade gazed at the familiar face before him. Even in the cool night air, sweat wet his upper lip. He stared at his father, Beau Bodine.

"No need to be nervous, son."

"I'm not your son anymore."

"No? When did you figure that out?"

Wade's knees weakened. Beau had cast doubt about his paternity for years, but Wade's mother had always avoided the subject. Still he stared back, unsure.

"Yeah, that's right," Beau said.

Wade stepped forward. The veins in his neck pulsed, and he clenched his fists. He knew he should calm down, but he didn't even know how. It'd been a long time since he'd had to. "Get out of here. Go back to jail where you belong," he said.

"Go on, take a punch, son, and you'll be the one winding up there. You should have been there instead of me anyway." Beau sneered.

Wade pulled back his arm, but headlights from a car

shone on them. The car pulled to the curb, and the driver's door flung open.

"Bert, no," a female voice called from inside the car. "Let's go home."

A large Hispanic man stepped out. "You two, hold it right there."

Wade lowered his arm. The man wore a suit, not a uniform, but he commanded a presence. A familiar presence. Large, imposing, loud. It clicked and Wade recognized him as one of the wedding guests. Wade relaxed his shoulders, and an ease settled over him. Fear hadn't taken hold, but anger held its place. It had been a while since he'd been in a fight, and he never ran from confrontation. Thinking of his great-grandfather, he unclenched his fists. *I can't screw this up again.*

"What's going on here?" The man asked.

"You best be minding your own business. We're having a friendly conversation here is all." Beau flipped the cap of the cigarette lighter in his hand, flicking the flame off and on.

The irritating click grated on Wade's nerves, but his gaze rested on the big man.

"You are my business. I'm the police chief here in Bay Town. Let me see your ID."

Beau raised his hands. "Hey, no disrespect, sir, I had no idea. I'm new here." He extended a hand. "Beau Bodine is my name, and I want no trouble."

Chief Bert narrowed his eyes and straightened tall to his full height. His broad shoulders pulled back, and he towered over both men. "I said ID. Both of you." Chief Bert pushed back his suit coat and revealed a badge clipped to his belt.

Wade pulled out a wallet and handed over his driver's license. "I'm with the catering company, sir."

The chief said nothing but pulled out his phone and snapped a picture of his license. He handed it back to Wade and stared. "So, how do you know Lacey Thompson?"

"Sir?"

"The girl at the wedding. The one who tripped on the dance floor."

He saw that? And why did he care? Questions flew through Wade's head.

"I never met her before, sir."

"You sure about that?" The chief narrowed his eyes.

Wade felt warm again. He hadn't met her before. The encounter on the run that morning wasn't a planned thing. He struggled with whether to bring that up. He didn't need any trouble. "I ran into her jogging this morning down at the gulf, that's all. But I've never seen her before that."

Wade's eyes shifted to Beau Bodine.

Beau smirked at Wade.

"Mr. Bodine, your license?"

Beau handed over the identification, and the chief snapped another picture. "Okay, boys, seeing as neither of you is from around here, you best take your fights elsewhere. Goodnight, gentlemen."

"Yes, sir." Beau Bodine tipped a hand to his head. "Wade, I'll see you around." A chuckle followed his grin.

Beau got into an older model sedan and drove off. Wade stared into the dark, and his heart still raced. Uncharacteristic gratefulness seeped in, but he shook it off. He'd always fought his own battles.

"Son? Are you all right?"

"I'm good, sir," Wade said.

"Who's the guy? How do you know him?"

"Just someone I knew a long time ago."

"I can sense trouble, and I think he's it. You best stay away from him."

"I will, sir. I plan on it."

"Good. Have a nice evening and give my compliments to the chef. You guys served a mighty fine meal tonight."

Wade watched the chief drive away, then headed to his vehicle.

On the short drive home, he took Beach Road along the gulf. Approaching the house where he'd seen Lacey this morning, he slowed. Wade rolled down the window breathing in the night-blooming jasmine. He stopped, letting his car idle. His pulse slowed, matching the purring rhythm of the engine, and he stared at the house. *Who are you, Lacey Thompson?* Whoever she was, she stirred something new inside of him. Something different from every other girl he'd met. Something fresh and clean.

Suddenly, the front screen door swung open, and Lacey stepped out. Dressed in pajama bottoms and a sweatshirt, she plopped on the front porch swing, cupping a mug in her hand.

Wade stepped on the gas and drove away. He hit the steering wheel. *"Stupid. Stupid. She'll think I'm a creeper."*

Arriving at an impressive mansion a mile away, Wade parked. He walked up the porch steps to the wrap-around veranda and inserted a key into the ornately carved wooden double doors. Once inside, he tossed his keys on the console table in the foyer. He winced as the jingly crash echoed throughout the quiet house.

"There's a valet for those, son." His great-grandfather waited.

"Yes, sir."

Placing his keys in the leather box muffled the noise. Wade walked into the vaulted ceiling living room and strode straight to his great-grandfather's side. Reginald Gardner sat in a leather, wing-back chair. Wade extended a hand.

The white-haired elderly gentleman shook it and waved toward a seat. "I'm glad to see you weren't out too late tonight." His great-grandfather still wore a gray day suit giving evidence that Wade's early arrival met with his approval.

"No sir, I worked."

"Glad to hear that. A catering job?"

"Yes, sir."

Wade sat across from his great-grandfather, hoping he wouldn't have to pass a test tonight. An interrogation to be exact. But he'd recently screwed up, and he had to pay his dues. He expected it.

"Which hotel chef?"

"Gardner Cottages."

Mr. Gardner uncrossed his legs, shifting a little in the chair. He rested an elbow on the arm and pulled at his goatee. "I'm surprised. Not The Jardin, or The Fleur Printemps?"

"No sir. The Gardner Cottage Chef."

"Did the food meet expectations?"

Clearing his throat, Wade took a moment to craft his answer. "Exquisite, sir. I sampled everything. Pretty near perfect."

"Pretty near?"

"I mean, perfect. I didn't hear one complaint, and the guests raved about the food."

"Raved?" His great-grandfather raised a trimmed white brow.

Wade pursed his lips. "They sent their compliments to the chef, sir."

"Did he go out to greet the guests?"

"Yes, sir. Directly to the bride and groom."

"And they were pleased."

"More than so, sir."

But Wade didn't think of the bride and groom. He thought of Lacey wearing a light pink flowing gown. Her thick brown hair piled atop her head until it fell. *Wow.* Wade sighed.

"Fine. You'll drive me back to New Orleans in the morning. We'll have lunch at the Cottages."

The command interrupted his thoughts, and Wade swallowed hard. "The morning, sir?"

Great-grandfather stared. "Why, do you have plans?"

"Coffee with a friend is all."

"What friend?"

"Someone I met at the wedding."

His great-grandfather's back stiffened. "The hired help doesn't mingle with guests. You know that."

"Yes, sir, but I met the girl jogging down at the gulf this morning, and she happened to be at the wedding."

A smile formed on Mr. Gardner's face. His eyes even twinkled. "The Thompson-Brooks wedding?" He tapped a square white envelope on the cherry-wood end table. A card scrolled with script peeked out.

Wade's eyes widened. "I believe so. Do you know them?"

"I do. The girl you met. Did she happen to be Lacey?"

Wade's mouth gaped. "How did you know?"

His great-grandfather smiled, seemingly amused.

"Were you invited? How do you know them?" Wade asked.

"I was invited, but I don't attend gatherings anymore. Your aunt would have attended, but she's in Europe." He breathed deep. "I'm tired. We'll discuss this another day. What time is your coffee with Miss Thompson?"

"Early. Eight-thirty, sir." Wade clasped his hands together and cracked his knuckles.

Reginald Gardner frowned and glanced at Wade's hands.

"Sorry, sir." But Wade's thoughts were preoccupied with why his family had been invited to the wedding.

"We'll leave when you're done, and you'll take me to St. Stanislaus for the second Mass."

"As you wish, sir." Wade chuckled. Great-grandfather always winced when he used the phrase, but Wade thought he secretly liked it, especially after he'd gotten the patriarch to watch his favorite movie, *The Princess Bride*.

"Good night, Wade."

Wade stood. Discussion over. *But how did he know Lacey?* Mr. Gardner, one of the wealthiest residents in New Orleans knew this little family from Bay Town and Wade wanted to know the connection.

"Good night, sir."

Wade walked over to his great-grandfather and extended his hand. When they shook, they shared a firm grip.

"Wade, tread lightly with this Lacey Thompson. She's a good girl."

Wade translated the sentiments to mean, *don't screw this up.* "Yes, sir. I will, sir."

"Providence, my boy."

"Yes, sir. Good night."

Wade walked up the grand staircase, into his room, and closed the door. He stepped to the tall window as a breeze blew through. Although the old house sat back on a massive front lawn the view of the gulf waters stretched out before him. The moon shone low over the horizon, but Wade felt restless. He stared at the private pier, jutting out from the boardwalk, and thought of going for a walk. A long one. He didn't expect to sleep well tonight. This Lacey messed with his head. And now Great-grandfather too, with his providence.

Wade turned, but a flicker of light under some trees caught his eyes. He squinted into the dark. A car sat parked. Closing the window, he drew the drapes, but peeked out one side. Headlights flashed on and off. He let the drapes drop and wiped his hands down his black trousers. He peeked again and watched as the car drove off.

Wade drew his hand through his hair and pulled. Trouble seemed to be encroaching by way of providence.

Sprawled across his bed, Wade woke with a start. His watch alarm went off, and he rolled over, but his clothes felt binding. No wonder, he thought. He fell asleep in his catering uniform. Grandpa would kill him for being so lazy. Wade jumped into the shower, dressed, flew down the staircase, and out the large, double doors.

Arriving at the Mockingbird Café, Wade chuckled at the eclectic joint and searched for Lacey. Not here yet, he grabbed a table by the window and sat. Then stood. The place wasn't too crowded for a Sunday morning, and it puzzled him. Ahhh, he breathed. This is a church going town. Not like New Orleans, where tourists filled the coffee shops.

Wade spotted a small sofa in a cozy corner. No other chairs, just the two-person setting. He walked over and sat. He fidgeted, then stood again. He glanced at the door—no Lacey. Running a hand through his hair, he moaned. No girl ever made him feel like this. And now he had the pressure of his great-grandfather.

"The swing on the porch is a nice spot." A large, curvy woman spoke behind the counter. Her hair hidden under a bandana, leaving a shining round face smiling back at him. "Seems like you're expecting a hot date this morning. Ain't I right?"

Before he could answer, a whoosh of air blew through the open door, and Lacey walked in. Wade stared. Beautiful. Her hair hung loosely around her shoulders, and the long, floral dress she wore made her green eyes pop. *Wow.*

"Oh my." said the woman at the counter. "Boy, you best be careful. She's the town sweetheart, and we's all watching out over her." She frowned at Wade but turned to Lacey. "Hey, Lace. Ain't you supposed to be worshipping this morning?"

"Hey, Jacquie. I'm going to the late service. What about you?" Lacey pointed.

"Evening service for me today." She glared at Wade. "You know this boy?"

Lacey turned red, and Wade loved it. *What girl blushed nowadays?*

"I guess you do. So, what can I get you two lovebirds?" The woman chuckled.

Walking forward, Lacey tripped but caught herself before Wade could. "Oh, no, it's not like we're together or anything."

"No worries, and whatever you want, it's on the house this time. If there's another time, I better get the okay from your mama first." Jacquie winked.

Wade laughed and warmed inside at Lacey's eye roll. They ordered, and he carried their drinks outside. Instead of the double swing, he led her to a tiny bistro table at the far end of the porch. As he walked by the window, Jacquie peeked out.

CHAPTER 4

"So, does everyone in town know you?" Wade asked, taking a big gulp. "Ouch. Oh, man. That's hot," he sputtered.

Lacey grabbed a napkin and handed it to him. "Well, yeah. It's coffee."

She giggled but stared past him. Wade turned and saw the back of a man walking into the café. An uncomfortable feeling arose. Something seemed a little too familiar. But Lacey's voice drew him back, and he focused on their conversation.

"Almost," Lacey said.

"What?" Wade dabbed his mouth.

"Your question. Almost everyone knows everyone. This is a small town, and everyone who knows Pastor Desmond knows me now." Lacey sipped her coffee.

"Who's Pastor Desmond?"

"Desmond Brooks. The man who married my mom last night." Lacey sighed.

Her mood changed with the sigh.

Wade stared back at her. The green eyes drove him crazy, and now nothing mattered but the sweet face in front of him. "Are you okay with that?"

She hunched her shoulders. "Yes, I am. I've wanted Pastor Desmond for my mom from the first time I met him." She giggled. "That seems so long ago. I'm so happy for them. He's a really, really good guy."

Her eyes lit up, and Wade lost himself in them. The green sparkles shined back at him and pulled him deeper still.

"Wade? Are you all right?"

He stared.

"Wade?" Lacey touched his hand.

He stared at her slender fingers. "What? Oh, yeah. Good, I'm fine." His muscles tightened so that his knees jiggled the table, tipping his cup.

Lacey grabbed it. "Are you sure? You seem like you're not all here."

He looked anywhere but at her and mumbled. "I'm not. I'm in another world. Seriously."

His eyes locked on hers. "This small town is not my thing. I mean, it's like a Hallmark movie."

Lacey giggled. "Are you kidding me? You watch Hallmark movies?"

"What? Ewww, no. My aunt does."

Now she flat out laughed. "And you watch them with her," she sang.

This girl is a Hallmark movie. "You know what I mean."

"I do." Her laughing stopped, and even the bright smile faded. "But it's not. I mean, the people here are nice like that. And very cool. We're all pretty close, but terrible things have happened here." Lacey swiped at her eye, while staring at a large oak tree.

Wade touched her hand. "To you? Bad things happened to you?"

"To a lot of us." Lacey sucked in a breath. "But that's for another time. What about you? What's your story?"

As if a pin popped an oversized balloon, the air gushed from Wade's lungs. "Maybe another time too. I live in New

Orleans with my great-grandfather, but he has a home here in Bay Town."

"That's right. You're Reginald Gardner's great-grandson." Lacey's eyes grew round as saucers. "I can't believe he's your family. We invited him to my mom's wedding, but he declined. Actually we invited him and his granddaughter, Summer."

"Yes, I heard. So how do you know them?"

"It's a long story. Your aunt was the maid of honor in a wedding my mom did in California. Then she hired mom to do her wedding and helped us move here."

"That's wild. But why did you move here?"

Lacey sighed. "We needed a fresh start. Anyway, thanks to Summer, your great-grandfather sold us the cottage we live in. I've only met him a few times, but he's like a—"

"Grouchy old man."

"No. Like a southern gentleman. Not many of those around, but that's wild. You're his great-grandson. I can't believe it." Lacey twisted her hair and threw it back over her shoulders, and Wade wished he could feel those strands between his fingers.

"Hey, what's that supposed to mean? I'm a southern gentleman."

She laughed, and their conversation turned to lighter things. The gulf, her mom's business, and their connection with Mr. Gardner.

"So, you're Summer's nephew. Is it your mom or your dad that's related to her?"

Wade stiffened. "Like I said, that's for another time."

He turned aside. Secrets were terrible, and this good girl probably wouldn't put up with a shady past. He ran a hand through his hair, shaking his head.

Her hand touched his once more, and the warmth felt like an electric current. A switch inside flipped, but he slid his hand away.

"Hey, we all carry baggage. It's taken me a long time to

work through mine. And I'm still working through it." She shook the watch on her wrist. "Oh, I have to go."

"Yes, of course." *Run, girl. Run as far away from me as you can.* "Yeah, sure. I think we're done here."

Lacey frowned. Confusion spread across her face, but she stood, then smiled. "Hey, why don't you come to church with me? I usually go to the first service, but the second one starts in a few minutes."

This time Wade frowned, then a smile tingled his face. "Wait a minute. You skipped church to meet me for coffee?"

Lacey rolled her eyes. The blush came back brighter than before. "It's not like that."

Wade leaned back in his chair and raised a brow. "Oh, yeah? It looks like it's all *that* to me," he teased.

Lacey began her retreat, and Wade stood. "Listen, I'd like to go with you, but I have to take my great-grandfather to the Catholic Mass thingy."

Lacey stopped. "Wait, you go to mass?" Her brows raised.

He patted his chest. "You hurt me, girl. What do you think, I'm going to hell or something?"

"We all are if it wasn't for Jesus." Lacey grinned.

"Did you just say the J word?"

"Weird, huh?" she shrugged. "But yes, because He's every-thing to me."

She tilted her head, looking and sounding every bit like an angel. Wade couldn't help but release a sigh. He felt himself grinning foolishly.

"If it weren't for Him and Pastor Desmond, I'd probably be flipped out on the streets by now." She looked down. "Maybe not that bad, but it's been a long road. And I'm headed down another one if things don't work out. Oh, never mind. I have to go."

"If what things, Lacey? What's wrong? Can I help?" Wade didn't know why he said that. He hadn't been able to help anyone but himself, and if it hadn't been for his great-grandfather, he might have ended up like Beau. Wade shivered.

"That's so nice of you. But no. I'll figure it out." She yanked her purse onto her shoulder. "Life, you know." She took a few steps off the porch.

"Right. Do I know?" Wade followed her. "Hey, can we meet again? I mean, would you like to hang out or something?"

Lacey's bright smile returned, lighting up her eyes. He liked this.

"Sure. That would be fun."

"Great." Wade pulled out his cell. "Can I have your number?"

They exchanged numbers, and Wade hated that he had to return to New Orleans today. Oh, how he wanted to spend time with this girl.

"Okay, then. Now, I do have to go," Lacey said.

He took a deep breath. "Right. I'll call you tonight."

He loved that a rush of color flooded her face. She beamed. "Cool." She stared back and seemed to be waiting.

Wade took the opening and reached forward, wrapping one hand around her shoulder, pulling her in for a light embrace. She took the bait and leaned in, but her hands remained at her side. Still, the warmth of their closeness lent a hope that he hadn't felt in a long time. A weird thought popped into his head. Providence.

Lacey left Wade on the front porch, waving goodbye from her car parked out front. He watched as she drove away. Wade's eyes moved upward, and somehow the blue skies were bluer, and the white clouds much whiter. He grinned.

A door slammed, and Wade turned. A rock sank in his stomach, and he took a step back. "Why are you following me?"

Beau Bodine ignored the question and leaned against the

clapboard structure. "So, you got yourself a girlfriend, eh? Hope she doesn't end up like the love of my life."

"You did that, not me." Wade stomped down the front steps. "Get out of here. I don't want anything to do with you." He walked to his car and clicked the fob. The lights flashed on a new model Tesla.

"Pretty fancy, there. Where'd you get that?"

Wade ignored Beau, got in, and drove off.

～

Beau Bodine walked back into the café. He strode to the counter and peered into the pastry case. "Well, darling, what's the best treat in there?"

Jacquie pointed. "The cranberry scones. They're my favorite. Hmm, mmm. But you can't go wrong with anything in here." Her body jiggled as she laughed. "So, you enjoying a stay in Bay Town? Or you just passing through?"

"I'm not sure how long I'll be staying." He grinned. "Why don't you give me one of them scones."

"Sure thing. Say, do you know that kid on the porch you were talking to?"

He narrowed his eyes. "Why do you ask?"

"Nothing, just never seen him or you around here. I pretty much knows everyone that comes in. Sunday mornings are slow 'cause of church. But the locals'll be here soon enough."

"So, do you know the little lady sitting with him? The kid, that is."

The woman set the white bag on the counter. With hands on her hips, she gripped them tightly and gave him a sideways glance. "So, now I'm asking you. Why do you ask?"

Beau chuckled. "She's a pretty little thing."

"Yes, she is." All friendliness subsided. "That'll be two dollars and fifty cents, sir."

He paid, and no more words were exchanged, but he ran into Chief Bert in uniform as he stepped foot outside.

"Well, well. If it isn't Mr. Bodine. That's a pretty familiar name. I can't place it now, but I will." The chief tapped his temple.

Beau's jaw clenched, but he took a deep breath and relaxed. "Well, you're right. It's familiar because it's common. Lots of Bodines in Mississippi, you know."

"So, how do you know that young man last night?"

Fishing. Usual for a policeman, but everybody seemed to know everyone's business around here. Beau wondered if the chief knew anything about Wade. Driving a fancy car, and living in a mansion on the gulf, curiosity gave rise to greater plans than the revenge he'd been plotting.

Beau glanced down the street, then back at the chief. "Do I have to answer that?"

"No, but if you cause any trouble in my little town here, you'll be answering to a lot more. I haven't run a check on you yet, but I will."

This time the clenched jaw wouldn't relax. Beau bored his eyes into Chief Bert. He'd find out eventually. "I'm a parolee. Just released from Central two months ago." After spending ten years in the Central Mississippi Correctional Facility, Beau had no intention of returning.

The Chief showed no surprise. "Good thing you told me. How long you been in Bay Town?"

"I arrived yesterday. I don't plan on staying, so no need to report to you my whereabouts."

"You don't need to report to me, as long as you keep it clean. Does your parole officer know you're here?"

"No, sir. The law says I can travel within the southern counties. My job had a shut down, so I took a drive. I haven't broken my parole." Beau cleared his throat.

"Well, make sure you move along then. It's in your best

interests to let your parole officer know everything. Better you tell him than me."

"What's that supposed to mean?"

"It means you almost had an altercation last night in front of a police officer. If I reported it, you'd be in violation."

Why the leniency, Beau thought. The law states that if an officer even questioned him, he should report it. "No altercation. Besides, I'm leaving now."

"Good." Chief Bert moved past him, opening the Café door. "Hey there, Jacquie. Got any donuts?"

"Bert, you know we don't serve those things here."

The chief let out a loud, unbefitting giggle. Turning back, he asked, "So, Mr. Bodine, what were you in the pen for?"

Beau bristled. "Manslaughter."

The chief pushed the door open further. "Do you and I need to have a little talk in here?"

"No, sir. Like I said, I'm not staying."

"Good."

Beau Bodine walked to his car. The door creaked as he opened it, and when he slid in and turned the key, the car sounded like a whining puppy. He slammed the steering wheel and stared straight ahead before attempting again.

That Wade, he'd pay. He'd pay with that Tesla. He'd pay with that mansion. Beau sneered. *He might even pay with that pretty little girl of his.* He cranked the key once more, and the car choked to what little life it had left. Beau turned to look at the Mockingbird Café, as the chief stood in the doorway, watching him.

CHAPTER 5

S unday morning service went as usual with greetings and announcements. The Yard Sale Fundraiser for missions seemed to draw the most attention, but as the singing ended, and the guest preacher began his sermon, Lacey daydreamed. She sketched on the back of the bulletin, then paused. Not a bad likeness, she thought. An ink drawing of Wade stared back at her.

Seriously? She scolded herself, then shifted her eyes to Aunt Charlene, who slouched, asleep beside her. She smirked at the quirky drawing of Wade, but a twinge of guilt set in. She hadn't heard a word, and the service dragged on and on. With Pastor Desmond on his honeymoon, the older reverend's dry sermon made it hard not to zone off. Lacey leaned forward and tuned in, trying to glean from the scriptures he taught.

A quiet, soothing sound breathed to her. She nudged her Aunt Charlene.

"What? Am I snoring?" Charlene said, causing the people in front to turn. "Oh, sorry," she whispered.

Charlene gave Lacey a thumbs up. She'd asked that Lacey nudge her if she fell asleep and confessed that she didn't have the attention span for the Bible as other congregants did. Aunt Charlene also voiced that some sermons were best preached to the dead. Still, Lacey loved her mom's sister. God wasn't done with her yet.

"Thanks, sweetie." Charlene patted Lacey's arm.

After the service, Lacey got caught up in the crowds. Everyone wanted to express their thanks for a beautiful reception. But the wedding dress drew the most accolades. Lacey received endless compliments about the design.

"Lovely wedding, dear." Bethie Cook patted her arm. "Your mama's elegant dress stole the show. I wish you could make my Roxanne a dress like that." She huffed. "If she ever gets married."

"Let me know when, and I'd be happy to, ma'am."

Bethie's lips turned down. "I will, but she's got to get out of that awful relationship." Her voice softened.

"I'm so sorry, Mrs. Cook. I'll be praying for Roxanne," Lacey whispered, but a tear in her heart ripped for all women in those situations. Something to be wary of.

"Thank you, dear, she needs it. We all do, don't we?" Bethie Cook squeezed Lacey's hand.

"Come on, Bethie," said Sally Trotman, pulling Bethie away. "Beautiful dress, Lacey, and God's spirit reigned at the ceremony. Wonderful. Just wonderful."

"Thank you, Mrs. Trotman."

Lyla stepped up and bear hugged Lacey. "Sugar, God has blessed you with talent." Lyla, Big Joe's wife, gushed. She loved fashion. Always the brightest figure in the congregation.

"Thanks, Lyla, but my mom can wear anything and make it look good."

"That she can, child, but she done outshone anyone on the Hollywood red carpet." Lyla wrapped an arm around Lacey's shoulders and pulled her in close. "Speaking of talents, what you sewing up for the Yard Sale Fundraiser?"

"Nothing. I'm baking brownies to sell."

"Perfect. Save some for Big Joe. He loves your baking as much as I love your designs."

Lacey appreciated the sentiments and felt the friendliness of hometown friends who had become family.

Charlene drove down Beach Road, and Lacey leaned her head out the passenger window. The air smelled clean, and no recent spring rains had churned up the smelly gulf.

"So, Bubba's Catch Shack it is?"

"Of course," said Lacey.

"Good. Nobody in D.C. does breakfast like him."

Whenever she came into town, Charlene never missed Bubba's All-Day-Breakfast Sunday Special. They drove to Pier One, she parked, and jumped out. Lacey gathered her purse and hat while Aunt Charlene ran for the short line outside the Catch Shack. A seagull squawked overhead, and Charlene ducked under the awning, covering her head.

"Hey there, Bubba. Give me a ton of French toast and sausage, will you?"

"What kind?" Bubba held a spatula, not a pen in hand.

Lacey grinned. He rarely wrote anything down and cooked to order.

"What do you mean what kind? I said sausage. What kind is there?" Charlene frowned.

"Give us the real stuff, Bubba." Lacey winked.

"Ewww. Don't tell me he serves that fake meat stuff. Why do you think I chose to come down here? I can get tofu or plant-base anywhere in D.C."

Bubba's belly jiggled when he laughed. "Oh, we got our health nuts down here, too, Miz Charlene."

"See, that's another reason I came here. He knows my name."

Bubba nodded and retreated to the grill.

The women grabbed a table, and Charlene pulled a metal chair, letting it screech across the concrete. She plopped down. "I thought that sermon would never end. I bet you can't wait till Desmond gets back. Who's preaching next week?"

"Don't know." Lacey plopped her shoulder bag on the

chair next to her. "I heard rumors that the volunteer youth pastor might do it." The flap of her purse had flipped open, and a crumbled paper flew out. She bent to retrieve it at the same time Charlene did, who got it first.

"Why the heck are you carrying around this soggy mess? And in your purse." Charlene smoothed open the damp paper and handed it over.

Lacey took it and stared, re-living her disappointment all over again. She handed the crumpled rejection letter back to her aunt. "I didn't get in."

Charlene grabbed it and squinted. "Are you kidding me?" She dropped the letter on the table. "You have to send them your sketches, and photographs of your constructed designs. Once they see what you can do, you'll be in. This isn't over."

"Yes, it is. I'm done."

"What do you mean you're done? I hate these fancy schools. Listen, let's keep the plan for you to move to D.C. We'll find something there. Anything is better than here, right?"

Lacey stared at the boats rocking in the harbor. She watched an older couple strolling hand in hand along the boardwalk. A couple of teens were snapping selfies against the rocks. Bubba served their French toast along with a large pitcher of maple syrup.

"I love it here." Lacey's voice trailed.

"But?" Charlene waited with widened eyes.

"Yeah. I guess there's not much opportunity." Lacey pushed up her sunglasses.

"You think?" Charlene leaned forward. "Lacey, you're young, and there's an entire world out there waiting for you. It doesn't mean this won't always be home. You have to get out there and use your talents, girl."

"I know. But maybe I'm not supposed to go to design school."

"Seriously? And do what then?"

"Well, the woman who sewed mom's wedding dress, Victoria, has a shop here in town. She carries some stylish lines but also has her own formal wear line, and her designs are pretty unique."

"What's she doing in little ole' Bay Town? Why isn't she in New York or California or something?"

"She used to live in California. She had a big job in the fashion industry there, but she's originally from here and came back. I'm not sure what her story is, but she seems happy."

"I can't imagine why. Who in Bay Town needs designer formal wear?"

"Right? I thought the same thing."

"Well, why don't you go talk to her?"

"I may do that. I'll be finished with the community college courses in another month. So I have some time to figure things out. Maybe I'll take a sewing job in New Orleans. Anything to get some experience in the industry."

Charlene's eyes narrowed, and she reached over and gripped Lacey's hands. "No. Not New Orleans." Her aunt's face grew pale.

Lacey understood. Her father died, possibly murdered, in a hotel in New Orleans. Her mom had been abducted there, along with Pastor Desmond. The largest metropolitan city near Bay Town didn't hold good vibes but had plenty of opportunity, and no place could be considered perfectly safe. When all that human trafficking stuff came down, she'd been attacked, right here in Bay Town. In her own carport.

"Hey, you know I'm not a mystical person. Spiritual, or whatever you want to call it. But I believe God guides, and I don't think He's guiding you back to New Orleans. If you want opportunity, let me talk to your mom. I'd love for you to spend the summer in the big city with me."

Shaking her head, Lacey huffed. "And like D.C. is any safer?"

Charlene sat up straight. "It is with me there."

"Maybe. I don't know."

Stabbing a piece of French toast, Charlene stuffed it into her mouth. "Mmm, this is the best."

Charlene got so lost in her meal that she never noticed Lacey pushing the same forkful around her plate. She'd barely taken a bite and dropped her utensil. Her stomach felt heavy. Life. Her life, her dreams bobbed along like the boats docked in the harbor. Going nowhere. Her eyes welled with tears, and she blinked, but not in time. The tears fell.

Charlene laid her plastic fork aside. "Oh, honey. It's all right. Things will work out. You're only nineteen."

"Almost twenty." She swiped a hand under her nose. "But if my life keeps going the way it has, I'm not sure if I will have much of one."

"You're strong, Lacey. Like your mom and me. We can get through anything. I know, losing your grandparents, heck, they were my parents too, then your dad, and now kind of your mom…although you asked for this." Charlene grabbed Lacey's hand and shook it.

Lacey chuckled. "I know. I'm so happy for Mom and Desmond."

"But that's them. Not you."

"No, they're always including me. I know that. Desmond wanted to acknowledge me in the ceremony, but I told him no. It's not that. I know they both love me. I couldn't ask for a better dad."

"No, you couldn't. Listen, I know it seems that Chris, your father, might have straightened out in the end, but he might not have either."

"But still, he was there when I needed him. When we needed him. But God chose to take him, anyway. And we needed Grandpa and Grandma, and God took them too. And I didn't do anything to deserve getting attacked in my carport." Lacey's eyes narrowed. "Why, Aunt Charlene? And now this. I just want to go to design school. It seems nothing I love or want is meant to be."

Lacey dabbed her eyes.

Charlene stood and moved to the chair closer to Lacey. She enveloped Lacey in her arms, kissing the top of her head. "Honey, I don't know much about this faith thing, but I know enough not to blame God. Hang on. Your mom and Desmond will be home in a week, and you guys can pray about it." Charlene laughed. "I can't believe I said that."

"Two weeks. I told them two weeks."

"Oops. I changed my flight and am heading back at the end of the week. Never mind. I'll change it again. I could use a two-week vacation."

Lacey pulled away. "No. No way. I'm a big girl, and you're going back to D.C."

"Then come with me."

"I have classes," Lacey said.

"Well, you're not staying here alone."

"I am. Tina is next door."

Charlene opened her mouth.

"Shhh," Lacey said.

"Don't you shush me."

Lacey tried to smile. "Sorry. I'll be fine. I'll figure it out, and I promise to call you if I need you."

"Oh, all right. You better." She pointed a finger.

Lacey passed her plate over to Charlene, who finished all her own food and ate half of Lacey's as well. They left Bubba's and headed to Beach Road, and Lacey's thoughts rolled around her head like clothes in a dryer. A jumbled, wrinkled wad of mismatched pieces. She listened to Aunt Charlene complain about nothing, and sadness enveloped her. She wanted to get away. *God, if you're willing, you can change anything. But maybe you're not willing?* She heaved a sigh.

As Charlene drove along the gulf, Lacey stared at the piers

passing by. Up ahead, a couple with towels around their shoulders were running from a pier to a car.

"Aunt Charlene. Stop." Lacey pointed. "Behind that Mustang."

"Cool car," mused Charlene.

Charlene pulled up behind a classic, blue 1965 Ford Mustang. Beautifully restored. The couple Lacey saw had popped the trunk and seemed to be teasing one another. When Charlene stopped Lacey jumped out. "Just a minute."

"Hey, Victoria?" Lacey called.

The woman who had sewn Melanie's wedding dress turned. "Oh, hey. Lacey." Victoria reached out to hug but pulled back. "I'm soaked." She frowned. "What happened to your hand?"

"An accident. But it's a long story."

"I'm so sorry." She touched the man next to her. "You've remember Art, right?"

"Yes. Hi. You're the youth pastor at Bay Town, right?"

"Volunteer, yes," Art said.

"Well, I hear the kids love you." Lacey turned to Victoria. "Thanks so much for sewing my mom's gown. You did an amazing job."

"Oh, my pleasure. But you did the hard part and I'm not sure that I've ever seen such an exquisite design."

Art nudged his wife and scrunched his nose. "Nobody uses *exquisite* in Bay Town."

Lacey laughed. "Thank you. Yeah, it's always been mom's dream that I could design wedding gowns to go with her business."

"Wow. A dream come true." Victoria said.

"Not exactly. Mom's dream, not mine."

"What's yours?"

"I'm not sure. Definitely design, but I'd hope to get into a design school." Lacey said.

"Great. Which one?"

"Well, not great. I applied to four and got rejected."

"Keep applying. There are plenty out there," Victoria said.

"Well, I'd hope to go somewhere in the fall, but it's not happening. So I guess I'll hit the job market in New Orleans. Good experience, right?"

Art snapped his fingers. "Work for Victoria. She needs part-time help."

"Oh, Art, Lacey's too talented for my shop."

"Is that so? Says the woman who got an order for a gown from a B-list actress who wore it to the Oscars earlier this year." Art boasted with his chest puffed out.

"Really? That's incredible," Lacey said.

"God. All Him." Victoria shivered. "Listen, I need to get warm. Art dragged me out here to jump off the pier."

Lacey scrunched her nose. "Why?"

Victoria laughed. "We used to do it all the time when we were kids. Listen, why don't you stop by my shop on Main Street?. We'll talk. I went to design school, and I almost hit it big."

"Almost?" Art feigned hurt, grabbing his heart.

"Okaaay. I hit it big with Art and Bay Town, and I chose not to go into the industry."

"But she had the chance," Art said.

"The best decision I ever made. It just took me a while to figure it out. You might pray about your decision," Victoria said.

"Oh, I have. And I am, but it seems like it's not happening." Lacey looked down.

"Like it's not going your way? Wait, and be willing to listen. God may have a better plan." Victoria touched her shoulder. "Come see me."

"I will. Thanks, Victoria," Lacey said.

She watched as the sweet couple turned back to their car. Art planted a kiss on Victoria's cheek before closing her car door. Lacey had a faint recollection of the first time she met them. But they weren't married back then. Lacey and her mom's first Christmas Eve in Bay Town when they attended the church pageant and afterwards went searching for a fruit-cake from Sally Trotman. She smiled to herself. That's right, Sally was Victoria's grandmother. Lacey wrapped her arms around herself. Small town.

She watched them drive away. *Did Victoria say be willing?* The tumbling mess in her brain slowed down, and she envisioned pieces of smooth clothing folded and neatly stacked. She began to think that maybe God had a plan for her. He always had before. She needed to keep trusting Him.

"Okay, Aunt Charlene. Let's go home."

"Who was that?"

"That? Providence."

"Oh, boy. If you say so."

Lacey chattered about Art and Victoria, and the pleasant ride home warmed her heart. When they arrived, her cell rang. Charlene parked the car and headed inside, but Lacey sat in the car and checked the screen.

CHAPTER 6

Her eyes widened. Wade. She counted to three before answering while stepping out of the car. "Oh, hey, Wade," Lacey said as casually as she could. Her heart soared. She hadn't expected to hear from him so soon.

"Yeah, well it turns out I'm still in Bay Town. My great-grandfather decided to stay in town, but I'm working tomorrow, so I wondered if you'd like to go get some ice cream or something tonight."

A date? Lacey stifled a squeal but cleared her throat. "I love ice cream. But I need to check if my Aunt Charlene has plans. Can I text you back?"

Wade sighed. "Sure. Let me know."

Lacey clicked off and squealed.

Charlene rushed back outside. "What's wrong. What's the matter? Are you all right? Do I need to call your mom?"

"No, sorry." Lacey giggled. "Listen, do you mind if I go out for a little tonight?"

"Yeah, sure. No worries," Charlene said.

"I can call Tina to come over and hang out with you." Lacey wiggled her brows.

"No. Are you kidding me? That woman wears me out. Our sleepover last night was a rager."

"A rager? Aren't you too old for that?"

"Hey, watch it, kid. Not really a rager. We didn't have alcohol or a DJ, but Tina doesn't need any of those to get amped. And look who's talking. You crashed early."

"True," Lacey said.

"What time will you be home? Not that you need a curfew or anything." Charlene patted Lacey's head. "You're such a good kid."

"I don't know. Not late. Maybe nine or ten?"

"Oh boy, do you know how to have a good time or what? Be back before midnight. I'm going to go read. Bye." Charlene walked into the house.

"But I'm not leaving till this evening," Lacey called after her aunt, but Charlene drifted out of hearing distance. Good ole' Aunt Charlene. Way laxer than her mom. A twinge of caution ticked her conscience, but she let it go and called Wade.

"Hi. Yes, I'm free. What time?...What?...Okay."

Lacey hung up and skipped up the front porch steps but stopped. She texted him her address, wondering if he'd remember the house from the jog.

Dusk settled over the bay, and Lacey sat on the front porch. A red Tesla soon pulled up and parked in front of her home. Wade got out and walked up the porch steps.

Lacey stood. "Hey."

"Hey, yourself." He raised his brows. "You look nice." Wade grinned and pushed back his unruly hair. The dark blonde curls contrasted nicely with the white collared shirt. Lacey stared, and her pulse quickened.

"Thank you. So do you." Heat rose on her cheeks. "Let's go."

"Wait a minute." Wade pointed to the house. "Shouldn't I meet somebody in there?"

"I guess you are a Gardner. Southern gentleman and all," Lacey teased. "My aunt is in the shower. We already said goodbye. But thanks for asking."

"Sure. Your carriage awaits, princess." He laughed. "Sorry, that sounded dumb."

Princess. She sighed, remembering that Chris used to call her that. The spin in her brain commenced again, but she shook her head. "So, where are we going?"

Wade reached out a hand to help her down the steps. She hesitated but took it, and once again, her skin charged. She let go as they walked to the car. He opened the door, let her in, and skipped around to the driver's side. "Did you eat dinner yet?"

"I did."

"Dessert it is then." Wade turned and grinned.

Her internal temperature shot up a notch, and Lacey lifted the hair off her neck, blew out a breath, and looked away.

Starting the engine, Wade pulled out onto Beach Road. "I hear there's an old-fashioned ice cream place in Waveland."

The temperature returned to normal, and Lacey stared straight ahead. "The Foster Freeze."

They drove in silence for a few moments, approaching their destination fifteen minutes away.

"So, you've been here before?" Wade asked.

Lacey pointed to the driveway of the Foster Freeze, and Wade pulled in. She stared ahead at the old rickety picnic table remembering when she had sat with her dad and mom eating banana splits. *Maybe this wasn't such a good idea.* "Hey, if you want to go someplace else, I'm good with that."

Wade laughed.

The neon lights on the sign blinked and a few of the letters didn't light at all. The building needed a fresh coat of paint. It didn't seem to rate a five-star establishment, but the crowded parking lot told otherwise.

"This isn't exactly what I would have picked. But I love good ice cream." Wade chuckled.

She gazed back at him. His dimpled, cheeky grin reminded her of Chris, and she'd worked so hard at putting those memories in their place.

She felt a tap on her shoulder. Warm and gentle. Then a squeeze.

"Are you okay?"

"I am." She blinked. "Come on, let's get that ice cream."

Wade ordered for them both, and they took their creamy concoctions to an indoor corner booth and sat. The garish fluorescent lighting was less than romantic, but Lacey liked how it illuminated Wade's handsome face. His large brown eyes stared back at her, smiling. If eyes could smile, his did—a lot like her dad's.

"So, I didn't expect to hear from you so soon," she said.

"Yeah, well, I didn't expect to bug you so soon, either." He scooped up a big spoonful of ice cream. Wade swallowed and put down his spoon. "You know, something tells me I should leave you alone, but I can't."

The light hair on her arms rose. "Why can't you?" she asked.

Wade shook his head. "I just can't. There's something about you, Lacey Thompson. I think maybe you're way out of my league." He laughed. "I'll just have to step up my game."

"Out of your league? What league am I in?"

"You don't party. Don't drink, don't do drugs." Wade winked.

"And you do?"

"Well, not drugs. I have a drink once in a while."

Oh, Mom would not like this. She frowned.

"It's not like I'm a drunk or anything." He shook his head, and that thick crop of hair fell over his forehead.

Lacey wanted to push it back. He did instead.

"But my dad. What a tool. A bad one." Wade said.

"Bad is subjective. My grandfather didn't think too highly of my dad."

Wade wrinkled his brow. "Why? I'm guessing you had a good homelife."

"I did, but my dad didn't raise me. I didn't get to know him till I became a teenager." She stared back at him. "He was a lot like you."

Wade leaned back. "You don't even know me."

"Sorry, I mean, you remind me of him."

"So, I'm the subjective bad?"

"No, not really." Her voice trailed, and Lacey squirmed.

"Not really? Wow. I don't stand a chance, do I?"

Lacey giggled, but inside, her heart pounded. *Stand a chance with me?*

"I had fun with my dad. He just wasn't ever around that much. I only remember what my mom told me. He did make it once a year for my birthdays. But when I hit my teens he started coming around more." Lacey paused. "Until he didn't." Lacey wadded the napkin she held and gulped. Her eyes watered.

Wade reached across the table, taking her hand. "You miss him, huh?"

"I do." Tears fell. "A lot."

Standing, Wade came around and sat next to Lacey on her bench. He put an arm around her. She couldn't help it. The dam broke loose, the flood rushed out, and she buried her head in his shoulder.

"I don't think much about him. But lately … at least since the wedding…"

Even through her grief, she felt his kindness as he let her sob for a few moments. But then she felt a gentle hand pull her hair back over her shoulders, and his eyes gazed into hers. Lacey had never been kissed, but she hoped this might be her first. She'd never been much interested in a boy other than crushes, but Wade Gardner tugged at her heart. A man, not a boy. She glanced at his lips as his face grew closer. Everything felt so right, and he lifted her chin.

"Lacey," Virginia squealed. "Hey, there, girl. I didn't know you had a boyfriend?"

"I don't." Lacey felt color flood her face and she took a sip of ice water, hoping to tamp down her rising temperature. Wade removed his arm, and Lacey scooted away. Virginia slid into the bench across the table.

"Um...this is Wade. A friend," Lacey said. "Wade, this is my friend from high school, Virginia."

Extending her hand, neon blue polish with white polka-dots wiggled out. "Hi, friend Wade." Virginia giggled.

"Where's Officer Blaine?" Lacey asked.

Wade stiffened. "Officer?"

"Come on, Lacey. You don't have to be so formal." Virginia pouted. "His name's Rodney, you know that." Virginia giggled and grinned at the slight, red-haired man standing at the counter. "That's my husband."

"Is he a police officer?" Wade asked.

"Yes, right here in Bay Town. Wade, you're not from around here, are you?" Virginia winked at Lacey. "He's cute." She pushed back her platinum blond curls. "Rodney. Come sit down. Look who's here."

Rodney brought two chocolate-dipped cones and handed one to Virginia. "Here you go, sweetheart." He nodded at Lacey. "Hey, Lacey."

"Hey there. This is my friend."

Wade offered his hand. "Wade Bodine. I mean Gardner. Wade Gardner."

Rodney scratched his head. "You're not related to a Will Bodine, are you?"

Lacey's eyes widened. "Will?" *Will Boudreaux had terrorized Bay Town with human trafficking involvement.* Lacey shivered.

Wade shook his head. "No, sir. Like I said, my name's Gardner. My dad was a Bodine, but he's been out of my life, and I live with my great-grandfather."

"*Thee* Mr. Gardner?" Rodney's eyes widened. "Owns all the big hotels in New Orleans?"

"Not all of them by any stretch." Wade looked away.

Virginia clapped her hands. "Oh, whoo-hoo. Lacey, you got yourself a good one."

Lacey rolled her eyes and felt the bench shift. Wade's knees jiggled like a bouncing basketball. Sensing his nervousness, she made an excuse.

"Hey, I need to get home. I have class in the morning. Rodney, good to see you, again."

"Nice meeting you, Wade," Virginia said. "And Lacey, bring your boyfriend to our place. I've fixed it up right nice since we got married, and you haven't seen it."

Giving Wade a nudge, Lacey slid from the booth. "Sure, that would be nice. Good to see you both."

Rodney stood. "Nice to meet you, Wade."

"Yes, you too."

Wade picked up the barely eaten banana split boats, the melting ice cream dripping over his hands. He tossed them in the nearest waste receptacle and grabbed a napkin.

Once outside, Lacey blew out a long whoosh of air. "Oh my. I am so sorry. Virginia can be a little awkward sometimes. But she's sweet."

"And gorgeous. Man, that girl is something. I bet she spelled trouble growing up."

Lacey's shoulders stiffened. She didn't like Wade talking about someone else like that, but she disliked herself more for having the jealous thought. They'd just met.

He chuckled. "How did she land up with a police officer?"

"Yeah, well, that's another story."

"Seriously, I'm just curious. Guys like that don't usually get girls like her."

Lacey spun around. "You don't even know her." Still irked at him and herself, she really wanted to leave. Where Wade had been a quick bright spot in her life, he smacked of a relationship she didn't need right now.

"I need to go home," Lacey said.

"Are you all right?"

"Why do you keep asking me that?" Lacey's voice rose. "I'm fine. I'm dealing with stuff. My mom just got married. There's a new man in our lives, and I can't get into design school. It seems I have nothing going for me right now." Lacey threw up her hands.

Wade grabbed one and pulled her back. He took her other hand, lacing their fingers together. He stepped closer. "Hey, I'm here."

He grinned that everything is going to be all right grin, like Chris. *But look where it got him.* Lacey let go of his hands. "We'll see about that," she muttered under her breath.

"Lacey?" Wade stood still while she kept walking. "I'm not going anywhere."

She turned, and the spring breeze cooled her cheeks. Her hair fluttered back.

He closed the gap. "Whatever it is. We'll work it out, you know."

"We? I've known you two days. Not even."

Wade threw open his arms wide. "Hey, it's providence."

His grin made her forget everything, and she reached in for a hug. Wrapping her arms around his waist, she buried her head in his chest. She could get used to this.

This time he pulled away. "Okay. I better get you home."

On the drive, Wade reached over and grasped her hand. She let him and smiled, warmth filling her all over …

BAM.

Something hit them hard from behind. The airbags deployed, and that's all Lacey remembered.

She didn't know how long she'd been out but woke to soft fluorescent lights overhead. She squinted and felt her face. Thick gauzy pads were taped across her brow and cheekbones. She tried to turn her head, but it hurt. So did her casted hand and wrist.

"Lacey, honey." Aunt Charlene patted her uninjured hand. "You're in the hospital."

"What happened? Where's Wade?" Lacey whispered.

She gulped, and her eyes burned. *Had he not made it?* She couldn't swallow. *God wouldn't do this to her, would He?* Sweat beaded on her forehead.

"The idiot driving the car? Wait till I get ahold of him," Aunt Charlene said.

"Aunt Charlene, he didn't do anything. Someone hit us from behind."

Her aunt's face went pale. "What? Why?"

"That's what we're trying to figure out." Chief Bert's imposing figure stood in the doorway. "Lacey, can you answer a few questions?"

"Sure, but I don't remember much. Where's Wade? Please, how is he?" Lacey's heart beat faster, and she tried to lean on one elbow. Her aunt pushed her down.

"Can't this wait?" Charlene's stern voice grated.

"I'd rather not. Wade's not hurt bad. He told the paramedics to take care of you first. They patched him up, and he's waiting outside."

Lacey's body went limp as she relaxed. "Oh, thank you, God." Her eyes felt heavy, but she forced them open. "Can I see him?"

"Lacey, who is this guy? We don't even know him," her aunt said.

"He's Mr. Gardner's great-grandson. Isn't that enough?"

"No, it's not. You need to tell me what happened." Chief Bert stared.

"We went for ice cream in Waveland, and on the way home, someone hit us from behind."

"Did Wade exceed the speed limit?" Chief Bert narrowed his eyes.

"I don't think so."

"Were you drinking?"

Charlene held up a hand. "Okay, that's enough. Lacey's a good girl."

"What about Wade?" the chief asked.

"No, we had ice cream. Just ask Officer Blaine," Lacey said.

Chief Bert pulled his shoulders back. "My officer Blaine? What's he got to do with this?"

"We had ice cream with him and Virginia at the Foster Freeze in Waveland before Wade drove me home."

"That's easy enough to corroborate."

"Good. Go corroborate, and please leave us so that I can call my sister," Charlene said.

"You haven't called Melanie yet?" Chief Bert's eyes widened.

"No. Please don't call Mom."

"I would have called her already, but I wanted to see how bad you were first."

"I'm fine, and Mom is on her honeymoon. Leave them alone. Aunt Charlene, I'll never talk to you again if you call her."

Charlene crossed her arms and glared at Chief Bert.

"Don't blame me. She's your niece. Okay, Lacey. So far your report matches up with Wade's. It appears to be a hit and run. Good thing he drove slow. Hitting a tree at a higher speed would have been certain death."

"Oh, thanks for the good news, Chief." Charlene rolled her eyes.

"Please, can I talk to Wade?" Lacey asked.

"I need to know. Who is this Wade?" Charlene asked. "Why don't I know this guy?"

"No one does. He's not from around here," the chief said. "I'll get him."

Lacey pulled herself up and brushed back her hair.

Chief Bert leaned out the door, searching. "He's gone."

Wade stepped out to call his great-grandfather. This wasn't going to sit well. The Tesla was totaled, and Reginald Gardner warned Wade. One more slip up, and he was on his own. Years ago, his great-grandfather had hired a private investigator to look for him. When they found him, he'd been surviving on the streets. Wade had had enough sense not to get into too much trouble. With his mother dead, and Beau in jail, he had no place to turn. Still, he didn't get into drugs but managed to get by with petty thefts. Just enough to live.

His great-grandfather took him in, and if not for the patriarch of the family Wade wouldn't have three years of college under his belt. But he had to go and mess it up with one bad semester. Still, he'd been working hard, and Great-grandfather promised Wade that he could go back to college when he'd paid his debt, and if he kept his nose clean.

"Yes, sir. I'm sorry, I don't exactly know what happened, but I wasn't drinking or driving fast. Yes, sir. I'll ask Chief Bert to call you. Thank you, sir. I'm going to check on her now. I'll call right away as soon as I see her. Good night, sir."

He blew out a harsh breath, and his exasperation peaked when he pulled a hand through his hair but winced. His right hand. The one that held Lacey's when they got hit. His fingers were bruised, but hers were broken. He must have gripped them during the crash.

"Rough night, huh?"

Wade spun around. That voice. "You hit us." Wade stepped toward the man.

Beau Bodine tipped a hand to his brow and walked toward the parking lot, avoiding the overhead lights.

Running after him, Wade yelled, "Why? What's your problem? You could have killed us."

He moved to a darkened area behind a dumpster and turned. "Oops."

Wade clenched his fists. "What do you want?" he huffed. "I didn't kill Mom, you know that."

"Don't call her that. She was never your mom. I don't even know who your real mama is, but now I got some idea. Why are you hanging around that big mansion? Who lives there?"

"Why do you keep saying stuff like that? What do you mean, never my mom?"

"We couldn't have kids, so we adopted you. My wife loved you like you were her own, and it's your fault she's dead now."

Wade couldn't swallow and choked. "I don't believe you."

"Then go ask whoever it is that owns that big house. Why'd they take you in? It don't much matter to me, except that I'm out of money, and you're going to get me some."

"I'm not giving you anything." Wade pointed to the building. "The Chief of Police is in there. I'm going to get him now." Wade moved toward the building.

"I wouldn't do that if I were you. I'll be gone before he gets out here. And I know who your gal is. She's pretty popular in this town, and I got an idea where she lives." Beau's eyes narrowed as he looked past Wade. "I got nothing to lose."

Wade turned to follow his gaze. Chief Bert stood at the entrance to the hospital and seemed to be searching the parking lot. If Wade yelled, maybe he could end this now. But what about Lacey? Wade turned and walked toward the exit. "Don't' you touch her," he called over his shoulder.

"I won't if you do what I tell you. Give me your number."

Wade had no choice but to comply.

"I'll be in touch." Beau slipped away into the darkness.

Chief Bert shined a flashlight through the parking lot, and Wade walked to meet the man.

"What are you doing out here?"

"I had to call my great-grandfather. He asked for you to call him."

The chief squinted and continued to flash his light around. "Is there something you're not telling me?"

"Why? Did Lacey have a different report?"

"Actually, no. You two line up." He pushed up his dark, thick-rimmed glasses. "You sure you don't know who might have hit you? Or why?"

"Sir, can I go see Lacey?"

"Yeah. Go on, kid. But if you remember something, you come see me, you hear?"

"Yes, sir."

CHAPTER 7

The white sheets felt cool to the touch, but they heated in her hands while Lacey scrunched them between her fingers. "Aunt Charlene, could you check and see if Wade's out there?"

"Why didn't I meet this Wade? Your mom is going to kill me."

"Because you were in the shower when he came to pick me up. Besides, I asked, and you told me I could go out, remember?"

"Yeah. But I thought you were hanging out with Allie or someone I knew. Not a complete stranger. How long have you known this guy?"

"I met him at the wedding."

"Oh, great. That's like a Hallmark movie or something. Only in the movies do you ever meet someone decent at weddings." Charlene huffed. "So, where is he now?"

The memory of running into him at the harbor arose. Lacey closed her eyes and didn't have the energy to go there with her aunt. But Aunt Charlene had a point. *Would he just leave her?* Maybe his great-grandfather made him come home or something. Her temples pulsed, and Lacey closed her eyes. "Why don't you go on home. I'm tired."

"No way. I'm staying here."

Lacey opened one eye. "Please, go. I love you."

Charlene stood. "If you're sure. I am exhausted. It might do us both good."

"I'm sure, but do you have paper and a pen? Just in case I wake up inspired."

Her aunt pulled out a yellow steno notepad, one pen, and one mechanical pencil. "Take them both. Live dangerously." She leaned down and kissed Lacey. "I'll be back in the morning. I hope for your sake that boy at least checks in on you. On second thought, it's probably better that he stays far away."

Knock. Knock.

Lacey's eyes riveted to the door and a wide grin crossed her face. Wade's wild, wavy hair fell across his worried brow as he peeked in. He walked forward and extended a hand to Charlene. "Hello, I'm Wade Gardner."

She took his hand and shook hard. He winced at her grip.

"So you're the one responsible for my niece's injuries?"

"Aunt Charlene, please," Lacey pleaded loudly.

"Well, there's nothing wrong with your lungs. Look at her." Charlene narrowed her eyes. "Do you want to tell me what happened?"

"Yes, ma'am. I wish I could, but all I know is that someone hit us."

"Who?"

Wade dipped his head down and stared at Lacey.

"Aunt Charlene, can we have a minute?"

"Okay, but we're going to have a talk." Charlene jabbed a finger at Wade's face.

Wade nodded. When the door closed, he glanced at Lacey's casted hand and walked to the other side of the bed. Sitting on the edge, he touched her good hand. "I'm so sorry, Lacey."

"For what? It wasn't your fault."

She hadn't felt this good since the accident, and she took

his hand. "I'm so glad you're okay. Are you okay? I've been so worried about you. That was wild, wasn't it?" Sentences tumbled out, and she didn't know whether the accident or the meds formed her words, but she meant it, and she couldn't stop them. "I don't know what I'd do if you'd been hurt."

Pushing back a crop of hair, Wade shook his head. "Yeah, well, I wish it had been me instead of you. I bet your aunt wishes that too."

"Never mind her. She can be a little cranky, but she'll like you when she gets to know you."

"I think I've got a strike against me already. Maybe two since I'm not from around here." He stopped, and his lips pursed white. "Lacey, I think maybe we should cool it a little. I mean, we just met and all."

Lacey stared at the monitor. She thought her heart had stopped. *He's bailing on me.*

Her dry mouth made it hard to swallow. How could she possibly tell him how she felt? How did she feel? Although the pain meds jumbled her thoughts, and nothing made sense, she knew one thing for certain. She wanted Wade around. She pointed to a cup of water, trying to buy some time to think.

He let go of her hand, but she wanted to grab it back. He held the cup, the straw to her lips, and she sipped, but he still wouldn't look at her. He wasn't thinking straight, that's all, she thought.

"Do you want anything? I can call for a snack or something?" Lacey said.

"Lacey, you, and me. We're not exactly a good match." He glanced at the door as if waiting for someone to enter. "I bet this town would agree."

"What do you mean?"

He scratched his head. "I don't know. We're so different. I wouldn't want you getting in trouble because of me."

Closing her eyes, Lacey breathed deep. *Whoa. True colors.* Her heart beat faster, and her chest tightened. Faces ran through her mind. Faces of all she'd loved and lost. Too many in a brief time. Too many in her short life. She turned her head aside and took a deep breath.

"You're right."

He stood a foot from her, but Lacey felt his body go rigid.

"What?"

"You're right. We're not a good match." She glared at him. "Because I wouldn't leave someone after something like this. I wouldn't run away because I feared what people thought about me."

"It's not like that." He touched her hand.

She pulled it away, finding strength in the action. "Fine. Whatever it's like, I don't want to know."

"You don't mean that."

"How do you know what I mean? You don't even know me. And I'm glad I found out who you were before I got in over my head." Lacey's voice lowered. "Go, Wade. Please." She closed her eyes tightly.

"Can you look at me? Please."

"No."

"I've never met anyone like you, Lacey Thompson." He sighed. "It's the accident. I'm responsible, you know."

She opened her eyes, and he stared at her. Every second melting her heart.

He sighed. "Okay, I know it's only been two days." He touched her chin. "Maybe we can take some time to get to know each other better."

Lacey's heart raced. She wanted that badly too, but didn't know if she could trust him. He bailed on her just minutes ago and it raised doubts.

"Listen, can I call you tomorrow? So we can talk."

Lacey huffed. "No." She threw an arm across her eyes. "Close the door on your way out."

The silence lasted too long, but she heard a click, and footsteps retreated. Tears trickled but she pushed up the lever on the remote and raised herself. She grabbed the yellow notepad her aunt had left and positioned it on her lap, draping her arm over the top of it. With her right hand, she started to sketch. She scribbled but crumpled up the paper and threw it. Draft after draft of wadded papers dotted the floor. But as the night wore on, creations emerged from her pain, hurt, and anger. Sometime during the night, she fell asleep and didn't remember.

The morning sun peeked through the blinds, awakening her, and a young nurse stood by her side. Lacey rubbed her eyes and focused on the walls. Her crumpled sketches were smoothed out and taped up on the wall.

The nurse stared as she took Lacey's vitals. "Those aren't wedding dresses, are they?"

Lacey chewed her lip. "Do you want them to be?"

"No. I hate weddings."

Lacey searched each paper. "Yeah, me too. Did you tape those up?"

The nurse rolled her eyes. "Not me. Must have been the night shift. Are you a designer? Those are pretty good."

"I wish."

Knock. Knock.

A blood draw technician walked in. He raised his brows and his eyes riveted to the nurse. "Good morning," he sang cheerfully.

They didn't answer.

"Hey, someone's got talent. Did you draw those wedding dresses?" he asked.

"They're not wedding dresses." A duo of voices snapped back.

He threw up his arms and pointed at Lacey. "You too?"

The nurse shook her head and left.

"You're too young to be a man-hater, like her."

Lacey squeezed her fist as the man poked her. "Ouch."

"Sorry about that. You're tense."

"It didn't hurt last time," Lacey said.

"It all depends. Say, those are beautiful dresses. Is one of them going to be yours?"

Lacey huffed.

"Ahhh. High school heartbreak?"

"I'm in college."

"Even worse." He pulled out a cotton ball. "Give him a chance."

"Nope. I think I dodged a bullet." Lacey's voice wavered. But she didn't really want to give up on Wade yet. *Did she?* "Besides, design is my passion. I don't have time for heartbreak."

"You mean, love?"

"Same thing."

The man laughed. "Okay, I'm done here. You have a good day." He walked to the door and turned. "Passion is a good thing, but don't let it take over your life. Got to enjoy the road trip, girl."

Lacey leaned back after he left. *Enjoy the road trip?* So far, her life had been a series of wrecks, literally.

After another night in the hospital, Lacey couldn't wait to get home. Aunt Charlene picked her up and chatted throughout the ride home. Lacey stared at her cast and thought of Wade. He had held her hand before the crash, but nowhere to be found now.

When they arrived home, Tina stood on her front porch with mylar balloons flickering in the sunshine. She waved, and Lacey marveled how she could jump up and down in those spike heels. Her tight curls bounced around her head.

"Hey, Lacey. Welcome home, girl," Tina squealed.

Lacey cradled her cast hand and hugged Tina.

"Oh, you poor thing." She jammed her hands on her hips.

"But you better call your mama. She's been calling me all morning."

Lacey gaped, then narrowed her eyes. "Aunt Charlene."

"Don't give me those eyes. I didn't call her. I've been ignoring her calls."

They looked at Tina.

"Whaaat? Of course, I called Melanie. But don't worry, I told her not to come home. Although I'm not sure she'll listen."

"Aunt Charlene, can you call her? Tell her I'm tired. I'll call her later."

"Oh, make me do the dirty work."

Tina handed Lacey the balloons.

"Thanks, Tina. Well, I think I'll take a little nap."

Charlene and Tina nodded, and Lacey heard them whisper as she entered the house. Her life had always been an open book. Sweet little Lacey. Melanie's incredible daughter. Mature beyond her years. She could manage anything. *Not anymore.*

Lacey walked into her room and closed the door. She lay on the mattress on the floor. It'd been that way since they'd moved to Bay Town. Lacey stared at the sketches and fabric swatches tacked up all over her room. The sewing dummy in the corner still had the mockup of her mother's gown. Lacey sat up straight. Every wall, covered floor to ceiling, had something to do with design. Her dream. Always had been.

Buzzing came from her purse, and she struggled to find it. The buzzing stopped. Pulling out her cellphone, she checked the texts. Wade had sent her five texts and a voicemail.

Voicemail. She thought of Chris. She hadn't heard it, hadn't wanted to, but Lacey recalled her mother telling her about Chris's last voicemail before he died. His last words. Lacey deleted Wade's texts and the voicemail without reading or listening to them. She stared again around the room. *This is my dream. Right here.* And no one could take it away, but as she thought of the rejection letters, an inkling of doubt rose within.

Her eyes riveted on her Bible. She hadn't read it yesterday or today. But right now, she needed to ask God to guide her and show her the next move. She grabbed the book and flipped the pages to the place in her reading schedule. Leviticus. What could she possibly learn from that book? She read through and waited. Nothing. No insights to write down. No lessons discovered. No promise to claim. Silent. God was silent. She closed her Bible.

Retreating to her desk, she grabbed a pen and pad, and made a list. Call Victoria about work. Look for an internship in New Orleans. Apply for a state school. She crossed off the last. Why waste money at a university when she needed experience?

Lacey had been so set on design school that she'd ignored all offers of internships. Her professors at the Community College had quit recommending her. Clearing off her desk, she pulled out everything she might need to apply for an internship in New Orleans. Tomorrow. A new day, and Lacey would seize it. She spent the rest of the afternoon and evening planning.

Hours later, her phone buzzed, and as she reached to turn it off, her mom's face appeared on the screen. She took a breath.

"Hi, Mom."

Her mother's tirade turned to tears, and remorse gripped Lacey, but with a cheery voice, she placated her mom's fears. When asked about the accident, she gave a few details about the wreck and Wade. She averted more questions by asking to speak to Desmond. Melanie didn't know about the final rejection letter, and Lacey had no intention of telling her on her mother's honeymoon.

"Hey, Pastor...Desmond. Can you keep Mom away?...I'm good. I'm fine...You guys finish your honeymoon, okay…Thank you. Prayers always help. Tell Mom I love her."

Lacey hung up but winced. Prayers weren't helping. Maybe because the difficulty of surrendering her desires, or just trusting God plagued her spirit. Even when Grandpa and Grandma died weeks apart, she trusted Him. After the attack she trusted Him. And she never stopped praying when Virginia disappeared. So when did the doubts begin?

Charlene brought in soup and crackers. "It's about time for some pain medicine, isn't it? How's your hand?"

"It hurts. Ibuprofen is fine. I can't take those narcotics."

"That's my girl. I got a bottle right here in my pocket." Aunt Charlene kissed her head and retrieved the meds. "Okay, kiddo. I'm heading to bed. Don't forget to read your Bible and say your prayers."

"I did that already." Lacey's stomach did a little flip. She really did, but it didn't feel like it.

"Good girl. You're a special one, Lacey. A little different, but in a good way. You're in a league of your own." Charlene winked as she closed the door and said goodnight.

I don't want to be in a league of my own. Do I? She thought she did, her sole focus previously only on design school, but now, what about Wade? *How fast life changes.* Finishing her soup, she flopped on her bed and finished some sketches, organized her portfolio, and finalized her plans for tomorrow. Meet Victoria at her shop first thing in the morning, then hit New Orleans in the afternoon.

CHAPTER 8

I t took forever for Lacey to dress in the morning. With her fingers bruised and swollen, even the slightest touch sent needles of pain through her hand. Not to mention her heart. She pushed out all thoughts of Wade's touch.

Lacey settled on a pale lemon-colored, cotton-waisted dress. The sleeves barely dropped off the shoulders, but the slight ruffle added a sweetness. It ruched around the middle and flared full from waist to just above her knee. *Cute.* The newest trend of the season hadn't hit the stores yet. She'd designed and sewn it herself inspired by a dress she saw on Spring Fashion week on the internet. Hopefully, any decent design house would know it wasn't off the rack. Not that her first stop, Victoria's boutique, qualified as a design house, but Lacey's sights were set on New Orleans in the afternoon.

When she arrived downtown on Main Street, Lacey parked in front of her mom's wedding shop "Quaint Affairs." Victoria's Dress Shop sat in the middle of the block. Getting out of the car proved to be as challenging as getting in with her bum hand. She began to resent the accident. Funny how the sentiment hadn't registered before.

The spring air smelled fresh, though dark clouds threatened overhead. She stepped down the sidewalk and passed The Pink Rosette. It smelled divine. Max, the florist owner, swept outside. Lacey chuckled at the British flag sticker tucked in the corner of the window.

"Hello, dearie." His flowing longish hair blew like hers. "What happened to your hand?"

Lacey raised her cast. "Got into a car accident."

"Oh my. Are you all right? Anyone else hurt?"

"I'm okay. Everyone is fine." Lacey cleared her throat. "It sure smells good out here." She pointed at the galvanized buckets of flowers lining the front entrance.

"Got a good crop of roses, I did. Did you want some white ones for your mum? They're her favorite. But I'll tuck in a rosette, just for you." He winked.

"Oh, thanks, but she's still on her honeymoon."

"Of course. How could I forget? Lovely wedding, and you did a bang-up job on her dress."

"Well, thank you. Victoria did an excellent job. She sewed it."

"But you designed it, and I think it's the prettiest one I've ever seen. Are you going to save it for your own? Could be an heirloom, you know."

Lacey forced a giggle. "Not anytime soon. Well, I have to go. Have a lovely day." She waved and walked on.

She passed a few more doors and stopped outside Victoria's. She stared at the store windows. Trendy streetwear took up one window, but in the other popped dazzling dresses. Formal wear. Victoria's favorite line. Lacey frowned. She still didn't understand the logic of choosing to set up shop in Bay Town over a glamorous career in California.

A nicely dressed man with curly hair exited the store. "Oh, hey there, Lacey." His grin almost buried his small eyes, and his face beamed, but then he frowned. "How's your hand?"

"It's fine." She wanted to get past it. "You're Victoria's husband, right?" She almost didn't recognize him from the other day. Swimming trunks and a beach towel gave him a totally different look from the casual business attire he wore today.

"Yup. The famous lady's husband with no name," he teased.

"I'm sorry. Of course, it's Art, right?"

He gave her a thumbs up.

Lacey locked on to his comment about Victoria. "Famous? Victoria is famous?"

"Well, she'll get there. I'm telling you, the word's getting out. That dress she made for that actress got some internet coverage." He crossed his fingers. "It'll be Oscar season before we know it."

"Oh, wow. I had no idea." She bit her lip. Maybe working here wouldn't be so bad. "Listen, I'm here about the help Victoria needed."

"Oh, good. Now I don't have to quit my job and start selling women's wear." He chuckled.

"Where do you work?"

"At the bank. I'm the tech guy," Art said.

"So, why didn't Victoria take that job in California that you mentioned?"

Art threw out his arms. "Me. She couldn't resist me." He laughed. "Seriously? All God's doing. Heck, I would have gone with her to California if she'd asked me. But both of us surrendered our lives to Him, and he worked it out better than we could have ever imagined."

"And she's happy?"

"Happy? How could she not be?" He thrust a thumb into his chest.

Lacey dropped her shoulders and gave him a look.

"I'm kidding. You should have seen the other guy. Talk about the Sexiest Man Alive candidate." He chuckled, but a sweet humbleness took over. "I can't believe she chose me."

Lacey cleared her throat, but it didn't stop her eyes from widening. "She had someone else?"

"Almost. Yeah, it's another world out there. I had to trust God that if he wanted Victoria for me, he'd have to make it happen because I sure couldn't. It's like that with anything, you know. Our dreams, our desires, our passions."

Why was he telling her all this? Lacey shifted her eyes, searching for an out, but he continued.

"You got to give those things to God. I never realized that Victoria had always been my passion. Like my idol or something. I found it really hard to give her up, but it's the best thing I ever did."

The front door opened. "Art? Who are you preaching at now?" A gentle voice rang out from inside the shop.

"Oh, hey, sweetheart." He winked and raised a finger to his lips. "Nobody, I'm standing on the street here practicing my sermon for the Youth Group."

"People are going to think you're nuts. You better get to work before you get fired." Victoria stepped outside. Seeing Lacey, she shook her head at Art and slapped his arm. "I should have known."

Art grabbed his wife and spun her around. Planting a kiss on her lips, he set her down and scurried down the sidewalk. He turned backward. "I'll see you at lunch, Babe."

"Don't call me...."

"Babe," he called back.

Victoria smirked. "My old boyfriend called me that. I hated it."

"The one from California?"

"Art told you?" Victoria laughed. "He's such a nut."

"You guys seem so happy."

"We are. It's not quite how I envisioned my life, but it's better than if I'd gotten my own way." Victoria's eyes sparkled. "Come on in."

Lacey followed her around the small retail showroom, but

when she took her to the work area in the back, Lacey's heart swelled. "This is like a real fashion studio."

"It is a real fashion studio." Victoria shrugged. "A small one, but it's all mine."

Lacey walked past the spacious table with fabrics spread out across. Tissue paper patterns lay in piles, and the overhead lighting proved more than ample. A clothes rack and two dress forms lined up in the corner alongside a bin of fabric rolls.

"You're for real." Lacey gaped. Her eyes grew large as saucers when she saw a framed poster with a Hollywood celebrity in a fabulous gown on the red carpet.

Lacey turned. "I remember this dress. It caused such a sensation last season. Is it yours?"

"It is."

"It's incredible." Lacey couldn't take her eyes off the poster. The black velvet gown shouted elegance. A strapless dress with an asymmetrical neckline, cinched at the waist, flowed to a full skirt, complete with bustle. Lacey touched the poster. "You added a slit in front. And elements I would have never incorporated."

Victoria raised both palms in the air. "What can I say? Inspired, and I could have never orchestrated that sale on my own."

Lacey continued staring at the poster. She walked over and swiped her good hand across the paper as if she felt the fabric.

Victoria asked, "What is it you want, Lacey?"

She cradled her broken hand. "I wanted to go to design school, but I didn't get in." *I want Wade in my life, too.* "That's all I ever wanted, but it's not what God wants."

"Do you know that for sure? How old are you?"

"I'm nineteen, almost twenty. I'm about finished at the Community College."

"Well, taking a gap year to work can't be a bad thing. Then apply again later."

"Is that what you did? Work before attending design school?"

"No. But I should have. I went to design school, then got a job, and it took me away from Art and Bay Town. Although I learned a lot, I almost made some terrible life mistakes, but faithful people surrounded me. Art, my grandmother, and your mom's new husband."

"Yeah, he's amazing. He helped me through a lot." Lacey warmed inside.

"You're pretty amazing yourself, from what I've heard."

Lacey shook her head. "I don't feel like it."

Victoria touched Lacey's shoulder. "Give it time. You have your whole life ahead of you. You may make mistakes, and things won't always go right, but with God, you'll get through it, and it'll be for good. He promises us that."

"Now, you sound like Pastor Desmond."

"I'll take that as a compliment." Victoria giggled. "So Lacey, are you here to apply for a job? I need a little retail help in the front of the shop. But if you'd like to use the studio back here, you're more than welcome."

"Are you serious? I could design back here?" Lacey's mouth gaped. "I mean if you hire me."

"You're hired." Victoria laughed.

"Just like that?"

"Your reputation precedes you. But I'm afraid the job is just part-time though."

"That's fine. Thanks so much." Lacey beamed.

"Yes, of course. Why don't you bring in some of your sketches, and maybe we can incorporate them into my line? I mean, they'll be under your name, of course."

"Oh my." Lacey struggled with her portfolio case. "I have them right here. I'm headed to New Orleans today. So I brought them to show. I'm applying for some internships."

Victoria frowned. "Be careful. Stealing designs is a real thing out there."

"They do that? People steal designs?"

"All the time. Not all houses, but some do. They come across innocent, young talented designers, work them to death, and put their lines out there in fashion week. If they're a hit, they never even get credit. Every big city has house designs like that."

Her phone dinged, and Victoria glanced down. "I'm sorry. It's a client." She texted back, then turned her attention to Lacey. "Do you mind if I ask who you're going to see?"

Lacey pulled out her phone and showed Victoria the interviews she had noted.

Victoria perused the list, but her phone dinged again. She raised a finger, quickly texting again. "I'm so sorry, Lacey. I have to answer this. I've been playing phone tag with this person." She finished, set the phone down, and glanced quickly once more at Lacey's list. "I'll be praying for you, and be wise, don't make any decisions today."

"Thanks for the advice," Lacey said.

Victoria continued a brief tour of the shop then covered the job requirements, but she did it with friendly grace. Lacey relaxed, and she felt comfortable with the decision to work there for now. Victoria released her for the day and asked her to come back when the shop opened in the morning.

An electronic bell sounded from the entrance. "Coming," Victoria called and walked to the storefront. Lacey followed, and she stopped. Her eyes rounded.

"Oh, hi y'all. Hey Victoria. Lacey? What are you doing here?" The stunning, tall blonde closed the door behind her.

"Lacey is my new shop assistant. Welcome home, Summer." Victoria hugged her.

"Oh, thank you." She smiled at Lacey. "And the wedding? You must tell me all about it. I am so sorry I missed it. I flew back last night." Summer Gardner, the gorgeous and wealthy woman who had helped Lacey and her mom settle in Bay Town. Wade's aunt. She stood before them, like a model on a runway. "Oh, my, what happened to your hand?" She asked.

Lacey stared back, hoping to let her question go unanswered.

"Your hand?"

Lacey held it up. "A car accident."

"Oh my. That's what you meant by accident." Victoria frowned.

Summer's mouth gaped. "Here in Bay Town? When?"

"Sunday night," Lacey said.

Summer's brows knit together. "But that's when my nephew Wade got in an accident," her voice faded.

"Your nephew? Is he okay? Does he live here?" Victoria said.

"He's fine, but no, he doesn't live here." She rubbed her temple. "In fact, I don't know why he'd be in town. Grandaddy is here now, maybe he requested Wade's presence." Her eyes rounded wide. "Oh my, Lacey. Were you with Wade when that car destroyed his Tesla?"

Lacey took a breath. "Yes."

"How do you know him?" Summer asked.

"I met him at Mom's wedding." Lacey's eyes shifted around the room, looking for an escape.

"And he took you out after?" Summer's sweet lips hung open.

"Actually, I ran into him running along the boardwalk the morning before the wedding." Lacey didn't want to say more, but the look on Summer's face pried.

"Hmmm. Go on."

"We met for coffee the morning after the wedding and for ice cream that evening."

"Oh," Summer whispered. "That was fast."

Victoria cleared her throat. "I'll leave you two, but I'll be in the back. Let me know if you need any help, Summer."

"Thank you so much." Summer turned all her attention to Lacey. "I'm so sorry. I sound like I'm interrogating you, don't I? I'm just concerned."

"No, it's okay." Lacey tried to sound casual. "On the way home, we were rear-ended. A random hit and run." Random, like her relationship with Wade. Time to move on, she thought.

Maybe Summer sensed that because she smiled that polite smile. That mannerism that all well-bred, southern ladies had down pat. But Summer's sincerity couldn't be mistaken. Not condescending, but caring

"Are you all right?" Summer asked.

"Yes, I'm fine. Thanks for asking, but I really have to go. So nice seeing you, Summer. Thank you, Victoria," Lacey called back towards the studio.

"My pleasure. Let me know how things work out," called Victoria.

"Bye, Lacey," Summer said but she followed. "Listen, um. You and my nephew?"

"We're not a couple. We just met. It's not a big deal. Besides I've got other plans." Lacey nodded, assuring Summer as well as herself, but her heart ached.

Summer blew out a breath. "Oh, good. He's a nice guy. Lots of fun and all, but he's still trying to get his life together."

So I've heard.

"You know what I mean?" Summer giggled. "He can be a real charmer, but I sure love that boy."

Tell me about it.

Stepping outside, Lacey's shoulders slumped as she plodded along the sidewalk. A man stood near her car, flipping a cigarette lighter. Something felt familiar about him. His slicked-back hair, his swaggering confidence. When she approached her car and struggled with the door, he sauntered over.

"Allow me, little lady." He opened the door. "How'd you break your hand there?"

Lacey looked around. Still early, and the street empty.

"Thank you, sir." She ignored his question, got in, and waited for him to close the door, but he hung onto it, staring.

"Better be careful, darling."

He slammed the door, and Lacey jumped. Resting her cast hand on the steering wheel, she inserted the key into the ignition with the other. She started the engine and gripped the leather wheel with her good hand. It slipped, damp from sweat. She glanced back at the sidewalk and sighed. *He's gone. Good.*

By the time Lacey arrived in New Orleans, she'd shaken off the silly scare. Her stomach growled. She'd only had a green smoothie for breakfast. Her mother wasn't even home, and she still followed the healthy protocol. The clock on the dash indicated that she had time for lunch. Pulling into a fast-food chain, she ordered and ate while prepping last minute details for her interviews.

First, a large, prestigious design house. Go big, she thought, but her hopes dashed when she walked in. The warehouse bustled with energy, her eyes buzzed with excitement all around. But Lacey soon joined a sitting area with the other hopeful interns. She stood against the wall. Every seat taken. An hour passed, and half the applicants had passed through the doors, but Lacey still sat. She glanced around the room. Scrutinizing everyone's clothing, then her own. Maybe she should have dressed up more, but she never went for the costuming styles. The fashionable trends of neon-colored hair, and white athletic shoes dominated, but the colorful, eclectic clothing resembled a Mardi Gras parade.

A tall, thin, mature woman stepped in front of the group. "You are all dismissed. We've chosen our interns."

"But please. Madam DeFleur, you'll be so impressed with my work. I'm sure of it." A young man wearing high-rise pants, a blousy shirt, and an edgy haircut begged. "I've come so far," he added in a thick accent.

Madam DeFleur released a heavy sigh and pushed back her long, smooth black hair. The glistening white highlights almost shined against the contrast. "You may leave your portfolio with your applications on my desk if you'd like. We'll return them by mail when we're done reviewing them."

"Fat chance," whispered an older applicant.

One by one, the remaining dejected candidates left. Everyone except Lacey, and she wondered why no one had left their portfolios. She walked to the desk and hesitated. Madam DeFleur removed her glasses. "Leave it and move on."

Lacey gripped her portfolio, then opened it. Pages fluttered out, scattering everywhere. Some landed on the desk, but most landed on the floor. Lacey bent down, but try as she might, her swollen, bruised fingers couldn't pick up the designs, so she laid down the portfolio and tried retrieving the papers with her good hand.

The tall woman stared down at her. "Are all these yours?"

Lacey's eyes riveted up. Madam DeFleur held a sketch in her hand.

"Yes."

"What house did you design for?"

"None. I mean, not yet. I'm still in college," Lacey said.

"What college?"

Lacey stood, leaving her designs on the ground. "I'm finishing up at the local community college in Hancock County. I wanted to get some experience before applying to a design school."

The woman smirked. "You didn't get accepted. Did you." It wasn't a question.

Lacey shook her head.

Looking across the warehouse Madam DeFleur snapped her fingers. A younger woman collecting bolts of fabric looked up. She immediately deposited them in a bin and rushed over.

A long braid down her back completed the plaid mini-skirt outfit, and combat boots. Edgy costuming, Lacey thought.

Madam DeFleur pointed at the floor. "Pick those up for…" She looked down her nose. "Your name?"

"Ruby," said the young woman.

"Not you. Her." She pointed at Lacey.

"Yes, ma'am." The young woman scooped up the sketches, and her eyes widened. "Wow. These are good. They're really amazing."

Madam DeFleur cleared her throat loudly, and Ruby stepped back.

"Your name?"

"Lacey, Lacey Thompson." She turned to Ruby. "Thank you."

"All right then, Miss Thompson. I can squeeze you into our intern program. You can start tomorrow morning. Eight to five, every day. We may need you for shows on weekends, but you'll be notified. Report here to me. But first, I need you to sign some papers." She turned to a large filing cabinet behind her.

Lacey whispered to Ruby, "Does she own the company?"

Ruby's eyes shifted back and forth. "Not anymore. But don't sign any papers," she whispered. "Not yet. You're too good." She hustled away the minute Madam DeFleur turned back.

"Sign here, here, and here," said Madam DeFleur, pointing with a pen.

Lacey's heart raced. Standing amongst bolts of fabrics, swatches of textiles, and racks of samples stirred up her passion. Across the room, she caught eyes again with Ruby who gave a side-to-side head movement that shook the braid hanging over her shoulder.

"May I take the papers home first and look them over?"

Madam DeFleur drew back her shoulders and raised her

chin. Snatching the contract from Lacey's hand, she stuffed it back into a folder. "Good day, Miss Thompson."

Lacey's mouth gaped and she gripped her portfolio with her good hand. With eyes burning, she swept out of the warehouse not bothering to look at anyone or anything. Outside, she shifted her eyes upward. *You won't even give me a break here, will you?*

CHAPTER 9

Ten thousand dollars. Beau's extortion demand might as well be a million. Wade wondered why Beau had waited days to call. But he did. Early this morning.

Wade threw his cell on the bed and stared at the window. On the horizon, the gulf waters were as slick as glass, and it amped his angst. He pressed his forehead into the double-paned window, and with each slow wave that rushed the rocks, he pounded his head against the coolness. Again, and again.

One short phone call, and Wade had agreed to meet his father. Adoptive father? Whoever he was, the man had forced his hand, but concerns for Lacey were what mattered the most. The one-sided conversation gave Wade no answers, only demands that left him with more questions and an unmeetable extortion. Ten thousand dollars. He had no choice but to meet with the man.

As his pulse quickened, he raised a fist, ready to smash it through the window.

"Wade?"

The door to his room pushed open, and the scent of gardenias floated in.

His heart quickened even more at the sound of his aunt's voice. He cleared his throat. "Come in."

"I'm sorry, your door was ajar. Just wondering if you'd be joining us for breakfast? Granddaddy is waiting."

"No."

"You missed dinner last night. Are you all right?" Summer asked.

"I'm fine."

"Grandfather is concerned." Summer's voice cooed sweetness.

Wade shook his head and turned. "Tell him I'll pay him back for the Tesla. I'll pick up more catering jobs at the restaurant."

"That's not fair, Wade. You know he doesn't care about that. He loves you, and he knows it wasn't your fault." Summer cleared her throat and walked to his bed. She sat. "I ran into Lacey Thompson yesterday."

His skin tingled, and a knot formed in his stomach, but he couldn't speak. He closed his eyes, trying to shut out what Summer had to say but anxious to hear. "So?"

Summer stared back at him.

She's fishing and here it comes.

"She's a nice girl, Wade. She comes from a good family, and her future holds promise."

Wade pushed back his hair and rested both hands on his neck. Elbows out. He opened his mouth but shut it. He spun around towards the window again. When he clenched his teeth, his chin quivered, and he knew nothing he could say would make a difference.

He heard a slight creak come from the bed but didn't turn.

Summer's light footsteps padded to the door. "You hold promise too, Wade. You're just missing the Lord. That's the difference between you and Lacey."

The door closed, and he gazed out the window. A flock of white whooping cranes flew over the gulf. A lone seagull shot up into the sky, disturbing the perfect formation. The cranes scattered as the seagull darted about. For an instant, the gull's dark silhouette glided across the sun, and a single crane flew by. The seagull followed.

You have promise. Put your hope in Me.

Wade looked at the door. No one lingered, but a ray of sunlight shined through the window and rested on the night-stand. It shone on a black Bible that he'd opened a few times. It reminded him of his mom. Or whomever the woman who raised him must have been.

She had often talked of God's promises, but not for her. Always on her knees begging for God's deliverance for Wade out of juvenile hall, but even more that he would love Jesus. Wade picked up the Bible and opened it to the Psalms. The only book in the Bible that made any sense to him.

We wait in hope for the LORD; he is our help and our shield. In him, our hearts rejoice,

for we trust in his holy name. May your unfailing love be with us, LORD, even as we put

our hope in you. Psalm 33:21-22

Wade read it and reread it many times then sat on the edge of the bed in silence. He clasped his hands but couldn't pray. He hadn't done that since his mother died.

Knock. Knock. "Good morning, son."

Wade's eyes rounded. "Sir? What are you doing up here?"

Mr. Gardner never maneuvered the stairs, and he leaned against the door jamb. Behind him walked in one of the house staff who placed a food tray on the desk. The breakfast comprised of bacon, Eggs Benedict, toast and jam, and a bowl of fresh fruit complete with a crystal glass filled with orange juice.

"May I?" Mr. Gardner didn't wait for an answer but tapped his cane across the hardwood floor, avoiding the plush Indian wool rug. When he reached the side chair, he lowered himself and slowly exhaled.

"I'm sorry, sir. You didn't need to come up here."

His great-grandfather waved him off. "You missed dinner last night."

"Yes, I'm sorry."

"Want to tell me what's bothering you? I suspect it's more than the accident."

Wade shook his head and stuck his hands into his pockets but said nothing. The silence hung thick, but Reginald Gardner had more patience than he, and Wade didn't know where to start.

"When you found me on the streets, you said we were related. That I was your great-grandson."

"Yes. That is correct."

Glancing around the room, Wade took in the opulence, accustomed to it now. The family spent more time at the big house in New Orleans than here. Sometimes they stayed at the Gardner hotels, but Wade liked it here. A little more down-to-earth. *Down to earth?* A relative comparison in the Gardner household. But it felt more like home, especially the last three days after meeting Lacey. And Wade often wondered, *Why me?* But he never asked for fear of losing it all and landing up like Beau.

"How did my mom end up with my dad?" Questions surrounding his paternity plagued him. *Did it matter? The man was bad news. The worst. How could you let her marry him?* Wade wanted to ask. *Were you as hard on her as you are on me? Did you push her too hard?*

Wade's eyes burned, but they were nothing compared to the rage that seemed to burn in his great-grandfather's eyes. His jowls trembled.

"Did you see him? I got word they released him from prison."

"You knew? You got word, and you never told me."

"We were assured he couldn't find you. That's why we changed your name to Gardner."

"A lot of good that did. I'm still a Bodine. I always will be."

His great-grandfather scooted out of the chair, leaned on his cane, and stood. "You, my son, are a Gardner. Your mother, a Gardner, and I loved her with all my heart as I do you, Wade. Unfortunately, she made bad choices, and I couldn't stop her. She fell deeply in love with the wrong man. I tried, but nothing could be done."

"But my dad said the woman who raised me wasn't my mother. Is that true?" Wade pressed. "If she wasn't your granddaughter, who was she?"

Reginald slumped. His chin rested on his chest, and it heaved. "Wade, can we discuss it this evening?"

"It's true, isn't it?" Wade clenched his jaw.

"My granddaughter birthed you, and couldn't care for you, so she gave you up for adoption. The mother you knew raised you."

Ringing in his ears almost drowned out his great-grandfather's words. Wade ran his fingers through his hair and closed his eyes. His stomach flipped.

"Adopted. That's what Beau said. So neither of the parents who raised me are mine?"

"Yes. That's so."

Wade stood. "So your granddaughter gave me up because she couldn't take care of me? Is that a joke? Look at this place?" He flung out an arm. "I crashed a Tesla, and it's nothing to you. What do you mean she couldn't take care of me? You refused to take care of me."

His great-grandfather's knees buckled, and he sat. "That's not true. I didn't know about you. She never told us." He closed his eyes.

Summer rushed in. "What's going on?"

"Ask him," Wade shouted.

"Granddaddy, what are you doing up here? Did you climb the stairs alone? Are you all right?" Summer's voice choked.

"I'm fine," he said.

She turned on Wade. "Are you crazy? How dare you speak to Grandaddy like that. You don't know what he's suffered for you."

"Summer, that's enough," Reginald said.

"Wade, Granddaddy has given you everything."

"Enough. Wade didn't know," Reginald said firmly. "He didn't know Spring was his mother."

Sweat beaded across Wade's forehead, and he moved backward, dropping onto his bed.

"You had to know something. We hinted. We tried to tell you, but you never let us." Summer gazed at Wade.

"After you found me, I figured my mom who raised me was somehow a Gardner. I didn't need to know more. I couldn't ask for a better mom."

"But you must have had questions. You were old enough to be curious." Summer pressed.

"That's enough," Reginald said. "Wade's adoptive father is out of jail. I just found out. Our private investigator notified me yesterday."

Summer gasped, her hand raised to her mouth. "Oh, no. Wade, I'm so sorry. Did he contact you?"

"Who is he?" Wade's jaw tensed.

Reginald and Summer exchanged looks.

"Please, son. May we continue this evening?" Reginald asked.

"Yes, yes. That's what we'll do," Summer said.

"Who was my real father?" Wade spat out the words.

Summer's eyes fidgeted between the men, and she blurted, "Beau Bodine's brother. Wade, please, let's talk tonight."

Wade's stomach knotted. So many questions. So many emotions. Relief one of them. At least he wasn't the son of a killer. "My mom was everything I needed, and she never gave up on me. Not like your granddaughter."

"Oh, Wade, you don't understand," Summer whispered.

"You don't understand," choked Wade. "My mom lived a saintly life, and it got her killed."

His eyes rested on the Bible still lying open. Memories seeped in. Long forgotten, happier times. Vacation Bible School, Christmas pageants, and his mom reading and praying with him as he grew up until he became a teen and refused to listen. His heart had hardened over the beatings he took from Beau and, worse, those he'd witnessed against his mother. Still, she would have wanted Wade to treat others with kindness.

Wade held Aunt Summer's gaze, then walked to the chair where his great-grandfather sat. He offered his hand and helped the elderly man out of the room and down the stairs.

Wade promised to be home by dinner but didn't bother to tell his great-grandfather he'd miss work at one of the hotels in New Orleans today. Too much on his mind as he headed for the bank. He rechecked his phone, hoping for a missed call from Lacey. Nothing.

Pushing open the bank's glass doors, he stepped aside as a woman exited.

"Wade? Right?" Her bubbly voice cooed, and she patted her tight curls.

"Uh, yes, ma'am."

"Tina? Me." A glittery gold nail pointed to herself. "We met at Melanie and Desmond's reception. I'm Lacey's neighbor."

Wade tipped his chin upward. A nod of recognition, and his heart sank. "Oh. How's Lacey?"

"Excuse me? I thought you two...are you not like together?"

"No, ma'am. Just friends. Sort of. Is she okay?"

"As far as I know," Tina said.

A horn honked, she peered past Wade, and waved. "I'm coming, Rudy. I have to go. My husband's picking out paint colors for a job, and he needs my help. Bye, Wade." Tina rushed past him, then stopped. She flashed a broad white grin. "Give Lacey a call. She's a little low right now. I'm just saying."

"Yes, ma'am," said Wade, without intention.

He slipped into the bank, deposited his tips, and asked the teller for his balance.

"Here you go, Mr. Gardner." The cute teller slid a paper to him.

But cute didn't matter anymore.

"Thank you." He stared at the receipt. Just about enough to pay off the lost semester at the State University or Beau Bodine. He crushed the receipt in his hands. He'd start with a thousand and withdrew that amount.

Wade walked toward the doors, staring down. He had no idea what to do. Beau had given him a week to come up with the funds. If he gave him the money, what would stop him from asking for more? If he went to the police and Beau suspected anything, Lacey might be his target. He walked, but something stopped him.

"Whoa, there."

Wade faced a man holding up his hands. "Oh, sorry."

"No worries. What's up, man? Hi, I'm Art. I work here." He extended a hand.

"Wade Gardner."

"Oh, one of them." Art winked. "Just kidding."

"Yeah. But no. I'm not one of them. Not really." He stepped around Art and moved to the door.

"Hey, is everything all right?"

Wade stared back at the man. Lacey told him about this small friendly town, but this guy? Too much. "No, nothing's right."

"Oh, sorry to hear that. Say, I'm good at listening, and I'm on my break. Can I get you a water, and we can go outside and sit a spell?"

Wade shook his head. "I don't think so. But thanks. I can manage."

"Okay, then. I'll be praying for you, Wade Gardner."

"Excuse me?"

"Have a nice day." Art grinned and waved.

Walking outside, Wade scratched his head. He stopped under a magnolia tree, and the large white blooms soothed his bothered brain. A memory arose.

Years ago, living on the streets, and sitting under a tree, Wade's stomach growled with hunger. He had nowhere to turn, so he stole wallets. He always took most of the cash and left the wallets near the place where he'd picked it. But one time a wallet held no cash, just plastic. He wasn't into credit card fraud, not yet anyway. So he sat alone in the bus station in New Orleans, missing his mom. Beau rotted in jail at the time. Not that he'd ask for his help, so he threw up a quick prayer. Wade grinned at the memory, and peace flooded his soul.

It didn't end there. That night a man approached him at that bus terminal—a dodgy guy in an army jacket with a baseball hat. Nice disguise, he remembered thinking. Wade figured any adult approaching him on the street to be a social worker. They were hunting him down to lock him up after he ran away following the death of his mom.

He had tried to run again, but the man caught him, and afterward he explained his business to Wade, offering him the world, the Gardner world. Wade thought about that prayer.

CHAPTER 10

Her first full day at Victoria's shop dragged. Learning the basics of retail wasn't that exciting. At the end of the day, Lacey trudged into her house and picked up the note that Aunt Charlene had left. She had another meeting. As a social activist, Aunt Charlene hustled hard righting the wrongs in the world, which kept her busy and often preoccupied. *Good.* Lacey huffed and threw her tote on the kitchen table while slinking into the closest chair.

The events of yesterday flooded back. The whole Madam DeFleur fiasco. *I blew it.* As negative self-talk invaded her mind, she found herself blaming God for things not going her way, but she knew better. He gave her a choice to make her own decisions, and she chose to ask the stupid question about signing the contract for the internship at Madam DeFleur's Design House in New Orleans. Lacey wrinkled her brow. Why did that girl warn Lacey not to sign anyway?

Her aching hand throbbed, and she realized she hadn't taken any pain reliever all day. Between her swollen fingers and the headache pounding in the back of her neck, misery invaded. Laying her head down, she stared at the dripping faucet. Her eyes landed on the bottle of ibuprofen on the counter, but she had no energy to get it. Not physically, not emotionally, not even mentally. Rejection permeated her body until it hit her heart. *Wade.*

Glancing at her tote, she tried willing her phone to buzz, but it rang instead. Lacey scrambled, hitting her hand as she did, but it didn't stop her.

"Ouch. Hello?"

"Lacey? What's wrong?" Her mother's voice flooded her battered spirit as if she could sense Lacey's despair.

"Mom."

Lacey didn't realize how her mom's absence had affected her whole being. Life had thrown her quite a few curves, and she'd never gone through anything like the past few days without her mom and her mom's faith. The little girl Lacey wanted to beg her mother to come home, but she stifled it and cleared her throat, asking instead about the honeymoon. Interrupting her mother every time she asked about the car accident. She forced excitement, telling her about working for Victoria. Finally, her mother asked about the application for the design school in D.C.

"I got rejected…I know. I know, Mom. God always has a plan."

Her mother's soothing voice helped, as well as Desmond who prayed for her on speaker. Lacey felt transported back to his office, listening to wise counsel. His prayers were like that. When he finished, he assured her that having doubts about how God worked were okay, but not to let them lie under a shadow. They had to be uncovered, through God's timing and His ways. Desmond encouraged her that God would wipe away her concerns if she'd let him.

"Thank you, Pastor." A load lifted off her shoulders, and she giggled. "I mean Desmond. Or should I call you Dad? I can't decide."

"I understand. But I'd be honored if you called me Dad."

Lacey sucked in a breath. Tired of crying, but the tears that rose inside brought joy. Still, she stuffed them down.

"Okay, Dad. Well, I have work to do. Tell Mom not to call again, and I'll see you in another week or so. Bye."

Lacey hung up before the flood came. Despair and conflicted feelings about her career and Wade poured out and with it a wave of relief that made her wonder why she hadn't taken her mother's calls earlier. She headed for her room. Her Bible lay on the floor next to her mattress, where she'd left it after church on Sunday. Lacey plopped down and grabbed it.

First, she closed her eyes, gripping the tan book in her good hand. *I'm sorry, Lord. Sorry, I've stayed away these last few days. Help me. I'm so mad it hurts. But I love You, God.* She squeezed her eyes shut and wanted to say more, but nothing came, except when her mind opened to Wade.

"God, touch his heart," Lacey whispered aloud. She wanted to ask God to bring him back into her life, but she knew better. Didn't she? Like the job in New Orleans.

Lacey prayed for everyone she could think of and once again found that her own problems diminished when thinking of others first. She read the Psalms when her words ceased, and before she knew it, darkness had settled outside.

The door slammed, and she jumped.

"Lacey? I brought dinner," Aunt Charlene called.

Trotting into the kitchen, Lacey hugged her aunt.

"Relax, it's just fast food." Aunt Charlene kissed Lacey's cheek and frowned. "Wow. No offense, but you're a mess. Oh, honey. Have you been crying? Come here, baby." She thrust out her arms.

Lacey wiped her eyes, ignoring the invitation to hug. "I'm good. I talked to Mom."

"Oh, thank the Lord. I've been avoiding her calls. Did you tell her about Wade?"

"Let's eat. I'm starved."

"You didn't, did you?" Aunt Charlene gave a sideways glance.

"Wade's not...he's not around."

"What do you mean, not around? The creep. He gets you into a car accident then runs."

"It's not like that. I didn't know him that well. We're too different, so he says."

"He dumped you, didn't he? Men. Arrrrgh."

Lacey reached for the white paper bag and slid out the contents. They spent the evening eating and chatting, and while Lacey glamorized the job with Victoria, she neglected the whole New Orleans fiasco.

Wade didn't know what to expect as he sat on Reginald Gardner's right, while Aunt Summer sat gracefully across the room. He'd hoped for more answers than the brief meeting from the night before. The warm glow of a table and standing Tiffany lamp lit up the library. Though Wade had never been a reader, the wall-to-wall shelves comforted him.

Hazel, the head housekeeper, stepped in. "Shall I bring in some sweet tea?"

"No thank you, Hazel. Just bring Mr. Simmons in when he gets here, please."

Hazel left, and silence deafened the room. Finally Summer spoke.

"Wade, there is so much to tell you. We don't know where to start."

"Why not the beginning?" Wade's long legs stretched out casually, but he entwined his fingers tightly, resting them in his lap.

Reginald cleared his throat. His sad eyes drooped but his stiff back controlled the mood. He glanced at Summer.

"Yes," Summer began. "Well. My sister, Spring, fell in love if that's what you could call it. Oh, truth be told, he was a scoundrel, and I hate him." Summer dabbed her eyes with a pretty floral handkerchief.

Reginald gave her a nod.

"All right. Well, Spring left home and ran away with him. Grandaddy sent a private investigator after her, but she refused to return. Apparently, things got really terrible, and try as we might, she remained adamant and wouldn't come home." Summer's voice cracked. "And we left her alone just as she insisted."

"You gave up on her?" Wade shot the words.

"No. Of course not. We kept the private investigator on retainer. Awful. Just terrible knowing how she lived and being helpless to stop it. The private investigator kept offering her our help, but then someone threatened his life. Said to quit nosing around. Our hands were tied." Summer sniffed again. "But years later she showed up at this house. On the doorstep, literally."

"My mother? This is my birth mother you're talking about."

Mr. Gardner cleared his throat. "Yes, son. That is correct."

"Why?"

Summer stood and picked up an envelope. She walked to Wade and handed it to him. "She left this for you. Maybe you'll find those answers."

"You have no idea why she did what she did?" Wade asked.

"Foolish love. I assume. It consumed her. But Wade, you must believe us, we would have taken her back. I loved my granddaughter. So sweet and kind, but perhaps too innocent." Reginald's lips worked a smile.

"My beautiful sister didn't have an unkind bone in her body. but when she came back here, she was unrecognizable." Summer drew a breath. "She shocked us. You know we don't often come here to Bay Town, but when we do, we send our house staff from New Orleans ahead of time. They open things up and get the house ready for our visit." Summer choked back a sob. "Hazel found her lying on the front porch."

Wade raised a hand to stop Summer. "Wait, a minute. How long? How long did she stay on the porch before you found her?"

Reginald swallowed so hard his Adam's apple bobbed, and he sighed. "A couple nights."

"A storm passed over, and it had been freezing that night. Hazel called the paramedics and the police. She didn't even recognize Spring at first." Summer gasped and tears fell. "Me neither. When I reached the hospital, I couldn't believe my eyes."

"How did she die? Drugs?" Wade asked.

Reginald shook his head. "Not directly."

Wade crossed his arms and pressed them across his body. Processing the story knotted his stomach.

Summer tilted her head. "She had none in her system, but the private investigator confirmed that she'd been using drugs for years."

"Then how did she die?" Wade closed his eyes.

"A lot of things. Her body just shut down. Influenza, bad liver. That awful life compromised every organ, and it showed. My poor sister." Summer covered her face. "Oh, Wade, she only talked about you. That and how she regretted her choices. Sorrow laced every word, and she made us promise to find you. To bring you back here. She didn't know what life you had, but she wanted you to be with us. Wade, you belong here."

The veins in Wade's neck pulsed, but he said nothing.

"And we wanted you too, Wade. Here, here with us." Summer pointed to the letter. "I hope you'll find the answers there but know that she loved you."

"Then why'd she give me up? She could have brought me here herself."

"I'm sure she would have if she could have. I suspect she wasn't allowed to leave her situation. He wouldn't let her."

Wade shot up from his chair. "What are you talking about? What situation?" *Wouldn't let her?* Wade's eyes widened. "Wait a minute. Did she prostitute herself?" Wade choked.

"Oh, Wade, hush. Don't say it. She had no choice."

"Everyone has a choice." Wade lowered his voice.

"Yes, son. We do, but sometimes the wrong choices leave us to face consequences with no alternative. That's why it's so important that we follow God's plan for our lives."

Wade laughed. "You're kidding, right? God's plan? How could she fall for a jerk like that?" Wade's eyes widened. "Oh no. Did he groom her?" Wade glared. "The guy pimped her out, right?"

Summer covered her ears. "Please, Wade."

Reginald straightened. "Son, we don't speak like that. Especially with ladies present."

Wade laughed again, and his voice rose. "He did. Didn't he? And this guy, he—"

The door pushed open, and a man dressed in a dark suit, white shirt, and striped tie entered the room. Wade recognized him as the man who had found him in the bus station years before.

"Wade, this is Mr. Simmons, our private investigator. I believe you've met."

Wade nodded.

"Well, he looks like he's turned out right nice. You've done a good job, Mr. Gardner."

Reginald Gardner cleared his throat. "Mr. Simmons, my grandson is a respectable Gardner now. He's a hard worker and an honest young man, and I thank you for recovering him. Please sit. He has some questions for you."

The man barely sat before Wade fired away.

"Was my mom a prostitute and my dad her pimp? What

about the mom who raised me? I don't even want to know more about Beau Bodine."

Mr. Simmons shifted his gaze to Reginald, then to Summer. "Yes on both accounts."

Wade's stomach churned, and acid burned his throat. He closed his eyes.

"Your father, the man that handled your mother has since died in a car crash. They tied him to a case of human trafficking here in Bay Town. Two separate cases, to be exact."

Summer sat up straight. "Lacey, Melanie, and Desmond were caught up in that."

"Lacey?" Wade's voice grew strong. "What did he have to do with Lacey?"

"The man that handled your mom went by the name of Will Boudreaux. He abducted girls and sold them to a human trafficking hub in New Orleans."

"Why have I never heard this?" Wade asked.

"The news channels and papers all carried it." Mr. Simmons shrugged. "Boudreaux kept some girls for his petty operation, but Chief Bert broke it wide open with the help of Melanie Thompson and Desmond Brooks."

Wade covered his eyes and groaned. "What about Lacey?"

"Don't know her story, but another guy presumed to be involved died in a hit-and-run. They found another dead in a hotel room after the bust too. I didn't investigate it. Lots of bad stuff happened. Lots of people hurt."

Wade couldn't believe his ears. Lacey's parents tangled with his assumed father, who proved to be a whole lot worse than Beau Bodine. This couldn't be real. He drew a shallow breath. "How did Will Boudreaux die?"

Mr. Simmons shook his head. "A car explosion. Pretty much an inferno, during an abduction. The woman had some serious injuries, and left Bay Town. They credited the mayor here as the hero."

Wade remained silent for a long time. So did everyone

else. The private investigator shuffled his feet and shifted in his chair.

"Would you like a glass of sweet tea, sir?" Summer offered.

"Yes, please."

"Come with me. I'll take you to the kitchen." Summer led the investigator out of the room.

"This is worse than I thought." Wade dropped his head in his hands. His fingernails dug into his hairline, and he wanted it to hurt. A growl gurgled in his throat, and he felt more lost than he ever had before. More anger, more hurt.

A warm touch cupped his shoulder. Red-rimmed eyes pleaded back at him, pooled with tears. "Son, please don't go there. You have a new life here, and your mother made sure of it. Know that." Wade's great-grandfather pointed to the letter that Wade had thrown down. "Your mama had a genuine faith, but she went astray. But much like the prodigal son, she came home, and she confessed and repented of her wrongdoings before she died. Her dying wish remains. That you would know the goodness of God."

"Goodness?" Wade said too loudly. "Then why would she leave such a good God? Why would my mother turn her back on Him? On you? On all this?"

"We live in an imperfect world, Wade. He is a good God who lets us choose. Read that letter. I'm sure the answers are there."

Reginald wobbled with his cane's aid to the bookshelf. He pulled out a small black book.

Wade shook his head. "I don't need a Bible. You left one upstairs in my room."

"Have you read it?" Reginald asked with his back turned as he held the small Bible in hand.

"Sometimes. Yes, this morning, I did."

"Good. Don't forget what you read. It's providence. And so is this. It's your mom's Bible. I gave it to her when she was a little girl. It's the only thing she had with her on the doorstep when they found her. That and your letter." Reginald's eyes pooled with moisture.

Wade stared back.

"It's all she had left." Reginald held it out.

Papers fluttered to the ground. Wade bent to pick them up. They were photographs of a baby—a baby in Spring Gardner's arms.

CHAPTER 11

Wednesday afternoon teen girls giggled as they checked out the shiny satin dresses that Victoria had displayed in the shop's center. Lacey had already asked if they needed help, but they were content with pulling dresses off the rack and holding them up, spinning around in front of the three-way mirror in the corner of the store. A petite teen with long, straight black hair frowned. She held the hanger folding it down at her shoulders, and the long dress pooled around her feet.

"I can never buy anything off the rack." She struggled to pull up the dress at the waist.

"Here, let me help," Lacey said. "Go in there and slip it on."

She grabbed some clips reserved for sizing wedding gowns, and when the girl returned, Lacey went to work. She clipped an inch at the shoulders and folded four inches of the hem. Lacey stepped back.

"Wow." The girl grinned back at Lacey in the mirror. "Can you fix it like this?"

"I think so. Let me check." Victoria didn't do alterations but recommended a tailor on the other side of town.

Lacey peeked in the back where Victoria worked and proposed the idea of making the alterations on the prom dress herself. Victoria encouraged her to go for it if her time allowed.

"Thanks, Victoria." Thankful to help the girls, Lacey secretly hoped her career entailed more than just alterations. Retrieving chalk and pins, she returned to the teen still holding the dress. A few of the girls giggled at the clips. Evidently, they couldn't imagine the final results. Lacey would make sure the girl would look stunning.

"Yes. I can do it. When's the prom?"

"Two weeks." All the girls squealed.

No problem. Without Wade in her life, she had time on her hands. She could easily take the dress apart and reconstruct the shoulders, waist, and hemline. The petite teen's raised brows stared back.

"Okay. Let me write up a work order. How did you want to pay for this?"

"My great-grandma wanted to take care of it. She's meeting me here."

A tiny woman walked in. Lacey recognized the salt-and-pepper hair and the stick-straight posture.

"Oh, Lacey. I didn't know you worked here," Mrs. Higa said.

Lacey grinned. She hadn't seen the older woman in quite a while. "Hi, Mrs. Higa. Yes, I started a week ago. Oh, is this your great-granddaughter?"

"Yes." Mrs. Higa pointed to the petite teen. "She has searched everywhere and can't find a dress. I told her I could make one, but she won't let me."

"Oh, Obaachan. You're too old." The teen covered her mouth. "I didn't mean that."

The other teens hid behind the circular rack of dresses, giggling.

Lacey's eyes widened, but she suppressed a chuckle when Mrs. Higa's face wrinkled so that her narrowed eyes barely glared out. The woman boasted over ninety years old and still worked her lobster and crab traps off the pier. Old yes, but not too old for anything.

"I didn't know you sewed." Lacey tried to subdue the conversation.

Mrs. Higa pursed her lips. "I helped design and sew over three-hundred kimonos for St. Joseph's Academy Mardi Gras ball back in the sixties. Right here in Bay Town."

"Ancient history, Obaachan," the great-granddaughter retorted.

"Yes. They used Ancient Japan for the theme, and don't you forget it." Mrs. Higa jabbed a finger at the girl.

"But we're Okinawan," the teen said. "You always remind me."

"Yes, and I taught those girls an Okinawan dance for the ball." Mrs. Higa giggled, but it bubbled into a full-blown laugh. "And no one knew it wasn't Japanese." She slapped her thigh and held her waist, laughing hysterically.

"I know. I know. All the papers carried the story, and you were on the front page," the teen said.

Lacey's eyes grew wide. "That's pretty incredible. You never told me that story." Pride for the respected woman swelled in Lacey.

Mrs. Higa threw her hands in the air, her face flushing red. "Anyway." She pointed to the dress. "Too long at the waist and shoulders. I can fix that."

"No, Obaachan. That's okay. Lacey said she can do it."

"Yes, and it'll be my gift," Lacey said.

She loved Mrs. Higa and didn't doubt her abilities, but Lacey wanted to reciprocate all the kindness the old woman had shown her for the few years she'd lived in Bay Town. She'd shared lobsters, crabs, and many delicious dishes she cooked. She also allowed Lacey to spend the night when her great-granddaughter Allie came over. Allie and Lacey were good friends and the one her mother hoped would move in and become Lacey's roommate.

"Nonsense. If I'm paying for it, I can fix it."

The teen chewed the corner of her lip and stared at Lacey.

"I'd love to help, Mrs. Higa. You've done so much for me."

Mrs. Higa frowned. "You think I'm too old too."

"No! Are you kidding? You can do anything. How about we mark the alterations here, and you can take the dress home and work on it there?"

Mrs. Higa threw off her jacket, hitting the gaping teen. She pulled glasses from her handbag. Stepping on the platform, she pushed her granddaughter forward and put a hand out to Lacey, who handed her the chalk and the pins as she worked.

The girl's face scowled the whole time, and her eyes pleaded with Lacey.

Lacey marveled at the old lady's curled fingers working slowly but meticulously. "You are a seamstress, aren't you?"

Lacey patted the girl's shoulders. "Your great-grandmother is pretty amazing. Only the best students in my sewing class at the community college would have caught the detail that your great-grandmother is fixing."

"So, she can do it?"

"Of course, I can. Do you think I'd waste buying you a dress then ruining it? I'm old, but I'm not foolish. If I say I can do it, I can do it."

"I'm sure you can, Mrs. Higa." Lacey directed her attention to the teen. "She's a talented woman. When she finishes, will you come back here and model for me?"

The girl beamed, and Mrs. Higa smiled.

Lacey rang up the purchase, covered the garment with a bag, and handed it over. "How's Allie?"

"Busy. Too busy to come see me. That nursing school has her studying too much. But I guess that's a good thing." Mrs. Higa grinned. "But she takes good care of me when she comes."

They said their goodbyes, and the store emptied in seconds. But the bell jingled again, and one of the teens returned by herself. Lacey noticed a spark of familiarity.

The teen cleared her throat. "If I buy a dress here, can you fix it for me too? My mama said she'd take me dress shopping, but she's pretty busy." The teen wrapped her arms around her ample waist.

"Sure. Hey, do I know you?"

The girl's smile glowed. "No, but you probably know my mama. Jacquie? She works at the Mockingbird?"

"Of course. Yes, you look just like her."

"Yup, that's what everyone says."

"You're beautiful, like her too. What's your name?"

The girl blushed and kicked her toes into the floor. "Destiny. Everyone calls me Desi."

"Well, Desi, I'd love to help you pick the perfect dress. It'll be gorgeous. I promise."

Desi's eyes went round, and she clapped her hands. "Can I hug you?"

Before she could answer, the teen ran over and wrapped her arms around Lacey's waist. She squeezed for a quick moment, then ran to the door.

"I'll be back," she called.

And back she came. So went the rest of the week. Soon, Lacey had to send the other girls to the seamstress Victoria had recommended.

"That's nice of you, Lacey. Those girls trust you, and you have a gift for helping them pick out what fits and becomes them, not just what's trendy."

"It's easy when you don't stock trendy. But you don't design all the rack gowns, do you?"

Victoria laughed. "No. I found an affordable supplier, and I avoid the 'trendy.' But I have to stay in business, and tourists like trendy beach cover-ups and sundresses."

Lacey laughed. "Well, that's easy. Do you design those?"

"No. I don't have time. As a former buyer in California, I have many connections from there."

"I could do it."

"Oh, no. You'll be spreading yourself too thin. With the alterations, school, and working here. You need time to be creative with your line."

"My line? I don't think that's ever going to happen." Lacy sighed.

"Have you been praying about it? By the way, what happened in New Orleans? We didn't get a chance to talk."

Lacey's heart beat a little faster. She hadn't told anybody about Madam DeFleur's, and it still gripped her.

"Oh, no."

"Well, keep trying. You'll never know if God's opening a door or closing one unless you try. Unless, of course, He's saying wait."

That's what Lacey didn't want to do, wait. She couldn't let go of wishing she'd signed the contract. Her conflicted spirit went back and forth. When she prayed and read her Bible, she had peace. But when she went back over her sketches, angst arose. Deep inside, she knew the struggle, but she wanted her designs out there so badly that it hurt. That wasn't the only thing that made her hurt. She hadn't heard from Wade in over a week.

"Hey, it's five o'clock. Let's lock up. I'm having dinner with Art at Manière Sisters. Would you like to join us?"

Lacey loved Manière Sisters restaurant, but family memories made her shake her head. "No, thanks. I have to get these alterations finished before prom."

∾

Arriving home after work, Lacey checked the mailbox and grabbed hold of the few letters, not bothering to look. She walked into the house and threw the mail on the kitchen table. A note from Aunt Charlene informed her that she wouldn't be home for dinner. Lacey opened the fridge. No leftovers. She and Aunt Charlene had eaten out almost every night since her mother had been gone. She dropped onto a kitchen chair and rifled through the mail. Her jaw dropped.

An express mail package. She ripped it open and pulled out an ivory envelope with a stamped return address flourished with MDD in the corner. Her mouth gaped as she read. The letter from Madam DeFleur's Design house offered her another chance for the internship. Lacey squealed out loud and kissed the paper. "Thank you, God." she said. The letter asked her to bring her entire portfolio, and Lacey ran to her room.

Pulling out the case, she organized her sketches. She placed those in the rough stages in one pile and her finalized full-color designs in another. A flutter stirred inside. *Where was it?* Her most important sketch couldn't be found. The variation of her mother's wedding gown. She searched the rough sketches one more time. Nothing turned up. She grabbed a stack of loose papers on her desk. Not there either. Lacey resorted to digging through the trash and smoothed out all the papers in there. Zip.

Finally, she opened the drawer where she stashed every design she'd roughed out for the last year. They were filed by date. Her stomach churned. Licking her finger, she touched each corner, flipping each one over.

"Phew," she said, clutching a very rough sketch of her mother's dress to her chest.

Lacey spent the next hour finalizing it as best she could from memory but couldn't get it right. She stopped, closed her eyes, and suddenly slapped her forehead. The gown itself was hanging in her mother's closet. Retrieving it, she finished the sketch but groaned. This sketch still resembled a wedding gown. She pounded her forehead again trying to recall every modification of the red-carpet variation. Closing her pad, she placed it aside and sat. She glanced at her Bible. Was the letter an opportunity? Or a test? Lacey wished her mom were here.

Ice cream. The random thought popped into her brain from nowhere. But it sounded good. A bit of comfort in the way of the creamy cold concoction always helped. Lacey stared back at her Bible. Mom would pray first, but she wasn't here. Lacey grabbed a jacket and walked to the kitchen. She slipped the letter from Madam DeFleur into her bag, pulled out her keys, and headed to Waveland's Foster Freeze.

She ordered her chocolate-dipped cone and walked outside toward the old picnic bench but slowed. Bittersweet memories arose of her dad. He'd sweep into town unannounced and take her mom and her to dinner at the Meniere Sisters Restaurant, then they'd land up here. But the last time they did it, it didn't end well. Chris's girlfriend called, and it spoiled their evening.

Lacey breathed deep the Sand Pine tree scent surrounding the picnic area.

Gripping her chocolate-dipped cone, she eyed someone sitting on the picnic table. Not the bench, but the table. His wild hair blew in the breeze as he yelled into his cell phone. Lacey froze. Déjà vu. Just like Chris yelling at his girlfriend. But it wasn't Chris. The guy slammed the phone to his thigh and jumped off the table. He spun around, and his eyes locked on Lacey.

"Wade," she whispered. Everything in her said to run. But her feet felt like they were stuck in cement.

He walked closer and stood a yard away. His sad eyes stared at her, and his shoulders drooped. "Hey, funny meeting you here." He tried to smile.

That's his greeting? He hadn't called in days, but she could blame the finality of her goodbye in the hospital for that. Her body stiffened, and she turned. A trashcan stood nearby, and she threw the untouched, melting ice cream away. Her fingers were freezing anyway.

"Lacey, I'm sorry. Please, can we talk?"

Move feet, move. But they didn't, and she turned. She looked anywhere but at him. She watched the wind rustle the trees. She stared at the stars, the moon, and watched the dark clouds drift across the sky.

"How's your wrist?"

"Fine. Five more weeks, and I get the cast off. And what are you doing here?"

He grimaced. "I just got off work."

"Don't you work in New Orleans?"

"I do. But I have a meeting tonight. Things going on. Listen, I'm so sorry. Are you able to work with it like that?"

Lacey's stomach growled, and she gripped her waist. "Yes. It doesn't hurt anymore."

"Are you cold? Here, take my jacket."

She stepped backward and stumbled, but Wade rushed to her side, touching her elbow, steadying her. The contact sent shivers up her arm, and she wanted to push him away but couldn't. Lacey bit her lip and stared back at him. He dropped his hand.

"I'm going to New Orleans tomorrow," she blurted. Not a lie, but an exaggeration. She had to call and make the appointment first.

"What for?"

"An internship," her voice rose. "It's at a big design house."

"That's great. See, things worked out." He shoved his hands in his front pockets. "What design house?"

He melted her heart. His joy over her good news. The hope of things working out. Lacey breathed in and out, and her pulse raced.

"Madam DeFleur's."

His head shot up, and Wade pushed back a thick hank of hair that fell across his face. "Don't take it, Lacey. They're cutthroat. My aunt used them, and she steers everyone away from them. Don't do it."

CHAPTER 12

Wade put his hands up, trying to stop Lacey from running away from him. "Wait. Hear me out. Will you?"

"Hear you out? Why? So you can ruin the one good thing that's coming my way?"

"MDD is not a good thing."

"Who is MDD?"

"That's what they call it in New Orleans. Madam DeFleur's Designs. Listen, I've had some experience with the owner. Well, not me, but Summer."

"Summer? Never mind. Who is the owner?" Lacey crossed her arms, narrowing her eyes like laying a trap.

"Madam DeFleur, the dragon lady."

"Ha! No, she's not."

Wade rolled his eyes. "She used to be. Don't let anyone fool you. She still runs the show, but her daughter and the board of directors took control after she messed up with some ethical issues. She still calls all the shots."

"I don't believe you."

"Don't then, but at least talk to Summer. She ordered her wedding gown from MDD, and when she went for the fitting, they had made a slightly different version of what she ordered. A scandal about a stolen design surfaced."

Lacey crossed her arms and tapped her foot, but she didn't run.

Wade felt terrible for spoiling her hope. He had intended to comfort her, but he couldn't. He'd be meeting Beau soon, and he could be risking Lacey's life if he reattached himself to her now. Terrible timing. He had to get this part of his life straightened out. Wade sighed. Not just this. Not just Beau. His entire life. His birth mom and dad. With stomach churning he looked at Lacey. She could never know. He shivered trying to throw off the grip that dug deep into his heart.

Wade stepped forward reaching for Lacey's hand, but she shirked away. He sighed, thankful that she did. Falling for this girl tore his heart up, but that heart pounded realizing that he wanted her in his life more than anything in the world. More than his great-grandfather's approval. More than owning a big hotel. More than his future.

He'd lived for so many years in survival mode, taking whatever he could get his hands on. But if he had any chance with Lacey, he had to change. The uncertainty of how rose in his mind.

The moonlight shining over Lacey disappeared, as dark clouds shaded her face. The clouds masked every feature, but the essence of Lacey remained. He felt her goodness, but her pain as well. He waited. The moon peeked out illuminating her face again, and her pained eyes stared back at him. Yes, waiting. Any hope of relationship with this girl would have to wait.

Wade took another step closer but was careful to keep a slight distance. Her fresh, floral scent surrounded him. He backed up. Too tempting.

"Lacey, do what you think is best. I'm not going to tell you what to do. I care about you a lot, but right now I need to fix my life."

Lacey pushed back her long, chestnut hair. When the wind blew, it tousled her wavy tresses, but Wade loved the messy look. She needed help, too, and oh how he wanted to be the one to do it.

"Me too," she whispered. Her green eyes sparkled, but not with joy. She squeezed her arms around her waist. The cast hand rested on top.

Wade covered her hand with his. He could feel the tension in her fingers release. Her face softened, and she blinked. The hairs on his arms rose. He couldn't help himself and pulled her body close to his. "I know, Lacey. This is hard. But you have your mom and dad. Trust them. You come from a good family."

She buried her head in his shoulder. "What about you, Wade? The Gardner's are good people too."

Wade dropped his arms and backed away. "But I'm not one of them. You don't know me, Lacey. Heck, I don't even know me."

"Then let's figure you out together." Lacey pleaded.

"Not now. But maybe later we can start over." Wade rushed back to her and took her hand, and he held it in both his and squeezed. "I promise."

A smile crept on her lips, and she nodded so hard that her hair fell forward. Wade reached up and tucked a strand behind her ear. He nudged closer, and his face closed within inches from hers. His mouth parted, and he wanted nothing more than to press his lips against hers. Soft, inviting. He tried to wait but knew nothing could stop him.

Lacey tilted her chin upwards and closed her eyes. Wade lowered his head.

Honk! Honk!

Headlights flashed on the embraced couple, and Wade stepped away. Lacey shaded her eyes.

More honking, beeping, and laughter came from the

parking lot. Wade's shoulders drooped and he blew out an exaggerated sigh. *Providence?*

~

Wade placed Lacey into her car and followed her home. He grunted his frustration as he drove back through town. He came so close, he could almost taste her lips. Relief flooded him that they weren't in the same vehicle. He wasn't sure he could control himself from taking her into his arms. With any other girl, it didn't matter. But Lacey was different, and something inside of him had changed.

Wade drove across the Bay Bridge and parked outside the Silver Slipper Hotel and Casino. When he had worked at his great-grandfather's grand hotels in New Orleans, he often utilized the valet services to remind himself of where he wanted to be one day. But that dream was changing by the minute.

He passed the doorman and a cocktail waitress. Before crossing the gaming floor a tall, broad-shouldered man blocked his path.

"Got any ID, son?"

The clanging slots and ka-ching of money deafened the chatter.

Holding a hand to his ear, Wade pretended he couldn't hear. The man sporting a casino badge held out a palm and wiggled his fingers, clearly not amused.

Wade carried his twenty-two years with streetwise confidence. The wild, bushy hair and the scruff on his chin lent itself to an older air, but his youthful, chiseled jaw and slim physique gave him away.

"Sure, here you go."

The man narrowed his eyes and checked the ID. "Have a nice time, sir."

Wade tipped a hand to his head but stopped. "Hey, where's the café?"

The man pointed around the outskirts of the slot machines, and Wade followed the swirled, multi-colored carpet path that led to a bright but small diner-type restaurant. Wade spotted Beau and approached.

"No buffet? After life in prison, I thought for sure you'd go for it. Oh wait, you didn't get life, did you?"

"Shut your mouth and sit." Beau narrowed his eyes. "You got the money?"

Wade reached in his pocket. "Here's a thousand. I need more time."

Beau raised an arm and laid it across the padded red bench. "You're stupider than I thought. I gave you plenty of time. You're lucky I waited this long."

"It's only been a few days. I had to work. Besides, I can't get 10,000 dollars. No way."

Beau leaned forward. "I know where your girlfriend lives."

Sweat beaded on Wade's forehead. Would the guy stoop that low? He already had. Wade fisted his hands under the table. He wanted nothing more than to punch his dad. A mixture of anger and relief filled him. Not his dad. All his life, he'd wanted to beat this man. But his mom said, respect your father. He didn't have to anymore. Wade forced an obnoxious laugh.

"She's not my girlfriend. She goes to church. Not my type."

"Don't knock it. My wife went to church. You were brought up better."

Wade straightened. "Are you kidding me?"

"I don't kid about my wife. She was a good woman."

"Then why'd you smack her around?" Wade's throat went dry, and he tried to swallow while remembering the sweet woman he knew as a mom. But all that had changed. He didn't belong to her, and he didn't belong anywhere except to two low-lifes.

Beau's shoulders relaxed, and his head dropped to his chest. "The booze. I dried out in jail, but too late." He pointed. "Your fault. You made it too late. I could have changed, and I wouldn't have even gotten that bad if you weren't in our lives. She doted on you. She cared more for you than me."

A young waitress with bright purple streaks in her blond hair stood at their table. A pretty girl behind all that thick eye liner and mascara. She wore a white shirt, unbuttoned too low, and Wade averted his eyes as she leaned forward, placing two glasses of water on the table.

Beau laughed. "You got it bad for that girlfriend of yours. Why you can't even notice a cute little thing like her." He winked at the girl.

She tipped her head, and her purple-tipped ponytail swished. She raised her brows at Wade.

Wade glared at Beau but turned his attention to the server and smiled. "Hi, there."

"Hi, there, yourself. What can I get ya'?"

"I'll have the thirty-two-ounce steak dinner." Beau interrupted and pointed at Wade. "And he's paying."

The girl licked her lips. "And how about you, handsome?"

Wade took a deep breath then touched her hand. "I'm not that hungry. But what time do you get off?" His stomach flipped as he voiced the stupid line. She looked older than him, but he had to do something to convince Beau that Lacey meant nothing. The thought ripped his heart.

"Well, I'm not exactly on the menu." She giggled. "But I just came in, so I'm not off till 2:00 am." Her lips pouted.

"That's okay, he's going back to his big rich home and his sweet little girlfriend." Beau stared at Wade, waiting.

"I can come back." Wade said. "How about I meet you out front at 2:00?" Wade grinned.

"Make it 2:30. I need to clean up and change." She scribbled on the pad. "Here's my number." Ripping a ticket off, she handed it to Wade.

He winked.

"Yeah, I'll believe it when I see it," Beau said.

Wade listened to Beau rant about how much he loved his deceased wife while continuing to blame Wade. Beau took no responsibility for her death as they waited for the steak dinner. He made excuses for his drinking rages, and Wade listened, hoping to hear hints of his past.

"I know my father was your brother."

"Is that right?" Beau laughed. "Rich too. Maybe not as rich as your—who is that that lives in that big fancy house, anyway."

"None of your business."

"I'd say it is because that money you're getting me is coming from somewhere."

"It's coming from me busting my back working two jobs."

"Yeah, right."

"Why do you think I only have a thousand dollars?"

"You got more than that, and I know it." Beau sneered.

"It's not my money. The guy living in that mansion is helping me out. He's just some philanthropist that found me on the street." Wade pulled at his collar. "He set me right in college, but I screwed up, and now I have to work off my college tuition from last semester. I don't have ten thousand dollars." Wade leaned in.

"Well, you'll just have to get it." Beau pounded the table. "Or that little girlfriend of yours may just have another accident."

"Here you go, sugar." The waitress laid down the heavy plate with a clang. She tipped her head at Wade. "I'm taking my break, but I'll be back in a few." She wiggled her fingers in a friendly goodbye.

Whatever, he thought as he almost rolled his eyes. Instead, a scheme arose, and he stood and followed her.

"Hey, where are you going? We're not done here," Beau called.

Wade swung both arms out wide and grinned. He threw a nod toward the waitress and skipped. "Hey, sugar…" He caught up and slung his arm around her shoulder. She beamed up at him, not bothering to remove the friendly gesture.

He had to make Beau believe. If he could get a picture of the girl and text it to Beau after 2:30 am, that might convince him. He lightened his touch on her shoulder, and a twinge of guilt hit his heart.

"So, where are you taking me?" asked the waitress.

"Lead the way," Wade said.

As soon as they were out of the café, Wade removed his arm, but she grabbed his hand and led him outside. Walking to an outdoor garden, she sat and patted the bench. She pulled out an e-cigarette and puffed.

"I hate this job."

"Why stay?" Wade asked.

She giggled, and her ponytail swished. "I'm not rich like you." She crossed her legs, shaking her ankle, and her short skirt inched up her thigh.

Wade averted his eyes. "I'm not rich. He thinks I am, and he wants money."

Putting the vape in her pocket, she turned and faced Wade, bringing her face too close. Her lips hung open, and she stared at his. "Ohhh, you poor baby. That's terrible."

Wade pulled away and grabbed his phone. "Hey, can I get a picture of you?"

Her eyes narrowed, and after a pout, she hunched. "Sure, why not?"

She wrapped her arms around Wade squeezing her cheek

against his. As he held the camera out to take a selfie, he counted "One…two…"

On three, she kissed him full on the lips just as his finger hit the photo button.

Instinctively he thought to pull away and wipe his lips. To tell her to get lost. But a new decency admitted his fault. He played her for Beau's sake. For Lacey's safety, he thought, and as the girl kissed him again, he complied for a few seconds before guilt riddled him. He pulled away and stood.

"I better get back in there. He's not a patient guy."

The girl frowned but stood and wrapped her arms around him again, leaning in for another kiss. Wade stepped away, taking her hand, and they walked hand-in-hand back into the café. He dropped his hand before they approached the table, but he brushed her cheek with a light kiss, in front of Beau.

"I'll see you at 2:15," she cooed sweetly.

"I thought you said 2:30?"

"I can't wait," she said while walking away.

Beau pointed to Wade's mouth. "You better wipe that lipstick off your face, or your little girlfriend will drop you like a hot potato."

"I told you, she's not my girlfriend. We had one date, and you ended that."

Stuffing a piece of red meat into his mouth, Beau chewed. His cheeks puffed out, and he pointed with the fork. "Whatever. If you can't get me ten thousand, I'll take five for now," he mumbled with his mouth full.

"I can't do that, I told you."

Beau swallowed. "You will do that, or I'll break into that big old house of yours and hurt whoever it is that's your meal ticket. You hear me?"

"When is it going to stop?" Wade stared back.

"What?" Beau stabbed the last big hunk of steak and shoved it into his mouth.

"The extortion. I'll go to the police."

Beau threw his head back and laughed, a big wad protruding from his cheek. "You go ahead and think like that. I'll hit anyone close to you before they even get a handle on where I am." He chuckled but coughed, and kept coughing, His face reddened. He clutched his throat, gasping for air.

Wade watched in slow motion. Could this be the answer to his problems? He hated the man, and all the memories of rage and abuse flooded back, but something stirred inside his heart, and thoughts crashed around his brain.

A voice yelled behind him. "Someone call 911. The man's choking."

Slipping out of the booth, Wade grabbed Beau and leaned him forward pounding his back. Then dragging his body to a nearby chair, he slumped him over it as he performed the Heimlich maneuver. He'd learned it in Health Education for catering protocol. After a few harder upward pushes a mangled chuck of meat flew out.

Beau gasped, and Wade let him slump to the floor. People rushed over, offering water and help, and someone helped him stand. His red eyes bulged, and he seemed to be focusing on Wade.

"Get away from me," Beau yelled at the crowd. "I'm fine." He stumbled back to the booth and fell onto the vinyl bench. "We ain't finished here." The words were harsh, but not the tone.

"Yes, we are. I'll get you five thousand next week, and you give me your word you'll leave me alone," Wade said.

"We'll see about that." Beau frowned. "Why'd you save me, anyway?"

"I don't know."

Wade left a wad of bills to cover the check and walked out. He stood beside the entrance and waited. Beau soon exited and Wade watched him drive from the parking lot. He then pulled out his phone and the receipt with the waitress' scribbled number. He texted.

"I'm sorry. I can't make it tonight."

Shoving the phone in his back pocket, he leaned against the building, a whoosh of air escaping from his lungs.

He felt like a jerk leading the girl on. The kiss. How could he justify letting that happen, even for Lacey's sake? Still, Wade felt some sense of justification in that maybe Beau believed it enough to leave Lacey alone.

Then the choking. Wade brushed a hand through his hair. That bothered him. He could have let the man die. His hateful anger could have had a hand in death. *But Beau deserves it.* The words triggered something.

We all deserve to die, Wade. We're all sinners and capable of anything. His mother's voice came back to him. He recalled once when Beau went after his mom. A rage took over and Wade took the blow. Wade wanted to kill Beau. Really kill him, but his mother stopped him, and Beau stormed out. While holding a napkin to his busted lip, his mother shared Jesus' love. There on the floor of the kitchen. Wade couldn't fathom it then. He begged her to leave, to run. She should have, but she wouldn't. Wade slumped to the ground and closed his eyes.

CHAPTER 13

Lacey stared at her cell phone. The number on the screen glared back as her finger hovered over the call button. She wanted to accept Madam DeFleur's offer. She toiled over the decision, but finally decided to decline. She didn't know why, but she trusted Wade's judgement.

But the call didn't go well. Madam DeFleur intimated that Lacey had just thrown away her career.

"Don't say I didn't warn you," Madam said.

A warning? About what?

Desmond and Melanie returned from their honeymoon. Glad to have them home, Lacey begged Melanie to go for a run before she returned to work. Running side by side, the two moved in sync. Just having her mom home somehow calmed Lacey's frazzled nerves. When they reached Bubba's, Lacey threw up her arms in a victory dance. For the first time, Lacey outran her mother. They each downed two cups from Bubba's lemon-water decanter, and tossed their used cups into the metal can.

"Whew. What a hard run. Why the fast pace?" Lacey asked.

"Me? I tried to keep up with you. You did it. You beat me." Melanie stood and pulled the elastic tight on her ponytail. Lacey did the same to her thick, messy bun.

Lacey threw her arms around her mother and hugged her. "I'm so glad you're home."

"Me too, sweetie. Not that I didn't have a wonderful time at the Alabama shore. It almost felt like Huntington Beach, but with Desmond."

Fluttering her lips, Lacey huffed. "That seems so long ago."

A flock of brown pelicans flew overhead. Lacey counted, and her mom joined in.

"Ten, eleven, twelve. That's it."

Lacey giggled. "Remember when Grandpa insisted he counted twenty-eight in a single formation once?"

"I do. He always outcounted us. Didn't he? At least he said he did." Melanie winked.

"He did. The most I ever counted was twenty." Lacey stared upward. "I miss him and Grandma too."

"I do as well, sweetheart."

"Why did God have to take them?"

Melanie sighed. "I don't know why God took them home, but it brought us here."

"But why couldn't they have come with us? I just don't understand."

"We may never understand, but it doesn't mean we can't trust God for our future."

"You sound like Desmond."

Melanie chuckled. "Lacey, this is what you wanted too, isn't it? You wanted Desmond in our lives. It's like the Lord granted your desire."

"I prayed that you would be happy, Mom. You were so sad after Chris died."

Melanie took a deep breath. The old pain showed on her face. "It tormented me, Lacey. I wanted Desmond so badly, but it didn't seem to be what God wanted for me. And I felt guilty that I didn't want Chris, even when he asked to come back to us." Melanie bit her lip. "And then he was gone."

"But you still got what you wanted, right? Desmond."

"I did." She gazed into Lacey's eyes. "What do you want now, Lacey?"

Lacey crossed her arms across her stomach, trying to silence the gurgle. She pulled out a metal chair, screeching it across the concrete, and sat. "I'm afraid to say. God took Grandpa, Grandma, and just when I wanted Chris, He took him too."

"Is there someone you want now?" Melanie lifted a chair out and sat. "The young man driving the car. Where did he come from?"

"Who told you?" Lacey narrowed her eyes.

"Tina. Who else? But I bugged her till she spilled the beans. Said you met him at the wedding but wouldn't share anything else." Melanie reached over and covered Lacey's hand.

Lacey's mind spun. She'd never held anything back from her mom. They were best friends, and her life always an open book. Until now. Where should she start? So much had happened in two weeks. So much so that she hadn't shared it with anyone. Anyone but Wade.

"What's wrong, sweetie?"

"Wade Gardner is the guy. Summer Gardner's nephew."

Melanie's eyes widened. "Ohhh." Her mouth formed a perfect circle. "Well, he can't be all bad. I mean, he wasn't drinking or anything, right? Wait a minute. A guest at our wedding?"

Lacey bit her lip. "Not a guest. One of the servers. He works for one of his great-grandfather's hotel catering services."

"Oh, so he's a hard worker." Melanie nudged. "Is he cute?"

Lacey frowned. "Mommm."

"Seriously, though, he means something, or you wouldn't be so secretive about him." Melanie kicked Lacey's foot under the table.

"He's got baggage. We had one date, and something happened to him after the accident. He said he had to get things straightened out before we did anything."

"Did anything? You shouldn't be doing anything."

"I didn't mean that."

"Lacey, sweetie, you're nineteen years old. What's wrong with just getting to know him?" Melanie straightened. "Although, if he's got baggage...What kind of baggage? You need to find out, Lacey. It's important."

"Mom, stop. I don't know. But I like him a lot. A whole lot."

"Oh, my." Melanie stared at her daughter. "You sound too much like how I felt when I first met your dad." Her eyes glistened. "Same age too. Nineteen," she whispered.

"I'm almost twenty. And Wade reminds me a lot of Chris."

"Oh, dear. You didn't do anything you'll regret, did you?"

Lacey's mouth tightened and twitched. She swiped a tear. "Yes. I let him kiss me."

A grin spread across Melanie's face. "Whew. Is that all?" Melanie whispered then added, "Maybe it is a little soon. How long have you known him?"

"Two weeks now." *But only two days when he kissed me.*

"And where do you stand now?"

"I told you, nowhere. He asked me to wait till he got things straightened out."

"Maybe I better talk with Summer."

"No. Please, give him a chance. I promise to let you know the next time he calls." Lacey stood. "More water?" She grabbed a paper cone and filled a cup. She filled one for her mom and handed it to her. "Let's go. Victoria is expecting me and has a surprise. I can't imagine what it is. Good news, I hope because I could sure use some."

"Lacey, just trust God. Don't let your emotions rule you. When a parent says they understand, believe me, I do." Melanie pulled Lacey into her lap and squeezed her like a little girl again. "I'm praying for you, sweetie. But I need to meet this young man."

"Yes, ma'am." Lacey had mixed feelings about the idea but decided that would be a good thing.

Lacey unlocked Victoria's shop and whooshed in, dropping bags on the worktable and hanging the dresses she'd spent all weekend altering. She felt thankful for the busy work that kept her from checking her phone every minute, but Wade hadn't called or texted in days. But then he had asked her to wait. How long could it take to straighten things out? Lacey huffed. Not just things, but life. *That could take forever.*

Lacey started the coffee and pulled out a mug and the creamer from the fridge. She stared at a magnet that read, *Trust in the Lord with all your heart.* But Wade didn't know the Lord. Did he? She didn't want to assume, but they'd had no conversation about faith or Jesus. *And Jesus is the most important thing in my life.* Lacey winced. Had Wade crept into that number one spot?

"Good morning," Victoria said.

Lacey spun around. "Oh, hey."

"Wow. You've been busy this weekend." Victoria pointed to the rack of dresses. "You finished all those?"

"I did."

Victoria examined Lacey's alterations. "Nice work."

"Thank you." Lacey clasped her hands. "So, the surprise? I've been waiting all weekend."

"Bring your coffee, and let's go sit in the dressing area."

They sat in corner chairs that faced the platform where a three-way mirror stared back at them.

"Remember that gown I sold last year to that actress?"

"Of course. I love that red-carpet poster in the back room."

Victoria's eyes widened.

"She didn't," Lacey squealed. "She's ordering another gown?"

"Sort of. She wants me to bring my designs to California. I'm meeting her in two days, and I want you to come with me."

Lacey's mouth gaped. "Are you serious?"

"Of course. I want you to bring your portfolio. Two are better than one, and if she doesn't like any of mine, I'm sure she'll find one in your collection. Either way, we'll show her both."

Jumping up, Lacey bumped her coffee, and it dribbled down her pale, blue t-shirt, but she didn't care as she set her mug down and hugged Victoria. "I can't believe it. Wait till I tell Wade." Lacey winced. "I mean, wait till I tell Mom."

"If that's a yes, I'll ask Art to book your flight. I already have my ticket, and hopefully he can get us seated together."

"He's not going?" Lacey frowned. "I mean, he's not worried about your old boyfriend?"

"Chad?" Victoria waved a hand. "He won't even know I'm coming, and if he did, I'd avoid him like the plague. Art has nothing to worry about."

"How did you know Art was the one?" Lacey asked quietly.

"I kissed him when we were in kindergarten. We have a lot of history."

Lacey laughed. "That is a lot of history."

Victoria sipped her coffee and held the cup to her lips. "What about Wade? Do you think he's the one?" she mumbled.

"We have no history, so I have no idea. But I've never felt like this about anyone before." Lacey breathed deep. "My heart actually hurts when I think about him."

"Pray, Lacey. You're young. Youth had a lot to do with my problems with Art."

"Well, kindergarten. Come on." Lacey chuckled.

"Right? But so many things can change when you're young. Trusting in God's timing is always the right thing."

"I guess so. I'm trying," Lacey said.

Two days later, Victoria and Lacey arrived in California. Art booked them at the Maybourne in Beverly Hills, and Lacey couldn't believe her eyes. Formerly the Montage, she had never stayed anywhere so lush. Thick terry cloth robes were laid out on the two queen size beds. She spread her arms wide and fell backwards on the bed like in the movies.

Smiling up at the ceiling she asked, "How can you afford this?"

"I know, it sounds shallow, but it looks good for business. All part of the game and Art suggested it. He said it's good investment because if I sell one gown, that covers the cost of this trip ten times over. It's just one night." She winked.

"You can command that price?" Lacey slapped a hand over her face. "I'm sorry. How rude. It's just that I thought celebrities paid double digits in the thousands, some in the millions for their dresses. I had no idea you were in that world."

Victoria laughed. "Hey, someone needs to keep me humble when Art's not here. But yes, I gave it a shot when I priced her dress last year, and she didn't blink an eye. If I priced too low, they won't think I'm worth it. Besides, do you know how many hours and sketches it takes to develop the final product? Not to mention constructing the mock-ups."

"And the cost of fabrics." Lacey said.

"Yes. Listen, if we get done with these ladies soon enough, I'll take you to the garment district. Now those fabrics are amazing."

"I would love that."

"Good, let's eat. Get a good night's sleep, and we'll wow our client in the morning." Victoria winked. "God willing, of course. And we should pray, now."

The next afternoon, as they sat at a table waiting, Lacey felt a bittersweet déjà vu. Chris had taken her to an outdoor Beverly Hills bistro much like this about the time he started re-entering her life.

"Victoria. How lovely to see you."

Lacey's mouth gaped. The woman who spoke appeared much different from the poster in Victoria's shop. But Lacey recognized her from a TV show and a couple of movies.

The dark-haired woman with thick dark eyebrows kissed the air around Victoria's face. Her bright red lips were only slightly fuller than the caterpillars above her eyes, but the wide grin and accented voice made Lacey feel even more uncomfortable in the posh setting.

Two more women smiled behind her. Lacey didn't recognize them, even after the celebrity introduced them.

"My girls need red-carpet gowns too, and since I gushed all about you, here they are." Her sweet British accent didn't match the persona.

All three women were dressed outlandishly. Loud, even, with bright colors and everything clashing. She felt deflated before she opened her portfolio and wondered what they saw in Victoria's designs. Her gowns weren't even close to their style.

"Well, let's get down to business. I'm sorry, we don't have time for lunch."

Lacey pushed her salad aside, and Victoria called the waiter over. "Could you box our lunches and bring iced tea for all the ladies, please."

Victoria pulled out her portfolio first. They were not polite or discreet in expressing disapproval over most gowns.

"No. No. No. Definitely, no."

They flipped the sketches back and forth, slipping some out of the pile and laying them aside.

"Lacey Thompson here has her portfolio as well."

"Who are you?" The B-lister asked.

"Uh…I…" Lacey felt herself flushing and hoped her face wasn't as red as one of the women's tight jeans.

"Lacey is a new designer," Victoria said. "She works for me."

They glanced up but busied themselves turning the pages in Lacey's portfolios. Lacey bit her lip, and the more they frowned, the harder she bit. They shook their heads.

"Nope. No. Not this one, either." One woman held up a design, stared at it for a minute, and let it flutter. "Sorry," she said.

When Lacey bent to retrieve it, a slender, perfectly mani-cured hand recovered the paper, but instead of handing it over, she stared at Lacey's 11 x 14 sketch. It covered the woman's face, but behind a floppy hat and expensive sunglasses, Lacey couldn't see her anyway. She handed the sketch to Lacey.

"Is this yours?"

Lacey had no time to answer when the woman silently acknowledged those around the table and left.

Whispering and gawking ensued by the others, and Lacey squinted. Her eyes went wide in recognition of the mysterious woman walking away. Lacey looked at Victoria, who nodded in affirmation.

"Do you know her?" One woman asked.

"Well, she did compliment me on my gown last year," caterpillar brows said.

"Oh, then can we see your portfolio again?" Another said.

"Mine?" Lacey asked.

"Of course not." The woman giggled. "Victoria's."

Another flush burned inside, and she felt mortified, hating herself for raising her hopes. The hour passed as they continued to ignore her, and the disappointment dug deep. Still, something warmed inside. When the women finally expressed a positive nod for one of Victoria's gowns, her expertise astounded them. Victoria squelched any doubts when she articulated with confidence modifications of the design specifically for each woman's taste and figure. Lacey stood and gathered her portfolio.

She mouthed *restroom* to Victoria and left. Lacey walked by the floppy hat super celebrity who lunched with a large group of ladies. They laughed and chatted, but the woman stopped Lacey as she passed.

"Excuse me? What designer do you work for?"

Lacey's throat sapped of liquid. She gulped and almost choked on nothing. She tried to breathe, but she couldn't catch a breath.

The woman giggled. "Never mind. What's your name?"

"Lacey. Lacey Thompson."

"Nice to meet you, Lacey. I'm Reese."

"I know." Lacey rolled her eyes but took the woman's hand and shook.

"Do you live in California?" Reese asked.

"Yes. I mean no. I used to live here, but now I live in Mississippi."

A wide grin graced the woman's face, and she removed her sunglasses. Her eyes sparkled. "Why, you don't say? I'm from New Orleans." Her sweet southern drawl drew Lacey in, and they had a connection.

"Oh, yes, that's only an hour away from Bay Town."

"Why, yes. Is that where you live? What a small world."

"Yes, but I'm a Southern California girl. Raised here, but my mother opened a wedding consultant business in Bay Town, and I work for Victoria." Lacey pointed. "She has a shop there, too, down on Main Street."

The women around Reese seemed to want her attention back, so Lacey edged away.

"Well, sure nice meetin' you, Lacey." Reese pointed a finger at her and winked. "You keep up the good work. Ya' hear?"

"Yes, ma'am." *Good work. Did she just say good work?*

CHAPTER 14

Wade's world had turned upside down. Not that he hadn't lived in crises mode before, but he'd had stability and peace for a few years now. But with Beau Bodine reentering Wade's life the same night as Lacey Thompson, nothing would ever be the same again.

Wade squinted at the sun shining through his windshield. He tried deflecting it but the glistening water on both sides of the bridge shined just as brightly. He drove once again across the Bay Bridge to meet Beau Bodine. The man had sense enough not to return to Bay Town and Wade wondered if Chief Bert had something to do with it. But Wade refused to meet at the casino. He still had the charade to keep up that Lacey meant nothing to him. But in fact, everything he did from this point worked to secure that she would be in his future. Perhaps even forever.

Forever? He'd never thought past the present, and now he contemplated the future while reconciling his past. Wade sucked in a breath. He wished he'd never found out about his birth mom or dad. He pulled up the console cover and reached for antacids. Popping one in his mouth, he turned on the radio.

Wade thumbed his hands on the steering wheel in time

with the beat of the music. The words of the unfamiliar song stuck in his head. The lyrics spoke of running to God.

The more he listened, the calmer he became. He didn't know whether to credit the antacid or the song, but when the DJ announced "Soul on Fire" by Third Day, Wade took note.

Running. He'd been running all right and it never worked. At least not in his life. He could use this renewed hope in life, and it got him thinking about God.

Following the voice of the Maps App, Wade pulled into a parking lot. He grimaced. The neon, All-you-can-eat Buffet sign flashed from a smeared window. It appeared to be one of the still-in-business shops at the sad strip center. Wade grabbed the entire roll of antacids before exiting. He hit the key fob.

"So, no more Tesla, huh?" Beau pointed.

Wade turned, and Beau leaned against a rundown older model compact car.

"Yes. You took care of that one," Wade said.

"Well, this BMW ain't bad. Better than what I'm driving." Beau narrowed his eyes. "I just may renegotiate our deal."

"And you just may choke on the food in this joint," Wade said.

Beau cleared his throat. "Let's go. My treat."

Confident he wouldn't be having anything more than cola in this sad excuse for a restaurant, still Wade wondered at Beau's generosity.

They found a table, but Beau sidled up to the buffet filling two plates on his tray. By the time he joined Wade, a server had already brought water and Wade's drink.

Beau dug in. Coming up for air, he wiped his mouth. "I know I said I'd see about the ten thousand dollars."

"You said five. I don't have ten." Wade's jaw clenched.

"Listen, I appreciate you saving my life, but I need a break here."

"So get a job. Like me."

"I got one. Had to for my parole. But it don't pay enough."

"Yeah, I guess that can be a problem." He pulled out an envelope stuffed with bills.

Beau stared, and instead of wide-eyed approval, his eyes dropped. He wiped a hand over his face. "Listen, Wade. I never meant for anything to go as it did, and I never meant to hurt your mom."

"Just me. You meant to kill me."

"The booze. It made me crazy. You know that. I never got over losing your mama. She meant everything to me, and the whole time in jail, I just wanted revenge. But, heck, you're all the family I have left."

"We're not family. You said so yourself."

Beau's eyes shifted. "But we are. We're related. You know that now."

Wade's throat constricted, and he couldn't swallow.

"You're my brother's kid. And it's the truth."

The thought sickened him. After finding out about his birth father, Wade didn't know what could be worse. Closing his eyes, Wade thought of Lacey, wishing this weren't true.

"We're family. That's why you saved my life, ain't it?" Beau said softly.

Wade drew a deep breath and the thought returned that he almost didn't. Maybe, if he hadn't ever met Lacey, he wouldn't have. But he couldn't tell Beau that and it wasn't Lacey that he thought of when he jumped in to save Beau. He followed the instinct to do the right thing. He stared at Beau for a long time, not answering his question.

"No matter. You did, and I guess all that good Jesus teaching that my wife taught you sunk in." Beau blew his nose in the napkin. "I'm grateful, son. I am, and if I weren't so darn desperate, I wouldn't ask for more money now."

Wade pushed the wad over, and his heart felt for the man, although he'd never felt anything but hatred for him in the past. "I wish I could help more, but I'm trying to get my life straight, and for whatever reason, I've been given a second chance."

"Your mama, she called it providence." Beau's chin dropped to his chest, and he snuck the napkin to his eyes. "I should have listened to her because I guess I'm getting mine now."

Whoa. Wade couldn't believe his ears. "Listen, if you start living right like Mom tried, maybe things will turn out. Maybe you'll cut a break like me. God knows I didn't deserve it."

"Who are those people, Wade? The ones you live with that give you them fancy cars."

"I work for those fancy cars. I mean, I have to pay insurance and upkeep and stuff. But yes, they give me a lot. A lot I don't deserve."

That word again, *deserve.*

"Your mama said we don't deserve Jesus." Beau swiped his nose with a napkin and threw it down. "Ahhh, no use talking 'bout that stuff. Look where it got her."

"Jesus didn't cause that." *You did.* Guilt slapped Wade, "We did. We were all wrong. I caused you guys a lot of trouble, and with Mom always defending me, no wonder you got mad." Words flooded from Wade that he'd buried. "She was a good woman, and maybe we can both make right by her."

Wade's cell buzzed. He stared, and his eyes widened. He hadn't contacted Lacey in a while, and she'd left him alone, until now. He couldn't help but smile. "Hey, I got to get this." Wade stood and stepped aside.

When Lacey answered, inviting him to dinner at her house, his grin widened, and dimples cratered his cheeks. Finally, he spun around staring into Beau's puzzled face.

"Only a woman can make a man feel like that, and I don't think that flashy waitress in the casino could do that. So, your little girlfriend is back in the picture, huh?"

Wade watched Beau's face and voice transform once again. Returning to the evil, conniving self-centeredness.

"No." Wade couldn't even remember the girl's name, but scrolled his phone, then thrust it at Beau. "See, here." The picture of the casino girl kissing him full on the lips repulsed him, but he had to show Beau. Anything to hide Lacey from him.

"Wow."

Wade chuckled at Beau's shock, and relief flooded him. He couldn't help but feel a little thankful for the charade. "Anyway, she called, and I have to pick her up. So, we're good here?"

Beau narrowed his eyes and stared. "Yeah, well, about that. What if I'm down and out again? What if I lose my job or something? Mind if I ask for a loan?"

Pushing back a hank of hair, Wade shook his head. "No, no loans."

Beau's eyes settled on Wade's phone, and his jaw slacked. His mouth hung open for quite a while. "Well, thank you, son. I appreciate that. I guess we're done. Except, could you get me another plate of spaghetti and fried chicken?" Beau grinned.

An inkling, a hitch, something told him to beware, but Wade complied. He left the table and filled a plate with chicken, spaghetti and added meatballs. He placed the plate in front of a grinning Beau and retrieved his phone from the table.

"Thanks, son. I hope you find what you're searching for." Beau's words somehow didn't sound sincere.

Still, Wade took them and left.

Wade stood on Lacey's front porch. One hand gripped a colorful spring bouquet, and the other hovered inches from her front door. Fisted and ready to knock. He closed his eyes, wondering what to expect.

The door flung open. Lacey's beautiful, fresh face beamed. He hadn't seen her in a week, but it felt like a lifetime, and he knew he never wanted it to be this long again. She fidgeted then grabbed his hand and pulled him in.

Wade wanted to fold her in his arms and kiss her. He breathed in her flowery perfume and wanted to stroke her loose long hair. The chestnut brown glistened as it waved down her back. He couldn't even speak. He just stared.

"Are those for me?" She pointed to the flowers.

"Huh? Oh, yes."

"Why, thank you." Her nose buried into the bouquet.

When she came up for air, Wade laughed at the specks of yellow pollen on her nose. He reached out and wiped them off in slow motion, and the electricity sparked.

She must have felt it too because her mouth gaped, and she blinked. They were both frozen in time.

"Lacey? Is that Wade?" A sweet voice came from the kitchen.

"Yes, Mom," Lacey called back, then turned to Wade. "I can't believe you said yes." Lacey squealed but lowered her voice adding, "I can't believe my mom invited you."

"She did?" Wade felt a knot growing in his stomach. Why hadn't he thought this through? *It's an interrogation.*

"She did. You'll be fine. When I told her you were Summer's nephew, she promised to talk to you before talking to her. But you know the Gardner name holds a lot of clout in Bay Town." Lacey giggled.

"Yes, well, I'm kind of the black sheep."

A tall man resembling the British actor from the Superman movie walked in. He extended his hand. "Hi, Wade, I'm Desmond."

He shook Desmond's firm hand. "Hello, sir. Thank you for having me."

"Hey, our pleasure. You're in for a treat. Melanie's a great cook, and Lacey here, she makes desserts like nobody's business. Come on in. The table's all set."

A slender woman, slightly taller than Lacey, faced him. She waved from the stove. "Hi, Wade. It's so nice to meet you. Thanks for joining us."

"My pleasure, ma'am." Sweat trickled down his back, but all anxiety slipped away when Lacey gave him a reassuring nod.

When they sat, everyone put out their hands as if forming a circle. Wade frowned.

Lacey laughed and took his hand. Her touch heated his whole body, and he feared grasping the other hand that her mother extended.

A warm squeeze tightened from Lacey. "Pastor Desmond is going to pray," she said.

This time, Desmond frowned.

"I mean, Dad is going to pray."

"That's better." He winked. "Let's pray."

And pray he did. Short and sweet, asking a blessing on the food and giving thanks for Wade. The simple words created a longing in Wade's soul.

Since he'd become a member of the Gardner family, his diet consisted of high-quality chef cuisine, and he couldn't complain. Yet this home-cooked meal tasted incredible, or just being here with Lacey made it that way. Wade chuckled watching Lacey eat the homemade mac-n-cheese. She closed her eyes and hummed. It was that good.

The friendly dinner chit-chat bounced back and forth, and Wade listened more than he spoke. But when Lacey went on and on about her visit to California, his heart dropped to his stomach. She went that far and never told him? He didn't know she had an independent streak. Not a bad thing, but the thought made him frown.

"So you didn't take the internship in New Orleans?" Wade asked.

Melanie's eyes shifted toward Desmond, and then they both stared at Lacey.

She hesitated, hunched with a chicken leg poised before her mouth. "Uh, oh…I didn't." Lacey stared at her mom and winced. "That's why I never mentioned it. Wade said it wasn't a good idea."

Melanie gaped. "Wade said?"

Oh, this is not good. The room's temp went from tepid to frigid.

He shook his head. "My aunt, Summer, contracted with the design house that Lacey interviewed with in New Orleans."

"You went there? To New Orleans?" Melanie's eyes widened. "Did he go with you?" She pointed at Wade.

"Of course not." Lacey lowered the chicken leg.

"Why not?" Melanie glared at Wade. "You let her go there by herself?"

Wade hid a smile. This was going all over the place. Maybe this perfect family didn't have it all together as he assumed.

Desmond patted Melanie's hand. "Hey, I'm ready for dessert." He stood. "Kids, why don't you hit the living room, and I'll clear the dishes. Melanie? Coffee? Decaf?"

Melanie's wide eyes stared at Lacey, and she stood. "Yes, that's a good idea."

In the living room, Lacey blew out a breath, fluttering her lips. "Oh my goodness." She glared at Wade. "I didn't tell my mom about New Orleans."

His eyes narrowed. "How would I know that? And you didn't tell me about California."

"Why would I do that? We weren't talking."

"No. We were just taking a break." Wade stuffed a hand through his hair.

"Yes, so you could straighten your life out. And I'm supposed to sit around doing nothing while you do that?" Lacey crossed her arms.

Wade's eyes softened. "I asked if you'd wait." He scooted away to the other end of the couch. "I guess I forgot to wait for your answer. I just assumed."

"Well, you shouldn't have. That's presumptuous, don't you think?" Lacey poked at him, a smirk on her face.

"Right." Wade huffed. He'd been too busy worrying about his problems, neglecting how much this meant to her. "So, you didn't take the job at MDD, and your designs didn't get picked up in California?"

She shook her head, and her body slumped.

"I'm sorry, Lacey. Something will turn up. It always does," Wade said.

"Does it?" Lacey bit her lip. "I sure hope so because other than you, I don't feel like I have anything worth fighting for anymore."

"Me?" Wade's eyes widened, and he grinned. "That's the nicest thing anyone has ever said to me." He scooted back over and took her hands. "Lacey, something good will happen. I know it will. I can just feel it."

Sweat suddenly beaded on his forehead and the reservation that he sat in Lacey's home flew out of his brain as his pulse quickened. She leaned closer, her eyes begging again.

"Brownies?" Melanie asked while holding a plate. Desmond followed, carrying a tray with a white coffee carafe and mugs.

Wade dropped Lacey's hands and scooted away once more. Melanie walked straight over and settled herself in between them. She smiled.

"Hey, honey, why don't you join me here?" Desmond patted the loveseat and winked at Lacey. "We're still on our honeymoon, aren't we?"

Lacey laughed while shoving her mom forward. "You're turning red, Mom."

"Not as red as you were a moment ago."

The end of the evening came too soon, and Wade sensed that Lacey's parents had no intention of leaving them alone again. He gave his thanks, said his goodbyes, and Lacey walked him out. He glanced back at the house and shoved his hands in his front pockets. Melanie and Desmond stood on the porch, watching.

When he got to his car, Lacey hovered close.

"I can't believe they're doing that."

"I think they call those helicopter parents." Wade laughed. "Usually for kids."

"Well, to them I'm a kid." Her green eyes sparkled. "You're a first, you know."

Wade winced. He wished he had met her a long time ago. But he'd never felt like this about anyone before. A first for him. He'd never cared about someone the way he cared about Lacey. He wanted so badly to hold her close, but it was a whole lot more than that.

His cell buzzed, but he ignored it, staring at Lacey. He brushed her fingers with his hand, and he couldn't tell whether the tingle emitted from the breeze or her warmth. It didn't matter.

His cell buzzed again.

"You better get that."

Wade pulled it out and his eyes widened. He gulped as his stomach twisted.

"Wade? Are you okay? Who is it?"

"I have to go. It's my family." He searched around, and he caught a glimpse of an old model compact car shaded under a large pecan tree.

Lacey reached for his hand, but he moved to his car. "I have to go. Lacey, remember what I said about waiting? Please, just trust me on this, okay. I have to—"

"I know, I know. You have to straighten things out." She huffed, and her sad eyes stared back. "Does that mean it'll be another week before we see or hear from each other?"

"I'm not sure. But I have to go."

Wade jumped in his car and threw his cell on the seat. He pulled away without looking back at the sweet girl on the street. He knew that Beau followed as he drove down Beach Road. Before reaching his great-grandfather's house on the gulf, Wade stopped, but Beau's car sped past him, and U-turned. Beau waved at Wade as he passed.

He grabbed the cell and opened the message once more. The photo of the girl kissing him glared back at him. Wade groaned. Beau had a copy.

CHAPTER 15

Wade's throat burned. How could this get any worse? He hit the steering wheel, but his cellphone rang, and he scrambled to retrieve a text message.

<You lied to me>

Returning the call, Wade held the cellphone to his ear. Beau answered, and Wade cursed at him, but Beau laughed and hung up.

Wade called again, but Beau didn't pick up. Instead, Wade received another text.

<Meet me at the casino tomorrow for breakfast>

He had no choice unless Beau had already sent the picture to Lacey. Wade closed his eyes. His heart and mind were spinning out of control. What could he do? He hated this rollercoaster. He hated caring so deeply for someone. He breathed deep, and guilt flicked his conscience for swearing at Beau, but the guilt wasn't really about Beau. A transformation taking place inside of him mattered most, and Lacey had much to do with that. He had to call her and explain.

"Hey, Wade. Are you all right? Is everything okay?" Lacey's voice soothed.

Phew. A breath whooshed out. She hadn't gotten the photo.

"Yes. No. There's so much I need to tell you. Lacey, I told you I had things to straighten out, right? Well, stuff is catching up."

"It's okay, Wade. It can't be that bad." She paused. "Just be honest with me, okay?"

"Yes, I will. I am. That's why I'm calling." He wanted to tell her about the photograph and Beau. But he didn't know how. Wade didn't know where to start. He remained silent.

"Wade? Is it okay if I pray for you?" Her voice was almost a whisper.

"Yeah, I'd like that," he said softly.

Lacey's gentle voice and simple words felt like a flood of water showering him clean. If only for the moment, he'd take it.

"And Lord, please draw Wade close to you. In your name, Amen."

"Thank you." Wade swallowed hard. "I have to go. Just remember, whatever happens, I lo... I like you, Lacey. I like you more than I've ever liked anyone before, and I don't want to blow this."

Silence.

"You're kind of scaring me, Wade. Is there someone else?"

"What? No," he blurted. "You're the only one, believe me. I like you a lot."

"All right," she said.

He waited, hoping she might say the same, but she didn't. "I better go. I'll call you tomorrow after work. Maybe we can get dinner," he said.

"Sure, that sounds great. Bye."

"Have a good evening, Lacey. Bye."

"Wade?" Lacey's throat cleared. "I like you a lot too."

"Really?"

"Got to go. Bye."

She clicked off so fast it made him chuckle, but the momentary joy faded. *I need to tell her the truth.* Wade gazed out his window. The dull, starless night held no hope. *Are you there, God?* He glanced at the Gardner mansion and saw the silhouette of his great-grandfather sitting by a downstairs window. Wade watched as the man made the sign of the cross and bowed his head. His throat grew tight, and he thought of his mom. Her faith. An empty, gaping hole burned in his heart.

The following day, Lacey tiptoed into the kitchen. Desmond sat at the table drinking coffee. His Bible lay open in front of him. She backed out, hoping not to disturb him, and trying to avoid any questions about Wade.

Still, the sight of him there warmed her and she wondered if he and her mom would ever move into his home near the woods. She walked into the living room and peeked out the bay window. The skies were gray again. April had the most beautiful clouds but always threatened rain. She looked out at the waters rippling across the bay.

Nope. Mom would never leave her cottage on the gulf, and Lacey didn't mind Desmond here anyway. She walked back to the kitchen and watched him quietly. He'd helped so much, and she might need to talk to him again.

Confusion muddled her brain. Although she enjoyed working for Victoria, Lacey didn't want to sell retail and make alterations all her life. True, she had an ideal place to design, and Victoria's inspiration proved invaluable, but it seemed every opportunity to work in a successful design house had fallen through the cracks. Hopes raised, then dashed. Except for Wade, and even that hung in the balance. Or did it? *Trust God.* She looked at Desmond.

"What did you say?"

He looked up. "Good morning."

Lacey smiled and reached up, tightening her ponytail. She stood and stretched.

"Time for a run?" Desmond asked.

"Yup. Want to come?" *Please say no.*

Secretly she hoped she might see Wade running too, but he could already be back in New Orleans.

Desmond shook his head. "Thanks, I'll wait for your mom. I think she may not be feeling well. She's still sleeping."

"Oh, that's weird." Lacey stretched her neck toward the hallway. "Mom?"

Melanie appeared, scuffling her feet on the wood floor as she shuffled along. Dark circles wound around her eyes, and her hair stuck out like an electric explosion. Lacey blocked the path to the kitchen.

"Mom, go comb your hair," Lacey whispered.

"What?" Melanie sounded annoyed.

Lacey threw a nod to the table where Desmond sat. "Trust me. You don't want your new husband seeing you like this."

Melanie chuckled. "He's the reason."

Her eyes grew round as saucers, and Lacey covered her ears. "Oh, man. Don't tell me things like that."

Grabbing Lacey's hands, Melanie pulled them away. "I'm just not used to sleeping with someone in the same bed, especially in my own home."

"I got a place to go to, you know." Desmond's voice took a teasing tone.

"Okay, I don't need to hear this. Maybe you both should go to Dad's house."

Melanie scooted past Lacey and kissed Desmond's cheek. He grabbed her waist and pulled her down into his lap. They laughed while Desmond nuzzled her neck.

"Maybe you should go comb your hair," he said.

Melanie slapped his arm and stood, but he reached for her again.

"I'm out of here." Lacey ran outside and let the door slam, thankful she'd escaped without questions about Wade.

She ran fast but slowed near Mr. Gardner's house.

Looking up, she searched each window of the massive home. It had been completely rebuilt after the last big hurricane, but the grand old house had returned to its former glory. In an upstairs window, a hand pulled aside a sheer drape and Wade appeared.

Lacey grinned and waved, but he disappeared. At least she knew he was home. She jogged across the street and ran up the walk to the wrap-around front porch. Wade opened one of the heavy double doors and stepped out. Lacey stared wide-eyed.

He wasn't wearing a shirt, and she gaped at his tanned, defined chest and arms. Lacey swallowed and glanced down.

"Oh, sorry." He ran inside and returned wearing a black hoodie. He zipped it up. "Hi."

She grinned. "Hi. Long time no see."

"Too long." He gazed, and his eyes deepened.

"I'm kidding. Dinner was kind of weird last night, huh."

"No. It was great. Your parents are great."

"I think so too." Lacey shoved him. "Want to run? If you promise not to trip me again."

"That seems like ages ago."

"Two weeks and two days. But who's counting." Lacey felt herself flush.

"Two weeks, two days—" Wade twisted his wrist, "—and one hour. Give or take." He touched her hand, but didn't take it, peeking past her into the street.

That's weird. She turned, but he pulled her shoulders to face him.

"I can't run. I have an appointment," he said.

Lacey paused. "Okay. I need to finish my run anyway, and I've got to open up at Victoria's this morning."

Wade leaned forward and brushed his soft lips across her cheek. The light scruff on his face tickled her, and she hunched, almost stumbling as she stepped backward. Wade caught her, and the touch almost sent her back down the steps.

Lacey raised her hands, but Wade's hand still cupped her elbow. She closed her eyes and swallowed, counting to ten. This taking it slow stuff. What did that even mean?

Wade stared back and sighed. "Me too, Lacey. Me too." He said it as if reading her thoughts. He dropped his hand and stepped back to the porch. "I'll call you tonight, I promise."

After Lacey finished her run, she showered, dressed, and drove to work, not remembering the motions, only relishing how magical her cheek felt. His kiss lingered.

"Good morning," Victoria said.

Lacey shut the door to the shop and leaned against it, closing her eyes to the euphoric cloud hovering about her.

"Wow. Someone had sweet dreams last night."

"Nope. This morning."

Pushing off the door, Lacey went to the studio in the back. Victoria followed.

"So, I heard from those ladies in Beverly Hills."

Lacey's eyes widened. Besides Wade, design news excited her more than anything. She winced and thought how she'd neglected her quiet time, recalling Desmond sitting at the kitchen table with his Bible open. How could she have forgotten?

"They ordered?" Lacey asked.

"They did. All three of them."

Lacey squealed, took Victoria's hands, and jumped up and down like a school girl. Victoria joined in. Suddenly, someone behind them broke the circle and joined in, but they stopped.

"Art?" Lacey's wide-eyes gazed at him.

The jumping stopped, but Art didn't.

"What? I thought we were doing our morning exercises."

Victoria pulled him into a hug. Wrapping her hands around his neck, she pulled his head down and kissed him. "You nut," she said. "We're celebrating."

"Oh, yeah. Retirement is coming early, baby. If you can manage those divas." He frowned at Lacey. "I heard they weren't the nicest princesses around."

"Well, they sure put me in my place." Lacey's shoulders drooped.

"God's got something else then. Believe it and trust Him."

"Thanks. I'm trying."

"No trying. Just do it. God is good," said Art.

"There he goes again." Victoria hung on his arm. "I don't know why you don't quit your job at the bank and join Lacey's dad."

Lacey glanced between them. "What do you mean?"

"Oh, your dad has been asking him to be a full-time Youth Minister since we got married, and he's stalling hiring someone because Art is volunteering almost full-time already."

Lacey glanced between them. Genuine faith like her mom and new dad. Something inside twisted and wrenched, and she thought of Wade. Did he believe? The thought hit her like an arrow piercing her heart. She knew better, but she'd fallen head over heels with the essential connection missing. Jesus. He had to come first.

"Lacey? Are you all right?" Victoria touched her shoulder.

"I'll be fine. You guys are so happy. And Christ is always at the center of your lives. Like my mom and dad."

"Well, the key is to find the right person. Don't give your heart away to the wrong one, and you'll have the same thing someday."

Lacey bit her lip. She couldn't hide the disappointment she felt.

Art glanced at her, but he kissed Victoria, excusing himself to work.

When the entrance door closed, Victoria took Lacey's hand.

"Anything you'd like to talk about?"

The flood came, and Lacey covered her face. "I think I've already given my heart away."

Victoria pulled Lacey to the work table, and they sat atop the stools. "But it's never too late. If you know he's not right, pull back. I was in the same boat, and I'm so thankful I listened to God." Victoria's eyes seemed to search.

Lacey stared up at the ceiling. "It's that surrender thing, isn't it? If I surrender him, then maybe God will give him back? He wouldn't take him away, would he?"

A deep sob arose in her throat as a knot swelled. Lacey flopped her arms on the work table and laid her head down. "Every time I surrender, God takes something away. My grandparents, my father."

"I'm so sorry, Lacey. I can't even begin to understand why or how God works. I just know we can trust Him." Victoria pulled back Lacey's hair and peeked at her. "Is it Summer's nephew?"

Lacey buried her face in her arms.

"I'll be praying for you. Trusting God is believing that whatever He does will be for the best. I know it's easier said than done. But when I surrendered Art, and he surrendered me—"

"But you landed up together. You were meant to be. How can I be meant to be with someone who doesn't even know God?"

"Do you know that for sure?"

Lacey shook her head.

"There's always hope, right? Lacey, you guys are young. I'm not saying you'll land up with him, but both of you have a lot of growing up to do. You never know. If he's the one, it'll happen. Maybe God will grow him up fast." Victoria laughed.

"Not that you should wait. You need to go about your business. Seek God first, right?"

Sitting up, Lacey straightened her back and stared at Victoria. She grabbed a tissue and blew hard. Honk!

The women stared at one another wide-eyed and laughed.

"As I said, you both have some growing up to do."

Victoria reached for a tissue and dabbed at Lacey's eyes. She took another and quietly blew her own nose. "And that's how a southern lady clears her nostrils." She winked.

Being around Victoria and Art felt like being around Desmond, and Lacey felt grateful. They weren't perfect, but they were a great example. All her life, adults made up her circle of friends, and she welcomed it. It was always the older women that guided her.

"Thanks." She lifted her hands to the ceiling and rolled her eyes. "Okay, I surrender."

The electronic bell rang in the front of the shop.

Victoria stood. "Please get cleaned up. You'll scare our customers." She walked to the front.

Lacey laughed and sidled up to the kitchenette counter. She threw water on her face and dabbed but stopped. Silence permeated the building.

Finally, Victoria called. "Uh, Lacey? Please come out here."

Lacey huffed. *What now?* She walked out of the studio and gaped at a cute, petite blonde.

"Why, hey there, Lacey Thompson. I'm so glad you told me you was down here on Main Street in little old Bay Town." Reese from Beverly Hills pulled off her sunglasses and grinned.

CHAPTER 16

Wade hesitated in front of the casino doors and wiped his palms down his jeans, hoping the same waitress wasn't on shift. He didn't want to run into her, and the chances were good that she still worked the night shift. He walked through the casino and found Beau in the café.

"It's about time." Beau stared hard as Wade approached.

He slid into the booth while his eyes searched the room.

"She ain't here," Beau said.

"Who's not here?" Wade's fingers rapped the table.

"You can't fool me, kid. The waitress. She ain't here."

"Like I care?"

"The heck you don't. Listen, son, I ain't stupid, and I don't drink no more, so I got a keen mind, and you ain't pulling the wool over my eyes." Beau tapped a finger to his temple.

"What do you want?"

"I told you, money."

"I'm not supporting you all my life. I can't."

"Why not?"

Wade brushed a hand through his hair. "I want this to end. Give me a bottom line and give me your phone."

Beau laughed. "Why? So you can delete the picture? No

way, that's my security." He pointed a finger. "And you're a liar."

Sweat beaded on Wade's forehead. "Bottom line."

"For now? I'll take the ten thousand dollars. Then we'll see about later."

"You can't be serious. I told you, I don't have it, and it will take me all summer to earn another five." He didn't think Beau believed him.

"Then talk to the old man. The rich guy." Beau leaned forward. "I'm not kidding here. I'll send that picture faster than you can blink."

Wade sucked in a breath. He thought they'd come to an agreement after the choking incident. Beau seemed to have had a change of heart, but his old self returned. Wade had asked Lacey to trust him, and soon he'd tell her everything. But he couldn't let Beau blow it for him. He planned on explaining his past, what he knew of it. And he hoped she would understand why he did what he did with the waitress. Wade blew out a breath.

"I can't get another five thousand dollars for at least two months. And I don't want you hanging around here for that long."

"Who said anything about five? I said ten."

Wade wiped a hand across the back of his damp neck. Beau wasted no time demanding more. "I gave you six thousand already," Wade said.

"And now I want another ten."

"No."

Beau pulled out his phone, holding up the photo. He sneered.

Suddenly a thought popped in, and Wade smiled. "You don't have Lacey's number. So you can't send it."

A frown crossed Beau's face, and Wade couldn't help but laugh. "We're both stupid. Here I worried about you sending it to her, and you can't because you don't have her number."

Wade stood. "I'm out of here. I'm going to talk to Lacey right now, so I don't care about the picture. I'll show her myself and explain everything. You just leave her alone."

Beau's mouth hung open. Speechless. Beau had nothing on him. Wade's heart slowed, and he finally felt in control. No more hiding and maybe Lacey was right. They'd straighten out their pasts together.

"I'm not giving you another dime." Wade left the café but heard a crash.

"Hey, mister. You're paying for that. You can't be busting glasses around here."

Wade kept walking, a load lifted off his shoulders, as he headed out to see Lacey. Things were working out. They'd get past this together. Before he could get into his car, his cell rang. Aunt Summer.

"Hey, what's up?"

"It's Grandfather. It's his heart."

Wade stopped walking. "How bad? Never mind, I'm on my way. What hospital?" Wade jumped in the car and sped to Bay Town General.

Rushing into the hospital, he asked for Reginald Gardner and the nurse instructed him to the Cardiac Intensive Care Unit, CICU. Summer stood outside staring into a glass walled room. His great-grandfather lay connected to IV's and oxygen, his chest bare and his skin ashen. Nurses surrounded him and two men in white coats hovered nearby.

"What happened?" Wade asked.

Summer dabbed her face with a crumpled tissue. She tried to talk, but her words were choked with sobs. Wade stepped over to the nurses' station.

"Please. I'm his great grandson. Can you tell me what's going on?"

A nurse stepped around the station and pulled him aside. "He suffered a heart attack. They're monitoring him now and trying to assess the damage."

"Can he talk? Is he responsive?"

She shook her head.

Wade spun around to Summer. "When did this happen? I should have been there. Did he do it climbing the stairs again?"

Summer sipped from a water bottle and swallowed. "After you left this morning, I came downstairs to have breakfast, and I found him slumped in his chair." Summer closed her eyes. "Just awful, Wade. I thought for a moment he might be —but then he spoke." Her shoulders shook as she sobbed. "I called 911, and they came immediately. Thank God."

Wade pulled her into a hug and held her. She laid her head on his shoulder. Wearing high heels put her at the same height as him, but she crumpled in his arms.

"Shhh. He's a fighter." He said it to assure his Aunt, but he'd only known the man for a few years. "He'll pull through."

"I wish my husband were here. He's trying to catch a flight back, but I'm not sure when he can make it. Without my sister, it's just us." She gulped. "Oh, Wade. I'm so glad you're here. Spring would be so proud of you."

Wade wanted to choke, and the knot in his throat did just that. *Proud of what?* If his mom, Summer's sister, had been what he thought she was, he didn't care what she would have thought of him. But still, if it hadn't been for Great-grandfather, he wouldn't be here.

Lacey stared at the celebrity, standing just inside Victoria's shop. Her heart pounded. The door framed the actress' cute, petite figure and her black, floppy hat dipped low over one brow. She twirled her oversized sunglasses in one hand. A studded tote bag hung from her crooked elbow.

"Hey, there, Miss Lacey Thompson," Reese said.

"What a surprise. Did you come all the way out here to see me?" Lacey asked softly.

"Well, to be honest, I had an appointment in New Orleans, but I thought why not look you up. May I take you to lunch? And I'd love for you to bring your designs." Reese smiled. "If it's okay with your boss, that is."

"Of course. Go on, Lacey. The shop is always slow in the mornings," Victoria said.

"Wonderful, shall we?" Reese opened the front door.

"I'll be right there." Lacey ran to the back, grabbing her portfolio.

"Have fun." Victoria said and gestured to Lacey with praying hands.

Lacey hugged Victoria and joined Reese outside. "Did you have someplace particular in mind?"

"Whatever the local flavor is. I love down-home cooking." Reese licked her lips.

"Then it's got to be the Meniere's Sisters." Lacey chuckled. "Or Bubba's down on the pier."

"Those sound like my kind of places. But I don't have too much time. Is either close by?"

"Let's go to The Mockingbird Café instead. It's around the corner, and they serve great salads and sandwiches."

"Why, that'd be just perfect. Lead the way, my dear."

The lunch crowd hadn't arrived yet, and Jacquie fussed all over Lacey and her guest. She touched Lacey's portfolio and wiggled her brows. After she took their orders, they chatted about living in the south until Jacquie delivered their salads. After refills on their sweet tea, Reese asked to see the designs. Lacey opened her portfolio and laid them out, one at a time.

Reese took her time, pursuing each one. "These are lovely."

"Thank you." Lacey laced her hands together.

"Hmmm," Reese hummed.

A familiar warning arose, and Lacey waited for total rejection. She sipped her tea. Gulped, more like it.

"Wait a minute." Reese narrowed her eyes. "Is this your original design?"

"It is."

Short, manicured nails tapped the sketch of Lacey's proudest creation, her mother's wedding gown revamped into a red-carpet original. Reese picked up the sketch and held it in front of her. "Where did you get the idea for this?"

"What do you mean?"

"Where did you get the inspiration? I don't mean to be rude, but did you copy it from someone?"

Lacey placed down her glass, sloshing the tea over the side. "Of course not. All my work is original."

Reese fumbled through her tote and pulled out a folded paper. She smoothed it out before Lacey. "I know sometimes we're moved by another person's work, but are you sure you didn't copy some elements here? Just a little bit? Maybe by accident?"

A sketch of Lacey's mother's gown—a polished, full-color mock-up stared back at her. Lacey's stomach flipped. The modified dress maintained her basic design, but in the corner were the initials MDD.

"That's mine. She stole it from me," Lacey blurted.

Reese cleared her throat and gave Lacey a sideways glance. "Honey, you can't be serious. I admit, they're shockingly similar but MDD is a prestigious house in New Orleans."

"But it's mine. I went to MDD for an interview, and I dropped my portfolio right in front of Madam DeFleur. When I got home, I discovered that sketch was missing. I had no idea where it went, and I searched everywhere. It never turned up, so I grabbed my mom's wedding dress and redid it, partly from memory." Lacey's eyes widened. She couldn't believe what she was seeing. "Madam DeFleur must have kept it."

Reese pressed her lips together. "Let's be honest. Maybe you've heard the rumors about MDD, but they're just rumors. That's why I went to her first. Why, I used to go there all the time, but their designs have been a bit boring of late." She tapped the sketch. "Until now. Madam DeFleur actually called me to come take a look at her new line. She promised me I'd be pleased. Most of the gowns weren't that impressive, except for this one."

"But that's not hers." Lacey's voice rasped.

"I did choose that one, but I thought I'd give you a chance anyway since I flew down here. You know we all need a break. But honesty is so important, don't you think?"

Her condescending tone shattered Lacey's heart. The woman didn't believe her. Lacey nodded. She grabbed her hair and pulled it up, sticking a pencil into a messy bun. She gathered her designs and stuffed them back into her bag.

"But I can take you to my house. I'll show you my mom's wedding gown."

Reese waved her off. "Don't get me wrong. Your other designs are gorgeous as well. It's just that maybe MDD influenced you more than you thought." She touched Lacey's hand. "Honey, keep trying, but be true to yourself." She reached into her purse and pulled out a card. "I don't usually give these out, but here's my personal number. I'd be happy to take a look in the future when you have a little more experience. Perhaps you'll draw from your own inspiration."

Lacey hesitated before taking the card, but her pain wouldn't let her be rude. "Thank you. Honesty is everything to me too. Someday, I hope I can prove that to you."

She didn't know how, but she meant it. Not just because of her reputation, but more importantly because of her faith. She wasn't afraid to share her beliefs, and now her walk was on the line.

Reese said her goodbyes, and left Lacey feeling as limp as her wilted spinach salad. Watching the woman model-walk down the front steps of the Mockingbird Café, Lacey's eyes noted every nuance of her fashion style that she'd previously ignored. Not ignored, but she had been so mesmerized by the celebrity status, she hadn't paid attention.

Jacquie worked the counter, but strolled over, wiping tables. "So, pretty exciting, eh?" Jacquie punched Lacey in the shoulder. "You go, girl. Are you designing for the red carpet? I heard she might be up for an Oscar come next year."

Lacey continued to watch through the window as Reese clipped down the street in wedged espadrilles, the ties wrapped around her slim ankles. Lacey turned.

"Nope. Not this time."

Jacquie picked up the business card that Lacey had laid on the table. One beautifully flourished name and phone number scrolled across the black card. Floral embellishments marked the glossy card matching the woman perfectly.

"Well, this is a good sign. You got her number, girl. Don't you give up hope."

"Thanks, Jacquie."

"Heck yeah. You just wait. Why she'll be begging you one day." Jacquie stood straight and rested a hand on her generous hip. "Besides, we need you here. Why, my little girl is so excited over the dress you picked for her."

"Desi, right? She's so sweet." Lacey recalled the teen in the shop.

"I never seen that girl so happy with herself." Jacquie slapped her backside. "She gets those extra curves from me, and sometimes it's hard for us to get the right fit." She giggled.

"Jacquie? I need you at the register," the barista behind the counter called out.

"Gots to go. Thanks Lacey, you is a sweetheart."

Lacey waved and packed up her portfolio. She crumpled the edges of the last design in her hand. Madam DeFleur's sharp featured face darkened her mind as she stared at the sketch. Her mom's dress. Not just any design. She stuffed it away and strode out of the café.

Gusts stirred up along Main Street, sweet smells of jasmine filling the air, but Lacey didn't feel the sweetness. She entered Victoria's shop and slammed the door.

CHAPTER 17

"Hey, back so soon?" Victoria stood behind the register, and her smile turned to a frown. "Oh, goodness. I take it things didn't go well?"

"It couldn't have gone worse." Lacey threw her portfolio into a chair. "Madam DeFleur stole one of my designs, and Reese accused me of copying it."

Victoria stared back, wide eyed. "What? That can't be. You never worked for her."

"I never told you, but I went to her warehouse. I waited for over an hour, but never got an interview. She filled all the positions before I got my chance. So I approached her with my portfolio."

Victoria raised a hand, stopping her. "Wait a minute. You actually talked to the woman? *Thee* Madam DeFleur?"

"I showed you my appointment list."

"I must have missed it. I'm sorry. Every local designer has heard of her. Her design house hasn't done so well lately. Previously, she reigned the red carpet. I'm not sure what happened."

"What happened is the woman is a thief!" Lacey told the entire story, and everything she held inside exploded.

"Arrrrgh." She retrieved her sketch and thrust it at Victoria. "She copied this one."

Victoria stared for a long time. Lacey had never shown her this one. Victoria hadn't seen the modified evening dress. "Oh, Lacey. This is amazing. And Reese didn't like it?"

"She loved it. But she accused me of copying the design from MDD."

"That's awful." She huffed. "Are you sure?"

"You don't believe me?"

"Of course, I believe you. I'm just asking if you're sure that Reese saw the MDD design."

"She showed me a full-color mock-up."

"Hmmm. I'm wondering why she didn't just go with it. I mean, instead of seeing you first."

Lacey rolled her eyes. "She said everyone needs a break. And when she saw mine, she thought it better, but accused me of copying it."

Victoria walked back to the studio, motioning Lacey to follow her. She flipped on her computer and searched. Page after page, she scrolled, then stopped. Her shoulders drew back.

"That's it," Lacey said, peering over Victoria's shoulder.

"I almost can't believe it. How could she have gotten it up so fast?"

"You know I got a letter from her offering me another internship. When I called and refused it, she threatened my career." Lacey rolled her eyes. "Why? Why does she care?"

"Because you're that good, Lacey, and her house hasn't turned out an A-list design in years."

"So, what now?"

Victoria handed back the design. "I don't think you can sue. You don't have proof."

"I do too. I have my sketches."

"They don't prove a thing. We need a time-stamp."

Lacey's eyes widened. "Mom's wedding gown. I'll get the

wedding photos. And I can ask the professional photographer for a signed confession or something."

"An affidavit. Yes. Why don't you pull all that evidence together? I'd be happy to help in any way I can. Although, I don't know any lawyers that work cases like this."

"I'll figure it out. That woman is not getting away with this. And if nothing else, I'll show Reese that I'm not a thief."

Lacey felt charged, renewed, but anger burned inside at being offended this way, and it fueled her resolve to see this through. No one would stop her now, especially not Madam DeFleur.

A flurry of tourist came into the shop and kept Lacey busy all afternoon.

Wade and Summer spent the night taking turns sleeping in a chair by Reginald Gardner's side in CICU, and in a family waiting room. Neither went home.

The next morning, Wade woke Summer coaxing her to return home, while he held down the fort. His great-grandfather's condition had neither worsened nor gotten better. Grave concern worried them both. She gathered her things.

"I'll shower and be right back, so you can do the same."

"Sounds good." He hugged his Aunt. "Summer, has a chaplain been here?" Wade had no idea why the thought popped into his head, but he found it comforting. Even more so, the thought of Lacey's dad. "I could call Lacey's dad. He's a pastor."

Summer sniffled. "Yes, Lacey's dad would be perfect. Granddaddy loves Lacey and Melanie. Oh, Wade, could you call him, please?"

Wade didn't know why he offered. He'd only met the man once, but it meant he'd get to call Lacey. He hesitated. The conversation he'd planned on having with her would have to wait.

"Sure, I'll call Lacey now."

The doctor treating Reginald arrived for the morning rounds and he beckoned Summer and Wade to follow. Outside, he led them away from the door.

"No change, but we need to take action. I've made calls, and I'm waiting on a consult."

"What do you mean?" Summer asked.

Wade placed an arm around her shoulders. "Doctor, what's going on?"

"Are you family as well?" The doctor glanced between them.

Summer squeezed Wade's arm. "Yes. This here is Wade, my nephew and Mr. Gardner's great-grandson."

"Well, Mr. Gardner is very weak. The angiogram showed nine blockages, and normally we would do a bypass surgery, but with him going in and out of consciousness, we can't. Besides, his age is a huge factor. In the meantime, I'm afraid he's in danger of another heart attack."

Summer sobbed. "You know who my grandfather is, don't you?"

"Absolutely. His donations have helped this hospital quite a bit, and I'm sorry we're not able to move him to one more equipped. If he improves, I promise we'll move him to New Orleans."

"Thank you, Doctor." Wade shook his hand and watched him leave. He turned to Summer. "Go on now and get a bite to eat before you come back."

"No, I can't eat. But I'll go home and shower. Please call me if anything changes."

"Of course." Wade glanced between Summer and his great-grandfather. The Gardners. His family. They needed him. "Hey, I'm not sure how to do this, but should we try and pray for him?"

Summer's teary eyes brightened. "That would be really nice, Wade."

Wade took Summer's hand and pulled her to Mr. Gardner's bedside. Summer entwined her hands with her grandfather's, and Wade rested a hand on his shoulder. They bowed their heads, and silence reigned.

"Go ahead." Summer sniffled.

"I don't know how to pray. You go."

"Why don't we both just pray silently," Summer offered.

Wade blinked. Wondering if God would even listen to him.

Lacey finished a morning on-line class and bustled to the shop. She'd yet to return Wade's call, and wondered why he hadn't left a message. As happy as it made her to hear from him, she dreaded reliving the ordeal with Reese. It wasn't something she cared to tell him about. Embarrassment over yet more rejection and accusation fueled a low-lying anger.

Tagging new bathing suit coverups, Lacey chuckled. Maybe she should design cruise wear. But the chuckle caught in her throat. *No. No one else is stopping me, now.*

"Lacey, your cell is ringing," Victoria called from the studio.

Knowing it must be Wade again, she drew a deep breath and hurried back.

"Hi. I'm sorry I didn't call." Lacey gasped as she listened to Wade. "Oh, no. I'm so sorry. Yes, I'll call him right now and I'll text you his number. I'll be praying, Wade. Talk to you later."

She clicked off.

"Everything okay?" Victoria asked.

Lacey's chin dipped to her chest, and her shoulders slumped. Grandparents in hospitals frightened her. Dreadful memories of first her grandfather, then her grandmother. "Wade is at the hospital. His great-grandfather, Mr. Gardner, suffered a heart attack."

"Oh, no. I'll call the Prayer Chain." Victoria reached for her cell.

"Okay, and I'll call my dad. Wade asked if he could go to the hospital."

Lacey punched Desmond's contact, but the phone went straight to voicemail at the same time the front door opened.

"Hey. How's my girl?"

"Dad?"

A grin spread across his face. "I like the sound of that." He flung his arms wide, and Lacey ran forward, burying her head in his chest.

"What's up?" he asked.

"Mr. Gardner is in the hospital. He had a heart attack, and Wade asked if you'd go down there right away." Lacey spoke softly but pulled away.

"Of course. What hospital? New Orleans?"

"No, Bay Town General. He has a house here, well, a mansion, down the road from us, and they were there when it happened."

"Okay, I'm on my way."

"Dad?" As unnatural as it sounded, the warmth that filled Lacey calmed her anxious spirit. Anxious for so many things, the least of which right now her career. "Why'd you come in here?"

"Prayer walking up and down the street."

"Are you still doing that?" Lacey asked.

"Always. It helps keep my mind and heart on the people that need God. So I thought I'd check in on my daughter." He winked.

"I like the sound of that too." She sighed. "Can I go to the hospital with you?"

"Well, that would be up to your boss, but I don't think the hospital will let you see him."

"I know, but maybe I could see Wade in the waiting room or something."

"Sure but check with Victoria first."

"Check about what?" Victoria emerged from the back. "I just called the prayer chain. Are you headed over there, Pastor?"

"Yes, I am."

"Did you want to join him, Lacey?" Victoria nodded. "Go ahead. I'll handle the crowd." She glanced around the empty shop.

"Thank you. Dad, I'll take my car and meet you there." Lacey grabbed her purse.

As she walked down the street, a man lingered by her car. Her stomach flipped. The same guy that closed her door a while back. She kept her eyes down while slipping past him, but he stopped her.

"Hey, there."

Lacey stepped off the curb.

"Hey, there, I said. I have something for you."

What could he possibly have for her? She reached for her door handle.

"You want this or not?" The man thrust an envelope toward her.

She had no choice but to take it. The man smirked. At the same time, she heard a voice call from a vehicle in the road.

"Good afternoon, Lacey," Chief Bert called from his squad car.

Lacey turned. She breathed a heavy sigh. "Hey, Chief Bert."

She looked back, but the man hustled down the street in the opposite direction. His head hung low, and his hands shoved into his jacket pockets.

"Everything all right, young lady?" the chief called.

She watched the man turn the corner. "I don't know. That guy—" Lacey pointed, "—do you know him?"

He squinted. "What guy?"

Lacey huffed. "He's gone. But he gave me this." Lacey opened the envelope, and she gasped. Her eyes riveted on a photograph of Wade kissing a heavily made-up, beautiful blonde in a low-cut waitress uniform.

CHAPTER 18

Wade sat by Reginald Gardner's side and waited for Pastor Desmond, hoping Lacey would be with him.

He gazed around the room watching the machines click and buzz. The rich had everything, but they couldn't buy life. Yet if it hadn't been for this man and his money, Wade wouldn't be here, either. Or would he?

Wade took his great-grandfather's hand and squeezed. "Please, God," Wade begged, and his throat grew thick, making it hard to swallow. "I know I don't deserve anything, but he does. Save him, will you?"

Laying his forehead on their clasped hands, Wade sighed. He'd never felt so lost, but the memory of his mom's death arose. The mother who had raised him. He searched for her final words again. *Trust Jesus.*

He felt a presence in the room and Pastor Desmond walked in. Wade stood.

"Thank you for coming, Pastor." He leaned out, searching around Pastor Desmond.

"Lacey is on her way. I'm sure they won't let her up here, but I imagine you can meet her in the waiting room when she arrives." He walked to the bedside and touched Mr. Gardner's other hand. "I'm so sorry, Wade."

Wade recognized genuine concern in the man's eyes. This man of God that everyone talked about. The one Lacey wanted for her mother since day one. Wade cringed, sure she didn't feel that way about him. At least not the first time they met. But he'd do everything he could to change her mind.

"Tell me about your great-grandfather," Pastor Desmond asked.

He opened his mouth, then shut it. What could he say? He didn't know much about the man, but Wade had heard how driven yet generous everyone knew him to be. The generous part, Wade experienced. The man's tanned, wrinkled skin gave evidence of an outdoorsman, even at his age. Wade looked down at the pale pallor taking hold of his face.

Many times, early in the morning, Wade watched him ambling out the long walkway from the house. He'd cross the street and sit on his private pier. Sometimes on benches in the sun, sometimes in the shade under the gazebo at the end. Reginald Gardner had the longest construction over the water along Beach Road. It's where he spent his days in Bay Town.

"He's crazy about the gulf. He spends hours just looking at the water," Wade said.

"I think we could all benefit from relaxing like that." Pastor Desmond nodded.

Wade took a deep breath, and he blew out hard. His mind darkened. "It's because of me that he's in here. I'm sure he hasn't relaxed much since I came into his life."

"He might disagree with you. We just need to trust."

Wade's eyes narrowed. That's what his mom had said. Trust Jesus. And then she died. "Yeah, I'm not so sure about that."

"Well that's your choice. God won't force you, but I can tell you from experience. Life is a whole lot easier if you do."

"I'm not so sure." He cleared his throat. "My mom—step-mom." He ran a hand through his hair. "I don't even know who she was, but she trusted Jesus. That's what she always said. Then Beau killed her." He stared back at Pastor Desmond, thinking that ought to shock him.

It didn't.

"I'm so sorry. That's this evil world we live in. I can't tell you why that happened, but I can tell you that your mom had peace."

"A lot of good that did."

"When you have that peace, you know this life isn't all there is. God's always been trustworthy. If you read the Bible, you'll see that."

"I don't need to read the Bible. God hasn't been trustworthy with me. If you knew my real parents." Wade brushed a hand through his hair. "I don't even know them. But they weren't good people. They didn't even want me."

"And how'd you land up here?"

Wade smirked, but a grin replaced it. He pointed at Desmond. "I guess you got me there. Luck, I guess. But I know, I don't deserve to be here."

"None of us deserve anything but death."

"Are you sure you weren't my mom's preacher?"

Pastor Desmond chuckled. "I would have liked to have met her." His eyes grew sad. "Listen, Wade, if you ever want to come into my office and talk, I'd like that."

"Yeah, well. I'm not sure you could relate. My life is a whole lot different than yours ever was."

"How so? There's much about my life that you don't know."

"But you're a preacher, and you're married to Lacey's mom. Heck, you're practically a perfect family."

"No one's perfect. Not even practically, and you have no idea what they've experienced—the doubts they've had. Life in Christ is not a cakewalk, but it's a journey worth taking. I wouldn't do it without Him. I tried, and when I lost my first wife, I wouldn't have made it without God."

Wade's mouth gaped. "You were married before?"

Heels clicked on the floor, and both men turned. Wade's heart skipped a beat, but his shoulders slumped when Summer entered the room.

"Hey, Pastor," Summer said.

He stood and wrapped an arm around her shoulders. "We're all praying for Mr. Gardner. I'm sorry, but God willing, he'll pull through."

"I hope so," Summer said.

A nurse walked in. "Only two at a time in here."

"I'll go," offered Wade.

"No, Wade. You stay. I'll go unless you need a break. I'd be happy to stay as long as needed," Pastor Desmond said.

"Sure, thanks. I need to shower and change anyway." Wade fingered the phone in his pocket. He hoped Lacey had texted, maybe even waited downstairs. "Thanks, Pastor."

He pushed the button, and the large doors buzzed open. He checked his cell as he walked through and took the elevator down to the cafeteria. *Why wasn't Lacey returning his texts?* He grabbed a cola, popped it open, and took a long drink.

"Lacey? Are you all right?" Chief Bert asked.

She gripped her side with one hand but couldn't release the photograph with the other. Who printed out pictures nowadays anyway? But where did he get this?

"Lacey? What's going on?" Chief Bert pulled into an empty spot and parked. His tall, broad frame eased out, and he approached her. "What you got there?"

She stuffed the picture into her purse and shook her head. "A photo." Her voice trembled. "That man." She searched the street. "He gave it to me, and I have no idea who he is."

"Well, let me see it."

"No. Can't you just go after him? Find out who he is?"

"No, I can't. Did he threaten you or expose something?" The chief pointed. "Is that photograph pornographic?"

Lacey choked back tears. "No. Of course not."

"Then why are you so upset?"

"It's a friend. That's all. I didn't expect it, and I have no idea who that man is or how he got this."

"You're not giving me any cause to go after the guy. Have you seen him before?"

"Yes," Lacey said. "He approached me at my car last week." She shivered recalling that encounter. "Now, can you please go find him?"

"Lacey, I didn't even see him. You got to give me more than that."

"He's stalking me, isn't he? Twice already?"

"Give me a description." Chief Bert took out a pad and paper. Old school. No electronic tablet for him.

She closed her eyes, trying to recall. Nothing came up.

"Hair color? Height, build. Any scars or tattoos?"

"Brown. Taller than me. He had an e-cigarette. Not from around here, I'm sure of it."

Experience told Lacey to be wary of the man, but after seeing the photo, anger replaced caution. He was a creeper, and obviously he knew Wade. Why had she been so stupid? Low-lifes like Wade played girls like her. He'd almost said as much when they'd first met. But she thought maybe she met him in the middle of a life change. It seemed like it, anyway.

Chief Bert nodded, put his pad away, and moved toward his car. "Lacey, I want you to tell your mom and dad and watch out for him. Don't be alone anywhere. In fact, where are you headed now?"

Lacey ignored the buzzing phone. Probably a text from Wade asking her to come to the hospital. *Forget that.* But her heart wrenched at the thought of him possibly losing his great-grandfather. She knew what that felt like, but did he feel the same way? He didn't seem that close to his great-grandfather. Lacey's mind went through every excuse not to show him any compassion, and the photograph fueled it. But her heart in Christ convicted her.

"Lacey? Are you headed home?" the Chief asked.

"No. I'm working today."

"Okay, then. I'm going to look for this guy." Chief Bert pointed. "At some point, I need to see that picture."

Her eyes widened, and she shook her head. "It has nothing to do with the guy, I'm sure of it."

"I'll be the judge of that. I'll stop by your house tonight. I need to talk to your parents."

"No. I'll talk to them."

"I don't know what you're hiding, girl, but I need your cooperation. I don't want a repeat of two years ago."

"Me neither, Chief." She turned, treading back to Victoria's shop. She slipped inside before Chief Bert followed her.

"I'm back," Lacey called. "I can't go to the hospital, so I can work the rest of the day."

Victoria peeked out, cell phone to her ear. "I thought Wade needed you. How is Mr. Gardner?"

"Oh, I promise you. Wade doesn't need me."

But as to his great-grandfather, she had no idea. Guilt got the better of her. That and compassion. Lacey pulled out her phone and texted.

<Any updates on Mr. Gardner?>

The response from Wade came immediately. <Where are you? No, he's the same. Not good.>

<Okay. I'm praying.>

Lacey clicked off and turned off all notifications on her phone. She threw it in her portfolio bag, sat down, and cried.

"Oh, Lacey. Did Mr. Gardner…? Oh, come here, honey." Victoria reached for Lacey, but Lacey stopped her.

"No. He's the same." She gulped and pulled the photograph thrusting it at Victoria.

Victoria's eyes narrowed. "Who is this? Do you know these people?"

"Wade." Lacey yanked the elastic from her pony tail. "It's Wade Gardner."

"What? Where did you get this? He didn't give it to you, did he? That would be horrible."

Lacey shook her head. "I don't know who gave it to me. But it's Wade."

"What do you mean? Why would a stranger give this to you?"

Lacey grabbed a tissue and blew her nose. "Does it matter?"

"Yes. Maybe it's an old picture. Someone obviously wants to rile you up. Why would Wade call you and ask you to come to the hospital? Why wouldn't he call this girl if she meant something to him?"

"I don't care if she meant something to him or not." Lacey shoved her finger into the picture. "Her lips are smashed against his."

"Exactly. She's doing the smashing, and he appears surprised. Like maybe he didn't know it was coming."

"It's a selfie. See the angle of his arm?" Lacey twisted her hair. "Forget it. I'm done with him."

"Lacey, he's hurting right now. I don't know what this is all about, and you don't either. Maybe you don't have a right to be angry. Let him explain."

"Explain? Explain what? I'm so stupid. I just met him, and all he does is hurt me. I'm such an idiot." *He said he had to straighten his life out. He asked me to wait and to trust him.*

"His great-grandfather may be dying," Victoria whispered.

A retaliation caught in Lacey's throat, but Victoria's words seared her conscience. Wade hurt significantly more than her right now, and she knew what this kind of hurt felt like.

The shop bells rang, and the women turned.

"Lacey? I waited at the hospital. I worried that something happened to you."

Wade stood just inside the entrance. His hair wet, his clothes rumpled. His tall, slender frame hunched, and his thick wavy hair fell across his defeated face. He pushed it back revealing red rimmed eyes.

Lacey's fists clenched.

CHAPTER 19

L acey wanted to scream. To throw the photograph in his face. He had a lot of nerve, but his hurt pricked her heart. Still, words failed her.

"I thought you were coming to the hospital," he repeated.

Victoria stepped forward. "Hi, Wade? I'm Victoria. I'm so sorry about your great-grandfather."

He nodded, his eyes still resting on Lacey.

"Lacey? Why don't you and Wade take the back room? It's more private."

"No." Lacey gripped the photograph, which guided her found words. "That's not necessary." She glared at Wade. "I sent my dad. He made it, didn't he?"

"Yes, but he said you were coming too."

"Oh, no. I couldn't get in anyway." Lacey tried to sound casual. She hated feeling this way for or about Wade. She only wanted to feel compassion for Mr. Gardner. "How is he? Any change?"

"No."

"I'm sorry. You should go back, right?"

He scowled at her. Looking as if he didn't know who she was. "I came home to shower real quick, but I wanted to see you, first."

Lacey cleared her throat. "Well, I need to get to work, and I'm sure you need to get back."

"Wow. Seriously?" He shook his head. "Yeah. I guess so." Wade backed away and left, slamming the door.

"Lacey, you can't do that," Victoria said.

"Do what?"

"Ignore his pain. It's bigger than yours right now."

"I know that. I just can't deal with it. I'm praying for Mr. Gardner, and I hope Wade doesn't lose him. But that's all I can feel right now."

"Go, Lacey. Talk to him. He has to know why you're acting like this."

"I can't. I'm so angry. I want to hit him. I've never cared about anyone like I do him. But I hate him. Victoria, I hate him, and I feel stupid for falling for him."

Victoria gazed back and raised her chin toward the door. "Sounds like a little pride creeping in. Wade needs you right now. The photograph is a separate issue."

"I can't."

"But God can, and it's called dying to self. You'll be sorry if you don't go."

Victoria grasped Lacey's shoulders and nudged her toward the door. Hesitating, Lacey stepped out, relying on Victoria's strength. She searched the sidewalk, but no Wade. Relief flooded her, and she turned. Victoria had closed the door.

Lacey looked in both directions on Main Street until she saw Wade standing across the street next to his car gazing at the bus station. He turned as if he felt her presence. She waited, but he didn't move. She crossed the street, still gripping the photograph, unsure what she would say.

"Wade, if there's anything I can do."

"Not anymore. You could have come down to the hospital. But never mind. I guess you're too busy."

He glanced at the little ticket booth next to the parked busses, and Lacey followed his gaze. She thought she saw someone move behind the building. Her eyes widened, and for a minute, she thought she saw the man who handed her the photograph. She stared down at the crumpled paper.

"I'm too busy? I think maybe you're the one that's too busy." She thrust the picture at him.

He unfolded the wrinkled mess, and his eyes widened. "Where'd you get this?" Wade pushed a hand through his hair. "It's not what you think."

Lacey crossed her arms. "Not what I think? It looks pretty clear to me, and unless you tell me this happened before we met, we're done here."

Wade shook his head. "No. But she's nobody. I don't even know her."

"Wow. That's even better. You just go around taking kissing selfies with random girls. Goodbye, Wade." Lacey turned into the street.

Honk. A car screeched to a stop, and Wade grabbed her.

"Lacey!"

He yanked her into his arms and for a brief moment, she melted at the hurt in his eyes. She pulled herself free, dodged cars, and ran into Victoria's. She slammed the door trying to push him out of her mind, but still felt his touch. Lacey wrapped her arms around herself and leaned against the door.

Victoria stepped by her side and hugged her. "Give it to God."

"No. I can't."

"What else can you do?"

"It never works out." Tears burned her cheeks, and she swiped them away.

"Lacey, you're young. Things will work out."

"Why does everyone keep saying that?"

"Because it's true. It may not be the way you want, but God's ways are always good. Go home. Why don't you work on gathering pictures of your mom's gown? Straighten this thing out with Reese. Start working on that for now. And sooner, better than later, hear Wade out."

Lacey shook her head. "No, I'll just finish the alterations for the prom dresses today. Maybe I can warn those girls to stay away from jerks like Wade."

Wade stood staring at Victoria's shop for too long. For an instant, he felt the lingering warmth of Lacey in his arms. He crumpled the already crushed photograph and slammed the top of his car with his fist. He yelled and turned toward the bus station.

Beau stepped out from the ticket booth. Laughing.

"I see she opened the little present."

Wade walked over and punched him, knocking him to the ground.

"Hey, I'm calling the police," the ticketing attendant called.

Beau jumped up. "No. I'm fine. Don't call the police." He wobbled.

Wade pulled back his arm and punched him again, this time splitting his lip.

"That's it." The ticket attendant tapped his cellphone.

Beau moaned and rolled over on his knees. He raised a hand as people gathered about. "I'm fine. Just a father-son scuffle." But his body stiffened at the sound of the siren. Beau struggled to stand, cupping his jaw. He turned and ran.

Both Wade's hands rested on his head. He couldn't believe he'd done that, but his cell rang. He ignored it. Seconds later, it buzzed. Wade checked the text message.

<Come quick. It's Grandaddy.>

He headed for his car but heard a loud voice behind him. "Hold it right there, buddy."

Wade turned to see Chief Bert. A small crowd gathered,

and all fingers pointed at Wade. Cell phones raised, taking videos.

"Put those away and get out of here, folks." Chief Bert stepped towards Wade. "Want to tell me what's going on?"

"Yeah, I can tell you at the hospital. My great-grandfather's dying, and I need to get there."

"Wait a minute, someone called in an assault, and all witnesses are pointing at you. You can't go anywhere."

Wade side-stepped the chief, heading for his car. Chief Bert took his arm. "Stop right there, son."

Anger flared, as well as fear. "Didn't you hear me? My great-grandfather needs me." Wade broke the chief's hold and ran for his car.

"Wrong move," the chief called as he made chase.

He caught up and pushed Wade to the ground, cuffed him and pulled him to standing in one swift motion. They shuffled to a squad car, and the chief pushed Wade into the back seat. Screaming obscenities, Wade kicked the seat in front of him but stopped when he saw the chief stoop to pick something up.

Chief Bert stared at a paper and shook his head. He got in the squad car and Wade stared at Victoria's shop. Lacey and Victoria peered out the large display window as the Chief pulled away.

He glared back at her. *How much had she seen?* It didn't matter. Nothing mattered right now but his great-grandfather. Still, he felt his heart tear. She stood there and watched. She didn't do a thing. Just like she didn't come to the hospital. Wade's head dropped to his chest.

After the chief placed him in a cell, Wade continued to yell about his great-grandfather.

"What's his name? I'll check on him."

"Reginald Gardner."

"*Thee* Reginald Gardner? He's your grandfather?"

"Great-grandfather."

"Wow. Okay, then. I'll make some calls." He returned minutes later. "They stabilized him, but he's still in CICU. Now, if you can calm down and I can take a report, I'd be happy to get you down there. So, tell me, what's going on? Who did you punch out?"

"My stepdad."

"A name. I need a name."

"Beau Bodine."

Chief Bert's eyes narrowed. "The guy you were shouting at after Melanie and Desmond's wedding?"

"Yes."

"Why that guy told me he's on parole."

"Yup. I need to go to the hospital."

"Bodine. I know I've heard that name. I'll have Blaine check him out. Why'd you punch the guy?"

"It doesn't matter. Do what you need to do to me but let me see my great-grandfather."

"Listen, we can make this easy if you'll just cooperate. I checked, and you don't have a record, but I'm curious how a guy like you can punch someone out so easily and not have a record."

"Juvenile Hall."

"Ahhh. I got it. So, this is your first offense as an adult. That's good. The other good thing is there's no victim to press charges, so if you tell me what I need to know, I can let you go."

"The guy is messing with my life. He wants money."

"Why didn't you tell me that before?" Chief Bert fingered a paper and shoved it through the bars. "And who is this?"

Wade shook his head. "Nobody. Just a waitress that I used to convince Beau that Lacey didn't mean anything to me."

Chief Bert's eyes widened. "Wait a minute. Lacey? I thought you were done with her after the accident? Are you messing with that little girl?"

"She's not a little girl. And I'm not messing with her. It doesn't matter since she saw the picture."

The chief scratched his head. "I'm not tracking. Come again."

"Beau found out I had money. I gave him six thousand dollars, but he wanted more."

"Whoa. Are you crazy, kid? So, he's extorting and blackmailing you? Where does Lacey come in?"

"I refused to give him any more, but he said he'd show Lacey that picture if I didn't give it to him. I didn't get a chance to explain it to her myself."

"So, she knows nothing about him?"

"No."

The chief snapped his fingers. "Bingo. That's the guy that approached her on the street a couple days or a week ago. And he's the same guy who gave her the picture."

"Can I please see my great-grandfather?"

"Yes. Come on, kid."

Wade followed Chief Bert. As they walked by Officer Blaine's desk, Chief Bert barked out orders. "Pull up everything you got on Beau Bodine. Find his parole officer at West Mississippi Correctional Facility and report him in violation."

The Chief dropped Wade off at his car and went looking for Beau. Once at the hospital, Wade rushed up to CICU, where Summer and Pastor Desmond sat by Reginald Gardner's side.

"Wade, where have you been?" Summer dabbed at her eyes. "We almost lost him."

"I'm sorry. I promise I won't leave again."

Pastor Desmond stood and offered his chair.

"What happened to great-grandfather?" Wade asked.

"Everything." Summer bit her lip. "His blood pressure dropped, his pulse weakened."

"But God intervened, and the doctors got him back on track. It's still a waiting game," Pastor Desmond said. "Listen, if you'd like me to stay, I will."

"Yes," pleaded Summer.

"No," Wade added. "No, you go. But can I talk to you for a minute?"

They stepped outside. "Sir, I've made a mess of my life, and I've been trying to fix it." He glanced at the room, his eyes resting on Reginald Gardner. "Thanks to him in there. But now I screwed up bad. Listen, I like Lacey. I like her a lot, but I hurt her." Wade paused for a long while.

"Go on," Desmond said.

Wade confessed about Beau, and about the girl at the casino. "I'm so sorry. I tried to stay away from Lacey. I never meant to hurt her."

Pastor Desmond's lips grew taut, but he rested a hand on Wade's shoulder. "I believe you. We'll get it straightened out. You're a good man, and I appreciate your honesty "

"No, I'm not." A nervous laugh escaped. "There's so much about me that you don't know."

"Sometimes our past catches up, but you appear to be going in the right direction. Wade, how's your faith?"

Wade shook his head.

"The Bible said a mustard seed is all you need."

"Maybe that's all I got. My stepmom and I'm told my birth mom believed. My stepmom took me to church, but I forgot it all, until recently." He stared back at Desmond. "Until Lacey. I want something more than just to get away from my past. More than making something of myself."

"Those aren't bad things, and neither is a good woman. But that has nothing to do with your faith. Jesus is what you should desire more than anything else."

"A lot of good that did both my moms."

"Look to Jesus, not to people. But they're sitting pretty good in eternity now, and that's the most important thing.

Under certain circumstances, sometimes serving God in our hearts is all we can do, but once we're gone from this earth, we'll be serving Him in heaven. Like we were meant to do."

"Yeah. I don't get it."

"Peace. God brings you peace. Jesus saves you, and the Holy Spirit guides."

"It's that simple?"

"It's that simple but surrendering to him is the hard part, after confessing that you're a sinner."

"I am. No doubt about that."

"Well then, the next step is to receive and believe what He's done for you on the cross. If you do that, then you can surrender the things you want so badly, and His peace will get you through anything."

Wade stared back. "So, my great-grandfather and Lacey?"

Pastor Desmond's eyes widened, and he drew a deep breath. "I didn't know you cared about her that much to put her in the same category. But yes, even them. One step at a time, son. Just pray and ask God each day to give you the strength to get through and make the right decisions. Trust Jesus with your life. Get to know Him, and you'll come to love Him." Pastor Desmond rested a hand on Wade's shoulder. "And leave Lacey to me for now. She's going to need time to process all this, and I'm going to pray for you now."

"Thank you, sir."

After Pastor Desmond prayed, Wade re-entered the hospital room. Summer stared up at him.

"Go home, Summer. Go eat, and sleep. I'll be here."

"Are you sure?"

Wade enveloped his aunt in his arms. "I'm not going anywhere."

After Summer left, Wade sat by Reginald Gardner's side, held his hand, and prayed.

CHAPTER 20

Lacey fingered her mom's wedding gown. The intricate detail, the bias cuts. She almost couldn't believe she'd designed it. But Victoria's expert sewing skills brought it to life. She made it perfect. Lacey needed to improve her garment construction skills. All the more reason she wished she'd been accepted into design school. She held up her cell phone and finished snapping full-length angles and closeups of her mother's gown.

She stood back and lost herself in the champagne lace and satin. The garment's beauty felt magical as she relived seeing her mom walk down the aisle, dance at the wedding, and do all the wedding things that brides do.

But she wasn't lost for long. Wade interrupted her thoughts. Could it have only been a few weeks ago that she'd met him? Fallen for him so hard, and now, she'd witnessed him hitting someone. She didn't know him. Not really.

Lacey shivered. Seeing Wade knocked to the ground and handcuffed like that embarrassed her. Like a criminal. Shame and repulsion joined her anger. Yet, her heart twisted, recalling his glare as Chief Bert drove him away while he sat in the backseat of the squad car.

"What are you doing, sweetie?"

Lacey spun around. "Mom, hi." She pointed to the dress. "Photos for my portfolio. Hey, can I get some of the pictures from the professional photographer?"

"Not yet. I'm so sorry." Melanie blew out an exasperated breath. "She got sick and hasn't been able to edit or get the digitals uploaded."

"Is she all right? When will she get them to you?"

"She's fine. But she's so backlogged, I told her that my photos weren't a rush priority, so take care of others first."

"What? But I need them."

Melanie hugged Lacey. "In due time. So did you have a nice day?"

Lacey forced a chuckle. Where should she start? With her stolen design or Wade's arrest?

"Hey, Manière' Sisters take-out is on the table. Come and get it." Desmond's voice called from the kitchen.

"Come on, Mom." Thankful for the distraction, Lacey pulled her mom to the kitchen. She dragged out a chair and sat.

"Someone's hungry," Desmond said.

"Did you just come from the hospital?" Lacey asked.

"I swung by and got your mom first, and we stopped for a cup of coffee."

"So, how's Mr. Gardner?"

"Not well. He's a sick man. He hasn't regained conscious-ness yet, and every minute is critical."

"And if he does come to?" Lacey's heart raced as she recalled her grandparents.

"We'll see. Hard to say. But lots of people are praying for him. God is a miracle worker, any way you look at it. Come on, let's pray for the food."

Their lighthearted dinner time took on a somber mood. Melanie, Lacey, and Desmond usually shared about their day, and the way Desmond slipped into their routine, she felt like he'd always been there. Lacey loved it. But tonight, she thought she caught glances between her mom and Desmond. Something brewing.

"So, did you see Wade at the hospital?" Lacey blurted out, then shoved a forkful of pasta in her mouth.

The glance again.

Desmond cleared his throat. "For most of the day. He left for an hour or so. He had a rough day."

"He had a rough day? You don't know the half of it," Lacey said.

"I think I do," said Desmond. "But do you want to tell me about it?"

"What's there to tell? The guy's a jerk. I got a photograph of him kissing some strange girl." Lacey wiggled her fingers like quote marks around the word *strange*.

Melanie touched Lacey's hand, but instead of comforting her, it angered her. She pulled it back, crumpling a napkin in her lap, wishing it were the photograph. *The photograph. What had she done with it?* No matter, she never wanted to see it again.

"Lacey, you need to hear his side of it, then decide," Desmond said.

"Oh, no, I don't. It just happened, and he didn't even know her. What a sleaze. Both of them."

Melanie's eyes widened, and so did her mouth, but Desmond spoke first.

"Lacey, hear me out. The most important thing is Wade and his great-grandfather. He may need you to support him. I think he's trying to trust God, but you're pretty important to him too, and if he loses you both—"

"He's not losing me because he never had me." Lacey stood. "I know he's hurting, I know what it feels like, and I'm praying for Mr. Gardner and Summer. But I can't for Wade right now. I'm sorry. I can't."

"You keep saying you can't, but that's not what God says," Melanie said.

"I know, I know. I can do all things through Christ who

strengthens me. But I don't want to be strengthened. I just want to forget about him and move on."

"That's a dangerous place to be, don't you think? Turning your back on God," Desmond said.

"Lacey, honey. I've been there. You don't want to go there. You have your whole life ahead of you, don't make the mistake of walking away from the Lord for something like this," Melanie said.

"Something like this? That's a joke. It's not just Wade. I didn't get into design school, and what's worse, someone stole my best creation. Wade's just the last straw."

She blinked, fighting back tears, but there. Now they knew. *I'm a loser.* She couldn't do anything right, no matter how she tried. Tears fell, and when she couldn't wipe them away fast enough, she ran to her room and slammed the door.

Lying on her bed, Lacey cried, and she cried out to God. *Why? Why? Why?* She heard a light knocking at her bedroom door.

"Lacey, honey. May I come in?"

She didn't want anyone. Yet, her mother always said the right thing, and she could use the comfort. Lacey hoped the silence would beckon her mom in. It did.

Melanie plopped on the floor next to Lacey's mattress. She stroked Lacey's hair and kissed her but remained silent.

"Is it about your design?"

"No. I can't do anything about that."

"Tell me about it?"

Lacey talked and cried through the whole mess. The interview at Madam DeFleur's, the letter, Reese's visit, and the humiliation of being accused of copying. The worst.

"She actually thought I copied MDD's design."

"She doesn't know you. She knows that design house in New Orleans, and for whatever reason, she trusts them. Lacey, I'll get the pictures from the photographer. We'll get a lawyer if we need to. But nothing is worth turning your back on God. Honey, you know, if we have nothing on this earth, we have eternity with Him, and our witness to others here is all that matters."

Lacey shook her head. "Great, I'm a failure at that too. My life is over. I give up."

Melanie chuckled but covered her mouth. "You're nineteen years old. I'd hardly consider that the end of your life, and hardly time to give up." She breathed deep. "I remember I felt like a failure at nineteen too, but that's when I found God, or He found me. And soon after, you were born. Aren't we glad I didn't give up or give in?"

"Oh, Mom." Lacey threw her arms around Melanie.

"Honey, you're human, and Christ in you will make you a wonderful witness. To Wade, to that Reese. Who knows, maybe even to Madam Da' what's her name?"

"Now that's a stretch."

"Not for God."

Lacey blew her nose and wadded the tissue. "You think I should let it go?"

"I think you should write a letter to Reese, send some wedding pictures, and I'll ask Desmond about the lawyer."

"Okay, I'll do that. But never mind about the lawyer for now. That's a lot of money."

"We'll see." Melanie touched Lacey's chin. "And Wade?"

Shaking her head so that her hair fell forward, Lacey brushed it back. "I can't, Mom. Not yet. I'm not ready to forgive Wade."

"You will if you hear his side of the story." Melanie turned towards the open door. "Desmond?" she called.

"He's listening?" Lacey's eyes widened.

"Of course not. Desmond, come in here, please." They waited, and just as Melanie stood, he knocked.

"Did you call? I took out the trash," he said.

Melanie raised a brow at Lacey. "See, I told you so. Yes."

Melanie pointed to Lacey's desk chair, and Desmond complied. "Sit. Spill the beans on Wade."

"I'm sorry that you're experiencing this," Desmond said. "But your faith has sustained you. You've been mature in managing the death of your grandparents and your dad, and here you are again."

"I don't feel so mature." Lacey sniffed.

"You are. And your experiences, coupled with your faith, can help Wade. He has no idea how to surrender these things to Christ. That's the hard part in faith, but it's what you did well, and you could help him."

She couldn't tell if her heart hardened or softened, but something happened. Desmond did that...or God did.

"He's being blackmailed by his stepdad."

"Wait, stepdad?" Lacey's eyes widened.

Desmond raised his hand. "Hold the questions till the end. You'll have a lot of them. Wade's come from a difficult past, and he's trying to figure it all out. Are you ready for this? His stepdad has been in prison for killing his stepmom. He just got out."

Lacey's jaw dropped, and her heart turned to mush.

"The stepdad found Wade in Bay Town, and when he found out he had money, he wanted it. He's the one who rear-ended you guys, causing the accident."

Tears filled Lacey's eyes, again.

"Wade gave him a lot of money. Half his savings, but it wasn't enough for him. When the stepdad found out you were important to him, he threatened to hurt you."

Lacey's heart melted, but a lingering doubt gripped her. "But what about the girl in the photograph? Are you saying she's not real?"

"Well, she's real all right, and Wade feels bad about using her, but that's what he did. He just didn't expect her to lip-lock him in the selfie."

Melanie's eyes widened. "Did you just say lip-lock?"

Lacey laughed, wiping away her tears.

Desmond waved her off. "He punched out his stepdad in front of a whole pile of witnesses. Anyway, you know the rest of it."

A knot grew in Lacey's throat, and she found it hard to swallow. Her eyes burned. "And he went to jail for me?"

"Pretty much. But ran from the chief because he just got word that Mr. Gardner had taken a bad turn and he wanted to get to the hospital."

Lacey dropped her head into her hands and choked. "Oh, man. I'm such an idiot. I wouldn't even listen." She straightened and wiped her face with her blanket. "I have to go down there, now."

Melanie pulled at Lacey's hand. "Honey, why don't you call him first. He might need some time. Maybe you can see him at lunch hour tomorrow."

"No. I want to go now."

The glance between her parents affirmed their agreement to let her go. *Her parents.* That sounded right.

"I'll drive you," offered Desmond. "The hospital will let me sit with Mr. Gardner while you guys can talk outside."

Lacey dressed quickly and pleaded with God on the way over. *Please God, save Mr. Gardner.* Then she asked that Wade would know and love Jesus. It was that simple, but she remembered Desmond's words. Surrender. The hard part.

Lacey stayed in the waiting room while Desmond went into the CICU. She watched the television, then flipped through some magazines but put them down. What the celebrities wore always sparked her interest, but she didn't care about that right now. She heard footsteps coming from the hallway and stood.

Desmond walked in and shook his head. "Let's give him time, Lacey."

"Is Mr. Gardner worse?"

"It's not that. Wade is having a struggle right now."

"With whom?" She swallowed hard. "With me?"

Desmond sighed. "Yes, but I also suspect it's with God."

"But I can tell him. I know what that's like. He can't turn away. Not now." Lacey reached for her phone.

"Lacey, let's go home. Why don't you call or text him later? You don't know how God's working in Him right now, and I don't either. I think it's good he hears from you. You can encourage him, but make sure what you tell him are God's words and not yours."

"You mean send him scriptures?"

"No, not a good idea right now. Read your Bible and pray. God will guide."

The quiet drive home did nothing to soothe her troubled spirit, and the bright full moon cast a shattered spotlight over the gulf waters, mimicking her unforgiving heart just hours before. But like the moon's shadow surrendering to rippling breaks on the surface, so did Lacey's heart. She had trusted God with almost all of herself but held back enough to build a wall around the parts that hurt the most. *No more, God. No more.*

CHAPTER 21

Lacey and Jacquie waited while Desi changed. She peeked out of the dressing room and stepped up the two stairs to the three-way mirror. A grin spread across her face, and she spun around. Her eyes sparkled, and she clapped her hands as she glanced over her shoulder at her reflection in the floor-length mirror.

"I love it," she squealed.

Jacquie beamed at her daughter, and her eyes glistened. She hugged Lacey. "Thank you," she said. "Thank you so much."

Lacey's sigh expressed satisfaction over a job well done. The light teal, crepe back satin prom dress graced every curve of the young teen's shape, and since Lacey had a knack for the trends, the girl's dress fit right in with the other girls' gowns.

"My pleasure. She's adorable, isn't she?" Lacey said.

"That's putting it mildly. Why she's about to shatter those mirrors if she shines any brighter. Now come on, girl, let's get that gown off. I gots to get to work."

With arms hooked around one another, mother and daughter left Victoria's shop, and Lacey commenced to pull out the next prom dress, ready for final fitting number three for the day. The business of prom season kept her from dwelling on the fact that Wade had not called. It had only been a day, but Pastor Desmond said to give him time. Still, her fingers itched to text Wade again.

Bells jingled as Art walked in. "Hey, Lace. I brought napoleons from the Mockingbird. Victoria's favorite."

"Mille-fueille. Mine, too," cooed Lacey.

"Huh?"

Lacey clasped her hands to her chest, closing her eyes. She breathed out, "Rich layers of crème, sandwiched between thin layers of oh-so perfect pastry crust." She opened her eyes and licked her lips. "Both the Danish and the Italian chefs claim to have first created it, but France is where that glorious concoction came to be, so that's why they call it Mille-fueille. Although Russia claims it as their favorite dessert."

Art shook his head. "You are one interesting young lady. You didn't learn that in one of your design classes, did you?" He chuckled. "Who cares? Let's eat."

Though Lacey didn't feel much like food, when Art opened the pink box, her mouth watered, and she reached for one. They both hummed while eating when Victoria walked in.

"Hey, save some for me," she said.

Art pulled the last one from the box and lifted it to Victoria's lips. "Eat, my sweet."

Lacey giggled and thought how cute they were.

When they finished, Art asked, "So, anything new with Cruella Deville? I mean Madam DeFleur."

Victoria gave him a sideways glance. "Be nice, Art. But Lacey, have you done anything?"

"Well, I drafted a letter with pictures to send to Reese just to clear my name, and Mom said we'd hire a lawyer, but it's too much money. I think I'll let this one go. The design is memorialized in Mom's wedding dress, and that's good enough for me."

"Wow. That's pretty mature." Art squeezed Lacey's shoulder. "I bet God's swirling even better designs in that brain of yours."

Victoria frowned. "He's right. But it's hard to let someone do that to you."

"Right? I have to keep putting it out of my head, or I'll start crying."

Art and Victoria moved in for a group hug.

"God's got this, Lacey." Art squeezed her shoulder. "Well, I have to get back to work. Hey, any word on Mr. Gardner?"

"He's doing better."

"Great. That's an answer to prayer," Art said as he exited. "Bye."

Victoria turned to Lacey. "I'm so sorry about Madam DeFleur. I know how you feel. But Art's right. God's got something better planned."

"I know. I just hate that she got away with this."

"Well, just get that letter off to Reese. It'll bring some resolution."

The shop remained quiet for the afternoon, so Lacey spent the rest of the day writing and rewriting the letter defending her design. She crumpled paper after paper, not sure how much to say. She pulled out her phone and scrolled through photos of her mom's wedding gown and wished the photographer had come through. But she finished, sealed everything up in an envelope, and dug through her purse for Reese's business card.

"Found it…Ugh. I can't mail it. She didn't put her address on here."

"Call her, then."

"Are you kidding? No way."

Victoria giggled. "She's a celebrity. Art will find it."

"How?"

Victoria picked up her cell. "Art, can you find Reese's mailing address?...Great. Text me when you get it." She clicked off, but holding up one finger, Victoria mouthed, *wait for it,* and within seconds her phone dinged. She showed the screen to Lacey.

"See."

Another day went by, and still not a word from Wade. Lacey sludged through her work without inspiration. Nothing felt right. Not Wade, not her designs. Even the girls' joy going to prom couldn't lift her spirits. Though they thanked her with various gifts, it didn't help. Jacquie even brought in delicious muffins from the Mockingbird, and Mrs. Higa delivered her freshly made sushi rolls, which Art devoured.

Lacey got up one morning, dressed for a run, and padded through the house.

"Can I join you?"

Lacey jumped and clutched her chest. "Mother. You scared me to death."

Melanie sipped a cup of coffee while leaning against the counter. Her eyes traveled to Lacey's running outfit. They matched.

Rolling her eyes, Lacey huffed. "Not unless you change. I'm not running matchy-matchy."

"Oh, come on. How long since we've done that?"

"Like never." Lacey walked back down the hallway and said over her shoulder, "I'll change."

Their feet hit the sidewalk simultaneously, and Lacey giggled to herself at their matching shoes. The day brightened without clouds and sweat dripped down her back.

"Let's pick it up, Mom. It's hot already." Lacey raced ahead.

When they reached their turning point at Bubba's, he waved, and they each grabbed a paper cone, filling it with water from the cooler. Lacey chuckled at a couple sitting at a table. Tote bags with a map of Bay Town and the surrounding gulf imprinted on the front gave a hint that they might be tourists. They waved at Lacey and Mel while sipping on bottled water. Melanie raised her paper cone. Though they'd lived in Bay Town only a few years, Lacey felt like a local. Drinking from Bubba's cooler instead of paying for bottled water proved it.

"Mom, I'm glad we moved here."

Melanie hooked an arm around her daughter's shoulders. "Me, too, sweetie."

Although she'd had her share of troubles in Bay Town, Lacey loved the people and couldn't be happier with Desmond as her new father. If it weren't for him, she felt her faith wouldn't have grown as it did, but her experiences made her feel much older than her nineteen years. She chuckled, thinking about the sixteen-year-olds she helped with prom dresses. They were only a few years younger than her, but somehow she felt old compared to them. She shivered a little and crossed her arms, and lifted her face to the sky, letting the sun bathe her. But she didn't warm up, and something inside made her turn.

The parking lot. A man leaned against a car with his arms crossed against his chest. Aviator sunglasses shaded his eyes, but something about his slicked-back hair made Lacey shiver. She tugged at her mom.

"Don't look, but a guy in the parking lot is staring at us. Do we know him?"

Melanie brushed back some loose strands of hair and tightened her ponytail. She turned toward the parking lot, and Lacey remained quiet while her mom did a runner's stretch. Melanie glanced at the man and froze.

Lacey felt her mother stiffen. "Mom, who is he?"

"A ghost," she said. "Come on. Let's finish our run." She started down the boardwalk, tugging Lacey along.

"See y'all," Bubba called out.

When Lacey turned to answer, she saw the man with the

aviator sunglasses getting into his car. "Mom, he's pulling out. Why would he be following us?"

Her mom ran faster, and Lacey followed. "Mom?" she asked again.

"He looks very much like Will Boudreaux."

Lacey's eyes widened. She squinted as the car pulled up alongside them. It slowed, and she recognized him. The man who gave her the photograph of Wade and the girl. She gasped, and the connection hit her. Wade's stepdad.

Melanie tugged at her, urging her to keep running.

He pulled down his sunglasses and stared through the open window out the passenger side.

"Afternoon, ladies. Nice day for a run, ain't it?" He leered back with his hand gripping the passenger headrest.

Lacey shot a glance at her mom. She took Lacey's arm and pulled her across the street behind the car, but it stopped.

"Be careful, ladies. Running can be dangerous." He laughed and sped off.

Lacey clutched her chest. "Mom. That's him," she whispered.

Melanie's hands rested on her hips as the car faded away. "I swear, Lacey. If Will Boudreaux had a brother, that would be him." She pulled out her cell.

"Mom, did you hear me? He's Wade's stepdad. The guy who gave me that photograph."

"What?" Melanie asked while tapping her phone. "Are you sure?"

"Yes, Mom, I am. Who are you calling?"

Melanie held up a finger and spoke into her cell. "Chief Bert."

"Good idea," Lacey mumbled, and dropped to the grass. She sat cross-legged, holding her head in her hands. *Why is this happening again?*

Melanie joined Lacey on the ground.

"Chief Bert? Wade's stepdad just followed us." Melanie

patted Lacey's hand. "Yes, Lacey recognized him and she's sure. We're headed home now. I'll get my car, and we'll meet you at the station."

The women ran home and didn't bother to change clothes when they got there. Desmond wasn't home, and Lacey's heart sank. She could use him right now. They both could. She gripped the grab-handle above her door as Melanie sped to the police station.

"So, you're sure it was him?" asked Chief Bert.

Afraid if she spoke, the dam would burst, she cleared her throat and nodded.

"His parole officer's been searching for him. Did you get the make and model of his car?"

"Sorry, we were a little shook up," said Melanie.

Lacey pushed back some loose hair. "An older model. Kind of beat up. Maybe black with peeling paint?"

Chief Bert made a phone call informing the parole officer, then sent Officer Blaine to patrol.

"Don't go home. Go to the Mockingbird or something."

"I think Desmond is at the church helping to get ready for the Yard Sale Fundraiser. Can we go there?"

Chief Bert grinned. "Ain't no better place as far as I'm concerned."

"Good, then perhaps we'll see you on Sunday." Melanie winked as she stood.

He let out that loud giggle, so at odds with his size and stature. Lacey welcomed the light humor.

"Awe, give me a break, Melanie. I've been going more since, well, I been attending almost regular this last year."

Melanie extended a hand. "Yes, you have," she said. "I'm sorry, I didn't mean to nag you."

"Aww, no worries. I need the nudge. At least you don't

hound me like my wife. Why Lina, she bangs pots and pans on Sunday morning to get me up." Chief Bert chuckled.

Lacey giggled. She could just imagine it. Grabbing her mother's arm, she glanced at Chief Bert but took a deep breath.

"Lacey, don't you worry. We'll get him."

CHAPTER 22

T he ring startled Wade, and he sat upright. It stopped. He frowned as machines whooshed and clicked around him. *Oh, right. Still here.* His face itched, and he scratched the scruff on his chin. Reginald Gardner lay still with his pale face blending into the white sheets. Wade's heart dropped to his stomach. What he wouldn't give to sit on the pier enjoying the hot gulf sun with Great-grandfather right now. He wondered if he ever would again.

The ring again, and Wade pulled out his cellphone. Chief Bert registered on the screen. He had more questions, and Wade didn't feel like giving answers. Beau hadn't contacted him in days. Fine by him. Hopefully, he'd moved on with the cash Wade had given him. Better yet, he hoped the parole officer would find him. Right now, Wade concentrated on his great-grandfather.

He reached inside his coat pocket, feeling for the letter. His mom's letter. Wade stared down. He pulled at his coat lapels. *I wore this for you, sir.* Wade had worn a sports coat and dress shirt every day at the hospital, sans a tie. *"A gentlemen can show a little respect by how he dresses,"* Reginald Gardner always said.

Heels clicked the tile floor, and he knew Aunt Summer

approached. Turning toward the window, he stuffed the letter back into his coat pocket.

Summer walked over and embraced him. "Wade, you go on home and get some rest. Go shower, and shave. Let me stay a spell."

"We can both stay."

"Here." Summer handed Wade a brown, cardboard take-out box. "It's a little late for breakfast so I brought you something to tide you over. A BLT."

Wade kissed his aunt's cheek and took the box. "Thanks."

"Now go, you can take it home to eat. I insist." She pushed him toward the door.

"Okay, but I'll be back. I want to be here when he wakes up."

"Me too." Summer's eyes teared. "Wait. Have you talked to Lacey?"

He didn't turn but shook his head.

"Honey, she might be a good support right now."

Aunt Summer didn't know. Not aware of their falling out, but she was right. He wanted Lacey by his side so badly that his heart ached.

"What happened to not being good enough for her?" Wade chuckled.

"Oh, Wade. I'm sorry. I'm long past that. I think maybe you two are meant for one another. Go on, call her. I'm sure she's waiting to hear from you."

"Maybe."

Wade didn't get far. He wandered into the waiting room outside the ICU. He opened the take-out box. The fat tomato slices, snappy green lettuce, and crispy bacon didn't squelch the ache in his stomach. Closing the box, he leaned back, and brushed a hand through his hair. Staring at the ceiling, he thought of Lacey.

Willing enough to forgive him for the photograph, but

what about his past? And what of Will Boudreaux, his dad, terrorizing Lacey, and Bay Town?

The letter. Wade trembled as he pulled it out. The letter emitted power over him, and his hand shook, but he opened it.

"My dear son, I call you that because I'm not sure if your father kept the name I gave you. Wade."

Finally, some truth to his identity.

"I'm embarrassed and ashamed, and I don't know where to start, but know this. I've loved you more than I've ever loved anyone."

Wade stared at the words. The paper shook in his hands, but he forced his eyes to continue.

I'm sick, and I'm dying, and I'm going home. I should have taken you and gone back to Grandaddy a long, long time ago. I know he's found you because you're reading this letter. Your great-grandaddy is a good man. He always was, and I'm sorry I hurt him so.

My son, I hope you've had a good start with your adopted parents because what I have to tell you about your father will hurt. When I discovered his true character, it infuriated me as it will you. I ruined my life when I ran away with him, and living became hopeless. But when you were born, hope returned for a short time. I wish I'd run home with you, but I couldn't. I hope, and pray with my last breath, by God's grace that you've escaped your father's life.

Will Boudreaux is your father's name, and he's a human trafficker. I'm so sorry. I never dreamed him capable of such a thing. I wish I would have listened to Grandaddy and my sister, Summer. They are wise, loving, and a God-fearing family. Your family.

After your father used me, shame prohibited me from returning home. Horrified at all I'd done. I was raised better than that, so I can't blame it all on your father. I chose to leave with him. I believed him, like all the other girls.

Wade's mouth dried up. His father used his mom? Did she mean abused? Bile rose in his throat as he reread *other girls.*

I know this news is devastating, but Wade, you are not your father, and the most important thing I can tell you is to follow Jesus. I walked away. I once was lost, but now I am found, and I'm going home to rest in His arms. I'm sorry that I can't hold you in mine. Please, please receive the Savior, I long to see you one day, and heaven is my only hope.

I don't deserve heaven. None of us do. But Jesus changed all that. I hope you'll embrace that. I'm so sorry, son. I love you so much. Your loving mother."

The letter crinkled in his hand. *True—all of it. I'm the son of a prostitute and her pimp. A human trafficker. A murderer.* His stomach lurched, and he ran for the men's room.

Hunched over the porcelain bowl, he braced himself in the stall. More thoughts haunted him, and he stumbled to the sink and washed up. Who else in Bay Town knew Will Boudreaux and had suffered at his hands? He stared at his reflection in the mirror. *How would he tell Lacey?*

Wade stood. He wanted to smash something. He wanted to kill somebody. But his dad was already dead. He threw the wadded letter against the wall and stared at it. Walking over, he retrieved it, smoothing out the wrinkled page, rereading the last lines.

"Please, please receive the Savior, I long to see you one day, and heaven is my only hope. I'm so sorry, son. I love you so much. Your loving mother."

Heaven is my only hope.

Just like his stepmom said. With all the terror in their lives, both mothers had turned to Jesus. And they wanted him to do the same. The words toiled against the hate he held for his dad and Beau.

Jesus is my only hope.

Wade exited the men's room and stopped a nurse in the hallway. "Do you have a chapel here somewhere?"

"Of course, sir. It's on the first floor, just behind the main lobby."

Wade rode the elevator and walked into the sanctuary-like room. The stained glass, green plants, and subdued lighting welcomed him, and he sat in the back and folded his hands. He leaned forward.

Time went by without his notice. He sat in silence and listened to the soft music filtering through hidden speakers. He recognized an old hymn his mother used to sing. His head dropped into his hands. Tears welled, but he wouldn't let them fall. *What a mess.* He took responsibility for screwing up his life, but this? The impossibility of living with it crushed him. *"I can't fix this, God. Please, help me."*

But doubts arose. *Why should he help me?* Wade pulled down the kneeling bench. He swiped at escaping tears. *I don't deserve everyone's kindness. And I don't deserve God's. Deserve.* He pondered the word. *It has nothing to do with deserving. Turn, believe, and receive.*

An eerie strength arose, and Wade looked up, ready to see someone. But no one, nothing appeared. So he waited, and a peace settled. *I'm sorry, God. I'm trusting you on this, and with my life.* An odd presence filled the room. He knew it. He felt it. He filled his lungs with clean air and blew out.

"Thank you," he said aloud, and stood.

Wade exited the hospital and stepped outside. He relished the warmth of the hot sun, but before the smile growing inside could reach his face, a loud voice called his name—an angry voice.

"Wade Gardner?" said Chief Bert. "Why the heck don't you answer your phone?"

"Chief."

"Beau Bodine is still here. He threatened Lacey and her mom earlier."

"What? Are they okay? Where are they?" His jaw clenched. *Not again. Not like his real father.*

"They're safe. Has he contacted you?"

Wade still grasped the wrinkled letter but stared down. "Did you know Will Boudreaux was my real father?"

The chief pulled his shoulders back, gripped his utility belt with one hand, and snapped his fingers with the other.

"Bodine. I knew I'd heard that name before. I suspected something but never had time to investigate. Will Boudreaux had many aliases. He used the Bodine name too." He frowned. "Are you sure?"

"I'm sure." Wade held the letter, not offering it. "This is a letter from my mom, Mr. Gardner's other granddaughter. She's dead, and this is her death bed confession."

The Chief's eyes softened with sorrow. "I'm sorry, son. Listen, I'm headed back to the station. Lacey and Mel are at Bay Town Community Church with Desmond. Maybe you should head there too."

"Are you sure they're safe?"

The Chief nodded.

"Good, but I can't face them. Not yet."

"This ain't your fault, Wade. You're not like your dad."

"He's not my dad."

"Your father. You're not like him or this Beau Bodine. You're a Gardner. You got good blood in you, son. Lacey will understand." The chief's voice trailed.

"How do you know?"

"She has a story a little like yours. At least when it comes to her father. He left Melanie high and dry before Lacey's birth, but he came back at the end of his life. He unknowingly collaborated with the human traffickers. As a real estate broker, he found them properties for housing women. When he found out, he turned on them. I think Will Boudreaux had a hand in killing him."

Wade pulled a hand through his hair. "Are you kidding me? Can this get any worse?"

"I don't know how well you know Lacey, but her dad wasn't a bad guy. Just got himself into trouble. Heck, I liked the guy. A lot of fun but irresponsible. Melanie and Lacey couldn't count on him."

Wade gulped. "Like me."

The Chief frowned. "No. Not like you. If you were like

him, you wouldn't be here. At the hospital sleeping by your great-granddaddy's bedside all worried about whether he lived or died. Although you're probably heir to his wealth."

"Don't say that."

Throwing his hands up, the chief gripped Wade's shoulders. "See. That's what I'm talking about. You're not like any of them. Chris, Lacey's dad neither. Heck, he even helped save a local girl, Virginia, from trafficking."

"Virginia? Officer Blaine's wife?"

"That's right. And I think that's what got him killed. We could never prove it, but the New Orleans Police found Chris dead in his hotel room the morning after the big bust."

"Oh, man. Lacey's dad. And now Beau's after her. Wait till I get my hands on Beau." Wade's fingernails dug into his palms.

"Oh, no, you don't. That's my job. Right now, just be there for your great-grandfather. How's he doing?"

"Better. He's out of the Cardiac Intensive Care Unit, but still in serious condition."

Chief Bert placed a hand on his shoulder. "My wife, Lina, is praying for him. I hope he gets out of the woods. I'm sure the good Lord has His hands on all the Gardners. They do a lot of good. As I said, you've got good blood, don't forget that."

Wade didn't believe it for a minute, but said, "Thank you, sir."

"Good, now go meet Lacey. Officer Blaine is patrolling your house and Lacey's. Whatever you do, don't go home. The church is the safest place right now."

Wade's eyes widened. "No, it's not. That's the first place I saw Beau when he got out of jail. Right after Pastor and Mrs. Brooks' wedding."

"Shoot." Chief Bert pulled off his hat and slapped his thigh. "How could I have forgotten that?" He gave orders into

212 | KATHLEEN J. ROBISON

his shoulder radio but told Wade to go back in the hospital and stay there.

"I'm sorry, sir. I can't do that." Wade whispered and ran to his car.

After he showered and changed at home, he'd have a clear head to plot his next move. Going after Beau. He opened his car door and climbed in. When he started the car, tapping sounded on the passenger window. He turned to look. He shuddered.

"Hello, Wade." The voice muffled through the closed window.

Wade's stomach soured and Beau hunched down, pointing a gun at him.

CHAPTER 23

Lacey grabbed a brownie and ate it in two bites. She reached for another and another. After the third, she stopped.

"Not a good idea," Melanie said.

Dropping the chocolate gooey concoction, Lacey turned and hugged her mom. "I'm worried about Wade."

"I know, sweetie. Me too." Melanie pulled away. "But making yourself sick with a sugar high won't help."

Desmond walked in carrying a box and plopped it on the table. "We got more desserts." He pointed. "Good thing. It looks like those won't last till the Yard Sale tomorrow."

Lacey rolled her eyes. "I'll make more."

A smile creased at the corners of his eyes. "No worries. I'm sure plenty more are coming." He walked over and grabbed a brownie. "So, what are we stressing about?"

Melanie gave him a playful shove.

"Sorry. I know this is rough, but Lacey, Chief Bert has got this, and Wade's a tough guy. Besides, he's safe at the hospital. He's been there day and night, and Beau won't make a move there. He'd be pretty foolish if he did."

"Men like that live foolishly." Melanie grunted.

"I know, girls. It feels like we're living another nightmare.

But let's not go there. God will get us through. He did before, remember?"

A tear splashed down Lacey's cheek.

"Oh, honey." Melanie pulled her daughter close, and Desmond joined them.

He prayed, and as always, Lacey felt the load lighten. It didn't disappear, but his words soothed her spirit. He knew scripture like no one else, and Jesus' words flowed from his tongue, lending her the strength to get through this. Wade needed God. *Oh, God, draw him. Please.*

"Group hug." A melodious voice filled the room. "Hey, y'all. What are we praying about?"

Virginia entered through the back door and with a loud breath, whooshed back a wisp of platinum blonde hair. She struggled with a large box in her arms. Desmond rushed over to help, took the box, and placed it across the room with all the other yard sale donations.

"I got more in the car," Virginia said.

"How can you have so much stuff? You and Blaine have only been married a year."

Chuckling, Virginia waved. "Oh, it's from the thrift store. Carol had so much extra stuff in storage, and most of it's old, like her."

As often the case, everyone had extra grace for Virginia's socially awkward comments. All the community admired her for overcoming her challenges and tragedies. She had an amazing story, and if it hadn't been for Carol, the previous owner of Second Chance Vintage Thrift Store, she might not be here. Still, everyone's eyes widened, and Virginia slapped both hands over her mouth but bubbled out a contagious laugh.

"Well, she is old."

"She's only like fifty," Lacey said.

"Oh well. Anyway, this stuff is just not trendy anymore. Carol is the coolest person I know, and she wouldn't want it in the shop anymore." Virginia scrunched her face. "Hey, has anybody heard from her lately?"

With the thought of Carol came the memory of Will Boudreaux's death and how Carol almost died with him. *Would they never get over Will Boudreaux terrorizing Bay Town?* Lacey looked at her mom, who nodded as if she understood.

"He's gone," Melanie whispered, kissing Lacey's forehead.

"But maybe he's come back from the grave." Lacey hunched and rolled her eyes.

Melanie cleared her throat. "I talked to Carol about a month ago. She's doing well in Arizona. I'm not sure if she's ever planning on returning."

"I hope she doesn't come and take Second Chance back." Virginia's bright red lips pouted. "I've been working hard to keep it going with Rodney's help."

"She wouldn't do that. She loves you." Lacey hugged her friend. "We all do."

"Awww, I love you too. After all, you're my family now. With Hilly and Will gone, I don't got nobody." She clasped her hands together, pressing them against her heart. "But I got Rodney. Oh my goodness. He's the best husband in the world."

Desmond gave Melanie a shove.

"Oh, next to Desmond, that is," Melanie said.

"Yeah, he's pretty hot too."

Desmond turned bright red.

"Look at you." Virginia squealed. "You're as bright as Rodney when he gets embarrassed. Well, I better go. I'm not sure when Rodney will be home tonight."

Lacey stiffened. "He's out searching for Beau Bodine. Isn't he?"

Virginia's face scrunched. "Who? Wait a minute, did you say, Beau? Why my uncle Will had a brother named Beau, but I never met him. Uncle Will said that Beau married some nice

Jesus lady, and they adopted a baby boy, and…" Virginia rambled on about her family history.

Lacey's knees wobbled. It sounded all too familiar. Virginia had it all mixed up. She tended to sensationalize things. Lacey grabbed her mother's hand and squeezed. Didn't Melanie say that Beau Bodine could pass for Will Boudreaux's brother? She searched her mother's face, but Melanie's eyes were closed, and she slumped against the counter.

Desmond draped an arm around Melanie but spoke to Virginia. "Does anyone else know about this brother? Does he know about you?"

"Don't know, and don't care. I'm done with them." Virginia turned to leave.

"Virginia? We could use some help here. Can you stay awhile?" Melanie perked up.

"I guess. But I want to go home and cook."

"Well, how about Rodney joining us when he gets off, and we'll order take-out?" Melanie added.

"Great idea." Desmond walked toward Virginia and pushed her towards Melanie. "You girls get started. I have to make a phone call in my office. I'll be right back." He moved to Lacey's side and whispered, "I'm calling Bert. Don't worry."

"Can I come with you?" Lacey asked.

"Sure, come on."

He opened the double doors, and the bright sun hit Lacey square in the eyes. Shifting her gaze, she breathed deep. "Dad, do you think Chief Bert knows? Does he know that maybe Beau and Will Boudreaux are related?"

"I don't know, but I'll alert him of the new information just the same. Are you coming?"

"No. You go on ahead. I'll sit in the Rose Garden for a minute."

"You sure?" Desmond asked.

"Yes."

"Okay. I won't be long. I'll join you in a few." Desmond squeezed Lacey's shoulders.

Thankful for Desmond, Lacey thought of him as another of God's blessings. He hadn't been her new father for long, but he had already slipped into the role as if he'd always meant to be there. Would Wade have that joy one day? Maybe not a new father, but a family where he could belong. She thought of Mr. Gardner.

"Oh, God. Please don't take him. Wade needs him."

Lacey walked towards the Rose Garden and pulled her phone from her pocket. She wanted to text Wade, but Desmond said to wait. He said to trust God. *Would God make all this right?* A shiver went up her spine, and as much as she hated the thoughts creeping in, she couldn't help but have a cold feeling overtake her heart. If Will Boudreaux was Wade's father, did Wade know it? Her young mind jumped from Wade, the man trying to be a responsible, decent human being, to Wade, the son of a murderer, a human trafficker, and possibly the one responsible for killing her father. *Could she ever forgive him if it were true?*

Lacey swallowed hard. She had nothing to forgive. Wade wasn't Will, and he wasn't Beau. He'd been trying to prove himself ever since they'd met. Lacey shook herself and sat on the stone bench, clasping her hands. She had to pray for Wade.

"Lacey?" Virginia called from the community hall doors. "Are you going to come help or what?"

"Be right there."

Lacey stood and turned. A flash caught her eye, and she saw a car turn into the parking lot. She didn't recognize the car and wondered why someone would drive to Bay Town Community Church during the week. An eerie feeling took over. She ran for the Community Hall and pulled the door shut behind her. With her back pressed against it, she breathed deep.

"What's wrong?" Melanie asked. Her hands shook as she gripped Lacey's shoulders.

"Why, you're as white as a ghost," Virginia sang. Her accent could be as soothing as Summer Gardner's southern lilt or as annoying as screeching nails on a chalkboard. The latter grated.

"Come on." Lacey pulled the women to the back of the room, but the doors swung open, and a significant male figure framed the doorway. The bright sun behind shadowed his face but blinded the women.

Lacey screamed, and mama bear Melanie reacted, waving her arms at the man.

"You go on. Get out of here," she yelled.

"What's the matter with you, girl?" The man let the door close behind him.

"Oh, my goodness. Big Joe." Melanie breathed out a sigh of relief. "You have no idea."

"Calm down. I do. Chief Bert asked me to come to check on you between my bus shifts. I hear we have another possible situation." He cleared his throat. "What I mean is, are you all right, ladies?"

"Whose car is that?" Lacey tried to calm her voice.

"That's my old clunker. The SUV broke down. Good thing I always kept ole' Betsey running. So, we's all good here?"

"We's good," Virginia said. "I have no idea why y'all are so jumpy. Would you like a brownie, Joe?"

"If Lacey made 'em." He took a big bite. "Mmm, mm. Don't tell Lyla, but Lacey, you make the best. Lyla's at home baking for the yard sale tomorrow too." He took another and raised it in salute. "Thanks, girls. You stay put here, okay?"

He pulled out his phone and tapped a number. As he left, Lacey heard him say, "Yup, Chief. They's all good. Snug as a bug in a rug."

She wished. Lacey followed Joe outside. She couldn't

breathe in the building, and as Joe pulled out of the parking lot, Lacey gasped. Wade's BMW sat parked at the far end of the lot, close to the Sanctuary. She squinted. No one sat inside the vehicle.

"Wade," she whispered and ran for his car.

She reached for the door.

"Well, hello, darling."

Lacey shivered at the voice behind her and spun around. He didn't look familiar in the oversized safari-type hat and large aviator sunglasses, but she knew. Wade's stepdad. He flashed a gun and signaled for her to be quiet. Hitting a key fob, he opened the front passenger door and shoved her in. He got in the driver's side, and drove away, keeping his gun pointed at Lacey.

"No need to buckle up, sweet girl. Now shove yourself down there so no one can see you."

Lacey ignored him and peered into the backseat. She gasped. Wade lay slumped on the back seat. Blood seeped from his forehead. She started to scramble over but felt the gun against her head.

"Down, now, I said."

Lacey lowered her shaking body, taking deep gulps of air. God had saved her before, and he could again. *Wouldn't He?*

"What did you do to him?" Lacey asked.

"Same as I'm gonna do to you."

Lacey crumpled on the passenger side floor. "You didn't kill him, did you? How could you?"

"I don't know. And I don't much care. My life is done now too. Because of that rotten kid, I lost my wife. Because of him, my parole's broke, and I ain't going back to jail."

"He gave you what you wanted. Why don't you just leave?"

"Shut up. Do you think it's all about the money? Don't you get it? I came to get revenge. My wife was the best thing that ever happened to me. Then that kid came along. My stupid brother pushed that kid on us, and my wife loved him too much."

Lacey tried to swallow. So, Will Boudreaux and Wade's father. One and the same.

Beau stared straight as he drove but kept his gun pointed at Lacey. "You know what? That kid back there, he loves you, and you mean an awful lot to him, just like my wife did to me." Beau laughed. "He wouldn't tell me where you was today, so I hit him. I walloped him good."

She gulped and held back tears. "Why blame Wade?" Her voice grew more assertive. "Your brother is to blame."

"I said, shut up. That's all done and over with. I ain't so dumb, you know. I knew the Chief was out looking for me. I saw his patrols around your houses and at the hospital. So I thought, where else could she be? Bingo. And here we are."

CHAPTER 24

For a crazy man, Beau drove with ease, but it frightened Lacey. He didn't seem to care about anyone, and the bizarre thing, he had a Christian radio station playing.

"Ohhh." A muffled moan came from the back seat.

Lacey popped up, and he pushed her down again. The car swerved, and her head slammed against the door handle. She ignored the sharp pain.

"Wade? Are you all right?"

"Stay down," Beau seethed. "I just as soon shoot you here. But if that kid is still alive, I want him to see me do it."

Lacey's eyes welled, but Beau wouldn't get the satisfaction of seeing tears fall. Fear and frustration held their place, but now hope. Wade, and sign of life in the backseat. She knew it.

Beau slowed and parked. An obscured view of a tall building rose through the back window. Hope flooded Lacey at the sight of Bay Town General. She glanced up at Beau. Clearly his plan would backfire. Even with his disguise, the surveillance cameras would pick him up. They'd find him for sure, and in Wade's BMW no less.

"Stay put, or I'll shoot him this time," said Beau.

He pushed himself out and yanked open the back door. He dragged Wade from the backseat. No sounds came from

Wade, but Beau slid him to the ground and shut the BMW's door. He turned to a beat-up vehicle in the next spot. Lacey's heart raced as Beau struggled to shove Wade into it. Soft footsteps approached.

"Stop right there. Put your hands up." Chief Bert stood by Lacey's side of the car.

She popped up but Beau pointed his gun at her. "I'll shoot her."

"Hold it, Beau. You got no place to hide. Give it up now. You haven't killed anyone. Let's keep it that way."

Beau laughed. "Not yet anyway. Throw down your gun and your car keys while you're at it."

"You don't want to do this. You got no way out."

"That's where you're wrong. I got two ways out." He threw a nod to Wade lying on the ground and directed the barrel of his gun inside the car at Lacey.

"Fine. I'm doing what you say. Just hold on there." Chief Bert edged away and did as Beau commanded. Lacey stared up at him, hope fading with every movement. Beau opened the car door, his gun still on Lacey.

Beau stepped back. "Girl, climb over here, real slow like, and get out."

Lacey peered through the window at Chief Bert, and everything in her pleaded, but Beau's growl swiveled her head.

"Girl, you best listen to—"

Wade sprung up and jumped across Beau's back, propelling him to the ground.

"Wade," Lacey screamed.

Chief Bert opened the passenger door and grabbed Lacey, pulling her out. Her knees scraped on the concrete, and she tried to stand, but Chief Bert pushed her down.

"What about Wade?"

She peeked up, trying to see, but a bullet whizzed by her head.

"Girl, get down." Chief Bert crouched, half-dragging her

behind the next car, and the next until they were several cars away.

She scrambled along with him, but her heart cried out for Wade.

Bert barked orders into the radio over his shoulder. They reached the hospital entrance, and he shoved Lacey in the double doors. His voice boomed across the lobby. "Lockdown. Nobody comes in or out."

He ordered instructions at the security guard. Lacey ran after the chief, but he warned her to stay put. With a last glance, he nodded assurance and ran out the door. The few people in the lobby whispered. Others ran to the window. Wide-eyed, they stared as police cars and SWAT team trucks pulled in.

"Everybody get away from the window and get down," shouted the security guard.

From across the parking lot, Lacey saw Desmond. Her eyes widened as she saw her mother running with him. She almost screamed as they were shoved to the ground. Lacey ran to the window and pounded. The security guard grabbed her and pulled her back.

Chief Bert turned and saw Lacey pointing. He instructed Desmond and Melanie's release and pointed to the hospital doors. The security guard manually unlocked them, and her mom and dad rushed in.

"Oh, Lacey. Are you all right?" Melanie sprinted toward her.

"No. He has Wade," Lacey screamed.

"Lacey? Look at me." Desmond took her shoulders. "Remember God never left us during our last trial. He won't now. He's always here."

Is he? But her dad had turned up dead. And everyone else made it out, everyone but him. And now, Wade. Just when he tried to make something of himself. Lacey closed her eyes.

God, reach his heart, please.

"Oh, for goodness sakes, you can't keep me in this gift shop. At least tell me what's going on out there."

All heads turned to the southern drawl.

Summer Gardner stood behind a sweet grey-haired volunteer who struggled to close the gift shop door. "Please, dear, wait."

Lacey connected eyes with Summer. *Does she know that Wade's in danger?* She rushed to the gift shop.

"Stop right there, miss," the security guard said. He stood in a wide-leg stance, his arms at a half-circle around his short but sturdy body. "Everybody's got to stay put. The hospital is on lockdown."

Desmond walked towards him.

The man eyed him with a sideways glance but kept his gaze on Summer and Lacey.

"You too, sir. Stop right there."

Desmond stopped, but Lacey called out. "He's Pastor Brooks. Can't he help?"

The man's eyes widened. His arms relaxed.

"You the pastor of Bay Town Community Church?" He snapped his fingers a few times. "Pastor Desmond, right?"

"Hey. Can we have some information here? I have to get back to work," yelled a young man wearing a knit beanie with ear pods stuck in his ears.

"Son, you best stay down. Look at that activity out there." The guard pointed to vehicles of SWAT and police. "I got no more information than you, so sit down." He turned back to Desmond. "My daughter and wife go to your church. They talk about you all the time."

Desmond extended his hand but pointed to Summer. "It's her nephew who's been abducted out there," he whispered. "I'm not sure she knows it."

The security guard's mouth gaped, and he waved at Summer. "Miss, come on out. Come join the pastor here."

Lacey led Summer to Melanie, and they found a quiet

corner in the lobby. Desmond thanked the security guard and followed. They took turns explaining the situation to Summer, each careful not to relay the horror of what happened, but Summer stared back wide eyed.

"Oh, dear God, no. Poor Wade. He's been such a big help. Why didn't I give him credit for the changes taking place?" Summer cried.

"We'll keep praying, and Chief Bert will find them. They can't have gotten far." Desmond patted Summer's hand.

Summer's light complexion paled even more, and Lacey noticed for the first time how little Summer and Wade resembled one another. Where her coloring glowed white as an Easter lily, Wade had a healthy, natural tan. Lacey shivered wondering if he resembled his father, Will Boudreaux. She couldn't remember him. She'd only seen him once a couple years back in that dark alley, with Virginia. Lacey shivered.

"And things were going so well." Summer opened her purse and took out an embroidered handkerchief, dabbing it to her eyes. "Granddaddy's awake."

Melanie squeezed Summer's hands. "Why, that's great news."

"Yes, it is, and he asked for Wade straight away." Summer's eyes watered more. "I came down here to get him. They've got an ambulance in the ER ready to take Grandaddy to New Orleans. There's a surgeon there that will insert a whole pile of stents in him."

"Wow. That fast?" Lacey stared back.

"Yes. Grandaddy isn't a candidate for open-heart surgery." She blinked back tears as her voice rose. "They were just going to let him die. But Wade..." Summer's voice hitched. "But Wade, he made a phone call. When he worked a medical banquet at one of Grandaddy's big hotels, he waited on a guest there, a young cardiologist. The best in New Orleans and Wade got his card."

Lacey's heart fluttered at the mention of his name. Wade must have had his great-grandfather on his mind all the time.

"Anyway, Wade called the cardiologist at some point during this whole ordeal. He connected Grandaddy's primary care doctor with the cardiologist, and they agreed that if he awoke and remained stable, they'd transport him to New Orleans and do the surgery there."

"Wait a minute," Melanie said. "I thought they couldn't operate?"

"He's not a candidate for open-heart surgery. But this is a coronary angioplasty. No one else around would do it at Grandaddy's age and condition." She sniffed. "Except for this doctor."

"God does work in mysterious ways," Desmond said. "And good for Wade." He nodded at Lacey.

"Yes, but the ambulance is ready now." Summer said. "And Grandaddy requested Wade to ride with him."

Lacey stared at Desmond. "Dad?"

He held out both hands. "Let's pray," he said as if reading her mind.

Listening to his intentional petitions, Lacey sighed. Silently, she expressed gratefulness once again for this man in her life, and wondered if Wade would ever have faith like this.

As he finished and they dropped hands, a few moments of silence permeated, and Summer asked, "But what now?"

"I'll talk to your grandfather, maybe you can ride with him to New Orleans in the ambulance instead of Wade. You stay here while I check and make sure the transport is still happening," Desmond said.

"Of course it is. This crazy man can't jeopardize everyone's lives." Summer stood.

Lacey's eyes riveted from her mom to her dad. *Didn't Summer understand?*

"I'm afraid there's more you need to know. Beau Bodine took Wade at gunpoint," Desmond said.

Summer dropped into her seat and cradled her face in her hands. Her sobs wrenched at Lacey's heart and shook her strength. "Dad, can't we do something more?" Lacey begged.

Desmond approached the security guard and had a short conversation before rejoining the group. "He's checking on everything. I'll go to the ER and see if the ambulance is there and what's happening. You ladies stay here in case the security guard makes an announcement."

"I'm coming with you," Lacey said, and she followed.

They stopped at the ER desk and were told that without police clearance, Mr. Gardner's transport couldn't leave, but she let them go back. Mr. Gardner lay on a gurney in the hallway with his eyes closed. Paramedics hovered over him, checking his oxygen and IV's. The police stood guard.

"Dad, he doesn't look so good."

"He's a whole lot better than previously," Desmond said.

Desmond walked toward Mr. Gardner, but the police stopped him, instructing him to step away. Mr. Gardner's eyes opened at the commotion.

"Hello, Pastor." Mr. Gardner's voice sounded surprisingly strong. "Let the man through, will you?"

The officers parted and let Lacey and Desmond approach. Mr. Gardner managed to smile and lifted his hand.

"Is this pretty young lady Lacey Thompson?"

Lacey's lips quivered. "Yes, sir."

"It's been a while since I last saw you, but my Wade has spoken mighty highly of you."

She turned for Desmond's support, but a police officer called him over. Left alone with Mr. Gardner who knew nothing of Wade's situation, Lacey cringed.

"Thank you, sir."

"I warned Wade to tread slowly with you. You're a mighty special lady to him, Miss Lacey. I suspect you may be the reason for the change in that boy. The good change."

Lacey's heart cracked. "Thank you, sir, but I think maybe you had more to do with it."

Mr. Gardner squeezed her hand. "Well, God used us both." He pulled her close with his weak grip.

Lacey bent her head easing her ear close to his lips.

"Still, I'm glad he has you," he said.

Has me? A doctor conversing with a policeman interrupted her thoughts. "This man's got to get in that ambulance. They're waiting for him in New Orleans."

The boxy red and white vehicle with the back doors wide open waited just outside the ER. Lacey walked over, where a uniformed paramedic stood. His eyes shifted to the forward of the vehicle, and he swallowed so hard his Adam's apple bobbed. Lacey peered in. The older model ambulance allowed for a clear view into the cab. She couldn't see the driver, but the paramedic in the passenger seat slumped over the armrest. He wore a hat, and something stirred inside her. She stepped forward, but a voice shouted from the driver's side.

"Let's get this show on the road," he said, and mumbled something Lacey couldn't hear.

The paramedic scooted to Mr. Gardner's gurney. "Listen, why don't we get him loaded, and when we get clearance, we can leave." The man's eyes shifted again, and he mopped his brow.

"Fine, but no one's going anywhere until we get that clearance," said a policeman.

Lacey stepped out of the way, joining Desmond. They pushed Mr. Gardner forward.

"Can one of you give me a hand?" asked the paramedic. He directed his words to the policeman.

"Hey, you up there, come here and help." A policeman pointed to the front of the vehicle.

The driver opened his door and walked to the back.

Everyone froze. He waved a gun. "Drop your weapons. All of you."

One officer hesitated, and Beau cocked his pistol. The policeman complied.

"On the ground, now," he barked.

Lacey dropped to the ground with the others, but Beau stepped next to her.

"Well, well, if it isn't Miz Lacey Thompson." Beau sneered.

He yanked her to standing, but Desmond rolled into his feet, knocking him off balance. Desmond rose to his knees, but Beau never let go of Lacey. Regaining his footing, he kicked hard at Desmond, knocking him back to the ground.

"You want to be the hero, huh? Well, this little lady's death will make you the idiot." Beau pointed the gun at Lacey's temple.

The slumped paramedic in the passenger seat turned. "Leave her alone."

Lacey's stomach lurched. That voice. Weak, but Wade's. She tried to yank free, but Beau clenched her arm.

"Wade?" Mr. Gardner tried to raise his head.

"Shut up." Beau turned to the paramedic. "Get the man in the ambulance, now."

"Listen sir, you don't want to do this." A policeman spoke with his hands in the air. "Let's talk this through."

"You're wrong. I so want to do this." He waved once more at the gurney. "Now, I said!"

The paramedic and a policeman wheeled and lifted Mr. Gardner into the ambulance and Beau motioned them to the ground.

Beau grinned at Lacey. "Miz Lacey, come take a ride with us. Now," he yelled while waving the gun at the policeman lying on the ground. "Call your chief and tell him Beau Bodine is leaving through the ER exit, and if anyone follows me, I'll shoot one of my passengers. I don't care which one. Do it now."

The police reached for the radio on his shoulder. "Chief Bert, Officer Lindsey in the ER here. Beau Bodine is in an ambulance with three hostages. He wants clearance to leave. He's got a gun and said he'll shoot."

Beau shoved Lacey into the back of the vehicle, and she stumbled forward hitting her head. She fell into a passenger seat.

"Lacey, are you all right?" Wade asked. "I'm so sorry," he said quietly.

She peered through the cab and stared at Wade. Seeing him stilled her anxious heart and replaced it with hope. At least they were together, and maybe God would get them all out of this safely. Wade pointed to his great-grandfather, and Lacey patted his arm and whispered in his ear. With his eyes closed, Mr. Gardner gave a thumbs up. Lacey buckled up, then wrapped her arms around herself, trying to control her shaking.

"You're clear," the officer said to Beau.

"Good. Shut the doors and join your buddies on the ground." Beau ran to the driver's seat.

CHAPTER 25

"Just let her go. Let them both go," Wade said.

"Yeah, fat chance." Beau laughed. "I couldn't ask for a better scenario."

"I can give you anything you want." His great-grandfather's voice echoed from the back.

"You can give me anything I want? Ain't that a hoot. That's if you live long enough, old man."

"What is it that you want?" asked his great-grandfather.

"I can't hear you," sang Beau. "But I'll take a guess. You're offering me something. Well, thank you for asking, sir, but all I want is your great-grandson and his girlfriend here dead. And you're just collateral damage."

Wade turned to look at Lacey, but his head pounded, and the effort made dots form before his eyes. Racking his brain to formulate a plan worsened the pain. He had to do something fast. While Beau drove, Wade had an advantage, but he had to be careful. One swerve could kill them all, and he knew Beau's crazy frame of mind wasn't above that right now. Wade closed his eyes and pleaded silently.

He turned and looked back at Lacey, giving her a reassuring nod. But when he strained to see his great-grandfather,

Mr. Gardner's eyes were closed, and his jaw clenched. His chest rose and fell slowly between breaths. Lacey squeezed his hand, and that gesture somehow brought comfort to Wade.

"Turn around," Beau said.

Wade faced forward and touched the brim of his baseball cap. He pulled, and removing it caused him to wince. He threw it down. The dried blood and matted hair stuck to his scalp. Pressure built from Beau's blow, and it squeezed his head like a vise. The blinding sun didn't help. He pushed up his sunglasses. Just the motion hurt, and Wade squinted while shading his eyes. Beau did the same, finding it difficult to see the road without sunglasses.

They'd been driving about twenty minutes, and having traveled the Chef Mentaur pass many times, Wade knew they were approaching the Pearl River, the border between Mississippi and Louisiana. He peered at the rearview side mirror. No one followed. The authorities had heeded Beau's demands not to be followed. Yet, Wade suspected that the Louisiana state police would blockade their end of the bridge.

"Let them go," Wade said.

"Like I said, fat chance, and like you got a say so. You're about to experience my pain. It's what I been feeling all these years." Beau's face hardened. The veins in his neck bulged. "You killed my wife, and I'm going to kill your girlfriend and your grandaddy there. And you're going to watch before I kill you." Beau sneered. "Unless you think you got some plan to kill me first."

"Not me. But maybe them." Wade pointed straight ahead.

Beau eased off the gas as he approached the Pearl River Bridge. Swirling red and white lights filtered through the sun's rays. A line of state police, troopers, and what looked like SWAT blocked the Louisiana border. Beau hit the brakes, and Wade's head hit the side window. Beau's frantic hands struggled to maneuver the vehicle as it slid sideways. His gun on the dashboard slid toward Wade.

He reached forward, but the van slid to a stop, and the seat belt locked. He jolted back. Unclicking the belt he lunged for the gun. A deafening rumble made him pause, and he recognized the thunderous slap of rotary blades snapping overhead. He reached again. Too late. Beau backhanded Wade and grabbed the gun.

"Step out with your hands up," a voice shouted from a loudspeaker overhead.

Beau waved his gun out the window, shaking it in defiance. The helicopter hovered a few moments, then veered off. Beau hit the steering wheel and peered out Wade's window. The entourage of various uniforms lined the bridge.

Beau shoved his shoulder against the door and grunted. He hit the window repeatedly, then stopped. He seemed to be staring at the river.

Wade followed his gaze and stared at the murky waters. It wasn't deep, but he knew alligators were abundant here as they were in all the river sources. He wouldn't put it past Beau to force them all in.

An ugly grin crossed Beau's lips. "Well, well, lookey there. Ain't that just perfect."

Wade struggled to focus but saw a flash of silver through the tall grasses along the bank. His eyes followed a stretch along the river, and he recognized an aluminum flat bottom boat abandoned on the shore. Old and rusted. Wade wondered if it even kept afloat. Beau wouldn't care. He'd pile them in and head downriver.

Closing his eyes, Wade held a palm against them and pressed hard. He knew Beau too well. They both knew the area. Along the river were abandoned shrimping boats. If that boat failed them, Beau would find another.

Wade breathed deep and opened his door.

"Stop." Beau swung around and pointed his gun.

Cautiously, Wade pushed open the door, but the effort

weakened him, and he clutched the handle. His body swerved with one foot out the door.

"Wade," Lacey called.

He ignored her and faced Beau. "All I have to do is run, and they'll shoot me, and you won't have the satisfaction of doing it yourself."

"I'll do it right now. Then I'll shoot her." He pointed his gun at Lacey.

Wade swallowed hard. Deja vu. Like reliving the moment when Beau had killed his own wife. He aimed for Wade but missed, and the knife sailed right past Wade, hitting the only other woman Wade had ever loved.

"Won't do you any good. I won't see it." Wade's voice grew strong, but inside he feared retching his guts out.

He gripped the door and placed his other foot on the pavement. The gravel beneath his shoes grated.

"I'll shoot her, I will," screamed Beau.

Wade turned his back. His teeth clattered, but he knew Beau couldn't hear or see. Summoning up every ounce of strength, he prayed for God's help. He straightened and called over his shoulder. "You're going to kill us all anyway. You said so. But you won't get the satisfaction of me seeing it."

As Wade took a step, he heard Beau scramble across to the passenger side. A voice blared over the loudspeaker. "Stop." It came from across the bridge. "Hands on your head. Slowly move to the ground."

Wade complied, hoping it would draw Beau out. He went down on one knee, but dizziness overtook him, and he wobbled, then fell to the ground. Lacey's scream filtered through the fog descending on his brain, and he heard clomping coming across the bridge. He tried to decipher all the noises. Whirring overhead. Footsteps crunching behind him.

"Throw down your weapons. Put your hands on your

head. Get on the ground." The voice from the loudspeaker overhead blared again.

"Shut up," Beau yelled.

A shadow blocked the sun, and Wade arched his neck sideways. Beau's silhouette straddled him. Wade turned his head and glimpsed a SWAT team exiting the bridge.

"I'll shoot him, now. Get back." Beau tugged at Wade. "Get up."

Wade struggled, but his body felt like jelly. *Get away, Lacey. Get away.* The only thought he had left as he strained to see the ambulance.

The back door of the emergency vehicle swung open, and Lacey jumped out and ran. He couldn't see her anymore, but a door slammed shut. The ambulance roared to life, speeding backward. Beau shot at it, but Wade rolled his body, entangling Beau's legs and knocking him to the ground. The gun dropped, and Wade's fingers scratched the ground for it. Then his shoulder seared with pain. A warm, thick liquid seeped from his body, and he reached for his shoulder. He stared at Beau gripping a knife stuck there. Beau yanked the knife, and Wade screamed as he saw the blade sailing through the air.

Beau picked up the gun. Wade rolled his head to the side and a momentary relief flooded him. *She got away.*

The gun cocked, but peace flooded Wade. *Thank you, Jesus.*

Bullets riddled the air, and before Wade opened his eyes, a heavy weight fell across his midsection. He grunted and glanced down. Beau's body. Voices shouted from all directions, and the deadweight smothered him. He couldn't breathe. Heavy footsteps approached, and someone pulled Beau off him. A uniformed officer applied pressure to Wade's shoulder while another took vitals.

Through narrowed eyes, he viewed uniformed men standing over him. Rifles pointed.

That deafening thunder overhead hurt his head, and the wind kicked up grit stinging his face. The helicopter drew closer. So close, the noise escalated the throbbing pain in his head. But above it, Wade heard a familiar voice.

"He's the good guy. Stand down," Chief Bert said.

Everything happened in rapid motion, and Wade couldn't move, but he heard running footsteps.

"Wade!" Lacey screamed.

"Let her through," Chief Bert ordered.

Her body dropped, covering his, but he couldn't see, couldn't hear, couldn't move.

"Wade? Open your eyes, please," Lacey whispered. Her face wet, and her hair matted, but she wouldn't leave his side. She gripped his hands, only letting go when nurses and doctors performed their duties.

"Miss, you'll have to step outside, please. Just for a moment."

Lacey hesitated but left the room and rushed into her mother's arms. Melanie and Desmond waited just outside the door and led her to the ICU waiting room. No one said anything for a while until she stopped gulping air.

"He'll make it, Lacey," Desmond said.

Staring at him, Lacey blinked and tried to smile.

"God's given that boy many chances. He won't waste it."

Lacey hoped her eyes expressed her thanks, but words wouldn't come. Couldn't come. Not yet. So she asked God to hear her prayers. She dropped her head into her hands. No tears, but silent mumbling, groaning erupted inside.

Desmond stood. "I'll go check on Wade. Mel, why don't you take Lacey home to wash up." Desmond grinned. "He'll want to see your pretty face when he wakes."

Melanie stood and gave him a playful hit on the arm. "Excuse me?" She cupped her daughter's chin. "She's beautiful." Swiveling Lacey's head, Melanie chuckled. "Well, I guess a little washing up would help."

Lacey grabbed her mom and reached for Desmond's hand. "Thanks, Mom. Thanks, Dad."

Desmond kissed the top of her head.

"But I'm staying. Pretty face or not, I want him to see me first." Lacey stood but dropped back down. Her eyes widened. "Mr. Gardner?"

"He'll be fine, Lacey. He's in New Orleans. He wasn't much worse for the wear. Thanks to your brave actions."

"Oh, let's not go there. Jumping in the driver's seat of that ambulance almost got her killed." Melanie gave a sideways glance.

"Kind of like her mother, eh? Good thing you guys have God on your side," Desmond said.

"But did Mr. Gardner have his surgery?"

"Yes. They took him straight to the hospital. Apparently, they stabilized him, and that cardiac surgeon that Wade contacted inserted eight stents. Can you believe it? No other doctor would touch that kind of procedure."

"What does that mean?" asked Lacey.

"It means no open-heart surgery. If it hadn't been for Wade and you, Mr. Gardner might not be alive now."

Lacey cleared her throat, and something that felt like assurance and joy floated in. *Wade's going to make it.* She smiled.

"Now, that's the pretty face I'm talking about," Desmond said. He pointed to the ICU double doors. "Why don't you go check on him?"

Lacey ran for the doors and stopped. She ran back to Desmond and hugged him again. "Hey, can you get me a burger?" she mumbled into his chest, then pulled away. "Maybe fries and a shake too?"

Melanie huffed. "Wow. I guess you're feeling better. You sure I can't bring a salad, maybe some fruit?"

Desmond waved Lacey off and pulled at Melanie. "A burger from Fat Boyz? You got it. Go on, Lacey. We'll be back later." He squeezed Melanie's shoulders.

Lacey watched as her parents walked away and her mother bickered about healthy choices. Lacey laughed, then took a deep breath. "Thank you, Lord," she said quietly.

CHAPTER 26

The amber sunset rippled across the sky helping to distract Lacey from the hospital setting. She turned from the window. Wade's white bandages contrasted with his tanned face and chest. They covered his head and most of his shoulder. His half-uncovered body rose and fell with the hum of the machines. Looming darkness tried to grip her mind, but she pitched it off. She had so many things to be thankful for. Glancing once more out the window, she admired the shades of red and purple overtaking the sky.

"Hey, you're a sorry mess for sad eyes."

"Wade." She flung her body across his.

"Ouch."

Lacey stood up straight. "I'm so sorry," she said, smoothing back her wild mane.

"I'm kidding. Sort of." He smiled, but his face grew stoic. "My great-grandfather?"

"He's doing great. That doctor you called did the job."

"Already?"

"Right away. You've been asleep for a day now. He's recovering with a bunch of stents. Whatever those are."

"That's good news."

One corner of Wade's lips lifted, and he winked.

Lacey melted and leaned her face close to his. She kissed his cheek, felt herself go warm, and pulled back.

"Well, that's a start." Wade grinned. "Seriously, you're the best medicine in the world."

Wade searched her eyes, then closed his.

Lacey waited, wondering what he was thinking. They hadn't had a normal conversation in forever. Her stomach knotted. *Had they ever?* Their relationship or friendship had been fast and furious. But she loved him. She knew it now. The thought of almost losing him without him knowing that made her gulp. She swallowed hard. "Wade."

"Lacey, I'm sorry. I'm so sorry I got you in this mess. You don't deserve to be mixed up with me."

Unsure, she leaned her face close to his and kissed him. As she pulled away his hand touched the back of her neck, drawing her close, kissing her back. Gently, deeply.

"Whoa. I guess you are feeling a lot better," said a cheery voice in the doorway.

Startled, Lacey pulled back. She covered her lips with the back of her hand and stepped away from Wade's bed. Heat flushed her face as she saw Jacquie from the Mockingbird.

"Jacquie? What are you doing here?"

"I told you, I have another job. I'm Meals on Wheels around here and I heard they admitted your friend." Jacquie winked. "I ain't supposed to bring him a meal yet, but how about you, Lacey? A sandwich? Some Jell-O or ice cream?"

"Mom's bringing me Fat Boyz," said Lacey.

"Well, call her and tell her to double that order." Jacquie laughed.

"Triple it," Wade added softly.

"We're praying for you, boy. I haven't heard all the details, but news is buzzing about that shoot-out and all. Uh huh. It seems like Bay Town stays clear of trouble being right here in the city, but we got our fair share of bad guys, don't we?" She shook her head. "But God's got his hands on little ole' Bay Town."

Wade nodded.

Jacquie grinned at the couple. "I'm so glad you're safe. Why, my little girl is going to need a graduation dress soon, and I'll need you to fix it." She smiled at Lacey.

"Yes, ma'am."

"And you." She pointed at Wade. "You keep this little girl out of danger, ya' hear?"

"Yes, ma'am," he said quietly.

Lacey's hand rested on the bedside, and she searched his eyes, but he looked away. Jacquie left and Wade said nothing.

"I'm not a kid," Lacey said, "And you didn't put me in danger."

"Yeah, right." Wade brushed his fingers through his hair but winced, stopping short of the bandages. "If we'd never met—"

"If, if, if. If God weren't in charge, I wouldn't have met you. Now are you going to argue with that?"

"You sound like your dad," Wade said, not smiling. "We're not good, Lacey. You're too innocent for this junk. My life."

As if a hand grabbed her throat, Lacey felt like she couldn't breathe. She wrinkled the white sheets between her fingers. "You listen to me, Wade Gardner—"

"It's Bodine," Wade's voice graveled, losing strength. "Bodine, Lacey. The same family that hurt you before. Your father's death rests in my father's hands. That's me. That's who I am."

"That's not true. Boudreaux. Will Boudreaux did that."

"He's Beau's brother. He's my father, Lacey. You have to know that."

She couldn't talk. No words would come. She stared at him, but his eyes were closed. Why did he remind her of those horrid days? Lacey's gut roiled. Nothing mattered except that

Wade made it out alive. Lacey gazed toward the window and searched the darkened skies.

"Go home, Lacey. I'm tired, and you should leave."

She stared at the night sky for a long time before glancing back at Wade, but she whipped her head back, as a flash caught her eye. A shooting star streaked by and faded. She reached to touch his cheek but drew her hand back. His words forced her to remember. He was right, but still, no one had died this time. No one but Beau Bodine.

"No, Wade. The Bodines, the Boudreauxs, they're all gone. God's given you a new life."

"Right. I know, I'm a Gardner." His eyes opened and he flashed a stern glare. "That doesn't change who I come from."

"You're right. It doesn't. But a new life in Christ does."

Wade stared back at her and held her gaze. She drew strength, knowing that if she left now, good would come of it. He needed to be alone. Alone with God.

"I'm going now." Lacey pressed her lips together. She wanted to press them against his once more but didn't. She stepped towards the door and wriggled her fingers goodbye, but he stared out the window.

"What in the world are you doing here?" Victoria stared wide-eyed at Lacey. "I didn't expect to see you for another week or so."

Lacey dropped her bags on the worktable and walked to the Nespresso. She grabbed a pod and popped it in the machine. Leaning against the counter, she crossed her arms but said nothing. Her lips formed a straight line.

Victoria joined her and wrapped an arm around her shoulders. "How's Wade?"

"He may be going home tomorrow. At least that's what Summer said."

"Are you two not talking?"

Silence. The machine beeped, and Lacey pulled her cup out. She sniffed the rich deep roast and sipped. Victoria waited.

"I am. He's not. I left him the day before yesterday. I thought he needed time to think." Lacey's eyes watered as she stared at the gown posters on the wall. She took another sip, then shrugged. "I think maybe I gave him too much time."

"Time is usually a good thing, Lacey. It gives God room to work."

"But what if Wade has turned his life over to God, and it doesn't include me?"

"I don't know, what if?" Victoria said quietly.

I'm not going there. Done with *what if-ing.* Done doubting God. With her heart breaking, she chose to trust God. Right here. Right now.

Lacey giggled, but a cry burst out. "Then it's good. Isn't it?" She hugged the woman not much older than her but a whole lot wiser.

Victoria stroked Lacey's hair. "You are one wise young woman."

"Me?"

"Yes, you. Lacey, you've got a strong foundation. Most young women or men don't know how to trust God like you."

"Trust? I've done nothing but doubt Him."

"No. I don't think so. But still, you've never given up on Him."

"He's never given up on me."

"And he'll not give up on Wade either. Time, Lacey."

The bell rang in the front of the shop, and the women broke their embrace, both ready to face the day. Lacey walked to the front and stopped short. Her mouth gaped.

A beautiful blonde with oversized sunglasses stood with her hand on the door. "Well, hello, young lady. I'm glad you're here. I was hoping you was working today."

"Reese?" Lacey gulped.

"I got something to say to you."

Victoria pointed to the back. "I have a call to make. Continue, ladies." She practically ran to the back of the shop.

"Yes, ma'am," Lacey said.

"Now, where do you live?"

"Excuse me?"

"How far from this here shop do you live?" Reese pointed outside.

"Less than five minutes. Back down Beach Road, across from the gulf."

"Oh, my. A beach front home?" Reese's eyes widened.

"Cottage. It's a small cottage. My mom got a great deal. Why?"

"Because I want you to take me there to see your mother's wedding dress."

Coughing and sputtering came from the back. "Sorry. Hot coffee," yelled Victoria. She peeked through the doorway. "Go on, Lacey. I've got things covered here."

Speechless, Lacey grabbed her purse and led the way.

Reese sat in the passenger seat of Lacey's car and chattered about nothing. She commented on the beauty of the gulf and how much she missed the south. Lacey soon parked in her carport and lamented that her mother wasn't home to witness whatever might happen in this moment.

They entered through the carport entrance into the kitchen. Lacey winced, wishing she'd brought Reese through the front door. The kitchen's sweet interior had a welcoming vibe, but her mom's living room looked like a Southern Living Magazine cover.

"Can I get you some sweet tea?"

Lacey hoped for a freshly made pitcher. Her mother always had some handy. She opened the fridge and her shoulders slumped. A single store-bought bottle rested on a semi-empty shelf.

Reese turned toward the kitchen table. Tossing her hat and sunglasses, she pulled out a chair. "I'd love a glass, thank you." She sat.

Lacey hid the bottle in front of her and reached for a tall plastic cup but then reached higher, grabbing an etched, stemmed glass instead. She poured the tea and placed it in front of Reese.

"Mmm, mmm. Nothing like homemade sweet tea."

She would say that. "Sorry, but it's not." Lacey hunched.

Reese laughed. "Well, it's good."

Lacey's cell beeped, and she pulled it from her pocket. A text message notification glared back at her.

"So, about that dress?" Reese wriggled her fingers. "Go on now. Show it to me, girl."

Lacey laid down the phone. She didn't much care about the dress right now. She just wanted to talk to Wade and hoped the message came from him.

Retrieving her mom's dress, Lacey returned to the kitchen. She held it up and peeked around.

Reese shot to standing and gasped. "Oh, my goodness. That is the most gorgeous thing I have ever seen in my life."

The southern exaggeration raised doubts in Lacey.

Fingering the bodice, then the neckline, Reese touched every inch of the garment. "I can't believe this. You made this?"

"Well, I designed it. Victoria, my boss, sewed it."

"Yes. I know who she is. I thought about commissioning her. She does beautiful work. But this." Reese shot a sideways glance at the wedding gown. She let go of the dress and stepped back. "I owe you a huge apology, and Madam DeFleur should be flogged. Or defrocked at least." Reese giggled but cleared her throat. "We'll take care of that soon enough."

"Oh no. I'm done with her. It's okay."

"It certainly is not. And from what my sources have uncovered, you are not her first victim. No worries, my dear. I'll take care of it."

"What?"

"Don't you worry your pretty little head. I need you to save all that creativity for my Oscar dress."

Lacey's knees buckled, and the hanger fell from her hands. The wedding dress crumpled on the floor, and Reese scooped it up. She rehung the dress and handed it back to Lacey.

"Excuse me? What did you say?" Lacey's eyes went round as saucers.

Reese took the hanger from Lacey and hooked it on the top of the door jamb. She grabbed Lacey's hand and pulled her to the kitchen table. White peonies tinged with a champagne hue sat in a square glass vase in the center. They were the same color as her mom's dress.

Reese cleared her throat and squeezed Lacey's hand. "Seriously, I am so sorry that I doubted your honesty."

Lacey wanted to chuckle. *This can't be happening.*

"And I am officially asking you if you would design my dress for the Academy Awards next year. It's only eight months away." Reese eyed the wedding dress once more, and her eyes widened. "I know you can do it. I'll fly out here to collaborate with you, but I'm sure we can handle much over email and text."

Reese rambled on and on, and Lacey knew she should be taking notes, but she couldn't concentrate. Just too good to be true. Now, she couldn't attend design school even if she were enrolled. At least for the next eight months. This design for Reese would take every ounce of her time and creativity.

"I do not doubt that what you design will be perfect." Reese waved her hands in the air. "No doubt."

CHAPTER 27

Wade stood, pushing away from the wheelchair. He thanked the nurse, glad to leave Bay Town General. He pocketed his phone as he slipped into the passenger seat of Summer's sporty car. Summer opened her purse and tipped the valet.

"Wow! Thank you, ma'am."

Generosity. The Gardner way. Wade checked his phone again. Lacey hadn't answered his text. He laid the phone on his leg and pulled the loose baseball cap down low over his brow. The bright sun wreaked havoc with his head.

"Wade, you sure we shouldn't just go to the gulf house? No need to go to New Orleans today. Grandaddy will understand."

"No, I need to see him."

She dropped her hand over his. "He's so proud of you, Wade. We all are."

What was there to be proud of? He put everyone's life in danger, and the sooner he left the better off everyone would be. He just needed to see his great-grandfather first.

The engine roared, and Summer pulled out. She hummed sweetly to the tunes emitting from the radio. She seemed to be respecting his space, and he appreciated her silence, until she mentioned Lacey.

"Have you spoken with Lacey?"

His fisted hand pushed into his chin, as he rested his elbow on the armrest. He stared out the window.

"Oh, honey. That girl's been waiting."

"Uh huh."

"For you, Wade. Lacey has been waiting for you," Summer pleaded. "You really should call her. Everything is good now, don't you see it?"

The car seemed to slow as Summer left Bay Town and approached the main highway to New Orleans.

"You sure you don't want to see her? I can still turn around."

"I need to see Great-grandfather."

He did, and he needed to do that first. But if he were a different man, he'd rush to Lacey's side. He stared across the gulf. The water seemed to jump and sparkle, much like her. If only his life had been different. He had a journey to take, and it wasn't with Lacey. She needed to forget him. He wasn't her type. Never was. Closing his eyes, the pain behind them heightened, but gratefulness eased a part of him. Aunt Summer had stopped pestering him about the girl he loved.

Wade looked over at his aunt. Her perfectly straight blonde hair hung over her shoulders, and her pale pink lips drew a taut line. Sorrow took another part of his heart. Sorry for the pain he'd caused the family. All of them. Even beautiful Aunt Summer sported light lines on her forehead above her furrowed brow. He wished that he could say something to change that expression. She'd done so much for him. Her kindness reigned even when she wasn't sure she should extend it. He'd made a mess of everything.

Wade turned his gaze from Summer and stared at the road ahead, dreading when it cut inland. They'd be coming to the Mississippi-Louisiana line again soon. The Pearl River.

He clenched his jaw, wishing they'd taken a different road. Although longer, the highway avoided the unpredictable beachgoer traffic on the coastal route. Still, it may have been a better choice. Seeing the rising struts of the rusted bridge reminded him that this spot could have been the demise of Lacey and his great-grandfather. Wade shook his head. No one else he loved would suffer or die because of him. He'd make sure of it.

The bridge loomed, and his eyes wanted to close, but he forced himself to stare. The grassy bank, the murky green water below. His heart quickened. The forceful pounding of his chest caused him to clutch his shirt. He stared at Summer, wondering if she heard it.

She attempted a smile that may have expressed that she understood. Her body jerked as she stomped on the accelerator. Usually a slow, cautious driver, Summer gripped the wheel and sped across the bridge, not giving Wade a chance to think, to recall details of a week before.

The thumping tires pounded across the wooden and metal structure. The sport vehicle launched at the end of the bridge. Wade grabbed the overhead door handrail, and the car landed with a thud, bouncing much like a car with hydraulics.

"Whoo-wee," Summer yelled.

The slam of the vehicle on the pavement and her scream jolted his system, and instead of giving into the panic attack, he shook his head at Summer's laughter. "You're crazy."

"How's that for some excitement," she said.

Wade chuckled. "Like I need that." He glanced over his shoulder, back to the bridge. *And here of all places.* The light moment faded.

Summer grabbed his hand. "Wade, give us all a chance, okay? Don't make any decisions. We're your people." She gazed too long.

"Hey." Wade pointed as she veered to the right, approaching the shoulder of the road.

Summer swerved back and slowed the car to the speed limit. "And you know Grandfather would love to have a great granddaughter-in-law like Lacey."

Wade rolled his eyes. "Come on. I'm not even going there." Wade's darkness returned.

"Well, you should. I'm just saying. You two make a cute couple."

He took a deep breath. Would she still think that if Great-grandfather had died? If Lacey had died? But his stepmom was dead, and Lacey's dad too. Wade rubbed his temple.

When they arrived at the hospital in New Orleans, Summer pulled to the front entrance. "Why don't you go on in? I'll take care of the valet."

"Sure," Wade said.

Summer put the car in park and stepped out. Wade did the same. He removed the baseball cap but blinked. The massive overhead shade blocked the glaring sunlight, but still he kept on his sunglasses. He chuckled at the two young valets. Both running towards Summer.

Her southern charm exuded, and they stumbled all over her. One handed her a ticket. The other took the keys. He jumped in, roared the engine, and the tires spun before he peeled out. Just as quickly, he slowed. He popped his head out the window.

"Sorry, about that, Miss."

"Miss? Not ma'am? Well, I'll take that anytime, sugar." She waved as she called back.

"Flirting with the younger ones, huh?" Wade teased.

"Why, nephew, I do not flirt. It's just southern courtesy. I can't help it."

"Right," Wade said, offering his arm.

"And you have become quite the southern gentleman yourself."

Summer and Wade waltzed into the beautiful lobby of the New Orleans hospital. It bustled with people coming and going, but many stopped, and heads turned. They were a stunning sight. Summer in all her svelte beauty, tall, thin, and statuesque. Wade athletically handsome. The sunglasses hid his bruises well. They gave the appearance of a celebrity couple, approaching the red carpet. Lush palm trees, designer overstuffed club chairs, and couches scattered around the lobby. Reginald Gardner's generous philanthropy showed everywhere. Even fresh flowers adorned every coffee and end table.

Wade pulled at his collar and glanced back at the entrance. A bellman stood in uniform. Wade walked to the receptionist's desk. Everything was so different from the Bay Town Hospital, or any other he'd been in. His jaw tensed. *I definitely don't belong here. Not in the Gardner world or Lacey's world.*

Summer pulled him back and stopped. With her hand clutching the inside of his elbow, she turned and gazed at him. "Wade, you belong with us, you know? You've lived this life for a while now. And we're all so proud of you." Summer waved a hand to the outside. "All that happened back there, it's over. Please don't disappoint Grandaddy. He has great plans for you."

Wade nodded. But his heart wasn't matching the affirmation.

～

After they'd checked in and rode the elevator, the doors opened, and Summer led Wade to Mr. Gardner's private suite. Great-grandfather sat up holding a newspaper in one hand and a fork in the other. His hair combed, good color on his face, and a meal tray in front of him. He lowered the fork and pushed the tray aside.

Wade finger combed his wild crop of hair and stepped forward. He extended his hand. "Good afternoon, sir. You're looking well."

His great-grandfather's firm grip shook Wade's hand. "Perhaps better than you, son."

Wade chuckled, but his smile disappeared, and he cleared his throat. "I'm sorry, sir."

"Sorry? Son, you saved my life. Why, you're a hero as far as I'm concerned."

Summer raised an arm and waved it high in the air. "I second that."

"No, I'm not."

"I can't imagine what you're feeling, but don't doubt yourself, son. And don't doubt God. We got through it, didn't we? And you had nothing to do with the cause. We live in an evil world, and the older I get, the more I'm looking forward to the one we were meant for."

Wade's head began to pound again. He pinched the bridge of his nose. *Maybe the world you were meant for.*

"Whatever you're thinking, stop. You're a bright young man. And you can add courage to that as well. You had to make some snap decisions, and you made good ones from what I gather. You're exactly the kind of man—"

"Sir, I'm leaving. I can't stay. I have about half the money I owe you for the semester. I'll work to get the rest."

"You don't owe me. Your debt has been paid."

Wade frowned. "No it hasn't. We had a deal."

"I'm the one who made the deal, and I can change it. You owe me nothing. And if you're serious about leaving, you'll need the cash."

Summer drew in a breath and opened her mouth to speak, but Mr. Gardner peered a warning back at her over his glasses. She stepped aside and Wade nodded, thankful for the space.

"I can't let you do that, sir. You've done so much for me already. I'll leave the money—"

Great-grandfather raised a hand, and the steely gaze that accompanied said it all. *It's finished.*

"Thank you, sir. But I still need to leave. I need to figure things out," he said.

"I understand. But believe me, this is where you belong. I think if you'd start listening to all of us, you might hear what God's trying to tell you instead of heeding those voices that are telling you to leave."

Wade started to speak, but Mr. Gardner raised a hand.

"Let me finish. A young man has got to do what he's got to do. And I admire you for that. Maybe you think you're still the boy we found on the streets. In some ways you are because there were a lot of good traits in that boy. But you've grown in so many ways. Now, go grow in God and we'll wait for you."

Wait for me? For what? He didn't plan on returning. He stared at his great-grandfather, and breathed deep, but no words would come.

"Here's my last words, for now. Finish school, take the job I'll have waiting for you." Mr. Gardner winked at Summer and glanced back at Wade. "And go ask that little gal to be your wife."

Summer squealed. "Why, Grandaddy."

"I may be old, but I know true love when I see it." His eyes glistened. "Why, I married your great-grandmother when she was just nineteen, God rest her soul. You're both young, but if it's real, and it's from God, why not?"

Wade wanted to laugh, but everything hurt too much. And it wasn't just his wounds. No matter how much they encouraged him, or how much they'd embraced him, he couldn't shake the fact that Bodine blood flowed through his veins. He shook his head. He didn't know who he was, but he feared the ugly genes would hinder any permanent change.

"Thank you, sir," Wade managed.

"Thank *you*, son. Do what you need to do but come back. We are your family. Always have been."

CHAPTER 28

When Summer and Wade left Mr. Gardner's room, they rode the elevator down without a word. He donned his baseball cap and sunglasses and offered a hand for Summer to exit the automatic doors first.

Once outside, before she could hand her claim ticket to the young valet, he started running.

"I got it, ma'am," he said as he ran for her sports car. She chuckled and turned to Wade. "Now, how can you possibly want to give up this life?"

Wade stared at the parking lot. He didn't want to, but he had to. He kissed Summer's cheek. "This is where I make my exit."

"What? No. I'll take you back to Bay Town."

"Summer, your home is here. I'll get a ride to Bay Town, and I'll pick up my things at the house."

"You certainly will not."

The valet brought her car around, and hopped out, jingling the keys. Wade placed a hand on her back, nudging her forward.

She lowered her sunglasses and stared at Wade. "Now, nephew. You're acting so rash. Let me take you home and we'll talk."

"Nope. I have to take care of some things, so I'll be around for a day or so. I promise I'll come say goodbye."

Wade walked her to her car, and she allowed him to help her into the driver's seat. He closed the door under her protests and stepped back. She stared back, wiping a tear before pulling out.

"Man, are you crazy?" The valet huffed. "She's a keeper, she is."

Wade chuckled but raised a quick palm to his forehead. As good as it felt to laugh, it hurt. "Yes, she is." *But she's not mine*, he thought, and Lacey popped into his head. *And neither is she.*

Grateful that he didn't have to drive, he enjoyed the hired ride back to Bay Town. A luxury he wouldn't be experiencing after today. His new life. He stared at the driver and struck up a conversation about the job and the income, thinking he might be pursuing it in the future.

"Yeah, it's not bad. I started doing it part-time, but then I lost my other job. It pays the bills, but my wife does it too. The key is to have a clean and comfy car, and then it's all about the tips."

Clean and comfy car? Well, that put that job out of reach. But the thought made him think of the money, the thousands of dollars he'd given Beau. Was it recovered? He added it to the mental list of things to check before leaving Bay Town. The money left in his savings wouldn't go far.

An hour later, the driver pulled in front of the Gardner gulf mansion. He grinned back at Wade.

"Nice." The driver whistled. "Give me a call anytime." And he waved as he drove off.

Wade stared across the street. The sun bounced off the water and he shaded his eyes. Something caught his attention and he peered. Lacey. Out on a run. Everything in him told him to hide inside, but now or never, he had to face her. She hadn't returned his text from earlier that morning. Maybe she'd given up on him. A good thing. It would make his exit easier. He watched as she approached. It would make his goodbye hurt less. Her wild ponytail swished, and she waved as she slowed. *Maybe not.* He waited for her on the sidewalk.

Stopping in front of him, she gushed. "Wade, I am so sorry, I got your text while I was in a meeting, then my phone died. It's been such a crazy day. You'll never guess who showed up at the shop." Lacey paused. She reached forward and touched his bandages. "Oh, I'm so sorry. Did you just come home? I thought you'd been out of the hospital and didn't want to talk yet." She grabbed his hand and pulled. "Come on, let's sit on your porch. I bet that sun is wreaking havoc on your head. Don't I know. My mom gets migraines. And I had that head injury when—"

"Lacey, stop." Wade let go of her hand. "We do need to talk."

"Of course."

Her sweet voice messed with his head, but he had to tell her. "I'm leaving Bay Town."

Lacey frowned. "You mean back to New Orleans? You can't. We have a big party planned for you. You're a hero. It's kind of what the community does. Celebrations are huge here."

"Celebrate what? I almost got you killed, and my great-grandfather too."

She frowned. The gold flecks in her jewel-green eyes shined. He stared back wanting to capture every feature.

"You're crazy," Lacey said. "You saved all of us. You had nothing to do with what Beau Bodine did. Just like you had nothing to do with your…" Lacey paused and glanced down.

"With my dad, right? With that Will Boudreaux who killed your father."

"They never proved that."

"He's my dad, and I'm his son."

Lacey stomped her feet, like a spoiled teenager. Wade breathed deep. She was a teenager. Nineteen. Too young to live what she'd lived through and all because of the Bodines.

"Wade Gardner, you are not them. Just like I wasn't my father. Sometimes things just happen." Moisture glistened in her eyes, and she took his hand. "Please, Wade. Let's give us a chance?"

Wade let her rub her thumb across the back of his hand, and he stared at the motion. It felt so good. So right.

"Wade?" She stepped closer. "You know, we've never even been on a real date." She sang the last sentence just like Summer when she cooed a request.

He laughed. "You sound like my aunt."

"Well, she's the first southern lady I ever met, so she's rubbed off on me. But seriously, Wade. Please." A tear fell, then more.

He ran a hand through his hair. His heart melted like ice cream on a cone, but it also ripped like the paper surrounding it.

"I can't, Lacey," he whispered. "I have to go, and I'm leaving before the weekend."

"The weekend?" Her body stiffened. "Fine. Just think of yourself. That's what you used to be good at." She started to run, but turned, running backward. She called back, "By the way, how'd that work out for you?"

Her arms pummeled up and down, and he thought he could feel the ground shake from her pounding steps. He huffed loudly, removed his cap, and threw it down. Before walking to the house, he kicked the hat.

"Need some help?" A voice screeched over a loudspeaker.

A Bay Town squad car idled along the curb. Wade peeked in.

"Oh, hey." He couldn't remember the name, but they'd

met at the Waveland ice cream place where he and Lacey went for their second date. Sort of.

"Hi." The officer pointed to himself. "Rodney Blaine. We met at the Foster Freeze in Waveland. Is that Lacey running?" He pointed.

"Yeah, and right. I remember you."

The officer looked down the street as Lacey disappeared. "You guys have a fight or something?" He raised his hands, "None of my business, but I know women. Me and Virginia can get into it sometimes, and I don't know how we even get there. It'll blow over."

"Oh, well, we're not together or anything."

"Are you kidding me? After what y'all been through? That's one of the things that brought me and Virginia together. But that's another story. Listen, thanks for saving Lacey and Mr. Gardner. You were pretty incredible."

Wade didn't remember this guy barely speaking two words at the Foster Freeze. No matter, he didn't want to continue this conversation.

"I sure hope that's the last of the excitement here in Bay Town. At least from the Boudreaux clan." Officer Blaine's jaw dropped. "Oh man, sorry. I shouldn't have said that. I just re-read the whole report on the incident."

"No worries." *That's why I'm leaving town.* "It's the last, I promise."

Blaine shrugged. "Listen, I don't know if you remember my wife, Virginia?"

Wade grinned. How could he not? Although he only had eyes for Lacey, Virginia's stunning appearance made her hard to forget. That night in Waveland, he recalled wondering how she'd wound up with Rodney Blaine. A good man, but not a heartthrob and guys like him usually didn't get those kind of girls. He winced at the ill thought.

"Anyway, she wanted me to invite you for dinner," Rodney said.

The officer's voice sounded foggy in Wade's brain. "What? What did you say?"

"Will you come to dinner at our house? My shifts are a little weird these days, but I'm off this weekend. How about Saturday evening?"

"Why?" Wade blurted.

"Why? Well, my wife, she has her reasons." A squawking came from the radio inside the squad car. "I have to go, but how about you join us at six o'clock." He started the engine.

"I'm leaving town."

"What? You can't." Officer Blaine paused. "Listen, just come to dinner before you go, please? Virginia will be awfully disappointed if you don't. I think it will be worth your while."

Wade frowned, wondering what he meant. "Okay, sure. I don't know where you live."

"The apartment above Second Chance, the thrift store." He drove away.

Wade stared at the official blue car. It headed toward Pier One. He picked up his hat and placed it carefully on his head. He stared at the big mansion. A shower seemed to be calling his name. A long hot shower.

Lacey's chest hurt, and she doubled over. She gripped her knees, gasping.

"Why're you running so hard?" a giggly sweet voice called out.

Turning her head sideways, Lacey saw a head of platinum curls gracing that sweetheart face. Bright red lips grinned back.

"Oh, Virginia. What are you doing down here?" Lacey grabbed a cone and filled it with water from Bubba's cooler.

"I'm just waiting for Rodney. We're having dinner here tonight. Hey, can you come for dinner this weekend? You and

Wade?" Virginia's eyes widened. "Wow. Amazing. He's a hero, you know? Kind of like your old dad and well, your new dad, Pastor Desmond." Virginia giggled. "Anyway. I'm making a nice pot roast. Rodney just loves a good hunk of tender meat. But I'll make us a good salad too. Do you like Feta and those little tomatoes?"

"Virginia, Wade and I aren't together."

"What are you talking about? Of course, you are. After what you been through. Why Rodney and I were just talking about it."

"No, we're not. He's leaving town."

Virginia waved a hand through the air. "Oh, he is not. We have that party at Bay Town Community planned for him."

No use explaining. Virginia often had a one-track mind.

"Anyway, I want you and him to come to dinner Saturday night. That's just a few days away."

A few days and Wade would be gone. He wouldn't be at the dinner. Lacey didn't feel like arguing. "Sure. What can I bring?"

Virginia clapped her hands together and squealed. "Dessert, of course. You're famous for your brownies."

"Thanks. What time?"

"Six o'clock."

"Okay, see you there."

Lacey hugged Virginia and returned to her run. The sun fell into the horizon, and she headed home, hoping Wade would fall away too. For good. Running faster and faster, Lacey's tears broke like a dam, flooding her face. The wind couldn't dry them fast enough.

CHAPTER 29

L acey ripped off her covers and rolled off her mattress. Trudging to her closet, she stood in front of it and stared. She didn't feel like getting dressed. She didn't feel like facing the day because it would be devoid of Wade.

"Coffee's ready," her mom called from the kitchen.

Like she couldn't smell the rich deep aroma, but it did nothing for her. She wanted coffee all right, but she wanted it at the Mockingbird with Wade. His smile rose in front of her while she reminisced how he'd sipped the hot cup and sputtered.

Lacey pulled a chunk of hair over her shoulder and twisted. Staring at it, she thought how much the color and thickness were like Wade's and her father's. Many things about him reminded her of Chris. Probably why she liked him so much.

No. She loved him. First love. Didn't everyone say it was the best but hurt the most? They were right. She looked at her closet, stuffed with dresses, tops, and folded jeans. Grabbing a pair of jeans, she slipped them on and reached for a cropped, white, oversized sweater but threw it back. It landed on the floor, and she kicked it.

Her door opened.

"Honey, I've got to get going."

Lacey grabbed another top, covering herself. "Mom! Ever hear of knocking?" Her annoyed voice grated inside. She really didn't care if her mom knocked or not.

"I'm so sorry." Melanie closed the door. "Honey, how about we meet for lunch? You know we never celebrated the Reese thing."

At least there's one thing worth celebrating. The thought didn't ease her cracking heart. "Sure, Mom. I'll walk down and get you at noon."

"I love you, Lacey. I'm praying for you, sweetie." Melanie blew a kiss and closed the door. But a knock followed.

"Come in, Mom. I didn't mean it. You don't have to knock."

Melanie stepped in and cleared her throat. "Listen, sweetie. I know you're having a rough time about Wade."

Lacey bit her lip, but it didn't stop the flood of tears.

Melanie pulled Lacey to the mattress and sat. "I know, sweetie. I know it hurts. I'm so sorry," Melanie said, wrapping her arms around Lacey's shoulders.

Melting into her mother's arms, Lacey went limp. Hurt? That was an understatement. She could feel her heart breaking through the gut-wrenching pain. They sat in silence, until all the crying plugged up Lacey's nose and she couldn't breathe. She grabbed her sheet, wiping her face, and pulled back to face her mom. She knew exactly what Lacey was feeling. Her mom had experienced the pain with Lacey's dad. And at the same age too. Too young and too soon, mom always said, and she had so much life ahead of her.

"How did you go on? Without Chris?"

Melanie swiped her face with the back of her hand and tugged the sheet away from Lacey. They laughed. "I had you." Melanie kissed the tip of Lacey's nose and sputtered. "Oh, yuk." She swiped Lacey's face. "And I had my mom and dad.

Their faith carried me until I embraced God on my own. Prayers of the righteous ones availeth much."

"English, Mom. Not King James."

Her mom chuckled, but a faraway gaze came into her eyes. "And then my sister. Did you know Aunt Charlene came for your birth? The only person with me until mom and dad showed up."

"Aunt Charlene? I'm surprised she didn't tear into Chris."

"Your father, Lacey. Enough of the Chris."

"Well, it does help to differentiate between him and Desmond." Lacey raised a brow. "And yes, I heard that from Aunt Charlene a million times. Like I owe her or something."

"I depended on my folks a lot. And now it's your turn. We'll get through this, Lacey."

"But Wade doesn't think he has anybody."

"Pray for him. It's a struggle he'll have to work through."

"Wow, coming from you, that's harsh."

"Surrender. You know what I mean." Melanie stood. "I have to get to work, and so do you."

Wade stepped out of his car and closed the door. The sun warmed his face, and the gentle breeze soothed. Faces smiled, and he felt sick. Life just wasn't that good. He walked into the police station.

Chief Bert sat behind his desk. "Wade. Glad you're here. I'd like to close this case as best I can."

"Me too, but it's only been a week."

"Two weeks, but it's pretty much cut and dried now. With Beau Bodine dead, there isn't much to tie up. He had some belongings on him that we've determined should go to you."

Wade shook his head. "I don't want anything of his."

"All right. I understand. But you might want this." Chief Bert handed over a thick manilla envelope. "Go on, open it."

He unfastened the brad, and peered in. His eyes widened, and a grin spread across his entire face. "I was hoping this might turn up."

"Count it, son."

Wade took out a mass of bills. Hundred-dollar bills. After a few minutes, he quit counting. "How much is it?"

"Five thousand dollars. About a thousand short of what you gave him, right? Seems the guy knew how to spend a lot of money in a short amount of time." Chief Bert whistled.

Stuffing the envelope full, Wade slapped the bulging wad against his hand. "Thank you, sir."

"So, how's Mr. Gardner?"

"Very well. They put in a pile of stents, and he'll be back on his feet in no time."

"That's crazy, man."

"Yes, he had a doctor on the cutting edge. He did what no one else would try."

"Someone told me you deserve credit for that."

Standing, Wade pointed to the door. "Well, I better go."

"What now? If you don't mind me asking."

Wade pressed his lips tightly. The envelope crinkled as his hands twisted. "I'm not sure."

"I got ya'. But a little advice? Don't leave Bay Town. It's a good place to be, and you're a good fit."

"Yeah, right," Wade whispered. "Thanks, but I need to figure some things out."

Chief Bert removed his hat and scratched his head. "What about Lacey?"

Wade moved toward the door, hand on the knob. "She's better off without me. Thanks for everything."

Before the chief's rebuttal, Wade stepped outside, taking long strides to his car. He sat for a few minutes with his hands gripping the wheel. With his window down, he rested his arm on the door.

Just a few weeks ago no one wanted him anywhere near

Lacey, and now they were pushing them together. How trusting could people be? Bad blood. Blood. He touched his head where stitches laced his healing wound. He could have died. The migraines still plagued him. But taking a hit for Lacey? He'd do it again.

Death had been close. Wade thought of his mothers. Both dead, but both of them spoke of Jesus dying for him, and maybe he finally understood it. Maybe he could even accept it. He'd start a new life that was clean. Try and live a good life, not tainted by spoiling others. But not here around people he cared about. Lacey and Great-grandfather. He shivered thinking again of how close they all came to dying.

"Hey, Wade." Tina walked up loaded with shopping bags. "What'cha doing?" she sang.

He couldn't help but smile. Her long gold fingernails dazzled, matching her high heeled sandals. She pulled at her tightly wound curls.

"Hey, Miss Tina. Doing a little shopping?"

She giggled. "Oh, just a little. I drive Rudy crazy when he watches baseball on TV. So he told me to go window shop."

Wade laughed. "Anything left in the windows?"

"Not much." Tina turned and looked down the street. "Have you seen Lacey? I stopped by Victoria's shop, but I didn't see her there. I found the cutest bracelets for her."

He sucked in a breath. He'd never bought Lacey a thing. And now he'd never have the chance. He stared down the sidewalk, and his eyes widened. Lacey stepped out of a shop a block away. He turned the key and started the engine.

"There she is." He pointed. "But I have to run. Bye, Miss Tina."

Backing out, Wade left Tina glancing back and forth between him and Lacey. He hoped Lacey hadn't seen him. No matter, Tina would say something. He'd said his goodbyes, and no one could change his mind.

The rest of the week, Wade took care of business. He

resigned from the catering company at the hotel in New Orleans, though they begged him to stay. He stopped by to thank the surgeon who helped his great-grandfather, and he got rid of most of his belongings from the gulf house, giving them to the staff. He emptied his bank account, and coupled with the retrieved money from Beau, he bought a used car. After driving the Tesla and BMW, he cringed climbing into the small compact. He parked Great-grandfather's vehicle in one of the garages and left the keys with the house staff in Bay Town.

As he drove the car off the lot, he settled into the seat, trying to get comfortable. He drove around the city, avoiding Main Street, and steered the vehicle to Waveland. Stopping at the Foster Freeze, he stared at the rickety wood picnic table, and thought he'd give anything to sit there and eat ice cream with Lacey again. Remembering their embrace, her sweet fresh scent. He closed his eyes, but they ached as much as his heart.

His cell buzzed. *Saved by the bell.* It was only his calendar, reminding him that he needed to be at Virginia and Rodney's for dinner. The last thing left to do in Bay Town. He turned the car toward Main Street and hoped he wouldn't see Lacey. It was almost six. She'd been off work an hour ago. *Safe.*

Wade parked in the alley behind Second Chance. The back stairs led up to a little loft apartment above the thrift store that Virginia had acquired. He trudged up the flight and knocked. A dog yipped, and Virginia peered out.

"Oh, Wade. Come on in."

The little white dog jumped. "Cute puppy," he said.

"Ain't he cute? But he's not a puppy no more." Virginia picked him up, and pulled Wade in. "Leave him alone, Officer."

"Officer?"

"Yeah, I got him from Will Boudreaux for a birthday present a couple years ago." The name rolled off her tongue like it meant nothing, but Wade bristled. Still, he wondered why his father would give Virginia a dog.

"When I lived at the Refuge house, I had a huge crush on Rodney, so I named the puppy after him. Officer."

Wade's head spun. She had lived at the Refuge House? The home for abused and trafficked girls. One of Will's victims? Wade's stomach flipped, and he turned toward Blaine, who had just entered the room.

"Good evening, Wade. Glad you could join us." Rodney shook his hand.

Wade had so many questions, but he couldn't ask. All the more reason he had to leave Bay Town. How many victims hung from his family tree?

"You're in for a treat," Rodney said. "Virginia went all out. I hope you like pot roast."

Wade breathed deep. The aroma of rich beef broth filled his lungs. "Love it, and I'm not sure when I'll get a home-cooked meal again."

Virginia busied herself in the kitchen. She set multi-colored pottery dishes at the bistro table with four wrought-iron chairs squished around. Gem-colored stemware held patterned napkins nestled inside like tulips.

Wade frowned at the table. Four. *Why four?* He pulled out a chair and sat.

"Are you all right? You don't look so good." Rodney reached for a water bottle perched on the counter.

"Who else is coming?"

"Lacey, of course," Virginia said.

Wade pulled at his shirt collar.

"She's always late so let's wait a few." A brightly colored apron with ruffles swished around her legs as she sat. "So, Wade. Did you know we're related?"

Rodney's mouth gaped. "Uh, honey, why don't we discuss this later?"

"Discuss? There's nothing to discuss, and my family's all gone except for my cousin here."

Wade's stomach rumbled, and he felt sick again. "Cousin?"

"Yes. My mama died at my birth, and my Aunt Hilly raised me. Uncle Will was her cousin. So that makes us cousins, don't it?"

Wade frowned, but Virginia kept going.

"He helped raise me."

She shot a glance at Rodney, whose hand covered his eyes.

"Oh, honey," she said. "It's my past, and I know we don't like to talk about it, but it's not like everyone doesn't know it already." She patted Rodney's hand, then jumped up. "I'll make the salad, and I better call Lacey. Go on. You boys talk."

Wade stared after her. *Unbelievable*, he thought, but Rodney interrupted.

"Virginia escaped trafficking by Will, thanks to Lacey's dad and Pastor Brooks. They saved her, and a bunch of other girls too." Rodney spoke quietly.

Wade gulped and looked at the door hoping to escape.

"Sorry. I know this is all hard to take in, but Virginia is settled with it. She had some good counseling at The Refuge, and she's pretty special. She's been able to give this over to the Lord like nobody I know. I suspect we may have to deal with it more sometime in the future, but I think the Lord's given her grace for now."

Grace for now? Is that what they called it? Maybe that's what he needed. Just some time so he could deal with it later. The thoughts in his mind swirled, and he recalled Desmond had offered to help.

"Yeah, it was a crazy ordeal. With Melanie's help, they were pretty much responsible for saving Virginia and busting a trafficking ring in New Orleans," Rodney said.

Wade wiped sweat off his brow and rubbed his damp

hands down his jeans. Rodney grabbed a paisley napkin from the stemware and handed it to Wade.

"It's quite a story."

A story? It's a nightmare. His nightmare. Wade's knees bounced, and he clenched his jaw so tightly he thought his teeth might break.

"I have to go," he whispered. "I can't stay."

"I understand, but Virginia will be awfully disappointed if you leave."

A knock at the door stopped the conversation.

CHAPTER 30

Lacey walked in and froze. Her eyes flashed at Wade but shifted to Virginia.

"What's he doing here?" she asked.

Wade stood. He'd never get out of here if he didn't leave right now. "I'm leaving."

"No. I'll go. I'm not hungry." Lacey backed away.

Virginia waltzed over and hugged Lacey, kissing the air beside both cheeks. "Oh, quit it, you love birds." She frowned. "What took you so long?"

"You never told me you moved here. I went to your house." Lacey crossed her arms.

The wadded napkin in Wade's hand dampened as he squeezed it.

"Oh, yeah, I forgot to tell you. It's just temporary." Virginia giggled. "We had a leak in the kitchen at our house. Who told you we was here?"

"Max the florist." She glanced at Wade as if explaining who Max was. "I caught him watering his lawn."

"Have you seen his flowers? He gives me fresh cut bunches every day. I can't believe how beautiful his garden is. I wish I could grow things like him. He must have a green thumb." Virginia giggled.

A smile edged on Wade's lips and Lacey let a little giggle explode.

Rodney cleared his throat, stifling a laugh. "Honey, he's a florist. He knows flowers."

"Oh, that's right. I forgot." She pranced back to the kitchen. "Okay, whatever. We're going to buffet it here and eat there." She pointed to the bistro. "And no one is leaving." Virginia waved everyone over to the kitchen counter. She wiggled her fingers. "Come on now, join hands."

Rodney reached for Virginia's hand, but Lacey ran over, wiggling between them. Wade felt a stab to his heart. How could he blame her? She wanted nothing to do with him anymore. He joined the circle, clasping hands with Rodney and Virginia.

"Wade, you bless the food," Virginia said.

Wade's eyes widened. "What? Wait. No, not me."

Rodney shrugged. "Got to start sometime."

"Why cousin, don't you know Jesus?" Virginia asked.

Wade gulped. His eyes darted around, and the small group stared back at him. *But did he? Know Jesus?* He seriously believed in God, and Jesus had been engrained in his brain as a child.

"Wade, that's what makes us different than Will or his brother, or anybody else out there that shares our name." Virginia squeezed his hand. "We got to stick together. And if you don't know Jesus, why not just confess, and repent now? Ask him to be your savior."

Rodney cleared his throat. "Honey, I'll pray."

"But really, Wade?" Virginia squeezed his hand, and her eyes pleaded.

Wade glanced at Lacey. Her face had softened. Her eyes glistened, and she looked like the angel he met at her mother's wedding.

"Sure. I'll pray," Wade said quietly. When he closed his eyes, it was like he was alone. He could barely feel the hands holding his. "God, I know I've messed up. Please forgive me. I guess I'm trusting you on this one." He ended the short, sweet prayer with an Amen, but added, "And please bless the food." He looked up and shrugged. A quiet peace seemed to settle his soul, but restlessness remained.

"Well, did you mean it?" Virginia asked.

"I did." He looked at Lacey, wishing he felt differently. He felt freer, but no less guilty for all the pain he'd caused her. He may have decided to try and live for God, but he couldn't change his past. "I'm so sorry, Lacey. I'm sorry for everything, please forgive me." Wade's eyes teared, and he turned to Virginia. "And I'm sorry my father hurt you too."

"Not your fault, cousin."

"But it is. And that's why I can't stay here."

"Don't you get it? You're free from all that." Virginia hugged him so tightly, he coughed. She pulled back. "Wade, it's done. Jesus' blood paid it all for you." She pulled everyone in. "For all of us. Just accept it. I did."

"We all did," Rodney said. "At some point in our lives, we all have to, otherwise Jesus died for nothing. You can't repent on your own, Wade."

Just accept it? Wade chewed on his lip. His body trembled, and he let go of Virginia's hand. He stepped away, feeling like his knees would give out. How many times had he heard those words? Words that angered him.

"It's that simple, Wade. I promise," Lacey whispered.

He'd been at many crossroads in his life. When Beau killed his mother, and Wade wanted to do the same back but didn't. When the private investigator found him on the street, he could have kept running. And when he could have let Beau choke to death in the restaurant. Could a life change be that simple? Just say a prayer. Make a decision. There had to be more.

"Oh for Pete's sake, Wade. It's not like you're doing it all alone. Jesus is calling you, you can't resist."

"You can choose another path," Rodney interjected. "But I'd advise against it."

"Come on. My dinner is getting cold." Virginia stomped her feet.

Rodney raised his hands. "Stop. Virginia, honey, this is Wade's decision, and maybe he just needs to go home and think about it."

"Think about it? What if he gets in an accident and dies first?" Virginia said.

Rodney placed his hands on her shoulders, leading her to the kitchen. "Honey, let it go."

"You let it go, Wade," Virginia said over her shoulder.

He looked at Lacey, and as much as he wanted to hold her and kiss her and never let her go, for the first time since he'd met her, he wanted something else more. He wanted peace, and something assured him he could have it. In time.

"I believe." Wade gazed at Lacey. "I do."

Lacey's eye's widened, but Virginia screamed. She leaped up and barreled into him. "Oh you ain't just my cousin, you're my brother now."

CHAPTER 31

Virginia's pot roast melted in her mouth, but Lacey didn't taste it much. The nice meal and the light conversation put everyone at ease. The evening ended in hugs and promises that Lacey wasn't sure that Wade could keep. Promises not to leave town. Virginia had coaxed and pleaded him into agreeing. Perhaps he placated her, but butterflies fluttered inside, and Lacey hoped. Hoped for what? That she could be with him forever. But something inside told her he needed to be alone.

Lacey lay sprawled across her mattress and pulled out her phone from under her pillow.

Four o'clock, she sighed. One hour until the church potluck and Wade probably wouldn't be there. She flung her arm over her eyes. He didn't come to church this morning, and afterward she had come home, sketched a little and cried till she fell asleep.

She forced herself up and stood before the full-length mirror. She pulled at the long curls that she'd waved this morning, and her eyes traveled down the floral cotton dress she wore. All wrinkled now, yet she'd taken such care to look her best for Sunday morning. Well, actually for Wade. *Had he left town after all?* Tears welled, and she brushed them away as she patted her puffy eyes.

"No more," she said.

Knock-knock.

"Yes, Mom. You don't need to knock."

"Uh, it's me," a deep voice responded.

Lacey wiped her mascara-stained cheeks. "Come in, Dad."

Desmond pushed the door open, took one look at her, and spread his arms wide.

Lacey welcomed the invitation but slogged into his arms. "It's so hard."

"I know. I'm sorry."

She hugged his waist and buried her head into his chest. "I know I'm supposed to give it to God. I know I'm young. I know he's got to do this himself. I know. I know. I know."

Desmond pulled back and tipped her chin up. "That's half the battle. But the hardest part is surrendering it. You don't know what God has planned, but you're assuming it's the worst, right?"

"Yes."

"Well, maybe it's time to quit doubting that He has your best interests at heart."

Lacey peeked at her worktable. Reese's designs were everywhere. She'd doubted when she didn't get into design school. She'd doubted when she didn't take the job at Madam DeFleur's. Now look how things turned out. Designing a dress for an A-list celebrity for the Academy Awards next year. She turned towards Desmond. And she'd always doubted she'd have a father. Now here, God had given her the best.

"Keep praying for Wade. If you love him as much as I love your mother, give him up. You can trust God's plan."

"That's easy for you to say, you got the girl."

"I got two of them. Now, let's get to that potluck. You made your brownies, didn't you?"

"Yes. They're all boxed up in the kitchen."

"Good. I might try one to make sure they're decent."

Lacey slapped his arm and followed him to the door. She closed it and leaned against the back. If only Wade showed up to try them too. She shoved off and headed for her closet.

The community hall wasn't decorated, but the buzz of friendly voices and the aroma of freshly cooked food filled the air. They had potlucks often, but the celebratory ones caused Lacey's heart to hitch. Her mom's too. The warm night caused perspiration to glisten on her brow. She'd said a few hellos and tasted a few appetizers, but she needed air.

Strong hands rested on her shoulders. She froze.

"You all right?" a familiar voice asked.

Lacey's shoulders dropped, but not from the weight of the hands. She nodded. "I'm fine, Art." Her voice laced with disappointment.

"He's not here, is he?"

"Nope."

"I'm sorry. I hoped he'd change his mind."

Lacey turned. "Did you talk to him?"

"Just this afternoon," Art said.

"When? Why didn't he come to morning worship? Where is he? Is he gone?"

Art threw his hands up in surrender. "Hold on, girl. He said he needed time."

"I knew it," Lacey seethed. "If Virginia hadn't bugged him so much."

"Virginia?"

"Never mind. I shouldn't have said that. She meant well."

"She always does, and it's kind of eerie how God uses her," Art said.

Lacey wiped her forehead. "Is it warm in here?"

"Not that warm." Art pointed to sweat trickling down her cheek. "I'd say you need some fresh air."

"That's a good idea." Lacey headed toward the door but turned. "So, they're not going to honor Wade tonight?"

"Nah, I think Pastor Desmond knew Wade wouldn't want that." He waved around the room. "But it's a good turn out just the same. Did you see those amazing desserts that Mr. Gardner sent over from one of his hotels? The chef made them special for tonight."

Normally Lacey would run for specialty desserts, but she headed for the back exit instead. Shoving the door so hard that it banged against the wall, she stepped out and squinted at the outdoor lamplight, remembering that here is where she first fell for Wade.

She stared at empty brown catering boxes, with a hotel logo on the side. The desserts had been delivered in them. Lacey kicked one and uttered a muffled scream.

"Hey, slow down. Sandals aren't exactly kicking shoes."

Lacey spun around. Too many words formed in her head, but none made sense.

Wade stepped into the porch light and offered a hand. Without a word, he led her to a bench under the old Sycamore tree. His hand shook as he gazed at the street.

She pulled him down to sit. "He's not there, Wade. He's gone."

"And I should be too."

Lacey took his other hand and squeezed. "I'm glad you're not."

His eyes glistened back at her. Even in the dark night, the hue mesmerized her. She searched his face, and her eyes rested on the scar barely hidden under his hair.

"Does it hurt?" She touched it.

Wade moved his head, and she felt he didn't relish her touch. Yet, he took her hands, holding them both. He kissed one. Then the other.

"I should leave, but I can't."

The heart that had been sinking fluttered. It beat so fast, perspiration beaded again on her forehead, but she didn't care.

"Why? Why can't you leave?" She cleared her throat. "I mean, not that I want you to, but I'm wondering. If you want to leave, why don't you?" She wanted to stop talking but couldn't. "After all, you did promise Virginia." She chuckled. "But Virginia—"

He kissed her. His lips rushed so fast that he caught her in mid-sentence, and she couldn't breathe. They were soft and warm just the way a kiss should be. When he finally pulled back, he leaned his forehead against hers. She closed her eyes and wished they could stay like this forever, but he pulled away and grinned. He yanked out a crisp, white handkerchief with an embroidered G in the corner and wiped her forehead.

Lacey should have been embarrassed, but she touched her lips, only thinking of the kiss.

"It's kind of warm tonight—" he started.

This time she leaned forward. Her parted lips held his and she wanted to savor the soft, sweetness of his mouth forever.

"Ahem."

They slid apart, and Wade jumped up.

"Wade. Glad you could make it." Desmond grinned.

"Yes, sir. Pastor Desmond, I'm sorry, I..." His voice trailed.

Melanie stepped forward. She opened her mouth to speak but promptly shut it. She nudged Desmond.

"Sorry, kids, but we stepped out and saw two shadows. Didn't mean to intrude."

"Yes, we did," Melanie said.

"Mom," Lacey moaned.

"I understand. I'm sorry. It won't happen again." Wade stuttered. "I…uh… I'll be leaving, ma'am."

"Wade, no," Lacey begged.

Desmond laid a hand on Wade's shoulders. "Please don't. The Lord brought you here, and you're clearly wanted. I spoke with your Aunt and your Great-grandfather today."

Wade nodded. "Yes, I wrapped up my goodbyes in New Orleans."

"Well, it seems they're not happy about that," said Desmond.

"It's for the best." Wade shuffled his feet.

"For whose best? Mr. Gardner says he had some pretty lofty plans for you." Desmond shook his head. "Forget I said lofty. Wade, he needs you."

"He's got plenty of guys better than me to help with the business."

"But you're his heir. He said so, and he's been training you to take over the business."

Wade blew out a breath. He didn't like being reminded of that. "Yes, I know, and I've thought about it." His eyes turned to Lacey. "Especially lately." Wade ran a hand through his hair.

"Wade, you're his great-grandson, but you being here? It's more than that. It's like he has your mother, his grand-daughter back."

"Whoa. I didn't see that one coming." He sat.

"See, Wade," Lacey whispered.

Melanie placed a firm hand on her arm, and Lacey understood.

"I'm not my mom," Wade said.

"But she's in you, and you have a chance to give her back to Mr. Gardner. But that's not all. He loves you, regardless of your mom or your dad. Regardless of the Gardner name, he loves you, and he couldn't be prouder of you. None of us could," Desmond said.

"I agree. I'm proud of you too," said Melanie. "You're a wise young man, and you've been through so much. But the most important thing is that you trust God, and I sense you're trying to do that. So have a little faith in everyone on this. We know the Lord has great plans for you. I don't know what you're thinking, and Lacey is young." She looked at her daughter.

Lacey closed her eyes. *Here it comes. Now he's really going to leave.*

"But she's lived through things that have made her grow more than any nineteen-year-old I know." Melanie's eyes watered. "Whatever the plans you have, I think you can accomplish them better if you stay."

Wade cleared his throat. "I guess it's not just all about me, is it?"

"Oh, no," Melanie huffed. "We all have to learn that lesson about turning off that voice that tells us we're not good enough. The one that says someone, or everyone, is better off without us." Stepping forward, she placed a hand on his arm. "Wade, please. Don't go breaking my daughter's heart."

Wade smiled and offered a hand to Lacey. She took his hand, and he pulled her in his arms. "Thank you, ma'am. I won't do that. I promise."

The four stood without speaking, and clicking cicadas enunciated the momentary silence. An occasional owl's hoot joined in. Lacey wanted to hoot with it. She radiated joy back at her parents.

Desmond straightened. "Well, then. Shall we?" He and Melanie held hands and walked back to the community hall. "Food's getting cold," Desmond called over his shoulder.

Laughter bubbled from Lacey, followed by sniffles, then she stared up at Wade. His stoic face gazed back as he sucked in a breath. Taking her face in his hands, he caressed her cheek with a thumb. She closed her eyes, and the warmth of his face grew close as his lips covered hers once more.

But he broke away. "I guess I have a lot to think about."

"What's to think about?" Lacey bit her lip.

Wade laughed. "You. Life here in Bay Town. I think I knew it all along. I just had to believe it."

"Well, you heard my mom. Don't go breaking my heart." Lacey tipped up on her toes, raised her chin, and closed her eyes.

He whispered, "Without a doubt, I never will." He kissed her deeply once again.

The End

ABOUT THE AUTHOR

Kathleen J. Robison is an Okinawan-American. Born in Okinawa, raised in California, Florida, Mississippi, and Singapore. Her travels are the inspirational settings for her stories. She and her Pastor husband have eight adult children. Seven are married, blessing them with fourteen grandchildren and counting. The diversity of their 31 family members provide the inspiration for more lively characters than can be imagined. Her husband grew up in the streets of Los Angeles raised by a single working mom, and that life provides fodder for many of the conflicts of her characters.

Tackling difficult life's trials with God's strength are the central theme of Kathleen's stories. She hopes to inspire her readers to trust God and with His strength, weather through and rise above trials and tragedies. If you like suspenseful stories with a thread of romance, you will enjoy Kathleen's Bay Town Series!

facebook.com/kathleenjrobisonauthor

instagram.com/kathleenjrobison

bookbub.com/profile/3794692396

ALSO BY KATHLEEN J. ROBISON

Bay Town Series

Shattered Guilt (Book One)

Revived Hope (Novella)

Restored Grace (Book Two)

Let Them Eat Fruitcake (Christmas Novella)

Shadowed Doubt (Book Three)

A GARDNER'S LIFE

SHADOWED DOUBT BONUS STORY

KATHLEEN J. ROBISON

CHAPTER 1

Too weak to knock, she scratched at the ornate wooden door and tapped. But no one answered. Huddling under the eaves of the porch, the woman sank to the ground. Pulling her knees to her chest and dropping her head, she shivered. The rain stung, and the wind whipped. Her teeth chattered. *Oh, dear God. Help me.*

"Miz Summer, please. You have to come to Bay Town now. Right now. I think it's her," Hazel cried. "I called 9-1-1. She's in a bad way, and I couldn't help her, none."

"Hazel, slow down. What do you mean?" said Summer.

"It's your sister, Spring. Oh, ma'am. Please come quickly. I need to go. The firemen are here."

"My sister? Firemen? What for? Wait, did you say 9-1-1? Hazel, you are scaring me." Summer's voice rose.

"They're at the door, ma'am. I'm sorry, come quick."

Leaving New Orleans in a rush, Summer and her grandfather, Reginald, rode in silence. They passed the creole French colonial buildings, out of the city and into the bayou. They soon crossed over the bodies of water called the rigolets. The dividing line between Louisiana and Mississippi. Turning off the main highway, Summer raced to the beach house across from the gulf in Bay Town.

She glanced at her grandfather. He paled, but he breathed steadily.

"Are you all right, Granddaddy?" She patted his hand.

He nodded but clenched the cane resting between his knees. "Was Hazel sure it was her?"

"As sure as she could be. Spring left so long ago, but she couldn't have changed that much, could she?"

Don't answer that. Summer shook her head, trying not to envision anything, especially what her younger sister might look like at this point. When she'd first run away, they hired a private investigator to find her, but she refused to return home. Every year, he checked on her and gave his report. Not good. Very bad, in fact.

Before Summer turned down the back lane to the five-car garage behind the house, she caught a glimpse of Hazel waving. Her starched pink uniform a compliment to her graying curls and dark skin. Summer pulled her Mercedes to the front of the grand old mansion.

"They took her to Bay Town General."

"Thank you, Hazel." Summer yanked the wheel, intending to make a U-turn but stopped.

"Hazel, are you sure?"

Hazel's red eyes teared. "She called out my name."

"Oh, honey. Get in the car," Summer said.

Hazel climbed in back, and Summer drove. Arriving at the hospital, Summer practically threw the keys at the valet. For a split second, a thoughtful appreciation arose in her mind, thankful for her grandfather's generous donations to the hospital that allowed the courtesy parking.

"Hazel, please help Granddaddy."

"I'm fine. You go on in, Summer." Reginald Gardner swung his door open, and the valet scuttled to help.

Summer managed to quickly get inside the hospital while running in high heels.

"We're here to see Spring Gardner."

The receptionist looked up. "Identification, please."

Summer opened her Gucci purse and flipped out her wallet, producing the ID.

"Oh. I'm sorry. I didn't realize you're a Gardner." The receptionist smiled and handed back the ID. She scrolled the computer and looked up. "I'm sorry, there is no Gardner here today."

"The name is under Jones." Hazel's voice came from behind.

Summer turned and rushed to her grandfather's side.

Hazel walked to the desk. "The paramedics brought in a Spring Jones about an hour ago."

Her brows furrowed, and the young woman checked again. "Oh, yes. She's on the second floor in the ICU." She pointed across the lobby. "Elevators are down the hallway."

"Go on, Summer. I'll follow with Hazel."

"No, Granddaddy. We'll all go together."

Reaching the ICU floor, Hazel chose to stay in the waiting room.

"Thank you, Hazel. Thank you for protecting our girl," Summer said.

"She's my girl too, ain't she?"

Summer smiled. "Of course, we're both your girls." She hugged Hazel. "I don't know what we would have done all these years without you. And here you are, saving my little sister."

"Go on now. We'll talk later. You tell your sister that I love her." Hazel gave Summer a little push.

Summer and Reginald walked slowly to Spring's room. Summer gasped, and Reginald grabbed the door jamb. Spring lay as white as the sheets that covered her. Except the for dark circles under her eyes and the matted blonde hair, the figure that lay before them blended into the white sheets. Summer led her father to Spring's bedside and pulled up a chair. She motioned for her grandfather to sit, but he waved her off.

Is that really you, Spring? The frail woman couldn't have weighed more than ninety pounds. Besides the IV needles poking into her hand and arm, scars laid tracks inside both limbs. *Oh, sister, what happened?*

Reginald touched Spring's hand. She didn't move. He curled his fingers around hers.

"Sweetheart. We're here. Ready to take you home."

The dark eyelids opened. Her eyes glistened. "Oh, Grand-daddy, I'm so sorry."

"Shhh. No need for that now. Welcome home, Spring." He pointed across the bed. "Your sister is here, too."

Summer leaned to kiss her sister's hair, ignoring the dirt and stench. She hugged her and cried inside, feeling the bones that protruded everywhere. "Spring, I'm so glad you're home."

Spring spoke in a hoarse whisper. "I should have come a long time ago. I'm so ashamed."

"Now, we'll have none of that."

Spring slowly turned her head. "Summer, I need you to find my son."

Reginald frowned. "Son? I have a great-grandson?"

"Yes, Granddaddy. His middle name is Reginald. After you."

He smiled, but pressed a hand to his chest.

"Are you happy? Does that make you happy? Oh, Grand-daddy." Spring coughed, and the cough spasmed.

He nodded and lowered himself into the chair behind him.

"Granddaddy, are you all right?" Summer rushed over.

"Fine. Spring, go on."

But she couldn't as she struggled for air, gagging on each throaty air intake. Summer rushed to get a nurse, who came and lifted Spring up, leaning her slightly forward. She gave her sips of water until the episode passed. "I'll get something for that cough. Excuse me."

"Don't talk, sister. You'll have plenty of time to tell me about my little nephew." Summer bit her lip. "He is somewhere safe, though, isn't he?"

Spring gasped, choking back another impending tirade.

"Never mind, we'll get to him. You're back, and before you know it, you'll be home."

Knock. Knock.

A man in a white coat stood at the door. Young, good-looking. He smiled at the family. Summer looked down at her sister, who closed her eyes, turning her head away from the doctor. Shame shrouded her face.

"I'm Doctor Fournier." He approached the bedside and shook hands with Reginald and Summer.

A nurse walked in with supplies, ready to bathe Spring. "Oh, I'm so sorry. I'm going to clean Miss Jones up a bit. I'll come back."

"No. Please proceed. We'll step outside. I'd like to speak with the family privately." Dr. Fournier motioned to the door.

Summer turned and touched the nurse's arm. "By the way, she is Miss Gardner. Spring Gardner, my sister. And would you mind shampooing her hair as well?"

The nurse smiled. "My pleasure, Miss Gardner."

"Thank you. Now Spring, don't you go anywhere. We'll be right back just as soon as I can get this doctor to release you. You'll be home, good as new." She turned and faced the doctor. "Isn't that right, Doctor?"

He smiled. "Please, come with me." They followed him to the waiting room where Hazel sat. "Please, have a seat. What I have to say is quite difficult."

Summer's brows furrowed. And Reginald let out a loud sigh.

"I'm afraid your sister is in liver failure. She doesn't have much time."

Summer stood. "What are you saying?"

"It's too late," Reginald said quietly.

"Grandfather! Why, we'll just have her transported to New Orleans. That's a much bigger hospital. I mean no offense, Dr. Fournier."

He held up a hand. "Your grandfather is right. It's too late. She has a few days, maybe a week."

Summer's knees buckled. She glanced from the doctor to Reginald and back. "No. Get her a liver transplant." Summer glared at her grandfather. "Granddaddy? You can do that, can't you? Can't you put her on the top of a list?"

The doctor shook his head. "She has pneumonia in both lungs, and her system is too weak to recover. Wherever she lived, I suspect it took its toll on her."

Everyone looked at Hazel. "She told me she'd been on the porch for nearly two or three days. She couldn't remember. When I found her, she wore a thin summer dress, no shoes."

Summer's mouth dropped open.

Reginald closed his eyes and rubbed his forehead. "The storm. She lay on the front porch throughout the storm."

Hazel's voice shook. "Yes, sir. I only arrived yesterday to prepare the house for your stay, and I used the back entrance like always. Why, if I'd checked the front door, I could have brought her in last night."

Reginald took Hazel's hand. Their wrinkled dark and light tones entwined. "You did good, Hazel, and we are forever grateful to you."

"Even if she didn't have pneumonia, her organs are beyond compromised. I'm so sorry."

"Doctor, there has got to be something you can do." Summer tapped her foot. "Right, Granddaddy?"

"I'll call the church. They'll send a priest."

"Granddaddy? Are you serious?"

"To pray, Summer. To pray for your sister."

"Yes." Hazel spoke quietly. "I called my church, and they were praying too, and I prayed with Spring before the paramedics came." Hazel smiled. "And you know, Spring prayed too. She knows Jesus. She said that's why she's still alive." Tears dripped down her face. "She said he kept her alive so she could say sorry and goodbye."

"Stop it. You stop it, Hazel. I won't hear that. If Jesus kept her alive, it wasn't to say goodbye. Now, Doctor, you do whatever it takes to get my sister well. You know money is no object."

"Summer, it's all in God's hands now." Reginald nodded.

"Miss Gardner, he's correct. I'm so sorry. We'll keep her comfortable, and you keep praying."

Hazel looked up. "What about you, Doctor? We need your prayers too."

He smiled. "Yes, of course. I'll pray too. I'm just not sure He…" the doctor looked upwards. "I'm not sure he hears my prayers, but I've seen enough miracles to believe."

"Well, Doctor. I'll pray for you too. If you just ask Him for yourself, he'll hear you."

Dr. Fournier smiled. "I just may do that, ma'am. Mr. Gardner, Miss Gardner, my sincerest apologies." He nodded and left.

Summer burst out sobbing. Pulling tissues from her bag, she dabbed at her eyes, cheeks, and chin. Still, the tears flooded. Hazel enveloped her and pulled her close.

"God's got her, honey," Hazel said. "And I think she's at peace with him. You go enjoy your time with her. Let's be thankful that the good Lord gave her back to us before He takes her home."

"I just can't believe he'd do that, Hazel."

"His ways are not ours, but we can trust Him." She

squeezed Summer's shoulders. "And we can always pray for a miracle."

Summer nodded and blew her nose. "Yes, we can. Thank you, Hazel."

A nurse popped her head into the waiting room. "Gardner family? Please come quickly. It's Miss Gardner."

CHAPTER 2

"Come, Hazel. You come too."

Hazel, Summer, and Reginald pushed the button for the automatic doors to the ICU. A nice-looking gentleman in a blue suit smiled and stepped aside. He smoothed back his already slick hair. "Ladies, Sir," he said as he nodded.

He slipped by them but turned. "Sorry to hear about your sister." He tipped a hand to his brow and sauntered toward the elevator.

"Excuse me?" Summer asked.

But he turned the corner before she could get his attention. No matter, Spring would tell her. She caught up with her grandfather and Hazel. Entering the room, she encountered doctors and nurses attempting to calm Spring. She thrashed, coughed, and babbled incoherently.

"The doctor ordered a sedative. It should calm her."

"What happened?"

"Her husband stopped by, and she seems upset by it."

"Husband? What husband?" Reginald asked.

Summer looked at her grandfather. "It couldn't be him, could it? That man that passed us in the hallway?"

"Yes. It was." Spring's voice faded.

"Who?" Summer asked. "I didn't hear you."

Spring's head flopped to one side, and her eyes rolled back before closing.

"Oh, sweetheart, please. Tell us?" Summer looked at the nurse. "Did you see him? Did he give his name?"

"You can check in the lobby. I'm sure he gave his ID." The nurse frowned. "Come to think of it, he didn't wear a visitor badge. Let me go check." She stopped at the door. "Whoever he was, he upset Miss Gardner."

"Summer?" Reginald waved toward the window, away from the bed, and she followed. "Do you have the number of the private investigator I hired?"

"Mr. Simmons?" Summer asked.

"Yes. Call him. He'll know the man's name."

"What good will that do? He's gone."

"I'm not sure there is much of anything we can do. But if we can get Spring to tell us who he is, we may be able to stop him from doing this to other girls."

"What do you mean?" Summer narrowed her eyes.

"I suspect she's not his first victim." Reginald rubbed his forehead.

"I don't believe it. I just won't."

Reginald sighed. "Summer, we've been over this before. You read Mr. Simmon's report."

She sighed as she rubbed her temple. "Yes, of course, then. We must stop him." Summer's eyes widened. "Oh, Grandaddy, you don't think he's…is he the father of Spring's son?"

"Miss Gardner. Mr. Gardner? You best come over here now." Hazel waved them over.

"Summer, I need you to do something for me." Spring's eyes were closed and her voice weak.

Lowering her head and placing her ear next to Spring's lips, Summer coaxed her. "Of course, anything at all."

"I wrote a letter to my son…I left it on the porch…under the mat…please…" Spring drew a shallow breath. "Find him and tell him that I love him." Tears rolled down her face. "Tell him I'm sorry. Tell him…tell him to follow Jesus."

Her body shook, and she closed her eyes once more. "I love you, Summer and Granddaddy." A weak smile crossed her face. "And you too, Hazel. I'm happy I'm going home to see Jesus."

"Now, Spring. Don't talk like that," Summer sobbed.

"Hazel, why don't you go home with Summer? I'll stay here with Spring."

"No. Granddaddy, that's ridiculous."

"Summer, lower your voice."

"Fine." She opened her purse and took out a valet claim ticket. "Hazel, you take my car and go home. I'm staying here with Grandfather."

Hazel chuckled. "I'm sorry, ma'am, but I ain't driving that thing. I'll call for a ride."

"Yes, yes, of course. I'll call for you unless you'd rather stay?" Summer touched her elbow.

"I best leave you two with Miss Spring. Please let me know if anything…"

"Oh, nothing, but for the better." Summer forced a smile.

"Fine, then. I'll see you two later." She took Spring's hand and squeezed. "Jesus loves you, Spring. He always has."

The hospital found an empty room with a single bed for Reginald Gardner. Summer tried to sleep upright in a chair by Spring's bed. When the nurse's shift change came, Spring never stirred. They took her vitals and changed her IVs. Summer tiptoed round them, peeking over their shoulder, and hoping Spring would awake. She didn't.

"Is she all right?" Summer asked.

Knock-knock.

"Good morning." Dr. Fournier went to Spring's bedside,

checking the tablet the nurse handed him. Pulling out a pen light, he lifted Spring's eyelids. One at a time, he shined a light in each eye. His lips pursed.

"What? What does that mean?" Summer asked.

"She's slipped into a coma."

"Well, can't you wake her up?"

Another doctor walked in and nodded at Dr. Fournier. He smiled at Summer.

"Miss Gardner, this is our Palliative Care doctor. He'll assist your sister from this point."

"No. We don't need him." Summer shook her head. "We're praying for a miracle."

"Miss Gardner, your sister is resting quietly. That's the best we can do right now. Enjoy your time with her. I'll be in the hospital all day."

Summer's tall frame slumped. "Yes. Thank you."

He stepped into the hallway where Summer heard him talking to her grandfather. Reginald walked in. He went straight to Spring's bedside and kissed her cheek.

"Summer, late last night, while you were asleep in the chair, the parish priest came."

Summer's eyes flew wide.

"Granddaughter, he gave the last rites." Reginald made the sign of the cross.

Nodding, she expressed her agreement, but Summer couldn't help but doubt that her sister had kept the Catholic faith. She glanced at the frail form. Warmth spread over the pain in her heart. But her sister had mentioned Jesus multiple times.

"Summer, I have news. My lawyer, Mr. Landry, called. He got a call from someone inquiring about Spring's trust. A man claiming to be her husband, and he said he had a letter from Spring with instructions changing her beneficiary."

"That's ridiculous." Summer stood. "How dare he come here."

"Who?"

"The man claiming to be her husband. We saw him. Yesterday. We crossed paths with him at the entrance to the ICU."

Reginald nodded. "Well, this man told Mr. Landry that he expected to pursue the changes to the legal extent of the law and then some."

"Let him. The letter is a forgery," Summer said.

"That's what Mr. Landry suspected, but he said the man claimed it was notarized."

"Do you believe him?"

"If it's the man she ran off with years ago and left her like this, yes." Reginald rubbed his brow.

"What will we do?" Summer asked softly.

"Once he gets the notarized letter, Mr. Landry will investigate."

Summer waved a hand in the air. "It's a forgery and hardly plausible. It's just a bluff, isn't it?"

"Whether it is or not, I imagine Spring would want her son named the beneficiary in her trust. As well he should be."

"But that man will just get his hands on the money if she does that." Summer said.

"Yes, I'm afraid so. Unless we leave the estate as is. Currently, you are the beneficiary. If we leave it that way, I trust you'll hand over the estate to her son when we find him."

"Of course. But what if the boy is not of age?"

"I suspect he's not. She left seventeen years ago. He has to be younger than that."

Pain replaced the anger, and Summer's breaking heart cracked wide. "Oh, Spring."

∾

Another day passed, and Spring didn't revive. Both Summer and Reginald left to shower and change, but returned immediately to her bedside. Mr. Landry joined them.

"I received the email with a copy of the letter. It looks official, but I'll call the notary. When Spring passes, you may change the beneficiary to her son when you find him. I'll set that up if you'd like. In the meantime, let's leave Summer as beneficiary." He looked at Reginald. "Isn't that what we decided?"

"Of course," Summer said. "Whatever you've discussed is fine by me." She swept back her hair. "But, please, can we not mention Spring's passing?" Summer's voice dropped to a whisper.

"Summer, dear. She is dying. You know that?" Reginald said.

"Yes, Grandfather."

Spring's eyes slowly opened. A hint of a smile graced her pale lips. "Summer, dear. I love you so much. I'm so sorry," she said.

"Shhh." Summer whispered. "Oh, Spring. We forgive you, dear. No need for apologies. I love you," Summer whispered.

Spring struggled to turn her head. "Granddaddy, please forgive me."

Reginald stroked his granddaughter's hand. "Honey, I did that a long time ago. Life is too short to hold on to past hurts, and I'm just thankful the good Lord brought you home."

"Me too, Granddaddy." Spring's eyes widened. "Please. Please find my son."

"I will. I promise I'll do everything I can."

"Thank you. I love you both." Spring pursed her lips and kissed the air. "I'll see you in heaven."

Summer entwined her fingers with Spring's, and her tears splashed atop their clasped hands. Summer and her grandfather watched as Spring slipped into a deep, peaceful sleep. The rise and fall of her chest labored, and within the hour, it stopped.

The machines ceased clicking, and a long beep sounded.

Two nurses entered the room. One tried to smile but left. The other made notes and silenced the machines. The first nurse returned with the Palliative Care Doctor.

"No," Summer groaned. She hugged her grandfather and felt his heaving body rise and fall against hers. Her tears dampened his suit jacket.

"I'm so sorry," The doctor said as he took the tablet from the nurse, making some taps on the screen. He looked up. "We'll leave you for a while." He motioned the nurses to join him as he left.

One nurse stopped. "If there's anything you need, please ask. I'll be just outside."

"Thank you," Summer whispered.

Summer and her grandfather stood silently next to Spring's bedside for what seemed like hours, but when Summer checked her watch, it had been only one. A nurse peeked into the room, and Reginald nodded.

"Summer, we must go. Say your goodbyes."

She choked. "But I can't. Grandfather, I can't. I only had her for two days. That's not enough time."

"I'm afraid it's all the Lord gave us, and His grace is sufficient."

They held a private burial for Spring. The skies were clear, and the sun hot. Summer's black, sleeveless silk sheath absorbed the heat. She couldn't help but wonder why her sister couldn't have come home on a day like this. Maybe she'd still be alive. But she didn't really believe it. Summer pulled the brim of her wide hat down, almost resting on her sunglasses. She stared at her sister's grave and laid a bouquet of pink-tinged peonies atop the casket.

"I love you, Spring. God be with you."

They stepped carefully around grave markers, and

Summer clutched her grandfather's elbow, leading him over the uneven ground. Leaving her sister's burial was almost as hard as saying goodbye in the hospital. She looked around at the house staff and close friends. Heads down, they dabbed at their faces with tissue. None of Spring's friends from high school were here. Why would they be? They'd lived the debutante life and gone to college, as did Summer, but her sister had given all that up. For what?

All remained quiet on the drive home until Summer interrupted it. "Why did she go with that man? What would possess her to give up our life? She missed out on so much."

"I don't care she didn't have that life, Summer. All that matters now is she's at peace with God. But by His mercy, we will find her son, and he will not live your sister's unfortunate life."

He tapped a wrinkled envelope against his fingers. The sealed letter Spring had written for her son.

Summer bit her lip, a question waiting to escape. "Will you open it?"

"I will not," Reginald said.

Arriving home, Summer followed her grandfather to the library. Reginald crossed the room, filled with wall-to-wall shelves of books, floor to ceiling. Next to a silver-framed portrait of a sweet-faced girl with smooth blonde hair, he pulled out a small Bible and placed the letter inside. Spring's Bible. He returned it to the bookshelf.

Summer joined her grandfather and picked up the photograph. "We'll find him, Spring. We'll find your son. He's a Gardner, like you. And he'll live the Gardner life." Summer kissed her fingertips and touched them to the glass. "God willing, we will find him."

Summer turned to her grandfather, sitting quietly in his nearby wingback chair. "How will we find the boy?" she asked.

"The private investigator. I imagine he has many leads.

Although, I can't for the life of me understand how he didn't know she birthed a child."

"Maybe he did but didn't tell us. We never asked."

"We will be asking many questions now. I've asked Mr. Landry and Mr. Simmons, the investigator, to join us for lunch this afternoon."

"So soon? Granddaddy, you must rest."

Reginald waved her off. "I want to take care of this now." His eyes glistened. "I want to find my great-grandson. He's all I have left of Spring."

Summer wadded the linen handkerchief she'd been holding and nodded.

When both men arrived, Hazel instructed the staff to dish out steaming bowls of shrimp gumbo and freshly baked biscuits. All sat around the large, gleaming wood dining table as Hazel poured sweet, iced tea into crystal glasses. Summer ate little, as did Reginald. Mr. Landry ate his share, but Mr. Simmons ate as if he hadn't had a good meal in weeks.

The staff cleared the dishes, and all retired to the library. Reginald sat in the wing-backed chair, cutting an imposing figure. His shoulders taut and his white hair a contrast to the dark brown leather. Summer nervously fingered the thick velvet drapes hanging from the cathedral ceiling. If she wore a hoop-skirted gown, she could pass for a southern lady right out of *Gone with the Wind*.

"Mr. Landry, what have you to report on the letter?" asked Reginald.

"Good news. The letter appeared coerced, I won't go into details, but it was signed and dated at the time of Miss Gardner's hospitalization. I doubt she could have participated in a sound decision at that time. And the notary is under criminal investigation. His license is pending."

"How dare he come to the hospital," Summer said. She shivered recalling the smirk he flashed when they passed him. "Why that man harassed my sister until her death."

"Yes, well, you may not need concern yourself. I think we have a good case against him."

"Who is he?" Mr. Simmons asked.

"Will Bodine," said Mr. Landry. "At least, that's the name he gave me."

"Do you think it's an alias?" Summer asked.

"Never mind," said Reginald. "What is important is my great-grandson. But do you know if this Will Bodine is the father? I imagine so if he's trying to get Spring's trust fund."

Glancing between all present parties, Mr. Simmons grasped his sweet tea and sipped. "I believe he is. About seventeen years ago, for a period of time, I lost track of Miss Gardner. Like she had disappeared. Then almost a year later, she was back in the on the streets. I mean to say..."

Summer pinched the bridge of her nose. "Never mind, we understand."

"We would like you to find this boy," Reginald said quietly.

"That might be difficult."

"Whatever it takes."

Mr. Landry's cell phone rang, and everyone turned. "I'm so sorry. Let me get this." He glanced at the screen and looked up. "It's Will Bodine." Without waiting for comment, he answered.

"Hello. Landry here...No, I did not, but we'll contest that the will is null and void...You may object all you like, but I checked, and your notary is under investigation. If you pursue this, we'll go to court. I doubt the judge will find anything in your favor."

"You tell him he is not getting one dime of my sister's money," Summer yelled.

"What? No, I don't think so...just a minute." Mr. Landry lowered the cell to his side. "He wants to speak with you, Mr. Gardner."

Reginald extended his hand. "Yes, let me talk to him,"

Summer strode across the room.

Her grandfather raised a palm, stopping her in her tracks. He took the phone. "Reginald Gardner here... Listen, Mr. Bodine." He spoke rapidly. "If you tell me the whereabouts of my grandson, I will reward you handsomely." Reginald pulled his shoulders back and moved the phone from his ear. He hit the speaker button, and laughter rolled from the phone.

"How about you reward me handsomely for not killing your great-grandson?"

Summer gasped.

"Shhh," Mr. Simmons covered the receiver with his hand and whispered. "He's capable of it."

"Mr. Bodine, please. We are reasonable people. What do you want?"

"I want the boy's trust fund. Better yet, I want your grand-daughter's trust fund. I'll phone you tomorrow. Be available to meet me at the Silver Slipper in Gulfport." He clicked off.

"Reginald, you can't." Mr. Landry pleaded.

"Of course not. Grandfather, no."

"You go, and I'll be close behind," Mr. Simmons said.

All eyes riveted on him.

"We can catch him in the act of extortion. I'll call the police, and we'll nab him there."

"And my great-grandson?" Reginald asked.

"In order to nab this guy, we may not get that information right off. But I'm good at what I do. I found your granddaughter, didn't I?"

"A lot of good that did," Summer huffed.

"I couldn't help it if she wouldn't come with me. Now you're great-grandson. He's another story." Mr. Simmons raised his brows. "With the right amount of money, I'm sure we can get him to agree to meet you all."

"Good day, sir." Summer walked to the door and yanked it open.

"Everybody, calm down. Please. Summer, sit. I think it's a good idea."

"Grandfather. You can't be serious."

"I want my great-grandson, and I expect to find him."

"Good. Let's arrange the meeting, and I'll write a list of questions for you to ask this Bodine. It will help in my investigation. The more he talks, the more information he'll give. If you don't mind, I'll wire you up, and then I can hear everything," Mr. Simmons said.

"Oh, my goodness gracious. Who are you, Denzel Washington, in the Equalizer?"

All eyes turned to Summer. Mr. Simmons smiled.

"I didn't think you'd watch a show like that."

Summer stuttered. "Well, I didn't. I just like him as an actor and read about it. Of course not. I don't watch R-rated movies with that kind of language and violence. A southern lady does not entertain such vices."

Mr. Simmons laughed. "Well, miss little lady, we're dealing with real-life vices, and I bet this Bodine could be a whole lot worse than the likes of Denzel. But don't you worry. I'll get you the boy."

"Enough of this cops and robbers business, Reginald." Mr. Landry reserved the use of a first name basis for extreme cases. "You can't give in to this Bodine's extortion. The police need to be called. If not, what's to stop him from asking for more?"

"We'll deal with that when the time comes. My first concern is my great-grandson, and I trust the good Lord to guide me." Reginald tapped the rolled arm of his chair.

The room went silent, and Summer grimaced. Her troubled mind swam with the scenario of her grandfather meeting the menacing criminal at a casino across the gulf.

"I'm going with you," Summer said.

"Yeah, I don't think so. I'll be right there with your grandfather. Besides, I work alone." Mr. Simmons tapped the armchair.

"Not this time, you don't," Summer said.

CHAPTER 3

Reginald stared stoically as Mr. Simmons taped the bugging devices to his bare chest. The old gentleman said nothing.

"I'll be listening and recording everything, so be sure to get the answers to the questions I've asked. You got those memorized?"

A single slow nod confirmed that Reginald knew precisely what to do.

"I'll be in a booth across the restaurant. I wish it were in a quieter place, but at least it's not in the middle of the casino," said Mr. Simmons.

Reginald buttoned up his shirt and one button on his gray suit jacket.

"Okay, it's show time. Let's go."

Reginald drove himself to the Silver Slipper Casino, valeted his car, and walked the perimeter of the casino to the nearby restaurant. The *ka-ching* of slots deafened the air. Reginald reached above his ear, tapping his hearing aid. He stopped at the restaurant's entrance and leaned on his cane.

He looked around when a man in a silver suit approached. A very nice, costly suit. Reginald's eyes traveled the length of the tall, well-dressed man. His gold cufflinks gleamed as he adjusted them.

"Mr. Reginald Gardner?" The man grinned. "I'm Will Bodine. It's a pleasure to make your acquaintance."

Reginald nodded. "I can't say the same. Shall we take a seat?" He perused the restaurant and saw Mr. Simmons seated at a booth across the room.

"I changed my mind. There's a bar in the casino. Let's go there."

Reginald's body stiffened, and he sucked in a breath.

Bodine touched his elbow with one hand and placed another on his back.

Reginald wondered if Bodine felt the wires. Hopefully not. He wore an undershirt, a tee shirt, a dress shirt, and his suit jacket. Mr. Simmons had done this before. Will Bodine pushed him slightly toward the center of the casino.

Breathing a sigh of relief, Reginald let Bodine lead him to a bar amid all the noise. Reginald didn't dare look to see if Mr. Simmons followed. Instead, he prayed silently.

"Take a seat, sir." Bodine pointed to a tall stool.

"No, thank you. I prefer to stand." Reginald hooked the cane on his arm and leaned against the counter.

"Suit yourself." He raised a hand and signaled the bartender. "Whiskey sour, please. Now then. Let's get down to business."

"Yes, let's do. I'm prepared to give you one lump sum of cash. I'd rather not mess with the trust fund."

Bodine laughed. "Unless the lump sum is as big as Spring's Trust Fund, you can kiss your great-grandson goodbye."

Reginald's fists clenched, and he didn't know what made him angrier. Spring's name being spoken by such a foul creature, or the threat of losing his only great-grandchild. But Reginald didn't amass his wealth by reacting to threats and unsavory characters. He knew how to deal with Bodine. Or so he thought.

"How much are we talking about?"

Again, Bodine laughed. "You tell me." His face grew red, and he slammed a hand on the counter, sloshing the liquid in his drink.

"Don't play games with me, old man. I got all kinds of tricks up my sleeve. Why Spring's pretty sister might even be a good replacement for that sad, sorry of a granddaughter of yours. She let herself go."

"That's enough." *If only I were a younger man.* The veins in Reginald's neck bulged, but when he saw Mr. Simmons drawing close, he gave a slight nod, hoping he'd stay away. "Mr. Bodine. You should know. I've informed the FBI of your attempt at this extortion."

Bodine's eyes widened, but quickly narrowed. "I don't believe you."

"Extortion? FBI?" A deep voice came from behind Will Bodine. A large man, both in stature and height, stepped around the seated and shocked Bodine. "Mr. Gardner, I'm Mr. Black. Will Bodine works for my employer, and I'll take care of this."

"This is none of your business." Bodine slugged down his drink and slammed his glass on the counter.

"I'm afraid it is. The FBI is not an organization we tangle with. If you know what I mean. Come with me, Bodine." Mr. Black patted his coat pocket and looked at Reginald. "You too, sir."

Reginald followed slowly, breathing heavily. He imagined what they planned for him. Was this the end? He'd led a long, good life, but the thought of dying at the hands of his daughter's killer angered him. Would he never see his great-grandson?

Mr. Black directed both men outside and led them to the far side of the parking lot. Reaching a black SUV, Mr. Black helped Reginald into the back seat and instructed Will to take the front. He climbed in and drove. They didn't go far before reaching a remote road into the forest.

"Why'd you follow me? I met my quota this month. You got your girls. This has nothing to do with you."

"Yes. It does. Your business is ours. I'm here to ensure you don't forget that."

Mr. Black drove for more than thirty minutes, but that's all it took to disappear into a thickly wooded forest. The car stopped, and Bodine yanked at the door handle.

Reginald wondered if his life would terminate here. As much as he wanted to see his great-grandson, if this ending for him also meant the demise of Bodine, he was thankful the man would be out of their lives. Summer and Mr. Simmons would find his great-grandson. Suddenly, he remembered the wires. Perhaps he could still help.

"Mr. Bodine, where is my great-grandson?"

With his gun, Mr. Black led both men through the forest. All three men wore expensive dress shoes that sunk into the mucky earth as they trudged forward. Reginald stumbled, and Mr. Black took his elbow, the Glock still pointing at Bodine, who didn't answer.

The deeper into the forest they went, the darker it became. The dense pines and oaks shrouded the sun.

"Stop." Mr. Black pointed toward a thick tree trunk. "You, sit there."

Reginald breathed hard and stomped his cane. "I will not."

"Fine. This won't take long."

Before Mr. Black turned, Bodine took off running. Reginald pointed. Mr. Black took aim and fired a shot. Bodine screamed and fell. He hadn't gotten far, and Mr. Black trudged through the muck. He stopped and pointed the gun at Bodine's face. Bodine squirmed, holding his upper thigh. With a swift movement, Mr. Black kicked Bodine's head.

Reginald turned away, but the thudding of hits and kicks continued. He heard a slow, rolling sound across gravel. Shifting, he saw Mr. Simmons's van. He struggled to rise but found strength, padding toward it. The sound of Bodine's beating faded, and Mr. Simmons ran forward, meeting Reginald. Grabbing Reginald, he dragged him to the van and jumped in. Mr. Simmons sped down the dirt road and back onto the highway.

"Are you all right?" He asked.

Reginald reached into his pocket and retrieved a small, dark glass vial. He popped one tiny pill into his mouth and swallowed.

"Do I need to take you to the hospital? What a close call, and what's with the guy in the black suit? I couldn't hear anything for all the slots clinking, and then you went out of range. You're lucky to be alive."

Raising a hand, signaling him to stop, Reginald nodded. "Take me home."

"Are you sure? Your daughter will kill me if anything happens to you."

"I'll call my personal physician when I get home. We'll talk then." Reginald closed his eyes.

Summer paced on the wide veranda. When she saw Mr. Simmons's van pull up, she ran to it and flung open the passenger door. "Grandfather! My goodness. You're so pale. Mr. Simmons, take him to the hospital now." She tried to close the door.

Reginald pushed it back open. "He will not. Just help me in the house."

Once inside, Summer called Hazel for water and led her grandfather to the study. She knew better than to question him right now. He needed to rest and gain composure. He

314 | KATHLEEN J. ROBISON

managed his heart condition well, and Summer had learned to trust God with that.

Hazel brought in a glass of iced water for Reginald and a sweet tea for Mr. Simmons.

"Thank you, ma'am." He sipped the tea and sighed. "What a close call."

"Close call? There weren't supposed to be any close calls. What happened? I knew I should have gone." So much for waiting. She couldn't hold back. "Did he take your offer? Did you find out where Spring's son is? Oh, Granddaddy, you should have let me come."

"Oh, no," Mr. Simmons said. "That would have been even more disastrous."

"What do you mean disastrous?"

Mr. Simmons looked over at Reginald as if waiting for a sign to continue.

"Summer, sit down." Reginald breathed deeply, then exhaled slowly. "I'm not sure exactly what happened, but I don't expect to be hearing from Mr. Bodine again."

"Do you know anything about the other guy?" Mr. Simmons asked.

"What guy? Another man?" Summer's shook her head. "Oh, this couldn't have gone worse."

"Oh yes, it could have. Your grandfather could have gotten shot."

Summer flopped backward on the couch. "Hazel!" She called. "Sweet tea for me, please. I can't speak. I just can't imagine."

Reginald raised a hand. "Mr. Black. He worked for Mr. Bodine's employer."

"Employer?" Summer asked.

"They conversed, and he instructed Mr. Bodine to leave me alone. They were concerned about FBI involvement. He wanted no part of it. That's all I know, except I think he killed Mr. Bodine."

"Killed? Oh, my heavens. And you got away?" Summer whispered.

"Thanks to Mr. Simmons here."

"Oh, bless you." Summer clasped her hands.

Hazel knocked lightly and peeked in. "Sir, there is someone to see you. Shall I let them in?"

"Are you expecting someone?" Summer frowned. "Hazel, who is it?"

"He said his name is Mr. Black."

"Bring him in," Reginald said.

"Grandfather!" Summer reached for her cell phone. "I'm calling the police."

"Please don't." Mr. Black entered the room.

He cut an imposing figure, and Summer's imagination went wild. *Was he a...was he like Bodine? Did he use women, too? Why did he come?* She didn't need to ask.

"I'm here to ask that you not mention this incident with Mr. Bodine to anyone. I assure you he'll never bother you again. Never speak of this to anyone, and you'll not hear from the organization or me again."

"Organization?" Mr. Simmons asked. "What, are you the mafia or something?"

"Something, yes. We are very organized. My employer owns the penthouse at Shell Tower Plaza in New Orleans. That's all you need to know."

Mr. Simmons whistled and shot a glance to Summer. "Why, that's the highest building in New Orleans."

"I know. I know. But what does Mr. Bodine have to do with it? With you?" Summer pointed but quickly pulled back her manicured nail. If this man killed someone, he was a murderer. Summer cringed, thinking of the life Spring had led. She wondered if her sister had encountered this man before. Would she ever have peace from her sister's passing?

"Our business is finished, if you understand," Mr. Black said.

"No, it can't be. Please." Summer pleaded.

Reginald leaned forward, planted his cane, and stood. He extended a hand. "We understand. May I ask a question, perhaps two?"

Mr. Black sighed. "I'm not sure I have the answers."

"Do you know the whereabouts of my grandson?"

"No. I do not."

"Is Mr. Bodine dead?"

"Let's just say he's indisposed for now. I promise you will not hear from him again."

Reginald waved toward the door. "Thank you. Hazel will see you out."

The door closed, and Reginald dropped into his seat again.

Summer looked at her grandfather's weak frame. Spring's sudden appearance and death and this ordeal had taken so much out of him, and she feared it weakened his heart. How could life possibly go on? It would never be the same. She sucked in a breath, trying to quell a rising sob.

"Summer, you must trust the Lord." Reginald's eyes were closed, and color seemed to be coming back to his face. "God has always cared for us, and He will see us through in this. You must have hope."

Hope? What hope? Spring gone. Their family ruined. This Mr. Black had entered and exited their lives, leaving a residue of impending fear. Summer nodded, holding back a deluge of tears.

Her grandfather said, "Mr. Simmons, please find my great-grandson. Spare no expense. Whatever you need."

Summer looked up and swiped her eyes. Hope. This son of Spring's brought the hope that grandfather spoke of. Yes, they would find him. They would welcome him. Spring's legacy would live on.

"Yes, sir. I'll find him."

"Thank you, Mr. Simmons. Bring him home, please." Summer smiled.

Reginald offered a hand to his granddaughter. "Whatever happens, Summer. Our life. The Gardner life is a blessed one. Don't ever forget it. God's hand is upon us. Good or bad. He is with us. He is our hope. Not Mr. Simmons, not my great-grandson. Not even you. But our hope is always in Jesus Christ."

"Yes, Granddaddy."

"And we will never speak of this incident to anyone. Ever again."

Summer nodded and looked up. "Yes. Thank you, Jesus," she whispered.